THEIR LITTLE GHOST

HOLLY BLOOM

PROCEED WITH CAUTION...

You are about to embark on a slow journey into depravity that explores the following dark themes:

- Domestic violence and coercive control
- A missing family member
- Stalking
- Child abuse and exploitation (physical/mental)
- Mental health issues (including self-harm, psychosis, and PTSD)
- Dub-con (including choking, forced orgasms, fire play, sexual acts while a person is sleeping, and BDSM)
- Sexual assault and attempted rape
- Recording without consent
- Murder and body disposal
- Torture (including branding, waterboarding, and electroshock)
- Forced drug use and medication tampering
- Imprisonment
- Arson
- Dissociation

Remember, your mental health matters.

'I desire the things that will destroy me in the end.'
- Sylvia Plath

PART ONE
WHERE MONSTERS ARE MADE

THE PAST

TWELVE YEARS EARLIER...

AIDEN

"WHERE ARE YOU TAKING ME?" I ask, even though it's pointless.

At nine years old, I already know adults don't listen, especially to little boys.

They didn't listen when I told them Mama got hurt.

Mama didn't listen when I begged her to stop letting them in. She didn't listen again when I told her to stop putting those pointy things in her arms. They made her sleepy.

No one at the park listened when I told them she'd slept for three days straight. Well, before the flies came. They soon listened to me after that.

I liked those three days. Just Mama and me. She never liked having me around before, so it was good for the two of us to finally be together. We watched all my favorite movies without her yelling or sending me off to buy her beer. I wasn't forced to stay outside when the trailer rocked until the sweaty men left, no matter how hard I cried. No, those three days were special. It's how it should have been. Just the two of us. That's the kinda Mama I wanted, even though she smelled bad.

I blame our neighbor. I don't know his name, only that Mama called him an 'interfering piece of shit'. He kept knocking on our door. Again and again. When I opened it to tell him to mind his own business, he vomited beer all over our front step. That made me mad, so I stabbed him really quick, once in the leg, because he was too tall for me to reach anywhere else.

Soon after, two men came to take me away. I told them I don't want to go. I can take care of myself. I make peanut butter sandwiches, packet mac and cheese, and I know which dumpsters to find the best food in. I could stay in our trailer forever. Just me, Mama, and the flies.

"Are we nearly there?" I ask again.

The strange men are driving me to a special place. A place that'll help make me better, or so they say. They ignore my questions. They're dressed in suits and look like secret agents. Everyone at the trailer park watched us go, and an ambulance flew by on our way out. I've already asked where they're taking Mama, but they won't say. I don't think I'll be seeing her again.

"What's the special place like?" I push for answers.

I hear Mama's angry voice in my head. *Don't talk to strangers, Aiden, especially when they're dressed in fancy clothes. They think they're better than folks like us, you hear me? They're trouble.* Mama wouldn't have let me go. *They have no business knowing our business. You keep your damn mouth shut if you don't want another hiding.*

I stare out the car window, pressing my nose against the cold glass. There's a weird smell, which I think might be me, and the men have cracked the window open to let some of it out. A winter wind whistles through my torn T-shirt. The cold doesn't bother me. I'm used to it. Heating costs too much.

I pass the time by counting every tree and bird I see. I've always liked being outdoors. Sometimes, I spend days playing in the woods behind the trailer park. I don't recognize where we're at now, though. I know the world is a real big place because I've seen it on TV, but I didn't realize it was *this* big. I expect the car to tumble off the edge of the earth, yet we keep going.

We've been driving for a while. A long time. We stopped once to buy milkshakes and burgers. I shouldn't take food from strangers, but it looked so good that I couldn't help myself. I clutch my tummy. It aches from being so full, but it was worth it. Maybe this new special place will have more burgers and milkshakes. I've decided they're my new favorites.

The driver turns. "We're almost there, kid," he says, pointing ahead. "See that?" I follow his finger to look at the large iron gates approaching. "That's your new home."

I gasp, putting my small hand up to the misty glass. "Wow…"

It's a castle with tall brick walls. It must have hundreds of bedrooms. I've never had a bed of my own before. I've always slept with Mama or on the sofa. I grin smugly. What will everyone think of the trailer trash who'd never amount to anything now? I'm going somewhere special, unlike them.

The gates come to life and open. The sun sets behind the roof, and a tall man in a long, white coat waits at the entrance. He looks down at a clipboard in his hands.

"Out you get, kid."

I expect the men to get out, but they don't move.

"What're you waiting for?" the driver encourages. "Move!"

I stagger from the car, almost tripping. The sole is coming away from the bottom of my sneaker, and I hope they won't turn me away from the castle because of it.

"Good evening," the man at the door greets me. He smiles, but something about it makes me want to run. I can sense bad men. They've come in and out of my trailer often enough. "My name is Doctor Acacia."

No one said anything about doctors. Mama says you can't trust hospitals. *If you go into the hospital, they'll keep you. Boys*

like you go in and don't come out. Do you want to get taken away?
I didn't want that.

I look back at the car that's already driving away, leaving me stranded.

"This is your new home." Doctor Acacia gestures up at the building. There's writing above the door, but I can't read it. To me, letters look like ugly drawings. Mama said reading and school was a waste of time. "Welcome to Sunnycrest."

"Sunnycrest," I repeat.

It sounds like somewhere people go on vacation. Vacations aren't for people like us. Like me.

"Let's get you settled in," he says, holding out his hand. "I'll show you your room."

I keep my arms at my sides, frowning at his open palm.

He chuckles. "I can see you're definitely in the right place, boy," he says, ruffling my hair. "You're very lucky to be here, Zero."

"Aiden," I correct, sticking my jaw out in defiance. "My name is Aiden."

"Not anymore," Doctor Acacia says. "You are Zero now."

EIGHT YEARS EARLIER...

ELI

"I WANT TO GO HOME," I whimper. "Please. Take me home."

A boy with a dead-eyed stare slides off the top bunk and lands with a thud on his feet. He turns to face me, casting me under his shadow. He towers above me, as tall as a grown man. I'm eleven, and he's thirteen, but he looks much older. Something about him is off. He isn't… right. No one here is.

"This is your home now," the boy says.

Tears drip down my dirty cheeks. All I wanted was to hitch a ride. It's not the first time. I've done it loads before. When the man picked me up by the roadside, he promised to take me somewhere special. I thought we were going to get ice cream, but I knew I was in trouble when he drove past the shop. I kicked and screamed until he pulled over, then everything went black.

"I don't want to be h-here," I stammer, struggling to breathe. "I want to go home!"

"Shh," the strange boy hushes, kneeling next to me. I flinch as he wraps his arm around my shoulder. "You have to be strong to survive here, okay? I'll look out for you. Don't let them see you cry, you hear me?"

I sniff and nod, feeling other eyes on us. We're not alone. We're in a room with four others. The other boys don't speak.

They only watch, quivering under their thin blankets like scared mice.

"Good," the boy replies, cracking a smile. "What's your name?"

I look at the number sewn into my new shirt. That's what the doctor who brought me to my room told me my name will be from now on. Twenty-Five.

"Twenty-Five," I say, not stupid enough to risk another blow to the head.

"Good." The boy nods, satisfied with my answer. He leans to whisper in my ear, "Don't let them hear you say anything else. To them, that is your name."

It's not the first time I've stayed silent to avoid a beating. Mom and Dad argued constantly, until one day, their arguing stopped.

I was there when it happened.

He pushed Mom down the stairs and laughed. Her body toppled like a pile of tumbling blocks, bouncing off every step. I watched her head hit the wooden floor and burst open like a cracked watermelon. Blood spilled out, lapping at my feet, and stained her pretty brown hair. While Dad ran, I stayed with her and stroked her hair. The soft hair that always smelled like fresh shampoo, hair that draped over my face when she sang songs, hair I cried into after scraping my knees. I pulled what was left of her head onto my lap and stroked her hair until the sirens got close.

The door to our room opens to reveal a woman. There's no sparkle in her eyes, and her lips are fused shut in a straight line. Not like Mom, who always smiled.

She clears her throat and checks her notebook. "Twenty-Five and Zero," she calls. "Come with me."

The boy who consoled me stands up, clenching his jaw and balling his fists. He catches my eye and tilts his head, encouraging me to copy him.

We follow the woman along a long, windowless hallway

with no pictures. After a few turns, the gray walls all merge into one.

"Where are we going?" I whisper to Zero as the woman quickens.

"Where we're going doesn't matter. Just remember what I told you," Zero replies under his breath. "Do as they say and don't make a fuss. That'll keep you alive."

I gulp. How much farther? We pass through so many doors with electric locks and keypads. My heart sinks. There's no sign of ice cream anywhere.

She leads us into an enormous white room. It's like a spaceship. Seeing men in lab coats makes me giggle. Zero elbows me sharply in the ribs to silence me.

"Zero," Doctor Acacia, the man who introduced himself upon my arrival, says. "We have a new subject joining you today."

"Yes, Doctor," Zero says, hanging his head.

"We will put him in the tub first."

The thought of having a bubble bath perks me up. Mom used to make bath time so fun. I hope they have nice shampoo. Shampoo that smells like her. This place can't be so bad after all...

"No." Zero steps up. "I'll do it."

"It's okay," I chime in. "I don't mind."

Zero's shoulders slump, and he glares at me. I've said the wrong thing, but I don't know why. Maybe he's jealous.

"See?" Acacia smirks. "He doesn't mind. Follow me, Twenty-Five."

Acacia takes me into an adjoining room. I cast a quick glance over my shoulder to see Zero staring after us. I don't understand the look in his eyes. It's almost... sad.

I frown at the deep metal tub that fills the space. Next to it, wires come out of strange beeping machines.

"Undress yourself," Acacia commands.

I do as he asks, and a few of the men in coats join us. I

open my mouth to tell them that I don't need any help washing myself, but I don't get the chance. One of them begins attaching the wires to me.

"Ouch!" I yelp as metal clamps grip areas of loose skin. I reach to pull them off, but Acacia slaps my hand away.

"You will follow my orders, Twenty-Five," he warns. "Get in."

Shivering, I step into the tub, trying to ignore everyone else. I squeal when my toe breaks the freezing water's surface. A firm hand on my shoulder stops me from jumping out.

"Sit," Acacia spits through gritted teeth. "Now."

My teeth chatter as I lower myself into the icy bath. Something is wrong. Very wrong. I focus on the symbols on the screens of the machines surrounding me, imagining that we're about to fly into space to visit another planet.

Once I'm seated, Acacia reels off a list of numbers and mentions something about an experiment. I can't think straight or feel my legs. It's even worse than last summer when I ate too many Popsicles and had a ten-minute brain freeze.

"Begin," the doctor says.

My entire body jolts as a bolt of lightning shoots through me. I scream. A bloodcurdling scream. The same noise Mom made before she fell. I grip the sides of the tub, thrashing and clambering to escape.

"Let me out!" I yell. "Let me out!"

Arms force me back down. Shocks keep coming, again and again. So do my screams. I don't know how long I'm there, but I pray for them to stop. Maybe this is my punishment for not saving Mom. I'd take a thousand of Dad's belt lashings over this. Eventually, I give up fighting. It's pointless.

Suddenly, it stops.

Someone fishes my limp body out of the water.

I struggle to stand as dry clothes are thrust into my arms.

"Twenty-Five," a man says. I can't remember his name now. "You did very well. That's it for today."

I smile, because that's all I can do, and put on the scratchy sweater and pants before I'm ushered into the main room.

"Take them back," a voice says.

I focus on putting one foot after the other. I'm back in the long hallway again, trying not to slip. My wet hair sticks to my face, and my mouth hangs open. I try to close it, but I can't. My body isn't under my control anymore.

"Twenty-Five," someone says. My eyes flit to the other boy with a black eye by my side. I wonder what happened to him. "Are you okay?"

I say nothing and keep walking until I'm pushed into a room.

"I'll bring food soon," a woman barks before slamming the door behind her.

We're alone again. The boy puts his hands on my shoulders and stares into my eyes, like he's searching for something.

"What's your name?" he asks.

"Twenty-Five," I mumble.

"No," he says, shaking his head in disappointment. "What's your *real* name?"

My voice trails off. "I…"

"I'm Aiden," he says.

"I'm…" I will myself to remember through the aftershocks. "Eli."

As soon as I say it, I'm brought back to reality, even though it feels like a terrible nightmare.

"I'll look after you, Eli," Aiden says with a big smile. "Together, we'll get out of here. You'll see."

TWO YEARS EARLIER...

LEX

AIDEN GRUNTS while face fucking the girl on her knees before him. He holds her head and thrusts hard into her throat. She gags before he blows his load. When he pulls out, she gasps for air, his cum dripping down her chin like milk.

Aiden's lip curls in disapproval before saying, "I had to put all the fucking work in there." He shakes his head at her. "Your turn, Lex."

My cock is already out and waiting as she crawls to me. All of the female patients willingly bow down for us. We rule Sunnycrest. Aiden, Eli, and me. Zero, Twenty-Five, and Forty. The three of us are the only patients to survive every experiment thrown at us, which has made us infamous.

We're not taking advantage of the girls. They practically line up to suck us off daily. We don't go for the ones who are completely batshit or high on whatever drugs Acacia feeds them, though. We still have some standards.

The girl, whose name I can't remember, creates a seal around my cock with her lips. Aside from the remnants of Aiden's cum, her tongue is as dry as sandpaper. Still, I groan while she gets to work. It's not a great blowjob, but it beats using my hand. Next to me, Eli lounges across the bottom bunk, legs outstretched and humming to himself.

"What's the plan for tonight?" I ask Aiden.

Aiden returns to his top bunk to stroke the giant rat that he keeps as a pet. The rodent gives me the creeps, but I'll never tell him that. When they die, he keeps the skulls, wearing them around his neck on a chain. In the real world, that'd seem crazy, but here? It's normal.

I owe Aiden and Eli my life for taking me under their wing. I've been in Sunnycrest for three years. They taught me how things work and how to survive. I was sane before I got here, but now… I've never been fucking crazier, despite what Acacia says.

I didn't talk when I first arrived. I had 'selective mutism due to trauma', according to my clinical notes. Watching your parents burn alive in a fire is enough to screw anyone up. No matter how hard I tried, I couldn't speak. I even stayed silent through hours of Acacia's experiments. That's why he liked me so much. I was his challenge. Countless other subjects endured less and didn't survive. It took him almost a year to coax a scream from me, and when it happened, my scream was the sweetest sound I've ever heard.

As we aged, Acacia moved us to a different wing in Sunnycrest. Usually, he likes to keep the experimental subjects separate. There's no point mixing them among the general population. The general population, or gen pop as we call them, are other patients who are here for therapy because of a criminal order—not kids like me, Eli, and Aiden, who were handpicked to take part in Acacia's torturous games. However, over the years, we developed a mutual understanding with the doctor holding us prisoners. They experiment on us, and we experiment in our own way with the other patients. Perhaps that's one of his experiments in itself.

"Acacia's yearly freak show will be the same as it always is," Aiden mutters darkly.

I exhale deeply as I come. A brief relief. The girl backs away, breathless, looking up at me for some kind of compliment. Her desperation is sickening, and I kick her in the stomach. She yelps, making me harden again. I'd rather she scream over my cock than suck it.

Not put off yet, the cum bucket turns to Eli. "Do you want me to do you next?"

He shakes his head. He doesn't fuck them every day. Only when he feels like it, and today, his head is elsewhere. Tonight is on his mind, too.

"Why are you still here?" Aiden says, making a shooing gesture with his hand. "You better practice sucking dick if you want to come back again."

She nods furiously. "I will."

She scampers out of our room, back to whatever hole she came from. Thirsty fucking bitch.

"So?" Eli asks. "What's our plan?"

"We're not allowed in the main hall," Aiden says.

I roll my eyes. "Obviously."

"But he'll parade us around in the lab for everyone to see," Eli mumbles.

It's the same every year. Rich white guys come to watch and torture us, taking bets on how much pain a human can withstand. We've been here for so long that we're conditioned not to feel pain, but Acacia is a sick motherfucker who keeps pushing limits.

Aiden's nineteen, and Eli and I are seventeen. Sunnycrest Asylum only holds youths up to the age of twenty-five. The older we get, the less interesting we are to Acacia's customers. Most prefer the young kids, but they're too unreliable. Acacia goes through them quicker than lab rats. Our endurance makes us special subjects and part of his longitudinal study, which is why we haven't been thrown into the furnace with the others.

Aiden peers through the tiny window of our cell to point at a car pulling into the lot. "Look who it is."

Acacia. We know his car. In fact, we know everything that

happens here. Acacia thinks he rules Sunnycrest, but we also have a big influence. Not just with other patients, but with the staff too. They fear us. I see it in the way they watch us; their fingers always flutter nervously around their waistband, making sure their stun guns are within reaching distance. We're mad and dangerous. Those that know about the secret experiments also know we're fucking invincible.

We gather to look through the glass. As is his yearly tradition, Acacia's wife and twin daughters join him for the open evening. The girls get out of the car. They're identical and impossible to tell apart, except one has bleach blonde hair. Even though I can't hear the blonde talking, I can tell she's confident from the way she throws her head back when she laughs. She's too confident. Arrogant, almost. The other—a brunette—shifts around uncomfortably, like she'd rather be anywhere else. She crosses her arms as if she wants to melt into the ground and disappear.

"I'm surprised he lets them come here," Eli says bitterly. "His precious fucking daughters."

We know all about Sarah and Erin. We hear Acacia talking to them on the phone and listen to the orderlies gossiping about the rich Acacia family. Those two bitches have everything, and they don't realize their father built their fortune at our expense.

Aiden grins and looks up at the vent above his bed. "Are you thinking what I am?"

I return a smile. "Right ahead of you."

"Eli?" Aiden prompts.

"Fuck it." Eli sighs. "Why not?"

They will tranquilize every patient this evening to ensure there are no disruptions, but we have an orderly under our thumb who pockets our medication. We don't need pills. Although, having them can be a useful bargaining chip sometimes.

Aiden unscrews the vent bolts and removes the metal

grate, then squeezes himself into the shaft. With his broad shoulders, it's a tighter fit for him than me and Eli. A few years ago, we started mapping the asylum's vents. At this point, escaping is still futile due to Acacia's security measures. We have to wait for the perfect time. Until then, navigating around through the ceilings has become our favorite pastime.

I'm next after Aiden, and Eli follows close behind. We slither on our stomachs like snakes. Many would find the tunnels claustrophobic, but they're oddly comforting to me. They give us the freedom we need.

We crawl until we're above a store closet next to the kitchen, where staff are busy preparing food for the annual event. Aiden painstakingly unscrews the grate, moves it aside, and drops to the room below. We follow one by one.

Through the hall, we hear the kitchen rumblings. The catering staff have all been called into the main hall. This is part of Acacia's routine. He briefs everyone ahead of the main event to ensure it runs smoothly.

"Come on," Aiden says, creeping toward the kitchen when we're sure everyone's vacated.

Hopefully, we can swindle some nice food. Anything will be better than the shit they serve us. We creep out of the closet. We're about to enter the kitchen when someone clears their throat behind us.

Fuck.

I spin to see a girl leaning against the wall, raising her eyebrows in amusement.

"What do you think you're doing?" she asks.

There's a smile in her tone, and an ease to the way she challenges us. Self-assurance like that only comes from having everything you've ever wanted.

Aiden doesn't flinch when he sees Acacia's daughter, drawing himself to his full height and crossing his arms. She isn't intimidated, though.

"That's none of your fucking business," Aiden growls menacingly. "Why don't you run back to Daddy?"

The blonde rolls her eyes. "I'd much rather do something fun." She takes a hip flask and a pack of cigarettes from her purse. "Is there somewhere we can sneak off to? These events are so dull."

"Sarah!" Another girl's voice floats toward us. "Where are you? Dad's looking for you."

Sarah freezes. "Shit."

Aiden seizes the opportunity to snatch the cigarettes from her hands and tuck them into his pocket.

She glowers at him but doesn't argue. Instead, she calls back, "I'll be right there, Erin."

"Sarah!" Acacia's voice booms, making the three of us shrink away, pressing our backs against the wall. "What are you doing back here?"

She catches my eye, and I put one finger to my lips. She grins and swipes her hand across her mouth in a zipping motion.

"Sorry, Dad," she says. "I got lost."

She winks before sauntering away, leaving us to retreat into the safety of the storage closet.

Acacia's voice is full of rage when he speaks to her. "Next time you get lost, you'll end up staying here."

PART TWO
POOR LITTLE RICH GIRL
PRESENT DAY

CHAPTER
ONE

ERIN

One year.

That's how long it's been since Sarah disappeared.

I'm stupid for expecting she'd come home today. In my daydreams, her rebellious eyes sparkle as she stumbles in with messy hair, swinging an empty liquor bottle, like no time has passed. She wouldn't understand our concern. She and Dad would argue, like always. But, for once, I'd be happy to hear them fight.

Yet, there's nothing. Only the same stifling silence that has consumed our table since she vanished. Mom lays the table, as she does every morning, with more food than we can eat. She puts out a selection of fruit, cereals, pancakes, sausages, juice, and a pot of coffee. No matter how early I wake, food is always waiting at the perfect temperature. It's always the same, even though nothing else is.

Mom's fork scrapes against her plate as she slices a banana into tiny pieces, setting my jaw on edge. She cuts her food up so small that it turns to nothing, then pushes it around until she declares she's full after three bites. She'd rather starve than gain a pound.

"My book club is holding a fundraiser at the weekend," she declares brightly.

Mom lives for social occasions and loves any excuse to buy new designer clothes. At fifty, she's beautiful and still turns heads wherever we go. She's the perfect trophy wife, befitting my famous psychiatrist father. People say we look alike, but I don't see the resemblance. Unlike my boring brown straight hair, Mom has blonde waves that naturally fall in all the right places, and wide blue eyes compared to my brown ones. Sarah used to dye her hair to look more like her.

Dad grunts in acknowledgement and keeps leafing through the newspaper. He's an imposing man at six feet tall with a sullen expression. In his youth, he was handsome with his angular jawline, dark hair and eyes. Now, wiry gray strands pepper his temples, and his lined forehead makes him look in a permanent foul mood. It's not helped by the fact he rarely smiles, and a perpetual cloud of negativity surrounds him. Nothing, and no one, is ever good enough or up to his exacting standards.

I pick at my food and look up at the faded spot on the wall where our family portrait used to hang. Mom put it up soon after we moved in, but Dad tore it down and declared Sarah a disgrace. We moved to the town of Pasturesville for a fresh start shortly after she vanished, and all of Sarah's belongings were left behind. He wants to erase her from our lives. We don't talk about her. Occasionally, Mom looks like she wants to say something when it's just the two of us, but she always thinks better of it. It's not worth invoking my father's wrath.

Dad slaps the paper down, and his shrewd gaze sweeps over me. "How was your math test yesterday, Erin?"

I cower under his scrutiny, wanting to blend into the fabric seat covers.

"We're still waiting for the results," I lie.

He nods curtly, letting me breathe easily once more. When he finds out I got a B+, he'll go crazy, but that's a problem for future Erin. I studied hard for the test, but I got distracted. All I could think about was Sarah. For the millionth time, I combed my memories for any clues that might tell me what happened to her.

Outside, a car horn beeps, providing me with a welcome excuse to leave. That'll be Mia, my best friend. She took me under her wing when I started at Stonybridge Academy. I'm not allowed a car, but Mia was the first in our class to get her license and gives me a ride to school every day.

I grab a granola bar for the road. "Thanks for breakfast."

Dad tsks. "You shouldn't start your day with sugar."

I freeze. Mom's shoulders tense, even though she plasters on a fake smile.

"A little sugar won't hurt," she says feebly.

Big mistake.

"Won't hurt?" Dad's incredulous face turns thunderous. He inhales deeply and puffs out his chest. "Do you know the dangers of a hyperactive mind, and what it can lead to?" I zone out as he rattles off the reasons on his fingers. "Lack of sleep, inability to focus, lack of concentration. Do you think this is what Erin needs for her senior year? She has college to think about. She can't eat this junk. I don't know why we even have it in the house!"

Mom lowers her head. "I didn't think…"

"You never do," he replies.

I put the granola bar down slowly, like I'm lowering a weapon, and pick up an apple instead. He can't have a problem with that, right?

Wrong.

He scowls. "Don't pretend you care now. I know what people your age are like, remember? I spend all day trying to fix the damage that's been done. You should be grateful that I'm here to guide you in the right direction. If it were down to your mother…" He shakes his head in obvious disapproval. "Who knows where you'd be."

"Sorry, Magnus," Mom murmurs, wringing her hands. "I'll do better next time."

He huffs and holds the paper up while Mia beeps the horn again.

"I better go," I say, slinging my backpack over my shoulder. "See you later."

"What extracurriculars do you have today?" Dad asks, unable to let me leave without knowing my entire schedule.

"Swimming and piano," I say. "I'm having an extra tutoring session with Mr. Meyer after school to make sure I'm ready for the concert on Monday."

"Only one extra session?" He scoffs. "What are we paying those school fees for?" He always finds a reason to complain. If there's a hole to pick in something, he'll find it. "I'll pick you up afterward. Don't be late."

"Yes, sir," I mutter.

"And one more thing." He picks up the pills hiding behind my coffee cup. "You forgot your medication."

I grab the colorful capsules and shove them into my mouth, swallowing without water. The giant rectangles sliding down my throat makes me wince. I've taken pills every day since Sarah vanished to help with anxiety.

"Have a good day, honey," Mom says.

I force a smile and hurry away. As soon as I shut the front door, my lungs expand fully, allowing me to breathe easier.

Mia beeps for the third time and lowers the car window to yell, "Hurry up!"

I roll my eyes as I head down the driveway onto the street. We live in one of the biggest mansions in town within a desirable gated community. We have seven bedrooms and baths, designer furniture, a kitchen that looks like a movie set, and a garage filled with four cars that no one drives, but we didn't always live like this.

Mia's arm drapes out of the window, and she taps her manicured nails impatiently against the side of her pink Cadillac. It has a custom plate and a sleek, white, leatherette interior. I joke that it looks like Barbie's car, but it suits her personality perfectly. The two of us are total opposites, which is why our friendship works. Mia's loud, confident, and completely unapologetic. She captures everyone's attention with her vivacious personality and stunning looks, while I'm happy being a bookish wallflower who can easily go days without speaking to anyone.

Mia checks her reflection in the mirror and applies a layer of sparkly purple lip gloss when I appear.

"I thought you were in a hurry?" I ask.

"No," she replies with a cunning smile. "But I knew *you* would be in a hurry to leave. Besides..." She adjusts the mirror and angles it at my neighbor's long driveway. "Your secret admirer is leaving too."

My cheeks burn as Nate Holt's car approaches.

"He's not my secret admirer," I hiss, simultaneously smoothing down my hair. "Drive!"

Mia doesn't move as the black Jaguar crawls to a stop beside us and lowers its window.

"Hi, Nate!" Mia chirps. "Fancy seeing you here."

Nate smiles, looking straight past her. "Hey, Erin."

"Charming!" Mia flicks her hair in feigned annoyance. "Am I invisible or something?"

"Hi," I murmur, avoiding Nate's gaze.

The Holts basically built this town, and it shows. At Stonybridge Academy, wealth doesn't instantly guarantee popularity as everyone who attends is already loaded. However, Nate's family history and his prowess on the football field have made him a local legend. Unlike most people, my father doesn't have a positive opinion of the Holts. He despises the way 'their arrogant son' swans around the streets like he owns them, even though he kinda does.

"Are you coming to the party after the game tonight?" he asks. "It's going to be wild."

"N—" I begin.

"Yes!" Mia interrupts. "Of course we are."

"Really?" Nate's eyes widen in surprise. "I didn't think you went to parties, Erin. Aren't you too cool for them?"

That can't be further from the truth. Before I open my mouth, Mia jumps in again. "She'll be there. I'll make sure of it."

"Sweet." Nate beams, showing off two perfect rows of Hollywood-style white teeth. "I'll see you there."

Nate's handsome in a clean-cut way. He has short brown hair, tanned skin, brown eyes, and a killer body. Although I live under a rock most of the time, even I know he doesn't date. His father doesn't want a girlfriend distracting him during the football season. Although, that doesn't stop Nate from having success with many girls, if the rumors are true.

"Mia!" I nudge her in the ribs as Nate speeds away. She's wearing a smug smirk and an 'I told you so' expression that makes me want to punch her. "You know I can't go. What will my dad say?"

"Come on," she says. "This is our senior year. He can't keep you locked away forever like some helpless princess. You told me that Sarah used to go to parties all the time, remember?"

"And look what happened to her," I mutter.

She went to a party the night she disappeared.

A party she never returned from.

Mia's expression softens instantly. "Shit, I didn't mean…"

"I know," I reply with a sad smile.

It's refreshing for someone to say Sarah's name aloud and to confirm that my twin actually existed outside of my own memories.

"This is our last year at high school," Mia says. "You're eighteen now. I know yesterday was the anniversary of Sarah's disappearance. You need a distraction. You can spend one night doing something normal, can't you? The party will be amazing."

Behind us, an engine whirs to life. The temperature drops

as my father nears in his car. He'll be heading to work now. He spends most of his waking hours there, when he isn't chauffeuring me around and acting like an overzealous bodyguard.

"Girls," he greets us curtly. "Is there a problem?"

This is his indirect way of asking why we're still stationary and not on the way to school.

"There's no problem, Mr. Acacia," Mia says. "I just dropped my lip gloss between the seats. Silly me!"

"You should be more careful next time." He frowns. "You don't want to be late."

"We're leaving right away, Mr. Acacia," she says, turning the keys in the ignition.

Thankfully, he's driving in the opposite direction.

I sigh in relief. "That was close."

When his car becomes a tiny dot in the rearview, I finally consider it safe to loosen my tie and undo the top two buttons of my blouse. Despite it being the twenty-first century, the academy still requires us to wear a uniform, which Mia deems an infringement of our human rights. For girls, it's a gray skirt with black thigh-high stockings, a purple tartan tie, and a matching gray blazer with the Stonybridge logo emblazoned on the right breast pocket. Everyone takes liberties with their uniform, though. When your parents are paying eye-watering fees, the administration can't complain. Mia's skirt barely skims her ass, and she's sewn bright patches onto her blazer jacket to give it extra pops of color. My parents prefer that I stick to the strict requirements.

"Don't take this the wrong way, but your dad seriously gives me the creeps," Mia says. She's not the only one. "Maybe it's because of what he does. What do you think it's like spending all day with psychopaths?"

Dad is the lead psychiatrist at Sunnycrest Asylum. Contrary to the name, the place is anything but sunny. It houses the most unstable under twenty-fives in the country.

There was an uproar when he first opened the facility. People were terrified that the patients would break out and cause carnage. However, he's since won the respect of the community by making generous donations to the mayor's office, school, and hospital, to name a few. As long as the money keeps flowing, everyone is happy to ignore how we're living so close to violent criminals.

"He enjoys his job," I reply impassively.

"Anyway, the party..." Mia changes the subject.

I groan. When she has an idea in her head, she's relentless.

"I already told you I can't go," I say. "What if my parents find out? They'll never let me leave the house again."

"They don't have to find out," she says. "Look, I have it all planned out. You can tell them that you're studying late at mine and stay over. You can even say my mom is helping by giving you tips for the concert."

Mia's mom is a world-famous pianist and also one of the nicest women I've ever met. She's warm, open, and friendly, just like her daughter. She doesn't yell when the bed isn't made right or the laundry isn't put away, and doesn't believe that eating a whole tub of ice cream is a cardinal sin.

"What if my dad finds out I lied?"

"He won't," she says. "It'll be so much fun."

I wish I shared her confidence. Dad has an uncanny way of finding out things you try to hide—probably because he spends all day raking through the darkest depths of people's minds.

"Even if your plan did work, I have nothing to wear."

"Puh-lease!" She laughs. "I have enough clothes to fill an entire shopping mall. You can borrow something. It'll be fun. You haven't stayed over in ages!"

"Your clothes are a little..." I struggle to find the right word. I love her, but Mia's outfits consist of an obscene amount of sequins and neon. They complement her gorgeous black skin, but against my pale Casper-like complexion, I'll look like a washed-out zombie. "Bright?"

"I'm sure I have something in the back of my closet that gives off a tortured poet vibe," she teases.

"I'm not a tortured poet!"

"Whatever you say, Mrs. Poe." She winks. "People are intrigued by you. You go to school, go to classes, and go home. Do you know how many people ask me about you?"

"People already know the most interesting thing about me. My sister's missing," I say. "That's all anyone is curious about."

"Not Nate," she says. "Didn't you see how he looked at you?"

Nate's popular. He can't seriously be showing an interest in someone like me. Butterflies flutter in my stomach as my mind wanders to what it would feel like to kiss him. Aside from a few games of spin the bottle in seventh grade, I've never kissed a boy—let alone had a boyfriend. Sarah was the one who all the guys flocked to.

I bite my lip, weighing up Mia's plan. "I don't know about this."

"What's the worst that could happen? You'll get grounded?" she asks. "That's no different from usual. You hardly left the house all summer. The party will be so much more fun if you come along. I need you!"

"You go to parties on your own all the time," I point out.

"But I don't want to." She pouts. "I want you to be there. And if you're not having fun, then I promise we can leave, okay? Pinkie swear."

"I'm not sure my dad will buy the excuse," I say.

"Oh, he will!" she says, then puts on her best British accent. While she hasn't inherited her mom's innate musical ability, Mia's a budding actress and can impersonate her mother perfectly. "I'm teaching Erin everything I know. She'll be the best pianist at the concert, after she's had a night of partying and sucking face with—"

I laugh. "I'm not sucking face with anyone."

"So, you're in?"

I know what Sarah would do. She wouldn't hesitate for a second. Maybe Mia is right. I don't think my father can get any more controlling than he already is. In some strange way, I almost feel like going to a party is a way to feel closer to Sarah again.

"Fine," I relent, despite my better judgments. "I'm in, but only this once."

"Yay!" she squeals. "This is going to be amazing. You won't regret it."

Mia continues to talk about outfit possibilities as we pull into the Stonybridge Academy parking lot. I nod and make noises in the right places to pretend I'm listening, but a pit of dread has taken root in my stomach as I wonder whether I'm about to make a massive mistake.

CHAPTER
TWO

ERIN

Mr. Meyer looks like he wants to beat me over the head with a violin after listening to his top student butcher Bach's Invention No. 1 in C Major repeatedly.

"You will be ready for the concert on Monday, *ja*?" he asks in his German accent. "College scouts will be there."

Mr. Meyer hopes I'll consider pursuing music at a professional level and constantly shows me brochures for amazing courses. There's no point in raising my hopes. I'll go to whichever college my father deems suitable. He wants me to become a doctor or a lawyer. Piano is simply an extra tick on my application to help me stand out.

"I'll be ready," I promise. "I'll practice this weekend."

He sighs in exasperation. "You best do. I can't have my star pupil letting us down."

"You have my word," I say.

I can play the pieces in my sleep, they come as easy as breathing. My fingers naturally know where to go and skip over the keys effortlessly, but I'm distracted because of the party and the lies I have to tell to get there.

Mia's waiting outside the rehearsal room and links her arm through mine when I'm done. "Ready?"

I quickly adjust my clothes to ensure my buttons are done

and tie is in perfect position, then nod wearily. "Ready as I'll ever be."

My father's car is already waiting in the lot when we approach, and Mia squeezes my arm in a silent show of solidarity.

"I wasn't expecting two of you." He frowns, checking his watch when I open the passenger side door. "You're late."

Four minutes late.

"Sorry, Doctor Acacia. That's totally my fault. I was listening to Erin play and didn't want her to stop," Mia gushes. "After hearing her, I asked my mom to let Erin play for her."

I say the words I've rehearsed like a mantra all day. "Ms. Moldova offered to give me extra tuition ahead of the concert next week."

"Extra tuition?" he snaps. "Why do you need that? I'm already paying Mr. Meyer for extra."

"She doesn't need any extra help," Mia interjects, "but my mom loves to support local artists, especially when they're my friends. She insists!"

"And, Erin?" Dad's eyes bore into mine, daring me to confront him. "What do you think of this offer?"

"Mr. Meyer's great, but he's no Ms. Moldova," I reply, accepting his silent challenge. "I could learn so much from her. She's a genius, and I haven't seen her for months."

"Tonight's not a good night," he says. "Now get in the car, Erin."

Usually, I'd drop the matter, but Mia clings onto my arm. She's the reason I don't give up instantly.

"I really think this will help, D-Dad," I stammer. "Who else gets the chance to learn from a world-class musician? It'd look great on a college application, and she might give me a reference."

"A reference?"

"Yes," Mia says. "She definitely will. One hundred percent."

"Hm." His knuckles grip the wheel, mulling it over. He hates me leaving the house but knows the benefits of a good reference. Plus, his daughter being trained by a world-class musician would give him bragging rights in his social circle. Eventually, he nods in reluctant agreement. "Fine, but I want to speak to your mother, Mia."

"Of course," Mia says. "I'll get her to call you as soon as we're home. She'll be rehearsing right now and doesn't like being disturbed when she's practicing. You know what creatives are like."

"What time should I pick you up?" he asks rhetorically. "I'll give you three hours."

"It's already six," Mia says. "Why don't you stay the night, Erin? It's honestly no problem. We have the space."

The way she says it comes out so offhandedly that it almost convinces me that this wasn't pre-planned.

Dad's brow furrows in suspicion. "Erin has a busy schedule."

"I don't have school tomorrow," I say, daring to push his boundaries further. "I'll be back first thing in the morning. Please, Dad? Just this once? Think about college!"

A long pause drags out, squeezing all the air from my lungs with it.

"Fine," he quips. "I'll see you tomorrow morning for breakfast. Do not be late again."

"Yes, sir."

I close the car door, not quite believing we've pulled it off. We say nothing until we're back in Mia's car, and my father's taillights are vanishing into the distance.

"Okay, your dad is officially the scariest man I've ever met," she says. "Holy shit, I thought he was going to drag you away. Did you see his face?"

"I can't believe he said yes."

I expected him to put up more of a fight...

"Well, he did." Mia cranks up Taylor Swift to full blast. "It's time to party!"

I giggle nervously. Well, I guess I'm doing this...

———

Two hours and a fake phone call to my dad later, Mia is in her element. I haven't seen her this excited since she modeled in a cosmetics campaign. Her room has been transformed into a runway, and she's hurling garments at me from all angles.

Her bedroom is an explosion of color: pink walls, a California king bed with a heart-shaped headboard, and a dressing table with flashing lights that give Hollywood vibes. My room looks like a nun's library in comparison.

"Try this dress," she suggests.

I hold it against me. It's purple, skintight, and has a plunging neckline that goes down to my belly button. "Absolutely not."

"Okay, fine." She ponders, then twirls her finger. "Turn for me."

I humor her and spin.

She bites her lip in concentration, then her eyes light up. "Okay, I have just the outfit."

She rifles around her rails in her adjoining walk-in, launching Jimmy Choos and Nikes at me. I duck to avoid being hit in the head.

"What the..." I pick up a bright pink, phallic object that lands at my feet alongside the pile of shoes. "Is this what I think it is?"

She turns and smirks. "Oh yeah, that. I figured I'd try it after being fingered by Oliver did nothing for me." She shrugs. "I thought there was something wrong with me at first, but no. It was all his poor technique and skinny fingers."

Oliver is Mia's long-term, on-and-off boyfriend, who is hosting the party this evening.

My cheeks flush as I throw the vibrator to the side.

"Poor Oliver," I say.

"Poor Oliver got the best head of his life from me, so don't feel too sorry for him. Besides, he's better now that I've shown him what to do." She wiggles her fingers and cackles. "All he needed was a little practice."

Hearing about Mia's sexual exploits is liberating, but I'd never talk so openly about sex myself. It's not that I don't have sexy thoughts or fantasies—I just can't imagine ever acting on them. At this rate, I'll die a virgin.

"You really should buy one," she says.

"Huh?"

"A vibrator," she says. "Actually, I can give you a spare…"

"Borrowing an outfit is one thing, but I draw the line at sharing sex toys."

She throws an unopened plastic box my way. "A brand-new bullet, never used. Consider it an early birthday present."

"If my parents found it—"

"They won't," she insists. "It's tiny, so I'm sure you can hide it. You'll be thanking me later."

I slip it into my backpack to avoid an argument, but vow to throw it away later. It being discovered isn't worth the risk. I don't want to be branded a sex addict and forced to attend some of Dad's colleagues' group therapy sessions. I've already sat through countless sessions in Sarah's absence. Despite patient confidentiality, everything I said somehow found its way back to Dad.

"Found it." Mia holds up a black dress. It's more under-stated than all of her previous suggestions. "Thoughts?"

"It's okay," I say.

"Try it on then."

I wriggle the dress on. Although it's tight, the fabric

stretches effortlessly, and it's buttery smooth. It's an off-the-shoulder cut with long sleeves and a sweetheart neckline that shows a tasteful amount of cleavage.

"You look hot, but it's missing something…" She scratches her chin then proceeds to find a studded belt and a velvet choker. "That's better. It gives me Princess Di's revenge dress energy with an edge. Very you."

I don't know what she's talking about, but I slowly rotate to check myself out in the mirror. It's the first time I've worn a dress like this. It matches my makeup: a natural soft glam look with silver eyeshadow, winged eyeliner, and neutral lips.

"Are you sure it's not too much?" I ask nervously, noticing how tightly the dress clings to my ass.

"This isn't just any old high school party where you wear jeans and chug kegs in the middle of some forest," she says. "This is a Theobald party. Trust me, this is enough."

As well as being Mia's boyfriend, Oliver Theobald is Nate's best friend and, quite possibly, the richest guy at Stonybridge Academy. His dad founded a major software firm that sold for an eye-watering amount. With his fortune, he bought a giant plot of land and built the famous Theobald mansion.

"I feel like we're going to the Oscars or something," I say, rolling my eyes. "Does my hair look okay?"

My brown hair flutters around my collarbones in loose, gentle waves that will probably fall out by the end of the night. Compared to Mia, I look positively plain. She's donning a white leotard with a glittering gold mesh dress layer over the top, which flaunts her sculpted long legs and gorgeous figure. With her dangling gold earrings, hair piled on top of her head, and bright red lips, she looks like a celebrity.

"Stop worrying. You look perfect," Mia insists. "This is your debut to the Stonybridge social scene. You need to make an impact. Nate's going to love it."

Nervous and excited butterflies flutter in my stomach. "I don't know about that."

Mia holds her phone out. "Let's take a picture."

"Fine," I say. Her enthusiasm is infectious. "But don't post it anywhere."

I avoided going on social media for months after Sarah's disappearance. Seeing her face splashed all over the internet alongside theories about what happened to her was too difficult. Every day, new posts appeared about people claiming they'd seen her in Wyoming, Ohio, Australia, and even Iceland. Not to mention the trolling...

"My ten thousand followers would eat up your beautiful face, but fine," she says. "Just get over here already."

We make a few jokey poses for the camera. Mia wraps a pink feather boa around my neck, and I sneeze while she kisses me on the cheek, leaving a lipstick mark behind. This is the most normal I've felt in... well, I can't remember. We giggle, and the heavy pressure that weighs on me most days lightens for a moment.

Is this how being eighteen is supposed to feel? Maybe this is why Sarah ran away. Did she want to chase this feeling of freedom? Despite a year passing, I still have no answers. Stepping outside of my comfort zone and into the world Sarah lived in could help me find them, or I'll learn that some secrets are best buried...

CHAPTER
THREE

ERIN

A SECURITY GUARD peers down at his list and barks, "Name?"

Behind us, our senior classmates are lined up, waiting to be admitted. Outside the Theobald mansion, rows of sports cars fill the street.

"Mia Moldova," she says confidently. "And Erin Acacia."

"Erin's not on the list," he replies with a deadpan expression, crossing his arms. "No name, no entry."

"Shit." Mia scowls and puts her phone to her ear. "I'll call Ol to fix this."

"It's okay," I say, cringing as the guard's glare deepens. "We can go."

"We're not going anywhere," Mia says firmly, then curses into her phone. "No answer. The little shit!"

Maybe this is a sign I shouldn't go to parties. We've fallen at the first hurdle. I should never have come. I don't belong here. Staying home is safe. Comfortable. Easy.

A figure appears like a knight in shining armor out of nowhere. "What's going on?"

I take a second to realize it's Nate. He's wearing a white shirt, the top few buttons undone, and a pair of pressed chinos.

"We have a gatecrasher." The guard points at me. "She's not on the list."

My cheeks flush scarlet.

"It's okay, Jay," Nate says, flashing me a smile that shows off his cute dimples. "Erin's with me."

I am?

The guard echoes my own thoughts aloud. "She is?"

"Yep," Nate says. "Right, Erin?"

Mia nudges me in the ribs and gives me a 'speak the fuck up' look.

"Y-yes," I stammer. "I am."

The guard shrugs and waves us past.

"Ignore him," Nate says, squeezing my shoulder in reassurance and making my skin tingle. "Ol's security loves throwing their weight around, but they're harmless."

"I'm going to kill Oliver," Mia huffs as we climb the stone steps to the gigantic oak door. "Erin's my best friend. I asked him to put her on the list."

"In his defense, I've never been to any of his parties before," I point out.

"So?" she fumes. "He should know better."

"I'll deliver the message that you're not happy with him," Nate jokes. "Again."

I snicker. While I hear about their relationship drama from Mia, Nate must get the other side of the story from Oliver. As much as I love her, the girl is high maintenance.

"Thanks for..." I begin, daring to look at Nate before we enter.

My sentence trails off when a loud chorus of cheers bursts out. A group of football players chants Nate's name as soon as they see him. "Holt, Holt, Holt!"

"You better go," I say.

"I'll find you later," he says, catching my eye and winking. "Maybe you can save me a dance?"

I don't have time to reply before one of his teammates pulls him into the throng of whooping high school students.

"It looks like someone was happy to see you," Mia teases.

"Shut up," I say, unable to keep the smile out of my tone. "Holy shit…"

My jaw drops at the sheer scale of the first floor. It makes my house look like a trailer. The entire downstairs is open plan and modern in design, with vast glass windows that flow around the sides. A sleek white staircase in its center splits into two, leading to different wings.

"Pretty amazing, right?" Mia says. "This place has ten bedrooms, and the basement has a cinema, indoor pool, and spa. There's even a basketball court. Oliver's dad had everything custom-made."

"It's insane," I say. "Doesn't his dad mind having the whole senior class over?"

It's damage waiting to happen in a building that cost him millions of dollars.

"He works away a lot, and Oliver's mom is staying in France with her sister." Mia shrugs. "Rumor has it they're getting divorced, but Oliver doesn't care as long as he gets the place to himself most of the time. Let me show you around…"

It resembles a night club more than a family home, with strobe lights bouncing off the walls. Rows of wineglasses and shots in every color cover the surface of an ornate bar. A U-shaped velvet sofa, large enough to seat at least twenty people, is directly in front of us, and a DJ booth playing house music is to its left. Beyond that, a sliding glass door opens onto an outdoor pool area where people are dancing.

"Mia!" Oliver, the man of the hour, greets us. Judging from his slurred speech, he's already hit the liquor hard. "You made it. You look…" His eyes trail up and down her body, and his Adam's apple bobs in longing. "Incredible."

I shift my weight from one foot to the other awkwardly,

trying to ignore the simmering sexual tension between them, when Oliver notices me.

"Erin?" He blinks hard. "Is that you?"

"Who else would it be, asshole?" Mia cocks her hip. Despite her sassy attitude, I can tell she's pleased her outfit got the reception it deserved. Oliver's not the only guy to have noticed her arrival; the hockey team is shamelessly checking her out too. Who can blame them? "Excuse us, we're getting a drink."

She barges past, leaving him staring after us.

"Everyone's staring at you," I mumble.

She laughs. "They're not looking at me."

My skin prickles as we move through the crowd of dancing bodies. I mimic Mia, holding my head high and smiling, but I'm freaking out on the inside. I'm not used to the attention. I'd prefer to watch from the shadows than be an active participant.

A guy I don't recognize wolf-whistles. "Looking good, Erin."

"Who is he?" I whisper.

"Some jerk from the football team," Mia replies. "Although he's definitely not the only guy thinking that. You're on fucking fire tonight."

While most guys seem incapable of looking at our faces, the girls have a less favorable reaction. Stonybridge Academy is full of cliques, and neither of us fit into them. While Mia could have been part of whichever she wanted, she avoids affiliating herself with any one group. The girls can't disguise their surprise when they see me, scanning my outfit like they're looking for a defect.

"Who are all these people?" I ask.

As well as the familiar faces I see around Stonybridge's corridors, there are many I don't recognize.

"A bunch of people from Rydell Prep are here," she says.

"I don't know why Ol bothers asking them, especially the football players. They're sleazebags."

Rydell Prep is the rival school in the next town and is full of equally wealthy assholes.

We slot into a gap that's opened at the bar.

"Shot?" Mia holds up a fluorescent green liquid and sniffs it. "Mm, apple."

"I'm not sure."

Aside from a few sips of champagne at a wedding, I've never drank alcohol before.

"You don't have to," she says. "But it might help take the edge off."

Anything is worth a try. I take the shot and drain it. It tastes like an apple flavor Jolly Rancher with a sour edge.

Mia waits for my verdict. "Well?"

"It's okay," I say, reaching for another. A blue one this time.

"Are you sure?" Mia asks.

I pass her one and arch an eyebrow. "I thought you said you wanted to party?"

She laughs and accepts the drink. "I never expected you to be the bad influence."

I hold up the shot in toast. "To Sarah."

Commemorating her on my first night out feels right. If the stories I've heard are anything to go by, she'd be the first to drink the bar dry and dance on the tables. Sarah lit up every room she walked into. Having fun is what she lived for.

Mia clinks her glass against mine. "To Sarah!"

The night passes in a blur. It turns out Mia was right about alcohol taking the edge off. Without the countless shots, I'd never have let Mia persuade me to join her on the dance floor.

The room spins, and my hips writhe to the music. Mia takes my hand and spins me around, pulling me back to her, laughing. Instead of feeling claustrophobic in the crowd, the heat of the other dancers brings me a sense of safety. Nothing can happen to us while we're here, together.

I stumble a little on the next move, almost twisting my ankle in my black heels. Damn them. A powerful arm around my waist stops me from falling, and I look to see Nate grinning down at me. My savior.

"Easy there," he says. "You promised me a dance, remember?"

I look at Mia, but she's conveniently vanished, leaving us alone.

"I… um…" Even though we're neighbors, we've never had a proper conversation. "I guess so."

Nate puts his hands on my hips. As if by magic, the previously bassy music switches to a sexy, slow song. Our bodies are pushed together, as more people join the floor, until my breasts press against his chest. All I can think about is the warmth of his fingers and the fluttery feeling between my legs.

Nate bends to whisper, "You look amazing tonight."

"Thanks," I reply, batting my eyelashes in a way I hope comes across as flirty and not like I'm trying to blink something out of my eye. "You don't look too bad yourself."

"Every guy in the room is wishing they were me right now," he says.

A cheesy, yet cute line.

"Oh, really?" My playful side comes to the surface. Usually, I'm shy and reserved, carefully picking every word before I say it, but the drinks have relaxed me. "And why is that?"

"Because they all wish they were dancing with the most beautiful woman in the room," he says.

"Does that line usually work?"

"Yes," he says with a lopsided grin, pulling me closer. "But I'm not just saying that with you. I mean it."

His hands slide to rest on my lower back. My body acts of

its own accord, swaying and wrapping my arms around his neck. We're close enough for me to feel the growing hardness in his pants. Knowing I'm having this effect on Nate Holt, the captain of the football team who all the girls want, gives me a newfound sense of power.

"You're a mystery, Erin Acacia," he says. "You have no idea how many times I've wanted to speak to you."

"Why haven't you?"

"Are you kidding?" He laughs. "You're fucking gorgeous and at the top of our class. Don't you realize how intimidating you are?"

"Intimidating? Me?" I snort in disbelief. "You're the most popular guy in school. Every girl has a crush on you."

His head dips closer. "Every girl?"

Our lips are inches away from touching. I stand on the tips of my toes. Just as we're about to kiss, a stumbling jock knocks into me, spilling a full glass of beer down my front.

Nate grabs the drink-spiller by the front of his shirt. "Watch where you're going, dickwad."

The drink-spiller cowers and musters a feeble apology, while a group of girls cackle. It was no accident.

"Are you okay?" Nate asks.

"I'm fine," I insist, even though I smell like a brewery. "I'll grab some paper towels to clean the mess."

"I'll come with you," he says.

Before he has the chance, he's swarmed by guys shouting, "Captain! Drink! Captain! Drink!"

While Nate gets swept into the chaos, I slink away to find a restroom, getting jostled back and forth as I weave through the gaps. My earlier euphoria takes a nosedive. People are too close. My head throbs from the pounding music. Everyone has drunk more than they can handle, including me.

Away from the safety of the dancers, the floor feels like it's turned to Jell-O. Each step takes more effort than the last, and I walk like an astronaut taking my first steps on the moon.

Mia is nowhere in sight, and I decide against calling her. I don't want to ruin her night.

"Do you know where the bathroom is?" I ask a nearby couple. They're too busy eating each other's faces to give me any directions.

I take deep breaths to steady myself, which only intensifies my dizziness. I make it to the stairs and lean against the banister to balance, then I hear his voice…

"Erin?"

I squeeze my eyes shut, hoping I've imagined it, until his firm grasp closes around my forearm. He grips so tightly it'll bruise.

"Erin!"

I open my eyes to see my father. I've not seen him this angry since the aftermath of one of Sarah's partying antics. His nostrils flare in fury.

"Dad," I stammer, "w-what are you—"

"We're leaving," he declares menacingly. "Now."

Onlookers snicker as he drags me from the house, yanking my wrist so hard my shoulder almost dislocates.

"Please, Dad," I whimper. "You're hurting me. I'm sorry, okay? I didn't mean—"

He marches me down the steps to his waiting car, ignoring my pleading.

"Dad—"

How did he even get past security? Surely he wasn't on the guest list?

"Don't say another word," he hisses, throwing me into the back of the car.

My lip trembles as the door shuts. Stupidly, I reach for the handle, but it's already locked. Of course it is. He's done everything possible to keep me confined. He won't stop now.

"After all I've done to keep you safe, this is how you repay me," he rages, getting into the driver's seat and revving the engine. "It's time I taught you a lesson."

CHAPTER
FOUR

ERIN

I STRUGGLE INTO AN UPRIGHT POSITION, getting thrown around without a seat belt. A particularly violent turn sends my head crashing into the window. Dad doesn't check whether I'm okay. His icy stare penetrates me from the rear mirror, watching with a look of disapproval that makes me want to hurl.

"You lied to me," he says.

"I..." I could make up an excuse, but he'll only see through it. His job has made him a human lie detector; well versed in sensing changes in people's body language and tone. "I'm sorry, okay? It won't happen again."

Apologizing is all I can do. Hopefully, if I sound sincere enough, he'll let it go. What started as a fun night has turned into a nightmare. Was it worth it?

"No," he agrees. "It won't."

We halt at a stoplight, and he sniffs the air.

"You've been drinking," he says. A statement, not a question.

Nothing sobers you up more than your dad crashing a party.

"Only a little," I admit, not that it'll make any difference.

He'll likely force me to attend Alcoholics Anonymous on a weekly basis.

"I'm disappointed," he says. The light turns green, and I'm thrown back again as he hits the gas hard. "After everything I've done to keep you safe, this is how you treat me. You broke my trust. A trust that I gave freely. A trust you'll have to earn back."

"I will," I say. "I promise I'll make it up to you."

"I know you will."

We drive past Stonybridge Academy and should take the next right, but he keeps going.

"You missed the turn," I remark feebly.

"No," he replies. "I didn't."

"But our house is that way…"

I'm tipsy, but I haven't completely lost my sense of direction.

"We're not going home."

A lump forms in the back of my throat, and I blink away tears. Crying has no effect on him. Whenever I hurt myself as a child, it was Mom who kissed my grazes better. He sees crying as a sign of weakness. Tears won't help me now.

Our town, Pasturesville, is close to a rocky mountain range, yet still within commutable distance to the nearest city, which makes it a popular neighborhood for families.

When Dad takes a left, leading away from the town, I realize where we're heading. The dirt track crawling up the side of the mountain is always deserted. Locals have dubbed it the 'highway to hell', and more suspicious folks tell stories about how the devil touches everyone who travels up it. Maybe there's some truth to that.

"Can we go home, Dad? Please?" I bargain. "I made a mistake, okay? I'm sorry, I—"

"Your words are meaningless after your actions tonight, Erin." He tsks and shakes his head. "How can I believe anything you say after you lied to me? You're lucky I arrived before you caused our family further embarrassment. It's bad enough that you went out dressed like a common whore, but drinking too? I expected more from you."

I pull my dress lower, but the fabric keeps bunching, making me extra conscious about the amount of thigh I have on show. I shouldn't have let Mia talk me into wearing this outfit, no matter how good I felt in it.

The road narrows as we continue, curving with the mountainside. Various signs along the sides of the road warn trespassers away in bold text. They needn't have bothered putting them up. No one comes here willingly. Beyond the trees, I glimpse the double chain-link electric fences that are there to prevent people from going in, and more importantly, to stop patients from getting out.

"Why are we here?" I ask.

Terror roots me to my seat as we approach Sunnycrest Asylum.

"I told you, Erin," Dad says ominously. "I've been too lenient with you, and look where it's got me."

He lowers the window and swipes his work card to gain access, jolting the gates into life. A security guard looks up from his post for a brief second as we drive by. He recognizes Dad instantly and waves a donut in our direction, not noticing me in the back of the car. It's not unusual for my father to work late, and he's often called in during the twilight hours.

I consider slamming my fists on the window, but it'll only make Dad angrier. Besides, the guard will never question his boss if he wants to keep his job.

Sunnycrest Asylum is a C-shaped building made from concrete slabs. Although we're at a higher altitude, that doesn't explain the change to the air here. The building is a vortex of misery, radiating a sinister aura that makes the hairs on my neck stand on end. Dad created it to treat, and contain, the criminally insane and most troubled youths in the country.

Sunnycrest has a top-of-the-range security system. I can't remember the exact details, but I've eavesdropped on enough of my parents' dinner parties to know that it cost multiple millions. No one gets in or out without special clearance, and technological advances have made it virtually impossible to leave the facility from the inside, meaning they've been able to cut the costs of the security detail outside.

"Get out," Dad commands.

I don't move, hoping this is a twisted joke. If he wants to scare me, he can consider it done. He marches out and storms to my side of the car, opening the door and grabbing my arm to force me outside.

"Dad, please," I beg.

My voice echoes around the courtyard, but I'm not the only one shouting. Wails from within carry through the whistling winds.

"Come with me," he hisses through gritted teeth, dragging me to a door labeled 'Authorized Access Only'.

"Can we go home?" I plead. "I don't like it here."

Although we're the only people around, I shiver, unable to shed the feeling of being watched. Tiny windows with steel bars are evenly spaced on the asylum's walls. I don't look up, too afraid to see who is looking back.

"You should have thought of that before you went to that party," he says.

He continues past the door and skirts around the back of the building. I stumble, struggling to keep up with his pace. There are no lights back here, and we come to a stone staircase that looks to lead into an underground basement.

"Move." He shoves me in front of him, forcing me to take the stairs first. I try turning around, but he blocks my path. He can easily overpower me, so fighting is pointless. "I said, move."

I gulp, taking cautious steps until I reach the bottom.

"Here." He passes me a rusty key from his shirt pocket.

I look at it in confusion. "What—"

"Unlock the chains," he commands.

Heavy chains and a lock block the door. I turn the key, hoping it won't open, but it does with a small click.

"Now remove the chains," he instructs.

I loosen them, and they drop to the ground with a clang. He then pulls a lanyard from under his shirt, which holds many fobs, keys, and cards. He doesn't go anywhere without it, and I'm pretty sure he sleeps in it too. With it, he opens the door.

He nudges me forward. "Inside. Now."

I can't see anything, only darkness stretching into the unknown. He has to be kidding, right?

I attempt to bargain one final time. "Please, can we just go home?"

He sighs, losing his patience, and pushes me with a force I don't expect. He propels my body forward, knocking me off my feet. I break my fall with my hands, narrowly avoiding smashing my face into the cold concrete. Before I'm back on my knees, he shuts me away from the outside world with a slam.

"Dad!" I crawl to the closed door and bash it with balled fists. "Let me out! Please! I'm sorry! I shouldn't have lied. I've learned my lesson."

He chuckles on the other side of the metal. Ironically, it's the first time I've heard him laugh for a year—aside from the fake one he uses when trying to impress visitors.

"You've not learned anything yet. This is what happens when you defy me," he says. "You will thank me for this later."

Tears fall down my cheeks in fat blobs and make my eyes burn from the running mascara.

"Please!" I whimper. "I want to go home."

"Obedient children get nice things," he says. "Bad behavior must be corrected. I'm doing this for your own good. I'll be back when you've had time to think about your actions."

Chains rattle, and I swallow the rising vomit as realization hits. He's really leaving me here.

"Don't leave!" I scream. "Come back!"

He doesn't answer.

I reach for my phone but remember it's in my bag, still in the car.

"Help!" I bang on the door. "Help me!"

It's no use. The asylum is full of people screaming from morning to night. Even if someone heard my pleas, they'd think I'm a crazy patient.

The smell of rising damp makes my stomach churn. My knees sting, and a warm trickle of blood oozes down my leg. My eyes adjust, noting the only shred of light comes from a tiny half-centimeter gap around the edge of the door.

I have to pull myself together. I grapple around, running my hands over the walls, trying to focus on what's in front of me. It's a grounding technique I learned from a therapist, only I never expected to use it after being locked in an underground cupboard.

What kind of parent does this to their own flesh and blood? No one ever questions the sanity of a psychiatrist, but he blurs the line between sane and crazy. How long can you spend around people who've lost their mind without losing part of your own?

"Bricks," I say, choosing to fill the silence than let it stretch out. "Breeze block." The space is compact. Ten feet by six, if that. "Concrete floor."

My shoe hits a steel bucket when I rotate. I kneel to inspect it and get assaulted by the pungent smell of stale urine. I retch, retasting the apple shot from earlier. Well, I guess that answers my question about going to the bathroom…

I carefully nudge the bucket. Despite the foul odor, it seems to be empty, judging by how easily it rattles, and I push it into the corner away from me.

"It'll be fine," I say. "It'll be over soon."

My words bring me no comfort. Dad wants to frighten me, not cause actual pain. All I have to do is stick it out until morning. He'll be back then and use this exercise as a teaching opportunity. Until then, I can get through a few hours being alone.

"Boo!" a male voice comes from somewhere above. It reverberates through me like a lightning bolt.

I inhale sharply, holding in air and hoping he'll go away if I stay quiet.

"I know you can hear me," the voice says.

His playful words don't match the underlying cruelness to his tone.

I'm a mouse that has walked straight into a trap that's about to snap.

I slap my hands over my mouth, struggling to control my breathing. I know what kind of people they lock up in here. Some patients have committed the worst crimes imaginable: murder, rape, and there's even a cannibal rumored to be in residence.

"You can't hide from us," a second voice says. It's deeper than the first, with a slight drawl to his accent, making him sound almost bored.

"What's wrong?" a third guy asks. He's British, which instantly makes him seem less intimidating. A Brit instantly conjures an image of a hero from an Austen novel in my mind. "Are you scared?"

"Let's find out," the first says.

I name them in my head. One, Two, and Three. Giving them names helps make them less scary than abstract figures.

A bolt from the ceiling falls at my feet. The tinny ping echoes around the tiny space, followed by the torturous scrape of more screws being loosened. I squeal as a sheet of metal lands to my right with a bang. They're in the ceiling, coming down a vent. *Fuck.*

"I love it when they scream," Three purrs, dashing my hopes of him being the next Mr. Darcey. Even a cute accent can't make that sentence sound good.

"Don't be afraid, sweetheart," Two says. "We only want to welcome you."

Their voices grow louder as bodies shuffle along metal above my head.

"Help!" I scream, breaking my vow of silence to pound against the door. They already know I'm here, so what harm can it do? I hear desperation in my hoarse voice, but I don't care. There's still a chance Dad is close by. "Help me!"

"Save your breath," Three urges. "No one listens when you scream here, except for me."

Help isn't coming.

CHAPTER
FIVE

ERIN

DID DAD PLAN THIS? Did he know they were coming? No, he'd never willingly lock me in a room with three dangerous psychopaths when he's made his thoughts about hanging out with boys clear.

I press my back against the cold metal door, and a chill snakes down my spine.

They're here.

Heavy panting comes from the vent and fills the space like a thick smoke. It crawls down my throat, choking me, but they don't move. Not yet.

They leave me hanging. Waiting is even worse than if they were to storm in. I'm hyperaware of every minute sensation: the goosebumps on my arms, my parched mouth, the strong beat of my heart pumping blood around my body. At least that's a reminder I'm alive. My legs scream for me to run, but my knees lock in place. There's nowhere to go.

"Are you afraid of the three big bad men who live in the walls?" One drawls.

"If she's not, she should be," Three says. "Why don't you scream for us again? What a sweet fucking sound. It's been so long since I've heard a woman scream that pretty."

Are they going to rape or kill me? Or both?

They're treating me like a toy. If these are my last moments, I want to show strength. I channel Mia's no bullshit energy, thinking about how my best friend would handle the situation. She wouldn't pray to be spared. It's too late for that.

"You're the cowards here," I say, mustering all the confidence I can. "Crawling around in the vents like rats."

Knowing they can't see my face makes it easier. They can't see my shaky shoulders or my trembling bottom lip.

Two laughs hard. A deep belly rumble that bounces off the walls.

One joins him, and adds, "This one has more fire than I expected."

This one? I bite my lip to stop myself from whimpering.

"Maybe we are like rats," Three agrees. "We crawl through dark spaces that other people choose to avoid. We slip into gaps that others overlook and make our home there. We're everywhere and nowhere. Always watching."

"It may be dark, but we still see you. You're trying to act brave when you're not," One says. "You can't lie to us. The question is, why did he bring you here?"

"I'm not like y-you," I stammer. "I'm not crazy."

They cackle. A maniacal noise that makes my teeth chatter and the hairs on the back of my neck stand on end. They're three separate entities, but the way they laugh together makes them appear interconnected.

"Everyone's crazy," Two says. "Those who can't see it are the craziest of all."

A metallic screech signals a body sliding closer. There's a deep breath, followed by feet dropping to the floor opposite me. I scream.

"There's that sound again," Three says from above. "Fuck, it makes me so hard."

I clamp my lips shut, determined not to make another

sound. My mind races through the possibilities of what could happen. All of them lead to the same outcome: Dad finding my dead body in the morning.

"What does she smell like?" Two asks.

One is here with me. He doesn't move straight away, but the heat radiating from his body warms my skin. His breathing sucks everything within range into a dark, destructive cloud, filling me with fear.

He takes a step. Slow and deliberate. He's in no hurry.

I try to remember everything Dad said about his work and how the asylum operates, hoping there's something that might give me a chance of surviving.

"What if an orderly finds out you left your rooms?" I ask, recalling that patients face sanctions for breaking the asylum rules.

Discussing punishments always makes Dad's eyes light up, whether it's limiting their access to the outside or extra sedation. He loves anything that gives him more control.

"Rules?" One scoffs. His voice has a gravelly edge to it. "There are no rules. This place is lawless."

"That's not true," I say. "I know—"

I stop, not wanting to give too much away. Finding out that I'm Doctor Acacia's daughter won't do me any favors.

"She seems to know a lot about the asylum for someone who isn't crazy," Two says.

"I watch a lot of movies," I reply.

"Tell me," One advances. "Who are you?"

His scent surrounds me, a hint of smoke, mixed with dirt, and an almost antiseptic clinical undertone.

"I'm no one," I say.

"Lies!" Three choruses from the vent, slamming his fists or feet on the iron like a drum. "Lies! Lies! Lies!"

One closes in. I shield my face with my hands. Although I can't see anything, I'm aware of his gigantic, looming presence. He rests his arms above my head, boxing me in with no escape. He's much taller than me, a foot at least, which makes him six-three, at least.

"Put your hands down," he commands.

I want to defy him, but I don't. Shaking, I do as he asks and drop my arms to my sides.

I once took self-defense classes in school, but my mind draws a blank on any moves that could save me now. All I remember is being told to gather as much information about your attacker as possible, on the off chance you get away. What good is that advice when you're locked in the darkness with only voices and smells to go on?

One leans closer. The tip of his nose nudges my cheek, and I turn my head, wincing at his touch. He inhales, breathing down the side of my face. My toes curl as he buries his face in the crevice where my neck meets my shoulder. He inhales deeply and groans with satisfaction. His moan vibrates through my core, and I whimper.

"What's she like?" Three asks. "Is she as sweet as she sounds?"

One's tongue shoots out of his mouth. I cringe but stay in position, with my left cheek pressed against the door, as he licks along my jaw like an animal.

"She tastes like cheap beer and virgin tears," he purrs. "What bad things did you do tonight, *Little Ghost*?"

"Nothing," I squeak. "I did nothing."

"More lies," he says. He grabs my chin to force me to look up, yet all I see is blackness. "Do you know what they do to patients when they lie?" His breath tickles my cheeks. "They do unspeakable acts. Acts that your innocent mind can't comprehend. Acts that are so depraved they'd make you question who you are. Acts that your fragile little body can't handle."

My thighs clench. The combination of his heady smell and sultry voice affects me in a way I don't quite understand.

"Do you want me to show you what we do to liars?" he

asks. "You came into our home, so every inch of you belongs to us now. Every sweet nook of your tight body is ours."

"Our new toy to play with," Two echoes.

Another body drops from the vent. His landing is lighter, showing he's nimble on his feet. Although I can't see him, the vision of a black panther springs to mind. A deadly predator who moves with laser precision.

"Please," I beg. "Don't hurt me."

Two laughs. His footsteps are gentle.

One moves aside, but I sense him standing close while Two approaches.

Two doesn't touch me right away. In fact, if not for the barely audible sound of his breathing, I wouldn't know he was here at all.

"We play rough," Two says. "Sometimes our toys break. Sometimes we like to make them snap."

I yelp as a piece of metal slides along my throat. It's not sharp enough to be a knife, but its coldness is like being swiped by an icicle. He paints me with the object, moving it back and forth across my throat like he's pretending to saw my neck clean off. A tear slips down my cheek, not that he can see it. This might be the end. The curved metal dances across my collarbone until it meets the dip in the middle and glides lower.

"Another one for my collection," Two says.

I squeeze my eyes shut as he withdraws momentarily, fully prepared for my throat to be slashed, when there's a snipping noise instead. *Scissors.* I don't feel anything being cut, though.

"Perfect," Two purrs. "I'll treasure this."

He's fucking insane. They all are.

"Can I come out yet?" Three questions. "I'm feeling left out."

Three is the one who makes me most uneasy. Perhaps it's

his obsession with screaming. They're all dangerous, but he seems to be in another league.

"Not today," One says. "But soon."

I sigh in relief, but my minute motion doesn't go unnoticed.

"Don't you want him to join us?" One mocks. "I'm not keeping him away for your sake."

"When I come for you, Little Ghost, I'll make you beg until you have no voice left," Three warns. "I promise I'll steal that pretty scream of yours. By then, begging is all you'll be able to do."

"If you're going to kill me," I say, "then do it already and make it quick."

Two snorts in amusement. "She's exactly what we've been waiting for."

"Tell us your name," One orders.

"Wendy," I lie, picking the first one that springs to mind.

A firm hand locks around my jaw, smothering the bottom part of my face. Fingers squeeze hard and push my cheeks together.

"Lies! Lies! Lies!" Three choruses. "Lies! Lies! Lies!"

"You will regret lying," One says. He's the one holding my face hostage, and he moves it left to right like he's a puppet master pulling my strings. His body closes in, and he whispers, "We'll make sure of that, *Erin Acacia.*"

He drops his hold, and my head flops.

"How do you know my name?" I stutter. "Why ask if you already knew the answer?"

The shadows slink away silently, scampering back into the dark abyss.

As soon as I'm sure they're gone, I slide down the door, pulling my knees up to my chest to hug them, and listen to them crawl away, leaving the lingering smell of danger behind. Those three monsters somehow knew who I was all along.

Hours pass.

I keep expecting them to return, but they don't. Perhaps the possibility alone is even worse. Mice scuttle around my ankles and strange noises, wails, and groans reverberate all around.

Finally, a rattle from outside brings me out of my daze.
The chains.

I stagger to my feet, ignoring the pins and needles tingling through my legs. I almost fall but catch the wall. Seconds later, the door opens and Dad stands in the doorway.

"Come, Erin," he says, moving aside to let me pass. "It's time to go home."

I hobble out, refusing to look back at that hellhole, and follow Dad silently to the car. I don't look up at the windows, but I feel their stares watching me. I won't give them the satisfaction of seeing my face.

Dad hums under his breath while we walk. Unlike last night, his simmering anger has subsided. He opens the car door for me, as opposed to throwing me in like a piece of trash.

After fastening his seat belt, he turns to face me. Despite his smile, his eyes let me know that my unacceptable behavior hasn't been forgiven.

"I hope you learned a valuable lesson last night," he says.

"Yes, sir," I reply, dutifully hanging my head in submission.

"Good," he replies. "Then we needn't speak of this again. Next time, I'm sure you'll make the right choices."

I swallow hard. "I will."

As we drive out of Sunnycrest's gates, I look back at the ominous building. What secrets reside within its walls? The border between its world and mine is thin. When we cross back into town and rejoin civilization, the neighborhood looks the same, yet everything feels different somehow.

I grab a strand of hair from around my face to twirl it, and my stomach flips when I find a chunk missing. One strand is at least three inches shorter than the rest. I choke down the vomit rising in my throat. The snipping. The scissors. His collection.

Although I've left Sunnycrest behind, a part of me remains there. With them…

CHAPTER
SIX

ERIN

"You're coming straight home after the concert," Dad orders as he drops me off outside the academy. "Remember, I'll be watching."

I nod solemnly. The last few days have passed in a blur. Aside from practicing piano and joining my family for dinner, I've done little else. Dad confiscated my phone as punishment and insists on driving me to and from school until further notice. He removed the television in my room, and I'm only allowed to use my laptop for schoolwork—anything fun is blocked by strict parental controls. He needn't worry about me breaking his rules anymore, though. I'll do anything to make sure I don't return to Sunnycrest.

Dad's blazing stare torches my back until I pass through the doors and find respite in the hallway.

Mia launches herself at me as soon as she sees me, almost knocking me sideways.

"Erin!" She hugs me tightly. "I've been calling you all weekend. Your dad wouldn't let me inside the house when I came to visit. Is everything okay?"

"Sorry, I've not been ignoring you," I say. "Dad took my phone."

"Someone said he showed up at the party," Mia says,

pulling away from our hug. Her eyes soften with pity, guilt playing on her lips. "How bad was it?"

I shrug, playing it down. Even though I trust Mia, I can't tell her what happened, especially when three psychopaths are involved. "Pretty much what you'd expect," I lie. "No phone for a week. Rides to and from school. I'm basically grounded for the rest of my life."

"I'm so sorry," she says, falling into step by my side as we make our way to our lockers. "It's all my fault. I shouldn't have pushed you into going to the party."

"Don't blame yourself," I say, feigning a smile. "I had fun."

"How did your dad even find out where you were?" she asks. "Is he tracking you or something?"

I shrug again. It doesn't matter. "He has a way of finding out things."

Mia wouldn't understand. Her mom is so relaxed. She has no curfew or rules. I can't imagine having that level of freedom.

"Are you sure you're all right?" Mia looks at me with concern and loosens my tie. "You seem a little on edge."

"I'm fine," I say. "It was an intense weekend, and I've got a lot on my mind. That's all."

She frowns but doesn't probe me further, for now at least.

"Your hair looks different," she comments. "Did you get layers?"

To balance out my hair after discovering the missing strand, I cut the other side to match, giving me choppy layers at the front. It's a little lopsided, but my waves disguised it enough for Mom not to notice.

"I fancied a change," I say, stroking the end of the strand Two cut. "I better go or I'll be late for English."

"I'll catch you at lunch," she says.

"Actually, I'm rehearsing with Mr. Meyer, but I'll catch

you later," I say, making a hasty retreat before she asks more questions I'm not ready to answer.

I stop at my locker to grab my books. When I slam the door shut, I jump out of my skin. Everything falls from my hands, sending papers and pens flying everywhere. Nate, who was leaning against the locker next to mine, kneels to help gather them up. He's wearing his school football jersey with purple sleeves and a white body.

"Shit, sorry," he says. "I didn't mean to make you jump."

"It's o-okay," I stammer, mentally scolding myself for being such a socially awkward mess.

We reach for the same piece of paper, and our hands brush. I flinch as if he electrocuted me. A man's touch reminds me of One and how he licked my face. His tongue was pointed with possessive intent, eager to claim me. My cheeks redden as I quickly gather the rest of my belongings and stand.

"Here." Nate passes me the books he collected, flashing a perfect, apologetic smile. "I'll walk you to class."

I nudge my head at the door opposite. "I think I'll make it without dropping anything."

"It was good to see you on Friday night," he says. "I heard your dad showed up?"

I groan. "Does everyone know?"

If the ground could swallow me up, that'd be great. I'll forever be known as the girl whose dad dragged her home from a party like a pathetic loser.

"Word travels fast," he says. "Your folks are strict, huh?"

That's one way to put it.

"My dad's protective," I say. I shouldn't defend him, especially after what he did, but it's second nature now. "Sarah's disappearance was hard on him. On all of us."

"Fuck, sorry, of course. I didn't think..." Nate runs his hand through his hair. "It's nice he looks out for you. All my dad cares about is how I perform on the football field. It sucks you had to leave the party so early, though. I was hoping we'd get to spend more time together. How about a rain check?"

Behind us, a group of girls watch our interaction with intense interest. Lindsay Polar—Nate's not-ex-girlfriend, because he 'doesn't date', but the girl he's hooked up with the most—is one of them. Lindsay's the head cheerleader and looks exactly how you'd imagine a stereotypical blonde pom-pom wielder: big boobs, skinny waist, perfect tan, and drop-dead gorgeous. After being with her, I don't understand why Nate would show any interest in me. From the glares she and her friends are shooting in my direction, she doesn't either.

"Maybe," I say, managing a tight-lipped smile and swerving around him to get to class.

"Did you hear she threw herself at Nate at Theobald's party?" Lindsay says, making sure she's loud enough for me to overhear. "It's pathetic. Look, she's practically stalking him now. Talk about obsessed!"

I ignore the giggling and keep my expression blank. Correcting them will achieve nothing. Besides, it only reaffirms why I've always kept my friendship circle small. Apart from Mia and a few other musicians, I avoid social interactions like the plague.

Safely away from Lindsay, I find my usual desk, right at the back of the class by the window. I carefully take out my book and line up my highlighter pens, ready to absorb myself in a Shakespeare play. A tragedy will help distract me from my problems.

Ms. Chi, our teacher, floats in on the bell, swishing her long-sleeved patchwork dress. She's my favorite teacher. Unlike the others, she respects my right to stay silent and doesn't put me on the spot to answer questions, even when she knows I know I'll get them right. Usually, she's in a good mood, but this morning, her expression is troubled.

"Silence, class!" she barks. Everyone sits straighter in their seats, taken aback at her sudden loudness. "The principal has an announcement."

Seconds later, a jingle echoes over the PA system. Usually, morning announcements take a few minutes. They include a quick rundown of sporting fixtures and club updates, read by a member of the school newspaper society. However, today, Principal Wire's voice fills the halls.

Principal Wire is a friend of my father's, who also sits on the town council. He's a serious man, well respected in the community, and he takes the academy's reputation very seriously.

"All students must report to the main auditorium for an emergency assembly immediately," Principal Wire says. "Teachers, accompany your students."

Everyone looks around in confusion. An emergency assembly has only been called once before, during my first week. My stomach rolls at the memory. He and the sheriff gathered all the students to request they come forward, if they had any information on Sarah's disappearance. Although Sarah never studied here, the sheriff thought visiting all high schools within a twenty-mile radius may be helpful. Needless to say, it gleaned nothing useful. Other students make the same connection as their heads swivel to look at me. Sarah's disappearance sets me apart from the others. People don't want to associate with me. I'm an unfortunate reminder that bad things can happen, no matter how rich or well-positioned your family is.

"Come on, class," Ms. Chi chides everyone. "Form an orderly line."

Whispered rumors fly through the halls as I join the crowd.

Nate appears beside me. "What do you think happened?"

Wherever I go, he seems to pop up. Whilst I'm flattered by his attention, he's ruining my attempt to meld into the background.

"No idea," I say, keeping my gaze forward.

"Some people are saying someone broke into the principal's office to steal exam papers."

"I don't think they'd break into the office for those," I say. "Besides, exams aren't for another few months. The papers don't get shipped that early, do they?"

Nate reels off various theories he's heard during the last few minutes as we head into the auditorium. I opt to sit at the end of an aisle, an easy position to make a quick getaway.

"Well, shit…" Nate mutters. "This can't be good."

I follow Nate's gaze to see Sheriff Brady talking with Principal Wire on the stage in hushed tones. Principal Wire looks like he's aged ten years overnight, his wrinkles more pronounced than usual. The excited chatter becomes more subdued as the chairs fill up. Four police officers guard each of the doors around the edge of the room. What's happening?

Principal Wire takes the podium and taps the microphone twice, causing a silence to descend.

"Students, I'm sure you're wondering why I've gathered you here today," he says. "We've received some alarming news that myself, the governors, and the sheriff's office consider necessary to share for your safety. Please listen closely."

He passes the microphone to Sheriff Brady. Sheriff Brady has held his position in the county for as long as I remember. He's as short as he is wide, with a gray handlebar mustache and red cheeks.

"I'm sorry to tell you this," the sheriff says in his thick Louisiana accent. "But there's been an incident at Sunnycrest Asylum. A number of patients escaped last night."

The crowd draws a sharp intake of breath. Some girls even gasp and clap their hands over their mouth in horror.

Sheriff Brady took the lead on my sister's case. Although he had good intentions, his investigation was a mess, giving me zero faith he'll be able to track down multiple criminals when he can't find one teenage girl.

"Wait, doesn't your dad run the asylum?" Nate whispers.

I slouch in my seat.

"Silence!" Principal Wire roars. "Pay attention!"

"These patients are extremely dangerous and pose a threat to our community," the sheriff continues.

"How many of them?" someone shouts.

"What do you mean by 'threat'?" another yells.

I didn't think it was possible for anyone to escape. It's built like a fortress and designed to be unescapable. That being said, the Titanic was an unsinkable ship and look what happened to that. Every design has its flaws, and the asylum is full of patients who aren't afraid to exploit any weaknesses they find.

"That's all the information I can provide at this time," Sheriff Brady says. "However, let me reassure you that the sheriff's office has the situation in hand. We are working closely with the asylum to ensure the patients are appre-hended. Until all prisoners—I mean, err, patients—are located, we are imposing a nine p.m. curfew for the town, effective immediately. No one should travel alone, unless absolutely necessary, especially women. In the meantime, I ask you to remain vigilant. If you see anyone you don't recog-nize or any individuals acting suspiciously, report it to the police immediately. But, most importantly, remember that there is no need to panic."

Telling us not to panic has the opposite effect. Total chaos erupts. People complain about the unfairness of the curfew. *What about hockey practice? What about my dinner plans? What about my birthday party?* There are so many questions. Too many for him to answer. His eyebrow ticks nervously. He tries to hide it, but he's worried. All of the officers are.

I grip my seat, struggling to take in the news. There are more than one hundred patients in Sunnycrest. The chances of the men I met in the shadows skulking around Pasturesville are low, right? My blood turns to ice as I remember they know my name.

"Quiet!" Principal Wire steps in to thwart the hysteria. "The academy will set up a buddy system to ensure no one walks to their cars alone. All students should travel in pairs. Until further notice, all extracurricular events, including the music concert, are canceled. Your parents have been informed, and we have officers stationed at the school for extra security until all patients are found to help you feel safe."

But we're not safe. None of us are.

"We will keep you updated with any news. Until then, you should all return to your classes," Principal Wire says. "I want you to continue your day as normal."

"Fat chance of that," someone scoffs.

An asylum breakout is the biggest event to happen in Pasturesville in years.

"Are you okay?" Nate asks gently. "You're shaking."

"I'm fine," I say, pulling my blazer tighter around my body. "Just a little cold."

When we get up to leave, Ms. Chi heads straight for me.

"Erin," she says. Her brow crinkles with concern. "Can I have a word?"

"I'll catch you later, Erin," Nate says.

"Aren't we going back to class?" I ask as Ms. Chi walks in the opposite direction.

"In a moment," she says, pausing outside the teachers' lounge door. "I'm sorry to pull you aside, but the sheriff would like to speak with you."

"With me?" My jaw drops. "Why?"

"Take a seat inside," she says, opening the door to reveal an officer with crossed arms lurking at the back of the room. "An officer will bring you back to class when they're done."

The officer doesn't speak as I sit on the squeaky leather

sofa. I adjust my position, crossing one leg over the other and back again. Did they find out my father locked me in the asylum? Do they think I know something?

I'm not kept waiting long before the sheriff arrives.

"It's good to see you again, Erin," he says, although his expression implies the opposite. He sits opposite me, his shirt buttons straining around his belly and threatening to burst. "How have you been after…"

"Sarah?" I prompt as his sentence trails off.

"One year," he says, rubbing his chin thoughtfully. "How time flies…"

"Ms. Chi said you wanted to see me?" I ask.

"Ah, yes," he says. "I'm sure the news about the escape must have come as a shock considering your fathers position at the asylum. None of his staff were hurt."

Is that supposed to be reassuring? Dad doesn't hire locally anyway. Orderlies and doctors come from out of state and can't afford to live in Pasturesville, so they tend to commute in. If something bad happened at the asylum, it'd be easy for no one in town to find out.

"That's good," I say feebly.

"Now, I don't want to alarm you," he says. "But I have to tell you this as a precautionary measure…"

He really needs to work on his uplifting speeches because I'm fully prepared for whatever's coming next to be awful.

"Because your father runs Sunnycrest Asylum, there is a small—tiny, really—chance that your family is at an increased risk of being targeted by the patients who got out," he says. "Only minimal, though."

"Targeted?" I repeat.

If I escaped from a facility with nothing to lose and no one to return to, I know who'd be first on my list to visit. The patients aren't only mentally unstable, they're convicted felons.

"We have officers stationed at your home, and one of my men will escort you to and from school."

"What about my mom?" I ask.

"We'll take care of her," the sheriff says. "You're in good hands."

Numbness spreads through me. He said the same thing when he promised to bring Sarah home. His words mean nothing.

"We'll have them herded up and back where they belong in no time," he says unconvincingly. "Officer Blackwell will escort you to class now."

The young officer loitering in the background scowls, clearly unhappy to be a teenager's bodyguard when a manhunt is underway.

"Okay," I say.

Officer Blackwell follows me down the empty corridor.

"I need to stop at my locker," I say.

It's been a long time since I've taken a Xanax, but I always keep a backup stash in case of emergencies. This is as good a time as any. I need something to take the edge off and calm me down.

Officer Blackwell merely grunts in response.

When I open my locker, a folded piece of paper with singed edges catches my attention. Someone has laid it neatly on top of my books. How did they get inside?

My heart thunders as I open it and read the words.

Have you missed us, Little Ghost?
Remember, we're always watching...

The cursive is surprisingly delicate. Swirling black ink letters with gentle curves that resemble calligraphy. Something fluffy brushes against my palm. With a shaking hand, I turn the paper to find a lock of my hair taped down. A cruel taunt at how they took it from me so easily.

"What's the holdup?" Officer Blackwell grumbles in bored disinterest. "Have you got everything you need?"

I should tell him. Instead, I stash the message quickly into my pocket. "Sorry, I'm coming now."

I slam the locker shut. Telling him would mean getting my father in trouble and admitting what happened. Besides, they somehow managed to invade my personal space and sneak into the academy undetected. The cops can't protect me.

"Move." Officer Blackwell makes a shoo motion. "Back to class."

They might be watching us right now, and we won't even know it...

CHAPTER
SEVEN

ERIN

ONE WEEK HAS PASSED since the Sunnycrest breakout. The entire town is crawling with journalists from across the country. Many are camped outside our house, desperate to get an exclusive quote from Magnus Acacia, the brains behind the asylum. Amidst all the drama, Dad has hardly been at home. When he isn't working, he's busy assisting the police with their inquiries.

After the initial public outcry, my father's reputation has remained intact after the sheriff discovered a security guard was to blame. Apparently, the guard confessed to letting them out in a note before taking an overdose. It's easy to blame one rotten apple and deem it a freak event. Whatever the circumstances, there have been calls for Dad and his board of directors to review their protocols, which they've promised to do.

MIA: Are you watching this?

I roll over in bed and click the link in Mia's text, which takes me to a breaking news bulletin. In light of the current situation, Dad begrudgingly gave my cell phone back.

I turn the volume up to listen to a news reporter, who

stands outside Pasturesville's sheriff's station, where a crowd has assembled.

Over the last few days, the press has released more information about the seven asylum escapees. So far, four have been caught. Two were found on the first day. They plummeted to their deaths in a ravine along the treacherous mountain path. My father claimed they suffered from severe hallucinations that would have easily led them astray. Another patient was discovered a day later, eating out of a Burger King dumpster and barking like a dog. The fourth, who they found yesterday, hitched a ride and made it three hundred miles. The cops finally picked him up from a gas station after he snatched a pacifier from a baby and rolled around crying until they arrived.

The men's faces are splashed over every newspaper, screen, and billboard for miles. I've committed them all to memory, wondering which faces belong to the voices I heard in the darkness. None of them seem to fit what I imagined. After studying their profiles, I discovered all the escapees were under six feet tall. Although, my earlier judgment of their height was probably impaired by the darkness and my drinking.

Since receiving their note, they haven't communicated with me again. I should have burned it, but it's hidden in my underwear drawer along with the vibrator from Mia. With the police going through our trash daily, it seems like the best place to keep it.

"There is a new development in the case of the escapees from Sunnycrest Asylum," Sheriff Brady announces. I sit up in bed, paying full attention. "We're delighted to announce that we have secured the final three patients. We picked them up on the Canadian border."

Mia's texts come thick and fast.

MIA: It's over?!

MIA: Thank fuck… I was losing my mind at
home!

Like many of our peers, she's struggled with the imposed lockdown. Everyone's been complaining about it at school. The entire town has been living in a constant state of fear, including me. Stores have closed early, people have upgraded their home security systems, and countless neighbors have given interviews about how their lives have been turned upside down. And now it's over, reduced to a shady time in the town's history… just like that.

Still, a weight lifts from my shoulders. Maybe I'll actually be able to sleep tonight. Lately, the slightest floorboard creak has broken me out in a cold sweat, and I almost fell out of bed when a moth fluttered in front of my face. Despite not hearing from the guys, I haven't been able to shake the feeling of being watched…

"All of the apprehended patients are being transferred immediately to another facility out of state," Sheriff Brady says. "We appreciate it's been a difficult time for our community. We've come together and united in the face of adversity. I want to thank the public and the staff at Sunnycrest Asylum for their continued support. From now, the Pasturesville curfew is officially lifted."

A round of applause and cheers burst from the watching crowd in response.

I fall back onto my pillow and laugh in relief at the thought of my tormentors leaving town for good.

MIA: Do you think this means the ball is
back on?

Normality has officially resumed again.

The Harvest Ball is a Stonybridge tradition to welcome fall. The administration is big on formal gatherings. Essentially, it's an excuse to get dressed up. In the past, Dad only let me attend because he was a chaperone. After my recent escapades, I doubt he'll let me go this year.

Mia sends a flurry of outfit ideas, drawing me back into a world where deciding what to wear to a dance is the most pressing issue. I text back with my opinions, knowing she'll look beautiful in whatever she chooses. She always does.

A smash from downstairs interrupts our messaging. I tiptoe and poke my head around my bedroom door, right on time to hear a heavy object bouncing off the wall.

I wince at my father's angry shout. "You stupid woman! What have I told you about going into my office?"

His office, in the basement, is out of bounds. I've only glimpsed inside twice, knowing it's forbidden. It's his territory. A land no one can cross into.

"I…" I strain to hear Mom's timid reply. "I was dusting. I thought you'd appreciate the—"

"Appreciate?" he fumes. "How many times have I told you not to go through my things?"

"I promise I didn't touch anything," she reasons. "I only—"

I flinch as his hand hits her face and the sound cracks through the house like a thunderclap.

I was six years old when I walked in on him striking her for the first time. Her right cheek was emblazoned with his handprint for hours after. I remember her telling me to stay upstairs and reassuring me that they were only playing a game. Since then, it's become a pattern. Whenever something doesn't go right for him, she takes the brunt of his bad moods and pretends everything is fine the next day. Sarah tried to intervene a few times. She yelled at the top of her lungs for him to stop and threatened to report him. He simply laughed. No one would believe that Magnus Acacia, the esteemed psychiatrist, beats his wife.

"Don't you understand how stressful the last week has been for me, woman?" he roars. "I've worked around the clock to protect our family while criminals have roamed our streets, and this is how you choose to repay me?" He picks up another object and hurls it. "Clean up this mess!"

"Yes, Magnus," she agrees like she always does.

I wish I were as brave as Sarah. There's so much I'd like to say—*want* to say—but I don't. Nothing will make a difference, anyway. She'll never leave him.

Slowly, I shut my door. Although I don't have three dangerous men to worry about anymore, I can't help wondering whether they're any worse than the monster I share my home with.

———

At breakfast the next morning, Mom overcompensates by preparing a mammoth feast, and my father acts extra appreciative.

"You've done a wonderful job with the eggs, Jocelyn," he praises, squeezing her hand.

Her entire face lights up. I push my plate away, suddenly losing my appetite. Her sole reason for existence is pleasing him, and even though I know she's a victim, a part of me hates her for it. Maybe if she stood up to him, I wouldn't be how I am. Maybe Sarah would still be here. Maybe the three of us could have had a happier life, but she'd choose him over her own daughters every single time.

"It's a beautiful day," Mom comments wistfully. "I see the reporters have left town."

"They've moved on to the next big story, I expect," he

says. "They're fickle. There's nothing to write about now that everyone is where they belong." Dad's eyes narrow at me. "Aren't you going to eat the food your mother has so lovingly prepared?"

Mom's pleading gaze meets mine. I play along, spooning grapefruit into my mouth. Sour to match my mood.

"I've been reading the latest digest from the academy," she says. Every week, parents receive a newsletter with updates from Stonybridge. "I see the concert has been rescheduled for the end of the week. Isn't that wonderful news, honey? You've been working so hard."

"Are you performance ready?" Dad queries.

"Yes," I reply.

"The Harvest Ball is coming up soon," Mom says. "Now all the nasty business is wrapped up, everything can finally return to normal again."

I chew the gooey grapefruit until it turns to slime.

"So it is," Dad says. "I expect you'll want to go to the ball, Erin? All students attend."

"I…" I almost choke. "I didn't think you'd…"

Dad's eyes flash a warning, letting me know I should consider what I'm about to say next carefully.

"I hadn't thought about it," I say. "With everything else going on, it seems kinda… trivial."

"Nonsense," Mom says, bubbling with enthusiasm. "I remember my own Harvest Ball. It's the social event of the season. We need to find you something to wear. I'll take you dress shopping! After the concert, you'll have earned a fun night out with your friends. Tell her, sweetheart."

Her excitement has given her a whole new lease of life. She's never worked. She keeps her days busy with beauty appointments, shopping, and social engagements.

"Your mother's right," Dad agrees, to my surprise. "We must continue as normal. You will perform at the concert and attend the ball. How will it look if my daughter doesn't go? We're a high-profile family. We have influence here."

"I guess I'll go then," I mumble. "We don't have to go shopping, though. I have plenty of dresses in my closet."

Unworn dresses she keeps buying that I'll never wear.

"You need something new. I'll go to the mall later today," she insists. Her tone becomes animated as her mind strays to browsing racks, searching for the perfect piece. "I'll find something for you."

"You really don't have to," I object.

"Let your mother spoil you, Erin," he says. He's always nicer after they argue, even if it never lasts. "Don't be ungrateful."

"Will you be chaperoning this year, Dad?" I ask.

His lips purse. As much as he wants to keep an eye on me, his presence will draw a lot of attention after Sunnycrest's recent publicity.

"I'm sure I can trust you alone at school for one night," he says. "Can't I?"

Mom laughs, but he's not joking.

This is a test.

A test I can't fail…

"PLACES, EVERYONE!" Mr. Meyer paces backstage. His wild, bloodshot eyes keep darting back and forth, while he mutters under his breath about symphonies, sheet music, and checks to see if the instruments are tuned. "We're almost ready to start."

Ten students are performing in the concert showcase for the academy board, parents, other students, and a select group of college recruiters. The academy's main auditorium stage is transformed for the occasion, now sporting thick red curtains and spotlights.

A violinist next to me turns gray and bolts to the restroom for the fourth time. The pressure is high. A few of the musicians, including the barfer, are scholarship kids, so tonight has the potential to decide their entire future. Even if I got offered a full ride on a program of my dreams, I won't be allowed to go.

A knock on the door interrupts Mr. Meyer's musings. A pimply freshman enters with a giant bunch of flowers in his hands.

"I have a delivery for Erin Acacia," the freshman says.

"Give them here!" Mr. Meyer snatches them from him and throws the purple carnations at me. "Is that all?" he snaps at the flower delivery boy. "Why are you still standing here? Out!"

The bouquet is gorgeous. Understated yet elegant. I hunt around in the petals for a note, but there's nothing.

"Someone has a secret admirer," a performer whispers in my ear. "Is it true you're dating Nate Holt?"

I blush. "We're just friends."

"Sure you are," she replies sarcastically, checking the strings on her violin. "That totally looks like flowers you send to someone you're 'just friends' with."

Mr. Meyer glowers at me. "If we're done with interruptions, we have a concert to play…"

He runs through the lineup for the millionth time, then hurries away to check whether the first performer has finished emptying his stomach.

I'm up last, so I've got plenty of time to kill. The atmosphere in the waiting room offstage is tense. Others practice tricky chords, but there's nothing I can do when the grand piano is already onstage.

"Psst!" Mia pops her head inside the room.

She's lucky Mr. Meyer isn't here, otherwise he'd combust.

"What're you doing here?" I grin, turning to another musician. "Tell Mr. Meyer I'll be right back if he comes looking for me."

He grunts like he doesn't give a shit whether I come back at all, until he looks up, and his eyes almost pop out of their sockets at Mia's low-cut neon pink top.

"Mr. Meyer will freak out if anyone else disturbs our preparations," I explain, grabbing her hand and tugging her down the corridor. "I didn't think you were coming tonight."

"And miss this?" She shakes her head. "I have to be there for your big moment. It's not every day your best friend is about to steal the show."

"I don't know about that," I say. "And you hate classical music, remember?" For someone whose mom is a legend, Mia hasn't inherited her love for it. "I'm closing the show, so you'll be waiting a while."

"I'll be here for ages anyway," she says. "Principal Wire convinced my mom to come as a guest of honor to impress the scouts. I told her to put in a good word for you."

"We both know my dad wants me to focus on academics, remember?"

"You can be whatever you want to be," she says. If only it were that simple. "You've worked so hard, and I've hardly seen you while you've been slaving away in the practice room. I want to be here to support you."

"Hey, Erin!" Nate calling down the hall startles me.

"It looks like I'm not the only one who came to support you." Mia nudges me playfully. "Break a leg!"

She slips away before Nate reaches me. His crisp white shirt and smart gray pants make him look like a magazine model. I smooth down my black dress that Mom insisted was fitting for the occasion. It has long, lacey sleeves, and a scalloped neckline. Apparently, it's very 'French chic', whatever that means.

"Hey," I say, smiling nervously. "If you're looking for the football field, it's that way." I point behind him.

"Funny," he says. "My mom dragged me here to 'become more cultured'. I was about to bail until I saw your name. I didn't realize you played piano."

"Uh-huh. Ever since I was five years old," I say. "But I don't blame you if you want to disappear at the intermission. An evening of Bach and Mozart is a lot for anyone."

"Even a football player can branch out from time to time," he says with his lopsided, dimpled grin that makes girls' knees go weak. "What other talents are you hiding? Every time we talk, I learn something else."

Nate's probably used to saying that line hundreds of times, but I can't deny that it feels good to be noticed. He's chosen to seek me out. That has to mean something.

"I'm really not that interesting."

He arches an eyebrow. "So, you're not hiding any dark secrets that I should know about?"

"If I told you, they won't be secrets anymore," I say.

He chuckles and scratches his chiseled chin. "There is something I've been meaning to ask you."

Nervous butterflies flutter in my stomach.

"I'm not allowed to date during the football season, but I wondered if you'd like to go to the Harvest Ball together? You know, as a non-date date."

"Um..." I hesitate. Like Nate's parents, Dad sees dating as an unwelcome distraction. However, if we're not technically going as a couple, it doesn't break any of his rules. "As a non-date date? Sure."

"Great." His face lights up, then he shrugs it off and acts casual again. "I mean, cool. That'd be cool."

"Erin!" Mr. Meyer's frantic voice reaches me like a ringing cowbell. "Erin! Where are you? I need you!"

"I won't keep you," Nate says, his eyes twinkling. "Good luck."

"Thanks," I reply. As he turns to leave, I call after him. "Oh, and, Nate? Thanks for the flowers."

"Flowers?" His brow crinkles in obvious confusion. "What flowers?"

"I thought..." My voice trails off, and I shake my head. "Never mind. Just ignore me. Pre-show jitters."

I have no time to dwell on the mysterious flower delivery as the night ticks on. Before I know it, I'm waiting in the wings and getting a last-minute pep talk from Mr. Meyer. It's a miracle he hasn't had an aneurysm with how stressed he's been. Luckily, it only happens once a year.

"On the third part, take it slow," he instructs. "Don't rush it. Remember what I taught you. Light touch. Feathery fingers. Then build up..."

"I've got it," I say, although it doesn't put him at ease.

"It's time!" He shoves me through the curtains. "Go!"

The spotlights warm my skin as I stride across the stage. I scan the audience, picking Mia out in the crowd because of her neon top. I try to pretend I'm alone, but my father's judgmental gaze still manages to burn into me. He'll accept nothing less than perfection.

Once seated, I inhale deeply and stroke the familiar white keys. My mind gets transported to another place when I play. I forget about the people watching and travel to my private bubble. A safe place. The song, Moonlight Sonata, is sad. As I play, I make up stories in my head. With this one, I think about doomed lovers. They push and pull as the piece progresses, vying for each other's attention. They resist and fight, but circumstances keep drawing them together, culminating in an explosive chorus. They're not meant to be, yet they can't be apart. No other love can compare, but they're doomed.

I'm halfway through when the atmosphere changes. A stir in the audience causes people to shuffle and turn in their seats. I stay focused, closing my eyes and letting the music flow, but gasps and scathing whispers grow louder.

A bloodcurdling scream from the back brings me back to reality. A woman clambers onto her chair, almost tripping over her long skirt.

"Rats!" she screeches like a banshee, pointing at the floor. "There's a rat!"

Chair legs squeal, while another whimper comes from the opposite end of the room.

"Another one!" someone else yells. "Look! There!"

"They're everywhere," another person says.

Light floods the auditorium, and I freeze in horror. An army of rats, at least fifty, make their way down the aisles. They scuttle under seats, their pink tails leaving a trail of destruction behind.

Complete chaos engulfs the hall. Women wail and hop on

their heels, knocking into chairs as they jostle to the exit. Some lose their balance, toppling over in their bid to escape. Accompanying husbands in smartly dressed suits try to stay composed, but many faces have paled, and they charge for the doors, shoving anyone who stands in their path.

Mr. Meyer runs onto the stage and grabs the microphone. "Everyone, if you'll please stay calm…"

"Calm?" A college scout in the front row scoffs. "This school is overridden with vermin!"

A large man next to him stumbles. To catch his fall, he grabs a handful of the red curtains around the stage. The fabric can't hold his weight. It tears with an almighty rip all the way up to the ceiling until it detaches. The thick velvet falls and buries people beneath it with the rats. They fight their way out quickly, but a woman insists her ankle was bitten.

"I…" Mr. Meyer stammers. "I don't understand. How is this possible?"

I look past the hysterical hordes and see a figure dressed in black at the back of the room. They stand frozen in place, a black mask covering their face. Dread settles in the pit of my stomach, and all of my instincts scream that danger is here. As soon as I blink again, the figure vanishes, leaving me questioning if they were ever there at all.

"Get up, Erin." Mr. Meyer takes my arm and heaves me from my seat. "We need to leave."

My parents are waiting outside the auditorium. Thankfully, neither of them has been mauled by furry concert crashers.

"Is this what you call a show, Meyer?" Dad snarls in accusation. "My daughter's performance was ruined."

"I…" My poor teacher's shoulders slouch. "I don't know what happened."

"The board will discuss this," Dad warns. "We're leaving, Erin."

Dad storms off, and Mom puts a gentle arm around my shoulders to lead me away. I smile apologetically at Mr. Meyer. Whatever happened here wasn't his fault.

"Rats," Mom whispers scathingly. "Can you believe it? I'm sorry about your show, honey. For what it's worth, you were brilliant."

"Thanks," I reply, although no one will remember my piece after what came after.

"Would you like to go out for dinner?" she asks. "We can try the new Italian everyone's talking about?"

"Can we just go home?" I sigh. "I'm not that hungry anymore."

On the drive, my phone blows up with messages from Mia.

> MIA: That had to be the best classical concert I've ever been to.

> MIA: Have you seen the videos?

Footage from the concert has taken off on social media. Rydell Prep students, in particular, are taking great pleasure in sharing it. Stonybridge will need to work extra hard to erase this scandal. As well as videos, someone even created a meme of me playing with the caption *Pied Piper*. Witty, but unoriginal.

"Can I make you some food?" Mom offers when we get home.

"Thanks," I say, trudging up the stairs. "But, after tonight, all I want to do is to finish my book report and go to bed."

Finally alone, I slump down at my desk, thoughts abuzz with giant rats. I watch every video I can find of the concert, slowing them down to study each face in the crowd. No one looks out of place. I scour the background, searching for the masked man, but find nothing. If I'd really seen him, surely there'd be evidence somewhere? No one can be that good at hiding.

After endlessly scrolling for a few hours, I mentally shake myself. There has to be a logical reason to explain the figure I saw—a shock-induced hallucination, perhaps? Yes, that has to be it. Finally more at ease, I pull back my bedsheets.

"Fuck!" I gasp and stagger backward.

Nestled underneath the comforter is a rat skull with purple flower petals neatly scattered around it. A note rests next to it, written in the same cursive that I've seen before.

Did you really think you'd got rid of us?
We live in the walls, Little Ghost.

I race to my en suite and throw up. I hug the toilet, consumed by uncontrollable shakes. Fear takes hold. It's no coincidence my performance was targeted. It was them. They've broken into my school before, but their latest message changes everything.

They've been in my space.

In my home.

My bed.

It's not over.

Yet, the police claim they found all the missing patients. My father was adamant about the number of patients that escaped. He can't have got it wrong, could he? I could tell him what happened, but that'd mean explaining what happened after he left me in Sunnycrest. I could go to the police, but they won't take me seriously. They'd take one look at my past, a history of depression and a missing sister, and take me straight to Sunnycrest for a permanent vacation. The men have to know that, otherwise they wouldn't be so brazen. No one will believe me, so I have no choice but to stay silent.

What do they want? Maybe if I don't give them a reaction and continue like everything is normal, they'll get bored and move on? What alternative option do I have?

I rinse the acidic bile from my mouth and scrub my face clean. They think they have all the power, but they'll only break me if I let them.

If they return, I have to be ready…

CHAPTER
NINE

ERIN

ANOTHER UNEVENTFUL WEEK HAS PASSED, only putting me more on edge. Sometimes, the hairs on the back of my neck stand on end when I walk the school hall or when I'm at home alone, sensing their presence. I'm probably paranoid, but my instincts tell me I'd be naive to think they'd forgotten about me already.

But I refuse to stay locked inside, hiding away. They can't control me. I won't let them. That'd be giving them what they want.

Mia admires my dress as I twirl. It's emerald green with a tight bodice and translucent floaty sleeves. Delicate sequins in swirling patterns catch the light as I swish the tiered skirt across the floor. I look like a forest fairy, which perfectly matches the autumnal season.

"You look amazing," she gushes.

"So do you," I say.

Mia straightens her golden tiara, which matches her flaming red ballgown. Vibrant orange fabric layered underneath her dress leaves a trail of flames with every step.

"Can I come in?" Mom asks, not waiting for our response before opening my bedroom door. She wells up, dabbing the corners of her eyes with a handkerchief. "You both look beautiful. You're going to have the most magical evening,"

Mia beams. "Thanks, Mrs. Acacia."

"When is your car arriving?" Mom asks, checking her watch. "It's almost seven."

"Any minute," Mia replies brightly, followed by an impeccably timed ring of the doorbell.

"Time to go, girls!" Mom claps excitedly like a giddy teenager. "Your dates are here!"

"Nate and I are just friends, remember?" I murmur, before she gets too carried away.

"Of course you are," she says, dancing down the staircase.

"No, really, we are," I insist. "Mom—"

"Gentlemen!" She throws open the door to greet them. "Come inside."

Nate and Oliver wear identical black tuxedos with bow ties, both clutching onto boxes containing a corsage. It's a school tradition that all girls wear them.

"Wow." Nate's jaw drops when he sees me. "You look great."

"Thanks." I smile shyly, a warm blush creeping over my cheeks.

Tonight, I'm going to be a ordinary teenager. I'll do something normal, without strange men crawling out of vents, rat skulls on my pillow, or threats.

Nate passes me the box. "This is for you."

Inside, peonies and blush roses are crafted into a beautiful arrangement. Mia has a similar one from Oliver in rich reds.

"We need a picture," Mom declares, whipping out a camera that I hadn't noticed earlier. "Gather together, everyone."

Dad appears out of nowhere. He brings the gloomy aura of the Grim Reaper, sapping all joy from the air.

Dad sniffs, looking the guys up and down in blatant disapproval. "Good evening."

"It's good to see you again, sir," Nate replies.

Dad's lip curls into a polite yet 'I don't like you' grin. "Likewise."

"We should go," I say, reaching for the door handle. "We don't want to be late."

"One picture," Mom begs. "This is your senior year Harvest Ball. It's tradition."

We awkwardly group together. I stand between Nate and Mia. Nate wraps his arm around me to rest his hand on my hip in a friendly pose. Dad's eyes crackle with fury as the camera flash fills the room.

"There!" Mom declares. "Perfect."

"Now, we really have to go," I say. "The driver's waiting."

"Don't do anything I wouldn't," Dad calls.

Everyone laughs, but there's a warning behind his words.

A white stretch limousine waits outside. Like a true gentleman, Nate opens the door for me, bowing his head slightly, and I slip inside. Glittering blue lights reflect off the white seats, and champagne is already waiting on ice. We may be underage, but being rich will buy you anything.

"Let's get this party started!" Oliver says, popping the cork and holding out the bottle. "Drink?"

Mia grabs a flute. "Fill me up!"

"No, thank you."

I choose to decline after what happened last time.

"Don't be boring, Erin." Oliver rolls his eyes. "You heard your mom. This is our last Harvest Ball."

"She said no, Ol," Nate says firmly, reaching into the mini fridge that's built into the lower seats. "OJ?"

I smile gratefully. "Perfect."

Mia and Oliver drink their first glasses and swiftly move on to another. I don't understand what she sees in him. He's a stereotypical Stonybridge asshat with more money than sense. She deserves better.

"I haven't seen you since the concert," Nate says. "It was… unexpected."

"That's one way of putting it," I agree, my lips twitching at the edges in a half-smile. "Usually, there aren't rats."

"I figured." He grins. "Shame about Mr. Meyer, though."

"He was a good teacher," I say. "I'll miss him."

He got fired. The academy board claimed it was because his teaching wasn't up to standard, but everyone knows they wanted to punish him for the concert disaster, even though he was innocent.

Nate raises his glass to toast. "To no rats at the Harvest Ball."

We all cheer in unison. "No rats!"

Nate's hand rests on my knee as we settle into a comfortable conversation for the rest of the ride. His warmth radiates through my chiffon skirt. Mia smirks and raises a subtle eyebrow as if to say *Go for it, girl*, which I choose to ignore.

"Looks like we're here," Nate says as we pull in.

He gets out to open the door for me. Life will never be perfect, but tonight, I can pretend to be a character in a movie. The ordinary girl on a 'non-date' with the star player of the football team sounds like a chick flick plot.

The Harvest Ball takes place in the school auditorium, leading out onto the grounds. The auditorium doors are open, leading into a giant white marquee that acts as a seating area. Circular tables are covered in linen cloths, autumnal flowers, and flickering candles. Soft orange lights create a warm glow against the marquee fabric, which will look even better when the sun sets. Smartly dressed servers move through the swathes of students, offering trays of canapes and sparkling drinks, while teachers turn a blind eye to the hip flasks being poured not-so-discreetly from suit jacket pockets. A banquet table provides a bountiful feast of fruits, olives, breads, and dips, alongside mini cakes and pastries, all fresh from the local bakery.

Inside the auditorium, a live band plays onstage. The oak walls are draped in golden fabric and hundreds of hanging fairy lights. White blankets cover the ceiling, reminding me of rippling waves. The usually drab wooden floor is replaced with sparkling white tiles, and trees with gold-sprayed leaves give it a Grecian vibe.

"They've gone all out this year," Mia comments in a low whistle as we take in the decor.

"They need to spend our fees on something," I say.

Our arrival hasn't gone unnoticed. Lindsay and her friends glare in our direction, seeing my hand interlocked with Nate's.

"I've got to meet Ol and the team," Nate says apologetically. "It's a football thing, but we'll catch up with you both later?" His eyes twinkle. "You owe me another dance."

"Oh my gosh!" Mia grabs my shoulders as soon as he leaves. "He's so into you."

I twirl a strand of hair around my finger coyly. "I don't know about that…"

"I saw his hand on your knee in the limo," she says. "Do you think tonight is the big night?" She wiggles her eyebrows. "I know Nate's a football player, but he's one of the good guys, plus he has a killer body. Have you seen his abs in the thirst traps he posts? I've heard he's great in bed."

"It's not a real date, remember?" I say, despite my mind lingering on the thought a little too long.

"If you say so," she replies, unconvinced. "Let's dance."

The quartet plays modern songs, giving a classical yet contemporary feel to the evening. After dancing and sampling the mini cake selection, I relax. The sun's going down, and the party has turned up a notch. Students are growing wilder with each drink, and even the chaperones are turning rosy-cheeked and merry. It's exactly what a school dance should be, made better by the fact Dad isn't loitering in a corner watching my every move.

Take that, Sunnycrest men.

If they had their way, I'd be cowering in my room like a rabbit in a storm.

Nate catches my eye from across the dance floor. Next to him, Oliver and Mia are wrapped in an embrace they won't be freeing themselves from anytime soon. Nate pushes his way through the crowd to get to me. Since we got here, he's been busy with his friends, so this is the first time we've spoken again.

He holds out his hand.

"Can I have this dance, m'lady?" he asks in a corny British accent.

I can't help giggling and wrap my arms around his neck, breathing in his scent. Fresh soap and cologne.

"You're stunning," he whispers into my neck, nuzzling into my hair, a hint of bourbon on his breath. "Do you know that?"

I embrace the moment, picking up where we left off at Oliver's party and ignoring the judgmental glares. Nate stays oblivious to the daggers Lindsay shoots our way. He looks at me like I'm the only girl in the room, Strong hands on the small of my back pull me into his chest. The music slows, and we sway together. Disco lights glimmer against the sequins on my dress.

He strokes my cheek tenderly, sending a longing tremble through me like a gentle summer breeze skirting over my skin. He leans in, his parted lips pausing for a brief second before brushing against mine tentatively, as if he's waiting for an invitation and checking this is okay. I kiss him back while he caresses my cheekbone, like it's a delicate flower petal. This is the type of kiss everyone dreams about.

Behind us, moody huffs threaten to ruin the mood. I won't let them. I'm too swept away, lost in his arms. His tongue softly probes my lips apart. I kiss him back with a new hunger, forgetting that we're surrounded by the rest of the senior class.

Eventually, when the song ends, he pulls away breathlessly.

"Come on." He weaves his fingers through mine. "There's something I want to show you."

I float across the dance floor after him as we leave the bustle behind.

Nate checks to make sure no chaperones are watching. They're too busy having fun, and the single moms crowd around our geography teacher. He's a single guy under fifty, who still has all his hair and a gut that doesn't expand beyond the original holes that came in his belt, so he's basically the most eligible bachelor in town.

"This way," Nate says, tugging my hand to lead me down the unlit hall into the main building.

He breaks into a run, dragging me behind him. My laughter echoes around the emptiness.

"Through here," he says, heading into the art room, which is on the opposite end of the building to the ball. "We can really be alone here."

Moonlight streams through the windows. As soon as the door clicks closed, Nate's hands are in my hair, sweeping me into another tsunami of a kiss.

"Fuck," he groans, pushing me back against a desk. "You have no idea how long I've waited for this."

His mouth is on mine again, ravenous and lustful, like I'm his oxygen. His fingers creep over my bodice and greedily grab a handful of my breast. The suddenness takes me off guard as he paws at me in a feverish frenzy that feels quite different to how it was on the dance floor. There's a desperate urgency to his movements, something almost animalistic.

"You're so hot," he purrs, pulling up my skirts. "Every time I see you, all I can think about is having you alone like this."

I catch his wrist as it reaches my knees.

"Hey," I whisper. "Slow down."

"Why wait?" he murmurs, pressing his erection into me. "You want this as much as I do, right?"

The liquor on his breath is suddenly all I can taste. He rolls up my skirt. Nate's been lovely until this point, but this doesn't feel right. It feels dirty. Sordid, almost.

I pull away.

"Nate," I say. "I really like you, but I don't want to do this here."

"Shit," he curses, stepping back. I expect him to apologize for taking things too far, but he pouts moodily like an entitled child. "I thought this is what you wanted. You can't kiss a guy like that and send mixed messages."

"Kissing doesn't mean that I want to have sex with you in the art room," I snap.

"Cocktease," he mutters.

I shove his chest hard.

"If you want to get your dick wet that badly, I'm sure there's plenty of girls at the ball who'd volunteer," I say, crossing my arms. "You should leave."

"Fine," he huffs.

He slams the door behind him, leaving me panting.

How can something so good turn bad so fast?

"What's wrong, Little Ghost?" an ethereal voice asks, sending a chill racing down my spine. "Did he leave you unsatisfied?"

Adrenaline kicks in. I dart for the exit, but before I reach it, a figure launches from the darkness. He must have been lurking in the shadows all along. I squeal in pain as he grabs my hair to yank me backward. His gloved hand covers my mouth.

"Don't make this more difficult than it needs to be," he purrs.

It's Two.

I recognize his voice.

I try biting down, but he'll feel nothing through his thick gloves. I struggle while he chuckles. His muscular arms contain me in a tight embrace, restricting all movement.

My eyes widen as the art room door opens. I hope—pray! —that it's Nate. Instead, a man wearing a black tuxedo and matching ski mask steps inside.

"Do you really think you can run from us?" the new arrival questions. "There's nowhere for you to hide. You're ours now. Our toy to play with. We're not letting you go."

Two's breath tickles my ear. "If I take my hand off your mouth, are you going to play nice?" I manage to nod against his grip. Slowly, he withdraws it. His fingers move to rest around my throat. He grips my neck, applying light pressure to my windpipe. "One wrong move, and I'll snap your pretty little neck. One wrong sound, and you'll be as dead as our last present."

"Who are you?" I gasp. "What do you want?"

One laughs. "So many questions, Little Ghost…" He saunters forward. His eyes scan my body, taking in every inch. "That's not what I'd be asking if I were you."

"What then?" I ask.

"I'd ask what we're going to do to you."

I notice something around his neck, and my stomach churns when I realize his necklace is made up of small skulls instead of beads. Just like the one left on my pillow. My breathing quickens as One runs a gloved finger along my collarbone. His hand dips lower, skimming over the boning of my corset. He keeps going, gliding down the soft fabric and tainting it with every stroke. I swallow hard when he reaches the top of my panties. The warmth from my mound radiates through the fabric and makes him pause before he meets my heat.

"What are you going to do to me?" I breathe.

One laughs, tearing his hand away.

"We're going to destroy you, Little Ghost. I thought you'd have realized that by now," he says. His mask is mere centimeters from my face. "And when we're finished breaking you, you'll be thanking us for it."

I can't let them see how afraid I am. I won't.

"Screw you," I snarl, sounding braver than I feel.

"There she is," Two says. "Our brave little ghost. You handled yourself well tonight. I wondered whether I should step in."

"I don't need your help," I say. "I don't want it."

"I think you're going to very much want what we're going to give you," One says. "In fact, you'll want it so badly that you'll stop trying to forget about us. Ignoring us won't work. It won't send us away. You're fighting it, but I know you want our attention. You enjoy it. You crave it, and soon, you'll crave us."

"Never," I spit. "You're crazy."

Two sighs, speaking to his friend, "He'll be sad to have missed this."

"What's wrong?" I rebuff. "Did your British friend not make it out of the asylum?"

Two cackles, tightening his grip on my throat. "We'll send him your regards. Although, I'm sure you'll be seeing him very soon."

My stomach churns.

"What's wrong?" One taunts, unclipping the front of my bustier. "Two of us not enough for you?"

He undoes one fastening at a time.

"No—"

Two's hand muffles my objections as the front of my dress falls open. I'm not wearing a bra, and my breasts shimmer in the moonlight, the tiny blue veins over them visible.

One's gloved fingertip trails across the tip of my nipple and makes it harden. He circles it, before catching it between his thumb and forefinger. He pinches hard. I cry out into Two's hand, wishing for a savior who isn't coming.

"A real man knows how to pleasure a woman," One says. "You deserve better than a high school fumble."

He wants to destroy me *and* bring me pleasure. None of it makes sense.

One's eyes penetrate me. They're an unreadable misty gray color, full of secrets, storms, and something else too… Damage. So much damage.

"Have you ever felt a man's touch between your thighs, Little Ghost?" One asks.

I blush. Although I can't see him, I imagine he's smirking underneath his mask.

"I bet you've imagined it," he says. "How it will feel to have a cock fill your tight virgin cunt."

I'm terrified, yet his words make my inner thighs clench in desire.

One drops to his knees. Two forces me to look ahead as One crawls under my skirts. I keep my legs pressed together, but One coaxes my knees apart. I whimper into Two's palm and move my head from side to side in resistance.

"Remember what I said about moving," Two growls ominously.

One's hand slips up my thighs. His glove grazes the front of my panties, and he pulls them down. He stands again, black panties in hand, and holds them up to his mask to inhale my scent.

"It's time we remind our little ghost who owns her," One says, unclipping his belt with his free hand. I swallow hard, my gaze drawn to the growing bulge in his pants. One hands Two the belt. "Tie her hands."

Two removes his hand from my throat. I open my mouth to scream, but One stuffs my panties into it to gag me.

"Hold still," Two growls, forcing my hands roughly behind my back and tying them in a leathery bind.

"No one can help you now," One says, pinching my nipple again to make a point. "On your knees."

Shaking, I lower myself into a prayer position. Two looms behind me ominously, while One shamelessly drops his pants and unsheathes his cock like a weapon.

It's the first time I've seen one in person. It's huge. Sometimes a tampon can hurt to put in, so I don't know how I'll stretch to fit something like that. He's around nine inches long, and I'd be able to wrap both hands around his girth.

One removes his gloves and spits onto his palm. He wraps his hands around his thick member, and I watch his foreskin slide up and down as he pleasures himself. He has no shame. He exudes confidence and keeps his eyes fixed on me the whole time. I'm repulsed and hypnotized. How would it feel in my hands?

"Don't look away, Little Ghost," One instructs as if he's read my dirty thoughts. "This is what I want you to think about the next time you touch yourself."

I look into his masked face, trying to take in as much as I can. Maybe I'll see something that could identify him, but I can't make out any real details. They don't do police lineups of muscular thighs.

"You're ours," he groans, quickening his pace.

I'm transfixed as his cock engorges.

I know what's about to happen before it does.

Nothing prepares me for his cum spraying over my tits. Ruining me. Tarnishing what's supposed to be one of the best nights of my high school experience.

"Look at her, all painted in my cum," One says. "It marks you as ours."

Two hands him a phone, and One aims it in my direction. A bright flash fills the room. I look away, disgusted that this is something he wants to commemorate.

"Behave," Two instructs, wrenching me onto my feet. He chuckles as he removes the belt from my wrists while One dresses. As soon I'm unbound, I grab my corset, pulling it up to hide my breasts.

One steps forward.

"This is only the beginning," One promises. He plucks my panties from my mouth and smears a droplet of his sticky cum over my bottom lip.

I keep my lips clamped shut, refusing to taste him. He's already taken too much from me tonight.

They say no more and leave, shutting the art room door quietly and leaving me alone.

No matter how hard I scrub my skin, I've been marked by them. And they know it too.

CHAPTER
TEN

ERIN

AFTER LYING about food poisoning to leave the ball early, I toss and turn in the darkness, staring up at my bedroom ceiling. My physical body is clean, but my mind…

Their words. Their touch. Their cruelty. Their dogged obsession has no limits. They're consuming me, creeping into every aspect of my life. They've invaded my thoughts, leaving no space for anything else.

I kick my blankets off. No position is comfortable. Every time I close my eyes, I see their masks… and his cock. How is it possible to be terrified and turned on at the same time?

I turn on the light and stroll to my underwear drawer. It's not like I'll be able to sleep, anyway. I rifle through the lace until I find my gift from Mia. The bullet vibrator.

A spark of adrenaline races through me as I settle back into position and slide it into my panties, knowing there's something so wrong about this, but I'm too intrigued to stop.

I bite my lip as the velvety silicone slides over my clit. Tingles spread between my thighs and down to my toes. I apply more pressure, and a tiny moan escapes from my mouth. A moan I wished they'd taken from me. Shit, did I really just think that?

The sensation builds, making my knees tremble as I hold it

in place, surrendering. I grind against it, coaxing the pleasure from deep in my core, and I visualize them. Their masks. His fingers pinching my nipples and kneading my breasts. Their power and animalistic desire to take whatever they want when they want it. I recall how his spit sounded, slathering his cock, and how his eyes stayed locked on me while he touched himself. It brings me a sick sense of enjoyment, knowing my body has that effect on a monster.

I writhe around as my orgasm arrives hard and fast at the memory of his cum spraying my skin. Claiming me as his. *Fuck. This is exactly what they wanted.* Finished, I lie, panting, disgusted at doing what he predicted, while simultaneously more satisfied than I've ever felt before.

Wailing sirens bring me out of my blissful haze. I throw the vibrator back into the drawer and race to the window. Blue lights fill my room, casting flashing shadows across the pink walls.

I gasp in horror at the scene. "Shit..."

The Holt mansion is ablaze. Wild, uncontrollable jumping flames fill the skyline. The fire devours the building, feasting on their possessions. Two fire trucks have pulled out front. The crew shout and work together, but it's already too late.

Thuds down the hallway grow closer.

"Erin!" Dad yells, throwing open my door. He's dressed in a full suit, while Mom stands behind him in her flimsy silk slip. "We need to go."

Shaking, I grab a hoodie to put over my pajama short set and fumble into sliders before racing out after my parents.

A firefighter is already waiting to greet us.

"You need to wait on the sidewalk until we get the fire under control," he says. "The wind is blowing eastward. There's a risk that the trees on your property border might be ignited by falling debris. It's better to be safe than sorry."

We follow him onto the street. We're not the only people

up. The entire neighborhood has woken and left their beds to stare in morbid fascination as the Holts' home burns.

"How did it happen?" Mom asks.

"It's too early to say, ma'am," he replies. "Hopefully, we'll have answers soon."

"Did everyone make it out?" I ask.

"Just about," he replies. "The son had to climb out of a window. He almost got trapped inside. He's a lucky guy."

Smoke catches in the back of my throat. Even though we're a fair distance away, the heat from the blaze warms my bare legs. In front of the Holts' house, Nate's mother sobs hysterically into his father's shoulder. I spot Nate a few feet away from them, sitting on the curb, his head buried in his hands.

"No!" Mrs. Holt wails despairingly. "God, no!"

An almighty power isn't listening. The upper floor caves in, succumbing to the flames with a gigantic crack. The fire crew hopelessly attempts to put it out, but it's no use. Even if they did, there'll be nothing salvageable.

"Why don't you see if Nate's okay?" Mom asks, gently nudging my ribs. "You were his date for the Harvest Ball."

Both Dad and I look at her aghast, but for different reasons.

"I told you, we're just friends, Mom," I say. "He won't want to—"

"She's not going anywhere," Dad declares, putting an end to the matter.

We're spared an argument by a neighbor crossing the street to speak to Mom.

Nate's shoulders shake. When he looks up, I see his eyes are puffy and his face is streaked with soot. He's bleeding from scrapes on his arms, likely from scampering down the side of the building. I should feel sympathy for him. That'd be a normal emotion, right? Yet, seeing him sob makes a twisted part of me happy. After how he treated me this evening, it's what he deserves.

A limo speeds past us, out of place among the emergency vehicles, and stops beside Nate. Oliver jumps out. He pulls his friend to his feet and bundles him into the back like a hero. Everything always works out okay for people like the Holts. Their houses can burn, but they have enough power and money to rebuild. Pasturesville's social elite have each other's backs, no matter what.

Nate departs with Oliver, leaving his parents to clean up the mess.

"Over here," a firefighter calls the assembled neighbors into a huddle.

"Following our initial assessment of the scene, there appears to have been an electrical fault," he explains to the group. "It was a freak accident, and the Holt family had a narrow escape."

"How awful," Mom gushes, reveling in the drama.

I zone out as he continues talking, watching the Holt mansion crumble in the background.

———

Three hours later, we're finally given the seal of approval to return home. The fire still smolders, but they're confident it has subdued enough to be of no risk to our property. Others still mill around, clearly disappointed that the ordeal is over, and a reporter from the local newspaper arrives to take photographs for tomorrow's front page.

Dad kisses Mom on the cheek woodenly, for the benefit of anyone watching from the sidewalk. "I'm heading to work."

"But it's a Saturday," Mom says.

"I have a lot to do," he insists. "I'll be back in time for dinner."

She nods, then turns her attention to me as we make our

way back inside. "Are you sure you're okay, sweetheart?" She rubs my shoulder. "Between the fire and food poisoning, your final Harvest Ball didn't turn out how you expected."

Yeah, that's one way of putting it.

"I'm fine, Mom," I insist. "Just cold."

"At least you don't have school in the morning," she says, kissing my cheek. "Sweet dreams." She smiles sadly, like there's more she wants to say, but decides against it. "Don't let the bedbugs bite."

I drag my body upstairs. I reek of smoke and head straight for the shower. It takes a while to wash away the stench. Ash has soaked into my pores and burned my nostrils, making it hard to shed the smell entirely. When I collapse back into bed, sleep envelops me.

I'm not sure how long I'm asleep for—maybe a few hours, maybe only a few minutes—but creaking floorboards and the overwhelming stench of gas rouses me.

Someone is in my room.

I keep my eyes closed. I already know it's them. I listen intently, only hearing one set of footsteps. Whoever it is, they're alone.

I stay paralyzed, curled on my side with my back to the wall, facing away from the intruder. They move around my space, opening my closet and my drawers, rooting around inside. They're not even attempting to be quiet.

"I know you're awake," a chilling British voice whispers. "I can sense it."

I say nothing.

His hand glides over the top of my blankets, across my shoulder, and down the side of my body. It takes all my effort not to flinch, and I keep feigning sleep.

"I won't hurt you. Not here. Not yet," he purrs. "I need more time to coax that pretty scream from the back of your throat." He leans closer, sniffing my hair like an animal scenting me. I hold my breath, not daring to exhale. "You smell sweet now, but you can't wash us away. We're under your skin, in the walls, creeping into your mind. We're here to haunt you. Your phantoms. Your darkest, filthiest fantasies." He strokes a strand of my hair to the side and rests two callused fingers upon the jumping pulse in my neck. "So quick. And ours. All fucking ours."

He stands again and continues his exploration. He picks objects up and sets them back down, marking his territory to make sure I know that nothing is private anymore. There are no boundaries to their twisted obsession.

The door handle turns.

"No one touches our little ghost but us," he says, before disappearing into the night.

His parting words confirm what I feared.

They started the Holt fire.

I don't move, even long after he's gone, for fear he'll return. When I'm finally certain it's clear, I jump up, racing to my door to prop a chair against it. It won't stop them from coming in, but at least I'll get a warning.

Dawn is breaking. When I turn to face my mirror, I see a smudge of black soot across my neck and another note taped up.

Strike a match and watch it burn.

If they burned down a house, what else are they capable of?

A tiny smile crosses my face. I raise my hands to my mouth in horror. What's wrong with me? Knowing they did that for me shouldn't feel good! Maybe Dad was right to take me to the asylum. Perhaps that's where I belong. With them.

CHAPTER
ELEVEN

ERIN

HOLDING a fundraiser for the Holt family is ironic, considering they have millions of dollars in the bank, but it perfectly captures the spirit of Pasturesville. The entire community has rallied around the Holts in the wake of the tragedy. The Stonybridge rumor mill has informed me that Nate's living with Oliver, while his parents have temporarily moved into their summer house. Once the school year ends, Nate will join them in the Hamptons, but he can't abandon football mid-season.

"How long do we have to stay?" I grumble, letting Mom steer me through the school gardens by our linked arms.

Despite my objections, Mom insisted I attend the fundraiser. I'm dressed like we're attending a funeral. A bland black dress with a demure pearl necklace. It's perfect. Plain. An outfit that won't attract attention.

The sun beams over the stalls erected in the academy's grounds. Local businesses are selling their wares and donating the proceeds directly to the Holts. Circular tables decorated with extravagant floral arrangements are spread over the lawn. Sparkling wine circulates on silver trays for parents, while their kids sneak glugs of champagne from behind the trees.

"We'll stay as long as we need to," Mom hisses through gritted teeth. She smiles, waving at another parent she recognizes, before dropping her voice. "Be nice, Erin. We're representing our family today. Think about your father's reputation."

For once, Dad isn't attending. Apparently, he has too much work. He's been exceptionally busy lately. When he's not at Sunnycrest, he's locked in his office and only comes out to eat. Not that I'm complaining.

It's easy to pick Mrs. Holt out in the crowd. She sits, dabbing her crocodile tears with a handkerchief, surrounded by other fussing mothers. Her sly smile hints she's enjoying all the extra attention.

"I'm going to find Mia," I say. At least she'll make the afternoon bearable.

"Oh, Nate!" I hear Lindsay before I see her. She and other students perch around the giant water fountain. "It's just terrible. I can't even imagine what you're going through."

Lindsay hangs off Nate's arm, pawing his leg like she's a supervillain stroking a cat.

"It hasn't been easy," Nate says. "But Dad's already started the reconstruction. He wanted to remodel anyway, so it almost saved him a job."

"I heard you almost died," Lindsay says. "Didn't the fire start right outside your room?"

My ears prick up.

"Yeah, it's lucky I noticed the smoke coming up under the door," he mumbles. Maybe he's more shaken up than he makes out. He catches me staring and jumps up. "Excuse me for a second."

I pace away in the opposite direction, cursing myself for sticking around to satisfy my own morbid curiosity.

"Erin!" Nate calls. "Wait!"

Shit. I can't exactly ignore the guy the fundraiser is in aid of. He jogs to catch up, and I turn to face him. We stand in silence, waiting for the other to talk.

"I'm sorry about your house," I say, being the first to break it. Thankfully, he doesn't notice my insincerity. "I'm glad you aren't hurt."

"Thanks," he says. "It's been crazy."

"I've got to find Mia," I say, trying to make a polite getaway and avoid causing a scene. "I promised I'd meet her."

"Before you go…" He grabs my wrist. "There's something I want to say."

His touch scorches my skin, and I wrench my hand away. The masked men's threat screeches through my mind. Touching me once got his house burned down. I don't want any blood on my hands.

"It's about what happened at the Harvest Ball," he says, then sighs. "Look, I was out of line. I had too much to drink and got carried away…" He looks away shamefully, tucking his hands into his chino pockets. "I really am sorry. Nothing like that will ever happen again, but… I really do like you. If you give me a second chance, I'll—"

"Look, Nate," I interrupt. "I don't date, and neither do you. The Harvest Ball was a one-off. I think we're better off as friends. "

His eyes widen in shock. Did he expect I'd give him a second chance because of his current situation? Lindsay would give him a blowjob for less.

"Okay," he says after a stagnant pause. "Just friends."

"Enjoy the rest of your day," I say, leaving him behind.

I know my worth, and an entitled football player doesn't cut it.

"There you are!" Mia creeps up behind me, pinching my hips and making me jump out of my skin. "Whoa, sorry!" She frowns. "You've gone as white as a ghost. Are you feeling okay? I thought you were better after that bout of food poisoning."

Since the ball, we haven't had time to catch up about what happened. The school play is approaching, and she's been busy rehearsing, which is a relief because it would have been hard to hide that I'm distracted.

"Sorry," I reply. "You just surprised me, that's all."

"I saw you speaking to Nate," she says. "How are things between you?"

"We decided that it's best we just stay friends," I say. "Nothing more."

"Shame." She sighs dramatically. "I thought you guys could go on a double date with me and Oliver. You seemed to get on well at the ball. Everyone saw you making out in the middle of the dance floor."

I shrug. "I don't have time for a relationship right now, and neither does he, especially after everything that's happened. It's better this way."

"Well, Lindsay already hates you," she says. "If you guys started dating for real, she'd smother you to death with her pom-poms."

I roll my eyes and change the subject. "How are things with you and Oliver?"

"Great," she replies, beaming. "I think things might actually work out between us this time. I know he can be a jerk sometimes, but…"

"Mia Jade Moldova!" Ms. Moldova joins us, wielding two empty vases. "Where have you been?"

"I've been catching up with Erin," she says innocently.

"It's great to see you again, Erin," Ms. Moldova says, then her eyes narrow at her daughter. "Can you fill these up? People are going crazy because there isn't enough water for all the flowers. You're supposed to be helping."

"But, Mom—" Mia whines.

"Mia!" Principal Wire intervenes, appearing from out of

nowhere. Instead of his signature suit, he's wearing a golf shirt and pants. Seeing teachers in their ordinary clothes is like seeing animals out in the wild. "This must be your mother." He smiles, a little too widely, and holds his hand out. "I don't think we've been properly introduced, Ms. Moldova. I hear Mia is doing wonderful things in our school play."

"I'll fill the vases," I volunteer, seeing an opportunity to escape and grabbing it.

"I'll help!" Mia offers, miraculously feeling more charitable.

"I'm sure Erin can handle the task on her own," Principal Wire says. No doubt he's eager to sidle up to a world-famous pianist. "Don't you?"

"I'll be fine," I say, shuffling away.

As the principal and her mom talk, Mia mimes, *Kill me now!*

I snicker, vases in hand, and head inside. A line has formed outside the restroom that includes Lindsay and her followers. To avoid any drama, I head to the girls' locker room. No one will hang out there.

The slow faucet trickle echoes around the emptiness. It takes forever to fill the vases halfway. I put them aside and splash my face with water. I'm not wearing any makeup, despite my mother telling me to apply some blush to make me 'look more alive' before we left.

A door slams behind me.

"Hello?" I call, spinning. "Is anyone there?"

A masked figure appears. He's dressed in black again: a hoodie over a pair of faded jeans, biker boots, and gloves. The Ghostface mask he's wearing is even more terrifying than the last one.

"I thought we made ourselves clear," Two says. He's easily recognizable from the Southern twang in his voice. "No one touches our toy."

He must have seen me and Nate together.

"We're always watching," Two says, reading my mind.

"What's your name?" I ask.

I've been thinking about what to call them since their last visit. I can identify them by their voices, but they're still abstract figures. Nameless ghosts who want to make my life miserable.

He crosses his arms. "Our names don't matter."

"If you're going to be in my life, then I'd like to know what to call you," I say, looking into the unreadable white face.

He tilts his head to the side, thinking hard.

"You can call me Eli."

"Eli?"

The name is ordinary, and he is anything but. Giving him a name instantly humanizes him, making him more than a figment of my imagination. Does that make him any more or less scary?

"And the others?" I prompt. "Are they here too?" I expect them to jump out. "What are their names?"

"It's just me today. I hope that doesn't disappoint you," he says. "If they want to tell you their names, that's down to them."

"Why are you here?" I ask.

He takes a step closer, leaving muddy prints on the white tiles.

"To remind you that you're ours," he says.

"Are you going to hurt me? Cover me in cum like your friend did?"

Unlike the others, I think I can get Two to talk. He laughs, a deep rumble, and takes something from his pocket. The missing lock of my hair.

"I always have a piece of you with me, Little Ghost," he says, waving the strand. "But I want to leave you with a lasting memory."

I step back. My spine presses against the cool sink as he advances, but there's nowhere to go.

"Turn around," he commands.

I raise my chin in challenge. "Why should I?"

"You're getting braver," he says, almost with admiration, then his tone shifts menacingly. "But you should be scared. A zebra doesn't laugh in the face of a lion when she's standing in his jaws. I won't ask you again."

"What if I don't do as you say?"

"Then, I'll make you," he threatens, resting his hands on either side of my hips to box me in. His manly leathery scent surrounds me, a forbidden musky aroma that I shouldn't like, but I do. "Don't make it any more difficult than it needs to be."

My courageousness wavers. "Are you going to hurt me?"

"No," he replies. "I won't hurt you, not unless you ask nicely. But I will destroy anyone who so much as breathes at you in the wrong way. Now, turn."

I comply, watching his masked face loom behind me in the mirror.

"Spread your legs wide," he orders.

Shaking, I do it, using the sink to steady myself. His gloved fingers tickle the backs of my thighs.

"Anyone could walk in," I say.

"So?" he says, moving his hand higher. "Do you like that?"

"No," I lie.

His fingertip strokes the laced edge of my panties and slides between my legs, gliding along the length of my pussy. This doesn't count as being touched, right? Not when it's fabric over fabric. I tremble, gripping the sink harder.

"Keep looking in the mirror," he says. "I want you to watch yourself when I make you come."

He rubs my clit; the friction ignites a lusty warmth that

makes me wet. He pulls the fabric taut, trapping my clit, before curling his finger and slipping it into my panties.

"Is this the first time your little virgin pussy has been touched?" he asks.

"No," I whimper.

"Liar." He pushes a gloved finger inside me without warning, and I gasp from the unexpected motion. "Don't lie to me, Little Ghost. I'm the first man to be inside your tight little hole, aren't I? Tell the truth."

He finger fucks me more aggressively, forcing my breath to come in short bursts.

"Yes," I gasp. "You are."

"Good girl," he praises, slowing his pace, then withdrawing. I stare into his masked reflection, wondering what he really looks like. He raises his hand to my mouth, the black glove glistening with my arousal. "Suck them clean."

"I—" He cuts off my sentence by shoving his fingers into my mouth. "Taste yourself, Little Ghost."

He pushes his fingers deep. I choke as he pumps them back and forth, brushing my tonsils.

"You're a natural," he compliments. "Suck my fingers like you're sucking my cock."

I splutter in shock, and he rams another finger into my mouth, stretching my jaw like he's preparing me for something bigger.

"Mmm. Do you want more, Little Ghost?" he asks. "Does your pussy want to be tasted?"

I gargle in response. Spit runs down my chin as he extracts his fingers.

"I'll give you what you need." His voice deepens. "All you've got to do is ask for it."

"Eli," I whimper. "I..."

"Hearing my name come out of your lips..." He groans, his erection digging into my ass. "Can you feel what you're doing to me?"

I back up, pushing my ass against him without thinking.

"Tell me what you want," he growls. "Say you want me to fuck your pussy with my tongue."

"I want…" I stare at my reflection. Flushed cheeks, hooded eyelids, and parted lips. "I want you to…"

"Say it," he pushes. "And I'll slide my tongue into your sweet little hole."

Saying it means confronting my desires and succumbing to my dirty fantasies. Every instinct tells me it's wrong, yet my body disagrees.

"I…I …" I struggle to get the words out. "I want you to taste me."

"Good girl," he says. "That wasn't so hard, was it?" He plucks a hair from my shoulder, rubs it between his fingers, then leans in. "You need to get used to asking for what you want, otherwise people will keep taking from you. People like Nate Holt."

"Hold still," he says, dropping to the floor. "Don't take your eyes off the mirror. If you close them, I'll know. You're going to watch while your virgin pussy baptizes my face."

All I can do is stay where I am, hyperaware that we're in the middle of school. But I don't want him to stop.

"Remember what I said, Little Ghost," Eli warns, gripping my thighs to root me to the spot. "I want you to see what a dirty little slut you really are."

He gently nudges the small of my back to reposition me, pushing my ass farther onto his face. My hands rest on the mirror for extra support as he rolls up the skirt of my dress. I shiver as the flat of his tongue slides over my panties, warming my pussy and making me conscious of how wet I am already.

"Mmm," he murmurs, sending a buzz through me. He hooks his fingers under my panties and moves them to the side to expose me. "Our filthy whore wants to be tasted, don't you?"

Before I can respond, his mouth meets my wet flesh. My vision blurs from the sensation, but I keep my eyes fixed on the mirror as he asked. I don't recognize the person looking back. The face of a girl whose pussy is getting eaten by a psychopathic stranger. A stranger who has likely done a thousand terrible things and is partially responsible for burning down a house.

He slurps loudly, drinking me. "You're so fucking wet." His gloved finger delves between my folds. "Your virgin pussy wants to be devoured. Do you like the feel of my tongue, Little Ghost?"

"Yes," I whimper.

He kisses along my slit and uses his fingers to part my pussy before his tongue delves inside me. I yelp, the fabric of his rolled-up mask pushing against me as he forces his tongue as deep as it'll go. He explores my inner walls, lapping at my insides until my thighs shake uncontrollably. He tongue fucks me like he's trying to taste the very essence of my soul and consume every twisted fantasy I've ever had.

"It's been a long time since I've eaten a pussy like yours." He sighs, his breath heating me as he pulls back to admire the view. No one has seen me from this angle before. "So innocent, yet dripping with sin."

He turns his attention to my clit, licking it like a sucker, then holding it in his mouth while it pulses. I moan as overwhelming pleasure takes over and I'm powerless to stop it. My back arches to give him better access, fully bent over the sink now, while he spreads my ass cheeks to bury his face deeper.

A flush of longing creeps up my neck as I keep watching myself. Watching how he can undo me with just his mouth. He's everywhere—his lips and tongue all merge into one, like a hundred wet fingers touching me at once.

"Oh yeah," he moans into my pussy. "Soak me, Little

Ghost. Soak me with your dirty desires. Don't look away, or I'll stop."

My orgasm builds to its earth-shattering conclusion. My eyes snap open, pupils wide. I stare at myself as he tips me past the point of no return, and my mouth morphs into a perfect O-shape.

Holy fuck, now I understand why people are so obsessed with sex…

My inner thighs tighten as his tongue slides inside my pussy, right on time for me to contract all over him. My moans vibrate my entire body as I clutch onto the sink to stop me from falling. He holds me in place, coaxing out every drop of pleasure he can, drenching his tongue.

"Fuck…" I gasp, shuddering.

When I'm done, my chest heaves from the exertion, and a bead of sweat drips down my face. The world looks different now, as if I've gained a whole new clarity. Mia always told me that orgasms were amazing, but this? It was even better than I expected, better than any orgasm I've given myself. But, most worrying of all, it's giving me a craving for more.

While I compose myself, Eli stands. The giant white *Scream* mask covers his mouth again. Maybe it's better I don't know what he looks like under it. I spin, very aware that my thighs are now coated in a mixture of my wetness and his spit. Evidence of what happened between us.

"You're ours," Eli growls. "Ours to touch. Ours to take from. Never forget that."

"Is that it then?" I breathe. "You're just going to leave?"

He chuckles. "I'm not leaving. You already know that."

He turns to go.

"Wait!" I call after him. "Is this how it's going to be from now on? You all just show up whenever you feel like it? Walking into my life like you own it? Treating me like your toy?"

"Would you prefer us to take you to dinner?" he mocks.

"Do you want us to be your dates at silly school dances? Or would you like to introduce us to your family? How about your best friend, Mia? Do you think she'd like to meet us? How about a double date?"

They know everything.

My silence is the only response he needs.

"I thought so," he says smugly. "We're your dirty secret. A secret that no one would believe. If you told anyone, they'd think you're crazy, just like your sister."

"My sister?" I ask, instantly forgetting everything else. "What do you know about her?"

"You're not ready yet," he says. "Don't you remember what we said before? We see everything."

"What do you know?" I grab his arm to stop him from leaving. "If you know something about Sarah, you have to tell me!"

With a fling of his muscular arm, he sends me flying across the slippery floor. I skid, falling and landing on my knees, while he storms away. I scramble to get up and dart after him. By the time I reach the hall, it's already empty.

What do Eli and the others know about Sarah? My stomach lurches at the sinister thoughts and images I can't shake. What if the man who ate my pussy had something to do with her disappearance?

Mom hurries to my side. "Where did you disappear to?"

"I was helping Ms. Moldova fill vases," I say. Well, that's half true. "You said you wanted me to help."

She frowns, but doesn't question me. Maybe that's a consequence of her being married to Dad for all these years—believing everything she is told. I'd like a time machine to go back and see what she used to be like. Was she a rebellious teenager like Sarah, or quieter and more reserved like me? Either way, that person is long gone. Her spirit was crushed by him long ago.

"Well, we better go inside," she says. "The auction is about to start."

We file into the main auditorium, where parents are handed bidding paddles. I scan the sea of faces. Most belong to students I recognize and families I know, but there are some I don't. I look at every man's face, wondering whether he's one of them. Is that a thought that'll ever go away? Am I going to look at every stranger who fits their rough sizes with suspicion from now on? I'd like to think I'd recognize them. The men who sprayed cum over my chest, tasted me, and watched me sleep. They've seen me in my most vulnerable states. Surely, that has to leave an invisible mark? Yet, as I inspect strangers' faces, I realize it could be any of them. There is one thing I know for sure, though. They'll be watching. They are here. As they said, they live in the walls.

"Stop daydreaming." Mom nudges me, while smiling politely at the other parents. "You're holding everyone up. Look." She points. "Two seats next to Mia and her mom. Let's join them."

While Dad makes his disapproval of Mia clear, Mom has a soft spot for her. I'm not sure whether it's because she actually likes her or is relieved her daughter isn't a total social pariah. In her glory days, Mom was the prom queen, the top cheerleader, and the Stonybridge 'it' girl. Although she left during college and in her early marital years, Mom grew up here in Pasturesville. Many others have stayed in town, and her high school popularity has carried over into adulthood, giving her an elevated status. You can see it in the way she's treated by other parents who knew her then. Husbands ogle her, and their wives eye her clothing enviously. Perhaps that's why Mom enjoys attending functions so much. She can reclaim her youth and cling to that part of her life.

"Having fun?" Mia asks, raising an eyebrow sarcastically when we sit down.

"Ignore her," Ms. Moldova says. "She's grouchy."

"I can speak for myself, Mom," Mia grumbles.

"Oh, I completely understand, Kim," Mom says, like the two of us aren't standing here. "Erin is always sulking. It must be their age. All the hormones. I remember what it was like in my day." She gets a misty-eyed look. "We were—"

Mom's nostalgia gets cut short by Principal Wire taking the microphone.

"Evening, ladies and gentlemen," he says, voice booming. "Thank you for joining us in the wake of a tragedy that occurred in our community. On behalf of everyone here, I would like to extend our well wishes to the Holt family. All the proceeds from tonight's auction will go toward rebuilding their home."

Applause erupts. I clap half-heartedly, resisting the urge to roll my eyes.

"We have very generous donations from friends of Stony-bridge Academy coming up," he continues.

Another round of cheering follows.

"If they clap this often, we're in for a long night," Mia mumbles under her breath, earning herself a reproachable look from my mother.

I zone out halfway through the auction. Mom wins a case of wine from the local vineyard for an eye-watering amount. Goods are auctioned away: monthly muffin baskets, spa days, a cabin retreat, Botox injections, a day with the principal, a private half-hour concert with Ms. Moldova, and more.

"Thank you everyone," Principal Wire says, gesturing for the eager student next to him to move the garish golden arrow on a display board. It marks cash milestones, reaching fifty thousand at its summit. He gestures proudly as the arrow hits the peak. "As you'll see, we've reached our target!"

"Does that mean we can go home?" I whisper to Mia as everyone around us erupts in loud applause.

She snorts behind her hand, while Mom kicks me in the shin. Considering I've stayed quiet for two hours, I think I've earned the right to be a little snarky.

"Before we end the auction, there is one last item to announce," Principal Wire says, dashing my hopes of an early finish.

He signals to his right, and a student wheels out a table from behind the curtain. A box covered in a black fabric sits on top of it.

"An anonymous donor has given a very special present to recognize one of Stonybridge's most talented sporting stars," Principal Wire announces. "I don't need to tell anyone here that Nate Holt is a skilled football player, but what you may not know is that he's an avid baseball glove collector. Sadly, Nate's fantastic collection was destroyed."

From what I heard, his gloves were yearly birthday gifts from his father, bought as investments. They'll have been insured.

"Please come up on the stage, Nate," Principal Wire requests.

Nate makes his way to the front like a celebrity, waving and posing for photographs as he goes. Watching him makes me question what I ever saw in him. Sure, he's handsome, but the longer I look, the more I see who he really is. Just another entitled rich guy. He doesn't understand true pain. How can he?

When he finally reaches the stage, Principal Wire shakes his hand like he's an award recipient.

Nate takes the microphone. "Before I accept this generous gift," Nate starts, dripping with confident arrogance. How have I mistaken his smug smirk for a smile before? "I want to say a huge thanks to you all. We wouldn't have been able to get through this difficult time without the support of Pasturesville."

Nate's front-row fan club swoons, like he's addressing them directly. Clapping ensues, which Nate waves off modestly, but I see through his act. He's lapping up the attention.

"Now, for the item…" Principal Wire declares.

I wait with bated breath, but not for the same reason as everyone else. Every surprise presents another opportunity for my tormentors to make an impact, and this is no different. A public humiliation would excite their sick minds.

He pulls back the black curtain, and everyone gasps to see a glove signed by a famous player I haven't heard of.

"We hope this will help you restart your new collection," Principal Wire says.

"Try it on!" Oliver shouts.

Nate stands next to the box, pausing and turning to the audience. "Should I?" Everyone applauds, including my mother. "Okay, okay!" Nate raises his hands, laughing. "I'll try it."

Principal Wire removes the Perspex box for Nate to remove the glove. Grinning, he slips it on. For a second, nothing happens, then his face falls. He turns a stark white, and his mouth curls into pure agony.

"Is everything okay?" Principal Wire asks nervously.

"My hand!" Nate staggers, clutching his wrist. "My hand!"

He screams and tears the glove off. His eyes water in pain as blood drips down his arm, soaking through his shirt.

"My hand, my hand!" he wails.

It's hard to make out what I'm seeing among the mess of bloody flesh. His fingers resemble chunks of raw meat. The offending glove falls to the floor, making a girl faint, while Nate fights to stay standing.

"Ambulance!" Mrs. Holt screeches, scampering onto the stage to be at his side. "We need an ambulance. Someone call an ambulance!"

Blood continues to spout from Nate's hand like a fountain. The unfolding scene is straight from a horror movie.

Principal Wire scoops up the glove and peers inside. His jaw clenches, and I read his lips as he utters, "Razor blades."

Mom covers her mouth in horror, while a doctor in the crowd races to Nate's aid. He's lucky to attend an elite private school, which guarantees some of the best surgeons in the country are already on-site.

"Oh my fucking God," Mia gasps.

No one chastises her for cursing, only sharing her horror as the school nurse sprints past with a dusty first aid kit. She joins the doctor, who tries to stem Nate's bleeding with his designer jacket. Those stains will be impossible to remove.

"Everyone out!" Principal Wire roars, almost rupturing my eardrums. "Now!"

People flock to the exits. A few are close to fainting and green-faced, while others linger, watching to see how things play out.

I look for a masked figure, or maybe a man laughing at his handiwork, but no one sticks out.

"Who would do something like this?" Mia shakes her head in disbelief as we're carried away in the crowds. "Everyone loves Nate!"

Well, not everyone…

It was them.

It had to be.

"Maybe it was someone from Rydell Prep?" Mia theorizes. "There's a game coming up soon. If Nate's injured, he won't be able to play. Wire said it was an anonymous donor. It fits, right?"

It was Nate's right hand. The same hand he touched me with outside. They must have seen it. It's the only explanation. Rydell Prep players would never do something so twisted. Nate touched their toy, and if people touch their things, they get broken…

"Possibly," I say.

"What is this school coming to?" a parent says. "First, rats at the music concert. Now, this! It's going downhill. Where are our fees going?"

"It's the children I worry about," another says earnestly. "How can Stonybridge ensure their safety?"

Principal Wire will have a mutiny on his hands, and the police will have to launch an investigation.

"Earth to Erin?" Mia waves her hand in front of my face. "Are you listening?"

"Huh?" I shake my head. "Sorry, I guess the blood has made me a little dizzy."

The truth is, no one is safe while my stalkers are roaming

Pasturesville. Everyone who comes into contact with me is at risk. If a jealous act ends in a slashed hand, where will it end? What if Mia does something they don't like? Will they hurt her too? What about Mom?

"I think I need to lie down," I groan.

"Come on, darling," Mom says. "Let's go home."

But home isn't safe anymore.

Nowhere is.

CHAPTER
THIRTEEN

ERIN

"Oliver says Nate's recovering well," Mia informs me as we stroll through the school halls. "It's a good thing the surgeon was there right away. If they didn't act so fast, he'd have lost two fingers."

Two weeks have passed since Nate's 'accident', and it's still all everyone's talking about. Nate returned to school yesterday and doesn't go anywhere without an entourage fawning over him like lovesick puppies. I've tried to keep my distance, which hasn't been difficult when he's constantly encircled by adoring fans. The police investigation has brought up no leads, and unsurprisingly, the anonymous donor is proving impossible to track down. The entire Rydell football team was interrogated, but they all had an alibi. Sheriff Brady will be tearing what little hair he has out.

"Are you sure everything's okay?" Mia asks. "You've been acting kinda weird and distant since the Harvest Ball. I know you said that you and Nate are just friends, but I get it if you're upset about what happened."

She's right. I have been pulling away from her. Throwing myself into schoolwork is the best way for me to protect her. I don't want her getting hurt.

Although my stalkers haven't contacted me again, I sense their presence everywhere. I seem to have developed a sixth sense for knowing when they're close. They taint the air and leave small traces behind. For example, little things around my bedroom look different. A picture frame moved a finger's width to the left, my toothbrush turned the other way, my pillow angled differently. Even my locker smells of them: smoke mingled with danger, secrets, and desire. Or maybe I'm losing my mind…

I've started looking for them everywhere I go, gazing through store windows, checking behind me in mirrors, and expecting them to be around every corner. Yet they haven't shown themselves again. Somehow, I can't help being disappointed.

There was a shift after my encounter with Eli. Instead of wanting to avoid them, I find myself seeking them out. Where do you start looking for men when there's no record of their existence? After running through different scenarios, I've decided it's up to me to make the next move. I have to do something that'll draw them to me, like moths to a flame. They're watching, and it's time to put them to the test, starting with the family golf competition tomorrow.

"I'm fine, Mia," I lie. "Really."

"Did something happen at the Harvest Ball?" she pushes. "Oliver mentioned Nate said he felt bad about what happened. He said he acted like a dick."

"He did?" I keep my expression neutral, knowing Nate won't have divulged the full story.

"Yeah, he said he got cold feet and left you alone," she relays.

Naturally, that's what Nate regaled to maintain his masculine bravado. God forbid anyone is immune to his impenetrable charm.

"It was nothing," I say.

"Hm," Mia huffs, unconvinced. "If you say so."

"Things seem to be great with you and Oliver this time, though," I say, changing the subject. "Have you talked about what will happen next year when you're in college?"

Her face lights up. "Well, we have—"

"Come along, girls," Ms. Chi chides. "Didn't you hear the bell?"

"We'll catch up later," Mia promises, hurrying away. "You'll be at the golf club tomorrow, right?"

"Dad won't let me miss it," I say. "It's an Acacia tradition."

Even though we only moved to Pasturesville last year, Dad insisted on us attending the golf tournament to charm the residents long before then.

Ms. Chi stands by the classroom door, blocking the entrance.

"Before you go inside, I wanted to have a quick word," she says.

I rack my brains. I'm pretty sure I haven't missed an assignment.

"Your father has been in touch," she says. "He's concerned you're falling behind with your work. Is everything okay?"

After allowing me to attend the Harvest Ball without him chaperoning, he's trying to reassert control.

"He's worrying over nothing," I say. "My dad's just protective. I've been hitting all my deadlines."

"If you ever need to talk, you know where to find me. Many students find it hard to live up to their parents' expectations," she says. "I know this time of year must be challenging for your family."

I feign a smile. "Thanks for checking in, but I'm fine, honestly."

Well, if you don't count being stalked by psychopaths...

"I'm glad to hear it, but remember, my door is always

open." Her sentence trails off with a sad smile, then she steps aside. "Let's start the lesson."

I can't concentrate for the rest of class, too distracted by the prospect of luring three men from their hiding place. They believe they have the upper hand, but they're not the only ones who can play games.

THE ANNUAL GOLF tournament is a day for all members to invite their family to the golf club. Really, it's an excuse to throw a lavish celebration and ensure members sign up for another year. Dad secretly detests golf, but he plays to keep up appearances. The club is a frequent jaunt for the Pasturesville elite, where the most influential people do business.

"Stop fussing," Mom says, batting my hand to stop me from adjusting my dress while simultaneously fluffing her hair. "You look lovely."

She's forced me into a red knee-length gingham sundress that cinches at the waist with a green cardigan and white sandals. I'm like a character from *Little House on the Prairie*, which isn't helped by the tight bun knotted at the nape of my neck.

"I don't feel it," I grumble.

Dad strides ahead of us to greet his golfing buddies on the opposite end of the veranda. The club house is a giant building nestled among rolling green courses, featuring a spa, fine dining restaurant, and bar. The day always starts with a drinks reception and light refreshments, followed by a brief tournament. There are golf cart rides for young children, alongside a magician and bouncy house to give parents a break.

I check my phone.

> MIA: Can't make it. Oliver's taking me to the city for a surprise shopping spree. Enjoy!

"Put your phone away," Mom hisses. "It's time to socialize."

Dad shakes hands with Robert Gilsmear, a wealthy CEO of a pharmaceutical company that supplies the asylum. Their relationship goes back years.

"It's always a pleasure to see you," Dad says to him. "I'm sure I can count on your attendance at Sunnycrest's upcoming event."

"Of course." Robert grins, showing off his new veneers. They're too big for his face, reminding me of a shark from an animated film. "You can always count on me."

I groan inwardly. How could I have forgotten about the Sunnycrest annual mixer? The only plus point about the event is Dad being out of the house more during preparations.

"Jocelyn!" Robert extends his arms to my mother. She simpers as he plants kisses on her cheeks. "And Erin, look at you!" He steps back to survey me. "How you've grown!"

His beady-eyed look makes me glad I'm wearing a conservative outfit. My inner alarm bells sound. Robert gives me the serious creeps.

"I still need a caddy for the tournament," Robert says. "What do you say, Erin?"

I glance nervously at my father. He's smiling, but he'd prefer me to be glued to his side all day.

"I don't know if Erin has the—" Dad begins.

"I'd love to," I interrupt, going against all my instincts.

The smile he returns churns my stomach.

This is the opportunity I've been waiting for. If my masked stalkers want to act overprotective, this is a man I won't feel bad punishing.

"Perfect." Robert claps his hands gleefully. "We'll tee off at ten. I will see you on the course, Miss Acacia."

"That was kind of you to offer, Erin," Mom says.

"I know he's an important asset for Sunnycrest," I say.

Dad's eyes narrow, going into shrink mode and trying to psychoanalyze me like one of his patients. It's an uncomfortable sensation, but a familiar one.

"Oh, look, there's Nate's mom!" Mom waves at her. "We have to say hello to our neighbors, Magnus."

She steers him away by the arm, giving me a rare moment of silence. I accept a glass of lemonade from the server and sip it, leaning against the fence overlooking the course. There are plenty of secluded areas and shrubbery. Are Eli and the others out there?

"Erin!" I jump as Robert's slimy hand snakes around my waist. "It's time for us to go."

"Sure," I say, forcing a bright smile.

The game doesn't start for an hour.

He leads me to a waiting golf cart and puts on aviator sunglasses, which he thinks make him look cool. His clubs are already loaded to save me from carrying them.

"Your carriage awaits," he announces.

He slips into the driver's seat next to me and drapes one ham-like arm around my chair. My nose crinkles from his strong cologne that does a terrible job at masking his BO. He slides closer, pushing me into his sticky armpit.

"We're starting on hole fourteen," he says, hitting the gas. It's the farthest hole from the clubhouse and renowned as the hardest on the course. "The other golfers will meet us there." His piggy eyes gleam like he's about to eat. "It'll be good to practice before the others join us."

"Yes, Mr. Gilsmear," I chirp.

My jaw aches from maintaining my fake smile.

"Please, call me Robert."

"Have fun, Erin!" Mom calls, waving us off as we speed past.

"We will," Robert says. His chubby fingers squeeze my shoulder and linger a little too long.

I've heard rumors about his appetite for young women. Due to his position, people brush the speculations off. Instead of calling him a pervert, like they should, they brand him an 'eccentric'. Even if he were caught, he has enough cash to brush anything under the carpet without consequences. His wife, who I haven't met, is ten years his junior. Mia swears she saw Mrs. Gilsmear hooking up with their gorgeous gardener once. Like many wives, she's probably unhappy, but won't leave her husband for fear of losing her comfortable life.

"How is school?" Robert asks. "You must be, what, eighteen now?"

"Yes," I reply. "It's going well."

"Your father told me you're shaping up to be a musical prodigy," he says.

We whizz along the perfectly maintained grass, through sloping hills, past the sandbanks, and around the edge of the small lake.

Are they watching us? I keep expecting to see a masked face, but there's no sign of them so far.

"He's exaggerating," I say. "Playing the piano is just a hobby."

"You're so modest!" He slaps my knee, not noticing my flinch. "I'm looking to hire a music tutor for my son. He's only eight, and he already plays the violin, piano, and flute. The little tyke can't decide which is best. He wants it all—a real chip off the old block!"

"He sounds very talented," I reply.

We take a left, trundling over uneven ground. Robert

steals a glance at my chest, watching my breasts bob with the motion.

"My wife is convinced we have the next Mozart on our hands!" He laughs. "Do you tutor in your spare time?"

"My schedule is pretty busy," I say. "My dad takes my studies seriously, so I don't have time for a job."

"I could have a word with him?" he offers. "You'd fit right in at our house."

I say nothing as we come to a halt at the hole.

"Why don't you help with my clubs?" he suggests.

We're in a deserted area, a row of conifers hides us from view. Maybe this wasn't my best idea…

His golf bag is huge. Based on my size, there's no way I'll be able to carry it single-handedly. I strap on my big girl panties and remember why I'm doing this. The masked men know something about Sarah. I need answers.

"Here." Robert places a lecherous hand on the small of my back as I attempt to haul the bag off the cart with a huff. His breath sends shivers down my neck. "Let me help you."

Not wanting to give up so easily, I tug the bag, causing them to fall with a crash.

Robert chuckles. "What am I going to do with you?"

I smile sweetly, ignoring my inner feminist and twirling a strand of hair around my finger the way I've watched girls flirt in the movies. "I'm such a klutz."

He checks his gold Rolex. The watch would look oversized on most people, but his large wrists make it look tiny.

"We still have time before the opposition arrives," he says. "Why don't we have a friendly game?"

"Golfing isn't my forte," I reply. "Music is my thing."

His face lights up. This is the response he hoped for. "I'm a great teacher." He winks and hands me a club. "Here."

I grasp it and focus on the hole, despite knowing I won't get anywhere near it.

Robert sidles up to me like a mangy cat, marking its territory. He slips his sweaty hands around my body and positions them on top of mine. "Let me show you how to swing."

I grit my teeth as something stirs in his pants against me. He wriggles his hips against my ass to get into position.

I scan the trees for movement. *Where are you?* They said I was theirs. This is their chance to prove it.

Robert guides my arms, and I strike the ball. It soars through the air, straight over the hill, landing in a cluster of trees. He steps away, clapping and pretending his erection hadn't been rubbing against me moments before.

"Bravo, Erin!" He applauds. "We'll make a champion of you yet! Next, we need to work on your aim."

I pass him a club. "Your turn."

"Oh no, I need to conserve my energy for the game." His eyes twinkle. "Into the cart!"

He gives my ass a friendly pat as I turn. Now I really want to see his hand removed.

My bright yellow ball is easy to find. Unfortunately, it strayed farther off course than I first thought, landing at the bottom of a large tree between gnarled roots.

"It'll be impossible to get out of that spot," I comment.

"Nonsense," he says. "All you need is special skill and training."

I brace myself, getting into position again.

"Before you hit, you need to practice your swing," he says, standing behind me. "We need to get your rotation right." He gropes my hips, pushing his disgusting hardness against me and rotating our bodies in sync. "See?" His fingers dig into my flesh. "All you have to do is bend forward a little to get that shift." He tilts me forward. "Oh yeah, Erin. Just like that." He wiggles his hips to rest his dick right between my ass cheeks. "What do you think of golf, Erin?" His voice grows hoarse with sickening arousal. "Do you think you're getting the hang of it?"

"I think I'm ready to swing now, Mr. Gilsmear," I say coldly.

"Oh, not yet, Erin." He continues wiggling himself back and forth. "You're not in the right position yet. Just bend a little more to get your back arched and shuffle back."

I stay frozen in place, horror-stricken as he continues moving in a rhythmic motion. His breathing grows ragged, filling me with disgust. He's using me. Sure, that's what the guys in the masks do, but there's something thrilling about them. Being gyrated on by a geriatric is quite different.

"I'm an excellent teacher, aren't I? You're built for sport. You're wasting yourself hiding behind a piano. A girl with a body like yours could do anything," he purrs. "I can teach you about more than golf, if you'd like?"

"I..."

A snapping twig makes Robert jump back and clear his throat, looking nervously at the rustling bushes. While he's distracted, I swing the club hard and launch the ball in the opposite direction.

In the distance, someone calls his name.

"It looks like the game is about to start," I say, relieved to be spared from any extra one-on-one tuition.

"That it is," Robert says, pretending like he hasn't just creamed in his pants. "May the best man win."

I spin, hoping to see a masked man emerge from the undergrowth, but no such luck...

My stomach rolls, both from disgust at what happened and for putting myself in that position.

The men are turning me into a person I don't recognize, and I can't get them out of my head, no matter how hard I try. Worse still, why am I so disappointed by their absence when it would be best for them to stay out of my life for good?

CHAPTER
FIFTEEN

LEX

"She's changing." Aiden comments, rubbing his chin thoughtfully, almost in amusement. Yet, there's no mistaking the darkness stirring behind his words. "She's growing bolder."

"Maybe she's more like her sister than we thought," I comment. "Their likeness is uncanny."

Aiden bristles at my side. A silent warning. We have an unspoken rule not to talk about her, and I know better than to break it. After seeing Erin's reaction when we mentioned Sarah, it's made me question how much she really knows. We thought she may have an inkling about what happened, considering she always follows Daddy's rules, but she seems oblivious. That, or she doesn't want to face the damage she caused.

"Look," Aiden says, drawing our attention back to the present situation. "She's asking for trouble…"

We watch them from our vantage point. Erin and Robert Gilsmear. We know all about him and his friendship with Acacia. He, like many others, knows about the experiments and does nothing to stop them. As long as he keeps getting Sunnycrest's business, Gilsmear is happy. Cash is all he cares about, making it easy for him to overlook how he's providing the equipment that fuels Acacia's depravity.

Eli clenches his fists. "We can't let him—"

"No," Aiden insists firmly, grabbing Eli's arm to stop him from charging across the golf course and tearing Gilsmear apart. "This is what she wants."

"But he's touching her," Eli says, shaking in rage.

His obsessive need for her rises to the surface. The feeling's mutual. We all want to rip Gilsmear's dick off. But this is only the start...

Eli has never been patient, though. When he has something in his sights, he won't let it go. It becomes his everything. He has obsessive compulsive disorder, but his troubles run deeper than that. Every single one of his twisted thoughts is now focused on her. She's become his very reason for existence. We're all obsessive when it comes to her. Although, unlike Eli, Aiden and I can keep ourselves in check. Eli says too much. He's unpredictable and lets his emotions get the better of him. He shouldn't have mentioned Sarah.

"Let him dirty our toy," I say in a cavalier way. "She is playing games. Taunting us. Look at how her ass is rubbing up against his shriveled old cock. She's frothing over him, begging for it."

While I don't want him touching our little ghost, it gives me a reason to punish her. We've made our intentions clear. Her breaking our rules justifies me breaking her. After this, Aiden might finally allow me more time alone with her. The virgin princess is turning out to be the dirty whore I knew she was.

"Lex," Aiden warns in a low growl, knowing I'm encouraging Eli. "Enough."

Aiden controls his emotions better than anyone. After everything Acacia put him through, it's a miracle he has any emotions at all. But he's possessive. He likes to claim what is his, and Erin is marked.

"But she's ours," Eli objects. "All fucking ours."

Although we'd always planned to use Erin to get what we want, I never expected her to turn into an obsession. Her stumbling right into our laps at Sunnycrest was a lucky twist of fate. That was the universe's way of begging us to take her. She is our payment.

"And this doesn't change a thing," Aiden says. He turns his phone to proudly display his screensaver. *Little Ghost on her knees.* His cum drips down her cheeks like tears, and her lips are parted in a silent moan, begging to receive every drop. "See? We own her."

"Maybe I can remind her of the fact?" I suggest.

"We'll see," Aiden says.

That's progress.

Gilsmear gyrates his hips, spilling dirty cream in his tartan pants over our girl. Fuck, she'll need punishing real good for this. If I had my way, I'd kill him, then fuck her against the tree and choke her until she begs me to stop. I'd keep going until she passes out, before showering her in my cum. My cock swells at the thought.

Erin's head swivels around. In that split-second, I see her intentions. She's not a rabbit in the headlights. She's laying a trap with her body. She wants this—not him rubbing all over her, her disdainful look makes that clear—but she's looking for something. *Us.*

Eli lunges, his weight crushing a twig underfoot.

"I said no," Aiden hisses.

"But—" Eli argues.

The look on Aiden's face makes him whimper and shut up. Aiden makes the rules. That's how it has to be. He's the only reason we survived in Sunnycrest and made it out with a shred of our sanity. Well, that's arguable...

"She belongs to us," Aiden says, his jaw clenching in determination, the way it always does when he's making a point. "And we'll show her that tonight."

"How?" I ask.

Aiden hunts around in his pocket and produces a pill bottle. Before leaving the asylum, we raided the medical supply closet. The orderlies aren't the only ones who have access to drugs. We know the combinations for every cabinet in the asylum.

I inspect the label and grin. After drugging her with these babies, she'll be at our mercy. Our toy to play with. Putty in our hands. Ours. All fucking ours.

We withdraw into the shadows again, watching as our little ghost readies herself for the game.

She fanned the flames. The question is, can she withstand the inferno?

"Wake up, hon!" Mom bangs on my bedroom door. "You'll be late, and turn that alarm off!"

My eyelids are heavy. I groan and put a hand to my thumping head. Little dots cross my vision, and everything's hazy. Maybe I'm coming down with something…

"I'm up now," I croak, heaving myself out of bed with great effort and silencing my beeping phone.

After being molested by Robert, I endured an afternoon of pretending it didn't happen. I followed him around the course and laughed at his stupid jokes. He found it especially amusing to make me cheer whenever he potted a ball.

When I returned home, I expected something to happen. I stayed up until three a.m., waiting. The slightest noise made my heart race in anticipation, but they didn't come, leaving me with only disappointment for company. Perhaps I'd lost my chance to get any answers about Sarah. They could have got spooked and left town for good.

"You have twenty minutes," Mom calls. "Your father will be waiting."

"Of course he will," I grumble under my breath, dragging my feet to the bathroom.

I take off my nightshirt, getting ready to jump in the shower, then catch my reflection in the mirror.

What the…

The stark contrast between my pale skin and the color red is first to draw my attention. Smeared bloody fingerprints cover my chest, like someone has grabbed my breasts and pawed at my hips. Next, tiny indentations from where teeth have sunk into the skin around my nipples leave possessive purple marks behind.

Marks.

Their marks.

How can I not remember? I part my legs and gulp, looking down to see bruises from where their ghostly fingers touched me. Another bite mark taunts me from my soft inner thigh. It stings as I run my finger over it.

I pull down my panties with shaking hands, half expecting to see blood, or worse, but there's nothing. I breathe a sigh of relief, spinning to check the rest of my body and find bloody handprints over my ass.

None of this makes sense.

As I turn, I inhale sharply. My hair… *Shit!* My hair looks like it's been hacked with gardening shears. Half of it has been crudely cut into uneven jagged lengths.

I'm not the type of girl who cares about her appearance, but we live in a town where image matters. Mom insists on taking me to the salon every six weeks for a cut and color. She'll lose her mind when she sees me.

I grab my nail scissors. It'll take a lot to tidy up this mess, but I start desperately cutting. My locks fall into the basin. How can they expect me to leave the house looking like this?

"Erin!" Father barks. "Where are you?"

I have seconds to react, managing to put on my bathrobe before he barges inside.

He glares at the scissors in my hand. His eyes narrow into

slits, like he's caught me standing over a dead body with a bloody knife.

"What did you do?" he spits through gritted teeth.

"I..."

I'm lost for words.

He grabs my arm. "You're coming with me."

"Dad, that hurts," I whimper, struggling to keep my robe together.

He doesn't listen and tightens his hold, digging his fingers into my arm so hard it'll bruise.

"Don't say another word," he hisses, dragging me down the stairs.

Mom hums to herself while clearing the table. When she sees me, she shrieks. A jug of milk slips from her hands and smashes.

"Your hair!" she shrieks in despair. "What did you do?"

"Do you think this is funny, Erin?" Dad yells. "This is behavior I'd have expected from your sister, not from you. Is this how you want to represent yourself at the Sunnycrest event this week? Are you trying to embarrass me?"

He doesn't give time for me to respond. Instead, he pulls me through the house and hauls me into his study, leaving Mom gaping open-mouthed after us.

"Sit down!" he roars, throwing me into the chair opposite his desk.

"Magnus..." Mom hovers in the doorway. "I have my stylist on speed dial. She can be here within the hour."

"No!" he yells. "Not today, Jocelyn." He points at me menacingly. "This is between me and her. Now, get out. Now!"

Mom bows her head. "Yes, Magnus."

He storms to his locked cabinet in the corner. It's the first time I've seen inside it as he keeps the key on him permanently. He rifles through its contents, hurling random pill bottles across the room while muttering to himself. I can't catch everything he says, but the words 'ungrateful' and 'spoiled' are hard to miss.

"We're increasing your medication." He slams three bottles in front of me. "Take one from each of these three times a day."

He lines up the pills. One yellow. One red. One blue. I'm already taking antidepressants he prescribed, and I've only just started feeling normal on them. I don't want to turn into a drugged zombie like the rest of his patients.

"I don't want—"

He grabs my face, squeezing my cheeks hard.

"Dad!" I thrash around, turning my head to get away.

He uses one hand to grab the back of my head, while forcing my mouth open with the other. He shoves the pills onto my tongue, almost making me choke.

"Swallow!" he commands, spraying me with spit. "Now!"

He snaps my jaw shut. I fight the urge to gag as the oblong pills slide down my throat.

"Open your mouth," he barks.

Trembling, I do as he asks. He swirls his fingers around my inner cheeks and raises my tongue to inspect underneath.

"I can't be too careful," he murmurs.

"I'll be late for s-school," I stammer, hoping this will get me back into his good graces. After all, education is what he values above all else. "I need to get ready."

"School?" He guffaws. "You're not going anywhere. You're not leaving the house until further notice."

Anger bubbles inside me. I've never lashed out at him before, partially because that was Sarah's area of expertise, and I wanted to avoid the consequences. It was easier to sneak into Sarah's room when he locked her up, or bring her food when he starved her as punishment for skipping dinner, rather than address the problem. Yet, with a grounding stretching ahead of me like a life sentence, I can't stop myself.

"I'm your daughter, not a patient," I say.

"Would you prefer an extended stay at Sunnycrest?" he asks. "One more word from you, and I'll have you admitted. I made mistakes with Sarah, but I won't make the same mistakes with you, Erin. I don't know what you were hoping to achieve with your little act of rebellion, but you will regret it. Until you earn my trust again, you will do as I say."

"But—"

He strikes me across the face, stunning me into silence. It's the first time he's hit me, and I cradle my burning cheek, cowering like a small child. All of my earlier boldness has evaporated.

"Go to your room. Do not come out until I return. Your mother will book you an appointment tomorrow to fix this mess before tomorrow night." He wrinkles his nose, plucking a strand of my hacked hair, then letting it drop around my face. "You will still be attending the function. I need to keep you where I can see you. Is that clear?"

"Yes," I whisper, a tear falling down my cheek.

"Good," he replies. "Now, get out of my sight. You're a disgrace."

I hold in a strangled sob and run upstairs. Mom ignores me as I pass, singing along to the radio as she wipes the kitchen surfaces with more vigor than usual.

"I'm heading to work, Jocelyn," I hear Dad say. "Erin is not to leave this house under any circumstances."

"I've called the academy to let them know she's unwell," Mom says.

"Very good," he says, before slamming the front door hard enough to knock a hanging portrait off of the wall.

Back in the safety of my bedroom, I sink to my knees. My head spins from the medication taking effect. The drugs must be strong for him to leave the house without worry of me escaping. I struggle to my feet, gripping onto my drawers for balance as my surroundings blur in and out of focus. My knees threaten to give way, but I grapple my way to the bed. I tug the curtains closed before collapsing into my cushions.

It's impossible to tell how much time drifts by. I curl into the fetal position, fighting to keep my eyes open, while my mind refuses to switch off. Every emotion comes to the surface: fear, anger, frustration. Whenever one rises, it gets tempered again and numbed, like they're wrestling to free themselves, drowning inside my brain while battling to catch their breath against an oncoming tide.

"I'm going to the spa, darling," Mom says from somewhere in the abyss. "I'll be back later. Feel better soon!"

I ignore her, pulling my blood-soaked robe tighter around me.

Silence stretches on until my bathroom door opens, and a chilling British voice says, "I thought they'd never leave."

I LOOK into Three's masked face. A balaclava with slits for eyes stares back. His long-sleeved black Henley is tight, hugging toned biceps, and his black leather gloves are pulled up to his elbows. I can't see any hint of his skin aside from a tiny opening around his neck, where his collar ends and the balaclava begins. I focus on that. The only thing separating him from a shadow.

"Are you real?" I whisper, unable to trust my mind.

He tilts his head to the left. "What do you think, Little Ghost?"

The motion makes his mask twitch, exposing more of his neck. Pink raised scars cover his skin. Burns.

"What..." My tongue feels too large for my mouth. "Wh..."

I wanted to see them again, but not as a mute mannequin. So many unanswered questions sit on the tip of my tongue, starting with what happened last night. Yet, I can't ask them.

He chuckles. He appears to be alone. Out of the three men, he makes me the most nervous. A dark energy engulfs him, and I know he wants to make me scream.

"Your daddy's medication doesn't interact well with ours," he says. "But you want to be used, don't you? That's why you let Gilsmear's dirty hands taint you. You put on a show for us like the filthy slut you are."

I shake my head, and slur, "I want—"

"That's your first mistake, Little Ghost." He holds up a finger. "Thinking that your wants matter. You thought you could get us to do your bidding by bending over for another man. It was foolish to believe you could summon us at will. Remember, you're not the one in control. We are. We decide what happens to you and when. That's how this works."

"Sarah…" I murmur. "What—"

He sighs, sauntering closer and sitting on the edge of my bed. I'm tempted to grab his mask and see the man underneath, but his intense stare holds me captive. His hazel eyes are flecked with bright amber, like tiny flames.

"I'm not here to talk about your sister." He picks a strand of my hair. "I'm here to remind you that actions have consequences. You toyed with us. The others already have their souvenirs, but I need you to be awake for what I want. Although…" His voice trails off and takes on a new hard edge. "Your father has made that more difficult."

"What do you want?"

"I'm going to make you beg," he says. He takes a lighter from his pocket and flicks it on. "You're going to scream until your throat is hoarse, and you can't make another sound."

He waves the flame in front of my face, heating my cheeks. I yelp as he swipes it across a strand of my hair, and it catches at the end. I pat it down as a horrible, singed smell fills the room.

"This is only the beginning, Erin," he warns, standing up. "We're just getting to know each other. Now, get on your knees."

I shuffle to the edge of the bed, swaying from side to side. "I…"

"Do it!" he roars.

I slide off and land on my knees before him.

He nudges me with his foot like I'm a dog, forcing me to crawl into the middle of the floor.

"Take off your robe," he orders. My momentary hesitation makes him more irate. "Off, now!"

I do as he asks, slipping the soft material from my shoulders and letting it fall.

"Look at their marks on you," he admires, walking around in circles while I keep my chin lowered, avoiding eye contact. "You may not remember them touching you, but your body loved every second of it. Your body needs us. It craves us. And, as you like games so much, it's time we played one together."

Terror builds in the pit of my stomach.

"Get on all fours for me," he commands. While I position myself, he acts fast. A rough leather band crushes my windpipe as he pulls it taut around my neck and fastens it. He gives the leash a tug. Adrenaline brings me out of my hazy, drug-induced state, knowing danger is here, and there's nowhere to hide. "This is how they used to chain us up in Sunnycrest."

He yanks the chain attached to my collar. The metal links rattle and jerk my head upright.

Although I've been in the asylum many times, I've never been on the wards. However, I've heard Dad talk about how they pride themselves on gentle rehabilitation. Three must be lying.

"You're our pet, and we're your owners, Little Ghost," he says. "I want you to remember this whenever you have another thought about letting another man lay their hands on you."

"I just wanted to speak to you," I breathe, realizing how stupid it sounds as I say it.

"Enough," he hisses. "All I want to hear from your mouth is pleading for me to stop."

He ruffles around with something. Clinking crystals

chime, then pressure from the leash builds. He forces my head up at an uncomfortable angle, drawing a choking sound from the back of my throat. I reach for my neck, struggling to breathe as it tightens. I move from all fours to a kneeling position and then onto my feet as the lifting chain manipulates me like a marionette.

"That's it," he encourages. "On your feet."

I hold the collar, clawing the material as it cuts into my skin. Above us, my chandelier jingles, and realization hits. He's created a pulley system—wrapping the chain around a chandelier arm, then back to his hands, leaving just the right amount of slack for me to stand. He tightens the chain, wrapping it around his fist to force me onto my tiptoes. It's the only way to breathe.

"If you try to escape, those crystals will shatter your skull," he says.

Why did Mom insist on placing chandeliers in every room in the house?

He swaggers forward with his lighter and holds the flame in front of my face, dangerously close to my eyelashes. "Are you scared, Little Ghost?"

I swallow hard and goosebumps spread over my skin.

"Yes," I whisper.

I'm hanging like a carcass, completely at his mercy, wearing nothing but panties.

"Good." The balaclava stretches across his face to form a grin as he flips the Zippo lid down. "You should be."

His index finger skims along my cheekbone, then down the curve of my chin and neck. My breathing deepens, my bare breasts heaving. He stops behind my ear, resting on my pulse.

"It's racing, Little Ghost," he observes. "The others are sad they can't be here, but they have other plans."

"What's your name?" I ask.

"Lex," he replies with no qualms. Sensing my shock, he

laughs coldly. "Knowing my name changes nothing. You can't trace someone who should be dead."

"You're a ghost too," I say.

"Something like that." He yanks the leash. I squeal, teetering on the very tips of my toes. "What's wrong? Is that too tight?"

"I can't…" I gasp. "I can't…"

"If you can speak, you can breathe," he snaps. "I need to retrieve my supplies."

He leaves me dangling while he searches a black briefcase balanced on top of my dresser. I'm not sure when and how he got inside the house, but there's no use in questioning him. They have their methods, and nothing can keep them out.

His case reminds me of one a Victorian doctor may carry. He unscrambles a scratchy combination lock into the right position, and it opens with a pop. His back shields my view, so I can't see what's inside properly, but his hands float a few inches over the objects while he makes his selections.

"This will do," he says, picking a mystery item.

He takes slow, deliberate steps, building anticipation as he moves behind me. I try turning, but it's too hard to hold my balance. I have to stay in the same spot, or I'll cut off my oxygen supply.

Heat radiates from his looming body like a burning fire, but his breath tickling the back of my neck makes me shiver. He tugs my panties loose and lets them fall to the floor.

"Spread your legs wide for me, little slut," he orders, loosening the chain slightly to give me room to move.

I step out of my panties and oblige as his palm slides down my spine, gliding over my lower back arch and down to my ass. His touch is fleetingly tantalizing, skimming the surface, like a breeze that's barely there but still chills you.

He notices me wince.

"What's wrong?" he mocks. "Don't you like being touched?"

I bite my lip and stay silent.

He spits on his gloves.

"You need to be punished," he purrs, sliding his hand between my ass cheeks.

I groan, expecting them to stray to my pussy, but I tighten instantly when I realize that isn't his intention. My thighs clench as soon as his wet finger rubs my asshole. The stitching of his glove caresses my entrance, and I pucker under it.

"You're going to take what I give you, Little Ghost." He tsks. "I never said I'd play nice."

He spits again, a wet sloshy sound, before returning. He's not gentle. He probes, pushing his finger into my ass. My eyes water. It's the first time I've had anything inside it, and the sensation is alien. He circles, stretching me, before pushing back and forth. In and out. I have no choice but to stand as still as possible while he fills me.

"Filthy whore," he chastises. "This is what happens when you allow old men to grind against your pretty ass. You need a reminder of who owns it." He withdraws from me. "You're ready now."

"Ready for…"

I yelp as he inserts a lubricated cylindrical object into my ass. It's smooth, silky, and a little bigger than his finger. He slides it in deeper, one inch at a time.

"That's it, Little Ghost," he compliments. "Let me see your ass eat it up."

He fucks me with the object, twirling it around. As I get more comfortable, it actually feels… kinda good. I arch my back but stay quiet, refusing to give him the satisfaction of knowing this isn't all bad.

He laughs, like he can read my thoughts, and stops abruptly, leaving the object buried inside me.

"Where are my manners?" he asks. "I'm sure you want to see."

He dismounts my mirror from the wall and lays it flat on the floor between my legs.

I hesitate before looking down and seeing my pussy splayed beneath me. My lips, puffy and pink from arousal, glisten.

"Look how wet you are," he says, noticing my wetness.

I imagine him smirking before I see the object in my ass.

A candle.

"You're not the only one who likes games," he says, flipping open his Zippo.

My jaw drops in horror. "You're not—"

"I'm not, what?" His tone is laced with bemusement as he lights the wick. "You better squeeze that virgin asshole nice and tight." He saunters around to face me and strokes my cheek. "Or I'll set your house alight."

I'm more worried about the wax melting inside me. How would I explain this injury at the emergency room?

"What do you want?" I ask through gritted teeth, fighting against my crippling fear.

If I tried to pull it out, I'd topple over, and I'm already struggling to balance…

"Come for me," he demands. "If you don't, I'll leave that candle burning. And if you're having any thoughts about trying to remove the candle, remember that I have no qualms about leaving you hanging."

"You're sick," I hiss.

"If you keep talking dirty, I'll set fire to your room and watch it burn with you inside it," he warns, catching my throat in a vise-like grip and squeezing. "Do you understand?" I blink away tears and clench as a drop of wax hits the floor. "I want to see your pussy drip, just like that wax."

He returns to his briefcase for another object, what looks like a metal stick with something bunched on its end. He dips it in an alcohol-smelling liquid, then walks in slow circles around me, enjoying every second of this.

Like a conductor directing an orchestra, he holds the rod end to the candle's open flame. With a theatrical flourish, the top of the rod lights up like a marshmallow over an open fire. I yelp in horror. His erection springs to life under his jeans, creating a giant tent.

"Are you scared, Little Ghost?" he asks. With his free hand, he catches a drop of falling wax and smears it onto my ass. The heat is mild, but I'm more concerned about the massive burning rod between my legs. "Touch yourself for me."

"I…"

To silence me, he edges the candle deeper inside me.

"Do it," he commands. "Or else."

What choice do I have? I slip my hand between my thighs. Every instinct is telling me to run, but there's nowhere to go when you're attached to a burning light. I clench my jaw to keep my adrenaline-induced shaking at bay.

"You know what to do," he says.

"I hate you," I moan, squeezing my eyes shut and imagining I'm anywhere but here while I touch myself.

Blindness provides momentary relief until a sting of heat bounces up my arms.

My eyes spring open to see Lex.

I scream as he rolls the fiery rod down the front of my chest, forgetting all about touching myself.

"That noise," he says, licking his lips under the mask. "Your scream is everything."

He twirls the wand in his hand, dancing the flames between my breasts. It only touches one spot for a nanosecond, long enough to heat and startle me, but not lingering enough to burn. Lex's amber eyes look almost red, hypnotized by the flames and the shadows they cast.

"Why did you stop?" Lex asks huskily. He sweeps the flickering flame across my nipple, making them harden instantly, and I scream again. "I'm a man of my word. Remember what you have to do."

My cheeks flush with shame as I touch my clit again, trying to separate my mind from my body.

"And don't think about faking it," he sneers. "I'll know."

Pleasuring myself has always been a guilty thrill. Going to Sunday school as a child taught me that sex should be reserved for marriage. Although I stopped believing in that notion long ago, part of that conditioning still lingers. But there's nothing thrilling about this. It's dirty. Sordid. Objectifying.

"Look at yourself," he instructs.

I stare at my pussy from beneath in the mirror, watching it soak my fingers while trying to ignore Lex's twirling fireball circus performance.

"That's it, Little Ghost," he says. "Keep finger fucking that ripe little cunt of yours. Look at that candle burning. You've not got long now. Tick tock."

There's about three inches left to burn, but I'm taking no chances. I massage my clit furiously, relishing the pleasure but hating myself—and this situation—at the same time. I always imagined sex would be pure and beautiful. A sacred act where you rolled around in silk sheets and whispered sweet nothings in a lover's ear, but this? It's nothing like that.

"You're getting close," he comments.

He holds the fireball to my ankle and bounces it up my leg. I yelp, but continue pleasuring myself. *Focus on your hands, Erin. Ignore what he's doing.* He goes higher, and the flames lick at my knees. I imagine that it's something else. A warm caress. A gentle touch. Anything to distract me.

"Maybe you need more incentive," he says, pushing the candle farther into my ass, so deep that I can feel its warmth.

Lex's flame wand continues rolling up my legs, whooshing back and forth. I gasp as it brushes my delicate inner thighs.

"Come for me, Little Ghost."

My orgasm nears. I push aside my self-consciousness and let my eyelids flutter closed, seeking the joy in the heat like a warm shower spray. There's no other way.

The first wave of pleasure rolls over me with a moan. The stuffed candle heightens the sensation, as if the orgasm is rebounding around my body, like an echo down a mountain range.

Lex yanks the chain hard, cutting into my windpipe. I choke and gasp for air. Dots swim across my vision while my pussy spasms, consumed by waves of toe-curling pleasure that are being squeezed from me, alongside my oxygen.

"Lex—" I gurgle, wobbling on my feet and about to pass out.

He releases the tension, allowing my lungs to swell.

When I come to, dizzy and in a haze, Lex faces me. He watches with a deep fascination that, while unnerving, reminds me he's under my spell, too. There's power in my ability to hypnotize a monster while coming undone. If only I can understand what they see in me...

"I've played your game," I say, glancing at the mirror. "Put it out."

He cackles. "Do you really think I play by the rules?" He leans close, his breath fanning my face. "Like you, I play dirty."

My heart thunders while he heads to my bathroom. The faucet runs, followed by a sizzle of him presumably putting out his flame rod. I thrash my neck from side to side, increasingly more panicked the shorter the candle gets.

"Lex," I yell, unable to keep the terror from my voice. "Put it out!"

He doesn't respond.

He simply returns to the room, gathers his supplies, and walks away with his briefcase.

"Lex!" I scream as his footsteps grow distant. Wax

continues to drip onto the floor and mirror. One drop lands on my inner thigh, scorching me. "You can't leave me here!"

The chandelier rattles as I grope the collar, fumbling with the lock. It's no use. A key is required. Frustrated tears spill down my cheeks.

"Help!" I plead. "Somebody help me!"

I scream in frustration. Not at Lex. Not at my masked men. But at everything. It's primal, coming out like a carnal roar.

Suddenly, the floorboards creak, and Lex nudges the door open.

He leans against the doorframe and purrs, "I knew you'd have a pretty scream."

This is what he wanted. To humiliate me. Shame me. Make me scream.

Lex calmly pulls the candle from my ass with a slippery pop. He blows it out and stashes the waxy stump in his pocket.

"I hope you've learned your lesson," he says, unlocking my collar, then holding my chin. He cups my face with a force that implies he won't hesitate to break my neck. "Never let another man touch you again."

Finally free, I fall to the ground, cradling my neck and spluttering for air.

"What do you know about Sarah?" I wheeze, reaching for his ankle but missing.

His shoulders tense. "If you want to know what happened to your sister, look closer to home."

Lex goes to leave again when, suddenly, he freezes. His body language shifts as he looks down at me. He shakes his head, as if willing a memory away.

Before I have time to question him further, he slips back into the shadows, where he belongs, leaving me with more questions than answers.

CHAPTER
EIGHTEEN
AIDEN

"She asked about her," Lex says, returning to the cabin and unpeeling his mask.

Sunlight slips through the windows, hitting his cheek to highlight the scars covering half of his face.

"What did you say?" I ask, swigging the last of my beer while Eli sharpens his knives at the table.

The rhythmic sound of his blade swiping against the sharpener is almost therapeutic. He does it the same number of times each day. Twenty-five. Another of his rituals.

"The truth," Lex says, beckoning for me to throw a beer. "That she should look close to home. He drugged her again."

"Bastard," I spit, although it isn't surprising. Acacia believes he can fix anyone by pouring pills down their throat or injecting them with poison. Just look at us. His daughters are the same—objects to use and experiment on. "Did she enjoy her lesson?"

Erin Acacia is our property. We've claimed her. When we lay our claim on someone, nothing but death can part us. We hold on to what we own because we know how it feels to have nothing. Too much has been robbed from us already.

"Let's just say she won't try to seduce anyone else anytime soon," Lex mutters.

"Good," I reply with a stiff nod. "Gilsmear won't be a problem for much longer."

Lex nods vacantly, not really paying attention. He glugs his drink and wipes his mouth with his sleeve. I expected him to return smug and eager to regale what happened. However, he's uncharacteristically subdued.

"What aren't you telling us, Lex?" I ask.

Eli looks up from his knife. He had his fun last night. A strand of Erin's hair pokes out of his shirt pocket, the perfect keepsake.

"It's probably nothing," Lex says, shrugging.

"What?" I snap.

"She just reminds me of her," he says, more confidently this time. "I thought I saw something… on her back… maybe I'm going crazy because I swear it was—"

"Enough!" I slam my fists on the table. "How many times do I have to tell you not to talk about her?"

Eli finishes sharpening and begins mumbling to himself.

"In the van, in the van," Eli chirps. "Carry the package. The package." He hits himself in the head. "Snap. Snap. Snap!" His hands slam into his forehead even harder. "Drop the package! Drop!"

"See?" I glare at Lex. "Look what you've done now."

Lex ignores me, staring off into space.

"The package," Eli mutters. "I'm a… I'm a… I'm a…"

"You're okay, Eli," I interrupt, gently grabbing his wrist to stop him. "He can't hurt you here. You're safe, okay?"

Eli's bottom lip trembles. "I'm safe."

"Yes," I say. "You are."

"Safe," he repeats. "I'm safe."

"You're safe," I confirm.

He exhales deeply and shakes his head in shame. "Sorry."

"You have nothing to apologize for," I say, then turn to Lex. "You should know better."

Lex rolls his eyes and grabs a discarded copy of the local

newspaper from the sofa. He holds it up. A photo of Sunny-crest dons the front page. In it, the building looks almost idyllic. No one knows what really happens behind those doors.

"Have you seen this?" Lex asks. "Fucking unbelievable."

"We'll be ready tomorrow," I say.

We always are. Only this year, it'll be different…

We're ready to disrupt his freak show.

We have friends in the asylum. Our eyes and ears are everywhere. And we can't stop—won't stop—until we exact our revenge. We've made it out, but it's not over. It can't be when he's still in control. We have to end this for good.

Her setting a trap for us shows she's ready for the next phase, but are we?

THE ANNUAL OPEN evening at Sunnycrest is an opportunity to showcase their advancements in the field of psychiatry and raise funds. Industry professionals, financial donors, and key influential figures—including the mayor, sheriff, and local business owners—all attend. It's also a chance to provide reassurance that it's secure following the recent breakout. Despite Dad's best efforts to brush the incident under the carpet, there have been whispers across town about whether it's still a safe place to have on the doorstep.

After yesterday's encounter with Lex and Dad force-feeding me more pills, I've spent most of the day in the salon. My stylist successfully evened up my cut with feathery layers that rest between my chin and shoulder blades.

"Ouch!" I yelp, accidentally catching myself with the curling iron.

Loose waves complete my look. Mom picked me a black dress with white pearl buttons and an oversized lace collar to wear. It sits below the knee, complete with puffy sleeves that go down to my wrists.

"Where are you, Erin?" Mom calls. "It's time to go."

I frown at the mirror. Blusher, lip gloss, and mascara don't stop me from looking ill, but at least foundation covers the bruising on my neck.

"Erin!" Dad roars. "We're leaving. Now!"

I hurry down to find Mom making the final adjustments to Dad's tie and smoothing his suit. They're dressed like they're attending the Oscars, Mom in a slinky white dress with a giant diamond necklace and Dad in a flashy tux.

"The driver is waiting," Mom says.

We always hire a car for the event.

As we leave, Dad grabs my arm to hold me back. "Have you taken your pills?"

I nod.

"Good." His grip loosens, but he glares in warning. "No funny business tonight."

"Of course," I reply. "I wouldn't dream of it."

He scowls, sensing a hint of sarcasm.

After Lex telling me to look closer to home for answers, I've made a plan. The first place to search will be my father's office, but it'll have to wait. Despite Lex's hint, I don't believe Dad can really be involved in Sarah's disappearance. Sure, he has flaws, but losing her changed him. He tried not to show it, but he was devastated when she vanished. Although he tried to control Sarah's life, he only wanted to protect her.

Our drive to Sunnycrest is filled with Dad bragging about tonight's guests, while Mom preens her hair. I shiver, recalling the last time I made this journey. The night everything changed. The night I met them.

Sunnycrest's gates open as we arrive. Guards, with rifles in holsters, patrol the yard.

"This way," Dad says, leading us inside.

Tonight's event happens in the grand hall, which is separated from the rest of the building by staff quarters and is only used for special occasions. The patients have their own cafeteria. They sedate and lock patients away for the night, making it suspiciously quiet. Nothing ruins a party faster than it being crashed by the criminally insane.

The guests are due to arrive in half an hour, so Dad busies himself with the final preparations by shouting orders at anyone he comes across. Mom and I take a seat at our table. A few of the supposedly 'reformed' patients have been given roles for the occasion. They wait with trays of drinks, wearing ill-fitting suits. They all have a distinct, glassy stare, like performing bears. Everyone knows the most damaged individuals aren't safe to be among the public. Not now or, quite frankly, ever.

"You look beautiful, darling," Mom says. "Although your hair is a little short. I don't know what possessed you to cut it yourself."

She drones on, and I let her lecture wash over me while watching the final touches being made to the venue. The event format is the same each year: a mixer with drinks, followed by a presentation from Dad about the asylum's work with other psychiatrists and doctors chipping in. It's followed by a three-course meal, and a brief recognition ceremony to reward local businesses for their continued support.

My phone buzzes.

MIA: Enjoy your night in Crazytown.

I smile at the irony. Unbeknownst to her, my home is crazier than this place.

"Oh, look!" Mom stands. "Our guests are arriving."

Dad beckons me to join him and greet the attendees. I smile politely and shake hands, avoiding conversation as much as possible. Sheriff Brady is accompanied by his wife. I like Mrs. Brady. After Sarah went missing, she sent trays of home-baked cookies. Of course, Mom threw them in the trash. To her, getting fat is almost as bad as Sarah disappearing. A few other officers and their wives trot in after them. I recognize a few doctors who always attend, some more esteemed than others. I can tell who the most distinguished guests are from Dad's posture changing and his fake friendly tone.

"I read your most recent journal article, Magnus," one says. "I'd like to discuss your theory on neuroplasticity. You make a compelling argument, but I disagree with your point on—"

Dad's eyes narrow, but he keeps smiling. "We can talk business later. Your table is over here."

He perks up as soon as he sees Devon Lewis. Devon has been the mayor of Pasturesville for twenty years. During that time, no one else has dared to stand against him. He's revered and feared in equal measure. His slicked-back blond hair disguises his early balding, and his third wife hangs off his arm. Every divorce brought a new wife younger than the last. As well as being mayor, he's an investor in the pharmaceutical industry and was key in Sunnycrest's opening.

"Magnus." Devon greets him coldly. "We have much to talk about."

"You're right," Dad says. The frosty atmosphere between them is hard to ignore. "It's been too long."

After everyone arrives, my parents work the room, giving me some breathing space. I slink off to find a quiet corner, wishing it were time to leave already.

Suddenly, someone coughs beside me. I spin to see a server—a guy around my age. Pockmarks cover his sallow cheeks, and he flushes when our eyes meet.

"Can I help you?" I ask.

"I..." His eyes skim the room, a bead of sweat dripping down his brow. "Are you Erin Acacia?"

"Yes," I reply, crossing my arms. "Did my father send you?"

He turns his back to the room, so no one can see what he's

doing. He passes me a folded piece of card from his inner pocket. "This is for you."

I eye it suspiciously, knowing better than to trust a patient. "What is it?"

"They said…" he stutters. "They said you'd know who it was from, L-L-L-Little Ghost."

I snatch it from his fingers.

"Is that all?" I ask.

He nods, shoulders sagging in relief, before hurrying away. Despite their escape, my tormentors must still have connections here. Judging by the look on their poor messenger's face, they're feared.

I glance around to make sure I won't be disturbed. Thankfully, everyone seems too distracted to pay me any attention. I carefully unfold the paper.

> *9:30 P.M.*
> *Take the first left after the kitchens.*
> *Bea will meet you there.*

Who's Bea?

I stash the note into my purse. What should I do? I remember what happened the last time we met here. This is their territory. If they can break out—and break in—I'll be putting myself at their mercy.

"Why are you hiding?" Mom asks, locating me. She links her arm through mine. "Come and join the party. There's plenty of people for you to speak to."

"Great," I mutter.

We spend the next half an hour circling the room while my mind is elsewhere. The hairs on the back of my neck stand on end, overcome with the feeling of being watched.

Finally, it's time to take our seats for Dad's presentation. I check the clock. Nine twenty. My knee jiggles nervously under the table as he takes to the podium. He taps the microphone a few times before his booming voice fills the space.

"Ladies and gentlemen, welcome!" Dad declares. "As you know, tonight is a very special evening for Sunnycrest. A chance to celebrate everything we have achieved in psychiatry, which wouldn't have been possible without your continued support. On behalf of myself and the Sunnycrest patients, I'd like to thank all of you. Peers, donors, and, of course..." He gestures to the table on our right. "Mayor Lewis."

Devon stands to bow. Dad's lip curls in distaste but he doesn't object, allowing Devon to soak in the admiration and applause.

"Secondly, I want to address the biggest challenge we've experienced. The recent breakout," Dad continues, when the crowd settles again. "It has been a year unlike any other. Thanks to the hard work of our sheriff's office, the patients were located quickly. The incident has made us reassess our security, which will be the first topic I'm addressing this evening. We've adopted cutting-edge technology to make this unit the most secure of its kind."

I observe my father's body language, noting how convincing he is. However, he must know that not all patients were found.

Dad invites a security analyst to the stage. I bite my inner cheek to hold back a laugh, knowing three monsters have been able to effortlessly infiltrate Sunnycrest tonight.

The clock hands tick on. Nine twenty-eight. Two minutes to go. I have a choice to make...

With my father in full flow, I whisper to Mom, "I'm heading to the restroom."

She waves her hand dismissively, engrossed in his presentation and beaming with pride.

No one notices as I slip out of the room and into the empty adjoining corridor.

A female voice comes from the darkness. "Erin?"

I'm not sure what I expected, but it wasn't a tiny girl stepping out of the shadows. She has a roughly shaven head with a few tufts at the sides. Her long white gown drowns her skeletal frame. Due to her size, it's hard to know her real age, but she looks to be about fourteen.

"Yes," I reply. "You must be Bea?"

She nods curtly. "Follow me," she says. "This way. Hurry! Keep your back against the wall, or they'll hear you…"

Against my better judgment, I follow her around a corner and through a set of doors that should be guarded.

"Where are we going?" I ask.

"Hush, hush!" she hisses. "No talking. Hush, hush! This way."

For someone so small, she walks fast. I follow her through the maze of corridors, only lit by red emergency lighting overhead. My heeled shoes click-clack on the tiles, creating an echo.

"Here!" She stops mid-corridor, next to a chair that looks out of place. "Go!'"

I frown in confusion. "What?"

She points up at a ventilation shaft, then jabs her finger at the chair to make it clear where she intends for me to go.

"No way," I say. "I'm not climbing in there."

Following her through the asylum is one thing, but squeezing into a tiny air duct? Yeah, that's not happening.

Bea sighs and opens her closed fist to reveal a bloody palm and a razor blade. She points the blade at me, tipping her head to the left. "You will go, or slick, slack, slice." She opens her mouth and slides the razor across her tongue, showing me more deep scars slashed across it. She licks her lips, painting them red. "Up, up! Go, go. Slick. Slack. Snip. Snap."

Fuck. I gingerly slip out of my heels and climb onto the chair.

"Hush, hush!" Bea urges. "Faster!"

Two loose screws barely secure the vent. After undoing them, I carefully remove the cover, trying not to make a noise.

"Give it to me," Bea demands. "Up, up!"

"Where do I go?" I ask, peering into the black shaft with nothingness stretching ahead. "There's no light."

"Listen and follow," she says. "Now, hurry. Move!"

I push my shoes into the vent first. It's now or never. I extend my arms, hooking my elbows, and haul myself up. My muscles ache from the exertion, but I wiggle my way inside. I slither on my stomach and start to crawl. The space is bigger than it first appears but still cramped. A clang from behind sends a shiver down my spine as Bea replaces the vent cover.

"Shit," I curse.

What have I got myself into?

I move forward on my front. The silver tin creaks beneath me as if it will collapse under my weight at any second.

I strain to listen.

Nothing…

And then it comes.

"Little Ghost." One's faint voice floats through the void. "Oh, Little Ghost."

I push through the darkness toward him.

The vent network must be how they get around the asylum. I reach a fork in the road, listening again. One's calls reverberate through the tunnels, everywhere and nowhere at the same time, beckoning me closer.

"Warmer," One says. "Very warm now…"

I take a left and shimmy on.

"Little Ghost!"

They're louder now.

A crack of light from around the next corner glints off the

metal. As I approach, another vent cover is removed to reveal a pair of staring eyes through slits in a black mask.

"You came," Eli says, the warmness to his voice is almost inviting. "We didn't know if you'd dare."

"Do you remember what you said to us before, Little Ghost?" One asks, hidden from view. "Who is the rat in the walls now?"

I scowl as I reach Eli. He hauls me out of the vent, throwing my body effortlessly over his shoulder, then gently puts me down onto my feet.

It takes a few seconds to adjust to the stark clinical lighting. The walls and floors are painted in a blinding white, giving the impression that the room stretches on forever. Glass doors line the walls, leading to smaller adjoining rooms. I've toured the asylum before, but never seen this place. It's like a futuristic movie set. In front of me, three masked men stand together, arms crossed.

"Where are we?" I ask.

"This is what your father is hiding," One says.

"Go on." Lex gestures around. "Look."

I explore, peering into the different rooms. Some have single beds, a toilet, and faucet, like prison cells. Others, along the opposing wall, are less cozy. One resembles a dentist's office with a reclining chair and trays of medical equipment. Another has an electroshock machine that looks about fifty years old, juxtaposing its modern surroundings. The next is empty, but heating components cover the walls, and another has a giant copper tub that would look luxurious in a home, but seems ominous here.

"This is your father's favorite," Lex says, tapping on the door of the final room.

My stomach lurches. Cuffs and restraints are mounted to the walls, alongside shelves of stainless steel instruments. I can't tell exactly what they are, but there appear to be speculums, blades, whips, and even cattle prods, to name a few. It's a torture chamber.

"Welcome to the real Sunnycrest," One says. "Now you're here, it's time we got to know each other better."

Then he takes off his mask…

CHAPTER
TWENTY

ERIN

For so long, they've been faceless, creatures of the night. Abstract forms that aren't human. What was I expecting to see when his mask came off? A monster underneath, or a smooth face with no features? Whatever it was, it's not this…

"I'm Aiden," One says.

His piercing gray eyes study my reaction. His voice matches his face, but I never thought he'd be so… beautiful. He's a six-foot-three powerhouse with huge muscles, but his face has a boyish vulnerability because of the faded freckles splattered on his cheeks. His nose has a bump in the middle, presumably from a break or two. He has short, brown hair, a defined jaw that's dimpled like a superhero, and a diagonal white scar on his left cheek. When he turns, I notice a tattoo on his neck. A faded zero in thick black ink, surrounded by a fresher outline of a ghost. The ghost linework has been done by single needle pokes, not a machine.

"Why show me your f-face now?" I stammer.

"Because you're almost ready," Aiden replies.

"Ready for what?" I ask, my voice increases a few pitches, more nervous than before.

He nods at Eli to remove his mask. Eli gives off a boy-next-door country vibe with his dirty blond hair, tanned skin, and full lips. He grins, his front silver-capped left tooth glinting off the light. His blue-eyed gaze meets mine, seeking approval. I gulp, desire stirring in my core as I spot a strand of my hair poking out of his shirt pocket.

"Ready for us to give you what you need, sweetheart," Eli says.

Lex takes his *Scream* mask off next. He shakes his wavy, dark hair free, showing me the right side of his face. His amber eyes are ablaze against his pale skin. He has pixie-like features and could easily model with a face you'd stop to look twice at. When he turns fully, I gasp. The other half of his face and neck is covered in burns. There are areas where it looks like he's had skin grafts years ago that haven't healed well.

"What's wrong? Never seen a monster before?" Lex raises his eyebrow and chuckles. "You're not the only one who has been touched by the flames, Little Ghost."

My cheeks heat, and I look at my feet. My shocked reaction doesn't come from a place of horror, as he suspects, but from my wanting to know more about him.

Conflicting feelings rise to the surface. They've done sick and twisted things, but they're also the most gorgeous men I've ever seen. They're nothing like Nate and the other preppy boys at Stonybridge Academy. They're raw and rugged with stories that leave a dark mark, not only on their faces, but on their souls. It's hard to guess how old they are. A few years older than me, perhaps. Although, their haunting stares make them appear wise beyond their years.

"You brought me here for a reason," I say, summoning my bravery. We don't have a lot of time before my parents realize I'm gone. "Tell me."

"You had to see this," Aiden says. "We had to show you what your father is doing. This asylum doesn't make people better. It's his playground. He treats people like lab rats and hurts them for fun."

I shake my head. My father has a brutal streak, but he

prides himself on his professional reputation more than anything else. He wouldn't do anything to jeopardize that.

"You've got it wrong," I say.

Lex smirks. "I told you she wouldn't believe us."

"Think about it, Erin," Eli says. "He locked you up here. He drugged you. What else is he capable of?"

His words stir a vague memory from the depths of my subconscious. Sarah's voice. A warning.

"You don't know what he's capable of."

I shake away the recollection, unsure where it came from. Probably my imagination. Spending time with these guys is enough to send anyone mad.

"He's not a monster," I say, defending my father.

Aiden steps closer, and I take a step back. His jaw clenches as we continue the dance. Him forward, me back.

"Are you scared of me?" he asks. "Even after everything we've done? Haven't we given you every reason to trust us?"

I raise my chin defiantly. "You've not told me what you know about Sarah."

A cold hard wall drops over his expression, and his fists clench at his sides.

"I need evidence," I say. "I have to know what happened to her. She's my sister."

"What about what happened to us?" Aiden asks. "We can tell you what really happens here."

My back hits the wall. There's nowhere to go. I'm cornered. Whatever I've stumbled on is bigger than myself, my father, and Sarah…

"Let us show you," he says.

I yelp as he lunges, grabbing my arm to tug me into one of the rooms. It has a desk with two chairs that face multiple screens, and shelves on the walls are filled with video tapes. There are hundreds of them. He forces me to sit in a chair, holding down my shoulders.

He bends to hiss in my ear, "Do you want to know the real reason your father holds this event every year?"

I shake with fear as Eli and Lex join us. They stand to the side, watching us and blocking the exit, but don't intervene.

"I don't—" I begin.

"He uses tonight to help fund his projects," Aiden interrupts. "Others are complicit. The mayor, the sheriff, and the rest of his sick friends. They all know what he does here. That's the real reason Sunnycrest opened, to do experiments no one else dares to and make money from them."

"No." I shake my head. "He wouldn't... He can't..."

"Do you want proof?" he sneers, nodding at Eli, who inserts a tape into the player. "We'll show you."

A blank screen in front of me powers on. Lines ripple across it until an image of a boy strapped to a chair appears. I recognize him instantly. Lex. In the clip, he looks around fourteen years old. His burns are redder and more raised. His ankles are bound to the chair legs, and his wrists tied to the arms. He thrashes to free himself. There's no sound, but I lip-read him screaming "Help" and see the sheer terror on his face.

No, Dad helps people. He does bad things sometimes, but he always thinks what he's doing is for the greater good, right? He wouldn't intentionally cause harm for the sake of it. I can't take the word of three criminally insane escapees over a medical professional. Can I?

I look away, but Aiden grabs my chin, forcing me to keep watching.

A man approaches Lex. My father. He's not alone. He's flanked by two men in white coats carrying clipboards. Seconds later, two more figures enter the frame. First, Devon Lewis. He laughs, unperturbed by the shrieking boy pleading for release. Next to him, Robert Gilsmear chuckles.

What are they doing?

"Keep watching," Aiden says.

My father selects a device from the host of mechanical appliances on the shelf. The footage is blurry, but I gasp as Dad fastens the object to Lex's face.

My bottom lip quivers, watching him drop a substance into Lex's eyes that makes him wail and convulse uncontrollably. The onlookers laugh, while the men in coats furiously scribble notes.

"No," I whisper.

My eyes fill with tears as my father picks up a cattle prod. His two helpers tug off Lex's sweater, exposing his chest. Even the pixelated footage doesn't mask his existing wounds. He's covered in bruises and gaping gashes.

"Watch, Little Ghost," Aiden says. "You need to see how your daddy was able to give you everything you ever wanted. Your music lessons, a beautiful house, and closets full of clothes you don't wear. This is how."

Dad jabs the prod into Lex's chest. Next, Gilsmear steps forward to take his turn. I wince when he pokes Lex even harder, debunking any chance that this was a medical procedure. Nothing can justify this. It's abuse. Pure and simple.

"Turn it off," I plead, tears dripping down my cheeks. "Please."

"Why?" Aiden sneers. "Don't you want to see what's been under your nose all along?"

"Make it stop," I whisper, wincing as they torture Lex onscreen.

"Your father takes money from people who want to experiment on children and make them suffer," Aiden says. "He'll do anything for a price. He likes to see how much pain a person can withstand, pushing them to the limits of what's possible."

"Aiden," Eli intervenes. "She's seen enough."

"Enough?" Aiden drops his hold on me, and his lip curls. "What do you deem enough, brother?"

I jump from the seat, clutching my stomach to keep its contents down.

"Why did you show me this?" I croak.

"You wanted to know what happened to your sister," Lex replies.

Aiden glares at him.

Lex has said too much, but he can't take it back now.

"Sarah…" My knees go weak. "She was here?"

This place is hell. Worse than hell.

"Not another word," Aiden scolds.

Lex shrugs. He isn't the same scared boy from the video anymore. Whatever my father did transformed him into someone else.

"Where is she?" I ask. "What did he do to her?"

"We can't tell you what happened to your sister," Aiden says. "Not yet. But you will find the answers yourself, if you look hard enough."

"What do you want from me, Aiden?" I ask, daring to use his name for the first time. "After everything my father has done…" Deep fear strikes me. Their obsessive stalking seems even more sinister now. "Are you going to kill me?"

Aiden laughs coldly and strokes my cheek, making me shudder. "Why would we do that, Little Ghost?"

No one knows where I am. I'm trapped in a secret room filled with torture equipment and three psychopaths.

"I'm his daughter," I say, stating the obvious. "Don't you want revenge?"

"We don't have to kill you for that, Little Ghost," Aiden says, his eyes lingering on my Cupid's bow. "In fact, you can help us."

"Help you?" I ask. "How?"

"By finding evidence and information," he says.

"You don't need me for that," I reply. "You seem to get in and out of my house on your own."

"If you help us, we'll help you. You want to know what

happened to Sarah, don't you?" Aiden says. "Don't tell me you've never considered that he was involved."

My shoulders tense. "What do you need me to do?"

His grin makes his scar twitch.

"See what you can find at home," Aiden says. "In exchange, we need your silence."

"How can you expect me to say nothing and pretend like everything is normal?" I ask. "This is… too big."

"We make the rules," he says. "Or do you need Lex to remind you of what happens when you break them?"

I dart for the door, but I'm too slow. Lex grabs a fistful of my hair before I reach it. I yelp as he pulls me into his arms.

"What's wrong?" Lex teases. "I thought you enjoyed our game."

"Fuck you," I snarl. "My father may be a monster, but so are you."

He smirks. "He created us in his image, after all."

"You're more similar to us than you care to admit, Little Ghost," Aiden says. "We saw the gleeful look in your eyes when the Holts' house went up in flames after what Nate did to you."

While Lex holds me in place, Eli plucks out a strand of my hair and wraps it around his finger so tightly that it turns the tip white.

"Evil can only surround a person for so long until it taints them," Eli says. "We see you, Little Ghost. You act like a good girl, but I've seen how your thighs clench when we touch you."

I blush as Lex strokes my arm with surprising tenderness.

"See?" Eli says. "You enjoy playing with monsters. You haven't been locked in an asylum, but you've lived under an evil tyrant for your entire life. We can set you free."

"I don't want to be like you," I say.

"Not yet, anyway," Aiden says. "But we're not going

anywhere. You're our property, and now you've seen our faces, it's time we claimed you for good."

I shut my eyes as Aiden licks across my brow, tasting the bead of sweat that's pooled there. He undoes the buttons on my dress and lets the front fall open.

"Look at our marks on her body," Aiden says. His hot hands slip into my bra and squeeze my nipple hard. I whimper, but he doesn't reduce the pressure, only pinching harder. The pain sends a warm tingle down between my thighs. "We don't share, Little Ghost. We refuse to."

I moan as rough fingers slip between my legs, kneading my delicate flesh. Their touch is gentle until they yank my panties down violently, leaving me fully exposed.

"Open your eyes when I'm speaking to you, Little Ghost," Aiden orders.

I squeeze my eyes shut tighter.

He slaps me across the face.

My cheek stings as I open my eyes from the shock. Aiden glowers at me, a mixture of hatred and lust locked in his stare.

"Let her go," he commands Lex, then addresses me. "I have something else to show you."

I try to cover myself, but Aiden bats my hands away, eyeing my pussy hungrily.

"Never hide from us," he says. "Look at the screen,"

I brace myself, expecting to see another torture scene. Instead, my bedroom appears on multiple screens from different angles.

"Watch," Lex purrs. "Watch what they do to you."

This is how they've known what I've been doing all the time.

They installed cameras.

I watch the recording of myself laid in bed with two masked figures prowling close by. One slowly pulls off my duvet, and the other undresses me. Their movements are careful, rolling me onto my back before tugging my panties down.

"I don't need to watch this," I say.

"Are you sure?" Lex's breath tickles the nape of my neck. His cock digs into my ass like a threat of what's coming. "It's hot."

"How long have you been watching me?" I ask, recoiling at what they might have seen.

Their gloved hands knead my ass on the big screen.

"Long enough to watch you touch yourself while the Holts' house burned," Aiden replies, confirming my fears and shattering any illusion of privacy I had. "Don't even think about taking the cameras down. We'll only install more."

"I should leave," I murmur. I've been away for too long. "They'll be wondering where I am."

"Leave?" Aiden's laugh chills me. "Not yet. When you return, I want you to be used and broken. Bend over."

"I—"

He doesn't let me finish my sentence. He pushes me forward aggressively, squashing my face to the desk and giving me a close-up of the video. I've never watched porn before, and they've turned me into the main character. I'm equally ashamed and turned on, seeing the two of them take it in turns to suck and bite my breasts while I sleep.

"This is only the beginning, Little Ghost," Aiden promises, unzipping his pants.

He spits, and his warm drool drips down my ass.

"I haven't done this before," I say, my voice muffled from the angle of my face. "I'm a vir—"

"I know," Aiden says, grabbing my hair and yanking hard to silence me. "That's why we'll make sure it's memorable."

He lines the smooth tip of his cock up to my entrance. Tears fill my eyes. I've never fantasized about losing my virginity on a bed covered with flower petals and surrounded by flickering candles, but I hoped it would be special. Maybe even with a long-term boyfriend, not like this. Not with them. I expect him to slide inside me, but he doesn't.

"Relax, Little Ghost," Aiden whispers. "You'll still be a virgin when we're done with you... in the place that counts, anyway."

I squeal in terror as his cock edges to my ass. He ruffles around for something in his pocket then squirts thick, slimy liquid over me.

"Take a deep breath," Eli purrs gently. "It won't hurt."

"Much," Lex adds.

I'm like a caged animal in a zoo or a museum exhibit. My skin prickles from their stares as Aiden's cock rubs up and down between my cheeks to coat us in lube.

"Please," I beg. "I don't think I can—"

He spanks me hard, making my body buck.

"Whether you like it or not, your tight virgin ass is going to take me," Aiden says.

I gasp as he slides his thumb inside me, rotating it to stretch me out.

"Breathe," Eli urges. "Good girl."

I know Aiden's big from our rendezvous in the art room, and I'm not sure how I'll take something of that size when I'm already struggling to fit his thumb.

"She's ready," Lex encourages. "Just fuck her already."

I expect him to ease in, but he doesn't. His throbbing cock pushes inside me with one violent thrust. My entire body jerks from the force. His soft hair tickles my ass cheeks as he holds on to my hips and groans, burying himself even deeper. I squeak, gritting my teeth as my insides burn.

"How does it feel to be filled by your worst nightmare, Little Ghost?" Aiden asks, his voice hoarse.

"I..." I whimper.

The sensation is all-consuming. It's painful and stings, but his added heat inside me feels... almost good.

Aiden keeps thrusting. I blink away tears as he yanks my

head back with every thrust, causing my scalp to burn. The sound of our slapping bodies fills the space alongside Eli's and Lex's deep breathing. Lex leans and swipes a falling tear from my cheek. I turn my head to see him suck it off his finger.

"I don't know what tastes sweeter," Lex says, licking his lips with a maniacal grin. "Your tears or your pussy."

I bite my lip while Aiden uses me like a limp rag doll. When he's finished, my ass will be red from his violent pounding.

"Why don't you find out?" Aiden suggests, lifting me upright abruptly while skillfully staying inside me.

Lex drops to his knees in a flash. My eyes widen as his tongue darts out and licks my clit. I tremble under his touch, and my eyes flutter closed, pain giving way to a new pleasure.

"She's so fucking tight," Aiden says, squirting more lube onto his shaft.

The pain lessens as my body becomes accustomed to Aiden's size. The initial ache eases as his cock slides in and out of me more easily.

"You're doing well, Little Ghost," Eli says, watching us from the edge of the room.

I almost find comfort in Eli's words until I see his hands wrapped tightly around his cock, pleasuring himself to the show unraveling in front of him. I thought he was one of the good guys, but getting off to this makes him just as sick as the others.

"Our virgin whore," Lex murmurs, sending vibrations coursing through me, before returning to feast on my clit like it's his last meal.

I moan as his tongue eagerly laps against my sensitive spot, then he catches my folds between his teeth and sucks. I yelp in surprise, and my toes curl from the intensity. I want to push him away, yet lean closer at the same.

"Her pussy is dripping," Lex comments, slipping two fingers into me. He curls them, stroking my walls, before returning to eat me.

His mouth and fingers, coupled with Aiden's motion, consumes my senses, whipping my body into a frenzy of horror and pure bliss. Most worryingly, the horror comes from how much I'm enjoying myself...

"You're all ours," Aiden says as he fucks me harder, pushing my pussy onto Lex's waiting tongue. "Eli, get ready..."

Eli steps forward while my knees tremble. I clench, trying to conceal my enjoyment. That'll only give them what they want. They've taken too much from me already.

"Fuck," Aiden groans. "Her ass is choking my cock."

That's a good thing, right?

My eyes meet Eli's. His pupils dilate, and my gaze strays to his fist that's furiously working his massive dick. A sick sense of satisfaction spreads through me, knowing the effect I'm having on him.

The longer I hold back my orgasm, the stronger it grows. I sink my teeth into my lip, drawing a little blood, as my pleasure peaks. My pussy convulses in waves, making my ass tighten and my shoulders shudder. Lex senses my body shift and clamps his mouth around my clit like he's trying to take my orgasm captive while Aiden plunders me from behind.

I quake as Lex's tongue flicks my clit in quick strokes. It accentuates each burst of my pleasure, the next wave stronger than the last. My insides clamp Aiden's cock so tightly that I swear I can feel his blood pumping through his throbbing veins. Every vise-like squeeze ricochets through me, setting my nerve endings alight and making me see stars. I have no choice but to ride it out...

"I'm going to fill you with cum, Little Ghost," Aiden says. His voice sounds far away, as if I'm having an out-of-body experience. "Tell me you want it."

Lex pulls back and stands, wiping my dripping arousal from his chin with his sleeve.

"No," I pant.

"Too fucking bad," Aiden snarls, thrusting as deep as he can and relieving himself with a grunt. Warm, sticky liquid spills into me. "Now you're ours." He slides out. "Eli, it's your turn…"

My eyes widen in surprise. Don't they remember this is my first time doing this? Eli's silver tooth winks at me, telling me he knows and doesn't care.

"Don't worry, sweetheart," he drawls, taking Aiden's place. He grips my hips and bends me over again. "You'll enjoy this."

I groan as he slides inside me. He's thicker than Aiden, but not as long. He thrusts deep and slow, taking his time. I'm aching after a round with Aiden, so Eli's change of pace is a welcome reprieve. There's less urgency and aggression in his strokes. He drags it out, wanting me to savor every inch of him, and I embrace it.

"Say my name, sweetheart," Eli commands.

I stay silent.

His voice turns harsher. "Say it."

Again, I say nothing.

He withdraws, leaving my chest heaving. I don't get a break for long. He forces me to face him, walking me backward until my ass perches on the table, then he forces my knees apart.

"Be a good girl," Eli orders. "Or I'll steal your virginity."

He rubs his cock over my pussy to show he isn't joking around.

I stare back in defiance, a silent challenge. Everything else disappears, suspending the two of us in a different realm away from our audience.

"This isn't what good girls do," I say.

A smirk dances on his lips

"No," he agrees, brushing a loose hair off my face. "It isn't." His cock circles my entrance. He's tantalizingly close, yet still so far. "But you like it anyway."

He gently strokes my cheekbone, then traces along the outline of my Cupid's bow, looking at me like I'm the most beautiful woman in the world. It completely takes me off guard, and I melt under his touch, wrapping my legs around his middle to draw him closer. Eli grins, knowing he has me.

"Fucking hell, what are you waiting for? Fill her or move," Lex whines, bringing us out of our shared moment and ruining everything. "I want my turn."

Any kindness in Eli's eyes instantly evaporates, and his demeanor changes. He yanks me upright and bends me over, spreading my legs wide before getting to work. He fucks me hard and fast, devoid of emotion, like a man on a mission. I was stupid to let myself believe that he might actually care about me.

"Eli…" I whisper.

He refuses to make eye contact. *Don't cry, Erin.* I focus on a spot on the wall as he uses me like a doll. Then, it's over. He comes and slides out, leaving more wetness seeping down my legs.

Lex shoves him out of the way, ready to take his turn, when Aiden clears his throat.

"It's time Little Ghost returned to the party," Aiden declares.

"What about me?" Lex sulks. "I've got blue balls here, Aid!"

"You have a hand," Eli snaps, narrowing his eyes as he re-zips his pants. "Use it."

A knock interrupts their argument.

"This isn't open for discussion," Aiden says. "Bea's here."

He opens the door to reveal Bea standing in the doorway. I yelp, trying to cover myself, but she doesn't notice I'm naked.

She's too preoccupied with examining a razor blade in the light, turning it back and forth, then giggling hysterically.

"Bea will take you back to the party," Aiden says dismissively.

"Tick tock," Lex says. "Daddy will be wondering where you are."

I quickly reach for my panties, but Eli gets there first. He stashes them in his pocket alongside my lock of hair.

"Do you always take souvenirs?" I hiss.

Eli doesn't reply. Instead, he mumbles to himself under his breath, "That's an order, Twenty-Five."

It's like he's entered a trance-like state.

"Eli?" I prompt. "Can you hear me?"

My anger turns to concern, even though he doesn't deserve it.

"Ignore him," Lex says, putting his arm around Eli's shoulders. "This way, brother."

"Time to go," Eli mutters as Lex leads him out of the room. "Time to go, Twenty-Five. Drop the package. Drop. No questions, Twenty-Five!"

"What was that about?" I ask.

"Do you think we escaped your father's torture with our sanity intact?" Aiden counters, silencing me instantly. "It's time you return to your dinner. Your father won't expect his good girl to leak the cum of two men all over the seats."

My cheeks burn.

"Hurry, hurry!" Bea snaps. "Not long."

"Here." Aiden passes her a knife. "For your time."

Her wild face lights up in glee, and she bows her head like he's royalty, cooing, "So pretty… all shiny…"

"Wait in the vent," he tells her. "She'll be up in a minute." He turns to me. "Turn around."

"Why? Defiling me wasn't enough for you?" I sneer.

"You should be thanking us for not deflowering you," he says. "You don't make it easy."

"Thanking you?" I shake my head incredulously. "You're unbelievable."

"Do you ever do as you're told?" He forces me to spin. "See? That wasn't so hard now, was it?"

He yanks down the back of my dress and inhales sharply.

"Fuck," he mutters, more to himself than to me. "Lex wasn't crazy."

"Hey!" I shrug him off. "Are you comparing notes or something?"

"We'll be in touch," Aiden says coldly, ignoring my question and avoiding my gaze.

Something's off.

"You're dismissing me like this was a business meeting?" I ask in disbelief, anger bubbling to the surface. "What about me? What's next?"

"Don't make me ask twice." Aiden's stormy expression sends a chill down my spine. "It's time for you to leave."

I begin to argue. "I—"

"Go!" Aiden roars, his spit spraying my face. "Now!"

I yelp and scurry after Bea, not wanting to stick around to see what will happen if I disobey.

Although, I'm not sure what I'm more afraid of. Him or the answers I'll find when I go looking for them…

CHAPTER
TWENTY-ONE

ELI

"Telling her was a risk," Lex says, pacing back and forth like a ravenous beast. "We showed her too much. How do we know she'll keep her mouth shut? She could run straight to Acacia and tell him everything. He'll increase her medication, then it'll be over. It could ruin everything!"

After what she saw tonight, I'm not sure how she'll act. She isn't like us. We've been dragged to hell and returned from the brink of death more times than I can count. We opened her eyes to the worst side of humanity, and there's no predicting what she'll do next. The Acacias are unpredictable…

"She had to know," I say. "It's all part of Aiden's plan."

"Where is he, anyway?" Lex blasts. "He should have been back ages ago!"

I'm starting to wonder the same thing.

"He'll have his reasons," I say. "You trust him, don't you?"

"Of course," he replies, despite his solemn scowl.

Aiden knows best. He's never led us down the wrong path and is the only reason we're still breathing. He taught us how to survive, and I'm not about to question his logic now that we've left Sunnycrest.

"She's our prize," I say, stroking her silky panties.

Her orgasmic moan fills my mind. Fuck. She's all I think about. Her scent, her hair, her sweet body, and that tight ass. I want to crawl inside her, burrow under her skin and never leave. I got lost in her, almost losing my sense of self entirely. She's intoxicating, addictive, her body the best drug imaginable. I never thought I'd feel this way again, but she's taken me by surprise. She isn't what I expected and keeps proving me wrong…

Sharing isn't a strong point of mine, though. As much as I love Aiden and Lex like brothers, I still struggle, especially with her. The compulsion to make her mine—all mine—is everything. My yearning to have her, whatever it takes.

When Aiden was with her, I imagined it was my cock fucking her. We're separate people, yet, as a group, we're one entity. We've functioned that way for so long that our psyches have blurred together, and we can almost read each other's minds. We know each other's weaknesses and have been through the lowest of lows. I've looked into the darkest recesses of their souls, and vice versa. That's why Lex spoke up when he knew I was tempted to take her virginity. We all agreed that we'd do it together when we're not rushed. Lex knows me too well.

When she pushed her pussy against me, I saw hope in her eyes. Hope that there was more to me than the monster she first saw. The truth is, she should fear my love the most. If only I were a ruthless sadist like Lex or controlled my emotions as well as Aiden. They're both batshit, but I'm the one she really needs to watch out for. My brain is messed up. Broken. I wish I could say I'd never hurt her, but that'd be a lie…

"I don't know why we couldn't stay behind," Lex says, cracking his fists. "I'd like to show Acacia who is really in control."

Since our breakout, Acacia hasn't recruited any more test subjects. Those who were previously part of his twisted experiment conveniently disappeared after we vanished, but he won't go long without new recruits. He needs to keep money coming in and, more importantly, satiate his sick desires. After all the negative press, he'll use tonight as an opportunity to reboot the program.

"We have to be patient, remember?" I say. "We'll get our revenge."

Let's hope she's ready for what's coming.

CHAPTER
TWENTY-TWO

ERIN

"Where were you?" Dad snaps as soon as I return to the table. Obviously, my absence didn't go unnoticed. "It's been an hour."

Servers put plates down in front of us, and my stomach heaves. Food is the last thing I want. I try catching the eye of the girl serving our food. She doesn't look back, but her blank stare makes me wonder whether she's been subjected to abuse at my father's hands. My entire reality has been turned upside down, making me question everything.

"I…" I murmur. "Upset stomach."

Mom puts her hand against my forehead and frowns. "You don't look so good, honey. You're as white as a sheet."

Dad scowls, as if I've purposefully become ill to inconvenience him. Little does he know that he's the one responsible.

I shuffle in my seat, struggling to get comfortable due to the lingering pain. I tried to clean myself up in the bathroom, but cum still soaks through the black fabric of my dress. Worse, I see the mayor, laughing and joking while knowing what's happening within these very walls. Who else is complicit? Does everyone here know? I push my food away and swallow bile.

"Maybe we should call the driver to take Erin home,"

Mom suggests, noticing we're receiving a few quizzical looks from our guests opposite. "We don't want to cause a scene."

"That's probably for the best," I murmur in agreement, my voice hoarse.

"Fine," Dad barks. He beckons a server to his side and hisses instructions in his ear.

Suddenly, clattering cutlery and a screeching chair make everyone's heads swivel.

The sheriff jumps up from his seat abruptly, and a hushed silence descends.

"An accident?" he says into his phone. "What happened?"

He has the attention of the room.

"Uh-huh." His expression turns grave, and the wrinkles on his forehead deepen. "I'll be right there."

He approaches our table, and my father rises to address him.

"I'm sorry to leave early, Magnus," Sheriff Brady says. "There's been an accident on the mountain. A car falling into a ravine. It's a nasty scene, so I've been told. My men and I have to go."

"Will the road be closed?" Dad asks.

Naturally, his first concern is whether this will affect his precious event.

"Temporarily, but I'll have it open again by the end of the night," he promises. "Officers are already out assessing the damage."

"Oh no, but Erin's unwell," Mom pipes up. Dad glares at her, but she continues anyway. "She was about to leave."

"I'll have an officer drop her home on our way back down the mountain." He winks. "Anything for the Acacia family."

A trip in a squad car beats staying here.

"Is it anyone we know?" Mom asks, thriving on the drama as usual. "The driver?"

"It's too soon to say," he replies. "We'll keep you updated, Magnus."

My father nods solemnly as the sheriff instructs a begrudging Officer Blackwell to drive me home.

"Feel better soon," Mom says as I trot away and mumble half-hearted goodbyes.

The cool night air nips my legs as we stroll across the courtyard to the waiting car. I clench my ass cheeks and waddle awkwardly to disguise my discomfort. If not for the evidence leaking out of me, I'd have questioned whether my debasement was a fever dream.

Sheriff Brady, ahead of us, speeds out of Sunnycrest's gates. His tires roar on the concrete, the noise carrying over the wind to join the wailing sirens in the distance.

"Get in," Officer Blackwell grunts.

"Sorry to be a pain," I say, hopping into the passenger seat.

He mumbles something under his breath. I don't fully catch what he says. Although, I can make out 'babysitter' and 'not a ride-along'.

I wrap my arms around my middle and shiver. Every person in town is now under my suspicion. Does Officer Blackwell know about my father's misdeeds? What about the sheriff? How far does his corrupt influence extend?

After a short drive, blue lights emerge from the tree line, slipping through the branches and illuminating the leaves. There's a flurry of activity where a group of squad cars gather.

Blackwell slows as we pass, lowering his window to speak to a colleague who is cordoning off a section of road with yellow tape.

"How bad is it?" Blackwell asks.

"A total wreck," the officer replies, shaking his head. "There's no way anyone survived. The bonnet's stretched around a tree. It's gonna take hours to get out. We'll be here all night."

"They don't call this the highway to hell for nothing," Blackwell remarks. "How did it happen?"

"Hard to say. My money's on them taking the corner too fast," the officer says. "That's the thing with sports cars. People don't know how to ride them on roads like this, especially with the frost."

"It's not a racetrack," Blackwell agrees.

The officer shines a torch past him to illuminate my face. "What's with the girl?"

"A favor for the sheriff," Blackwell replies, rolling his eyes. "I'll be back soon."

We drive away, and Blackwell cranks up the police radio to stay up-to-date with what's happening. Sheriff Brady's voice crackles, shooting orders left and right.

"We have the registration," an officer, who must be near the wreckage, radios. "G01 DY3."

A chill runs down my spine.

I know that plate.

"Run the plates," Sheriff Brady orders.

"You don't need to do that," I say.

"What?" Blackwell lowers the volume in annoyance. "Did you say something?"

"I… um…" I shouldn't have said anything, but it's too late to hold back. "I know who the car belongs to."

"Who?"

"Robert Gilsmear," I reply.

Blackwell jumps into action, responding to his colleagues.

I bite my inner cheek to stop myself from smiling. My men didn't let Gilsmear go unpunished for touching me. Some men bring women flowers, but mine deliver bodies. I never thought I'd be a fan of the latter, but I'll make an exception in Gilsmear's case, especially after seeing him torture Lex in the video. Crashing into a ravine seems almost too kind.

"It looks like there was only one person in the car," a voice says over the radio. "We'll have to wait for dental to get a true identification."

Although Gilsmear's wife was screwing their gardener, I'm pleased she wasn't in the accident. Although, I'm sure the guys didn't care about collateral damage.

"The plates match Gilsmear's," someone confirms.

Blackwell puffs out his chest proudly, and I fight the urge to say, 'I told you so'.

"Thanks for the ride," I say as we come to a stop.

"No problem, kid," he says, more chipper than before.

He doesn't waste any time in driving away, eager to return to the action.

Despite my aching, I have an added spring in my step as I let myself into the house. Although, that quickly disappears when I remember that hidden cameras are probably watching. There's no point searching for them if they'll only put them up again. Wherever I go, I'm watched.

The clock chimes, and I notice the door to my father's office is ajar. Usually, he keeps it locked, but he must have forgotten in his haste to leave. After a quick dash upstairs to change into a clean pair of clothes, I return to check I didn't imagine it.

Nope, the door is definitely open. I tiptoe down the hall, even though no one is around, and nudge it gingerly open the rest of the way. Gilsmear's accident will delay my parents' return, and I might not get another chance to look for evidence like this...

Driven by a new sense of purpose, I cross the threshold into my father's secret realm. Academic books fill the shelves on the walls, along with many framed certificates documenting his achievements. Was there even a time when he really wanted to help people, or did he always have a twisted agenda? I'd like to think positively, but I'm not so sure...

I scurry to his foreboding desk. It's neatly organized. Pens are lined up in a row from smallest to largest, and unread mail sits next to his computer. Where does he keep his secrets? He won't leave them out for anyone to stumble upon...

I sit in his chair and start with the desk drawers. They're clutter-free, only containing stationery and envelopes. Nothing screams 'I run experiments on people' and, more importantly, there's nothing related to Sarah.

I sigh. *What am I supposed to be looking for?*

Next, I search the filing cabinets. There are three of them, alongside a locked medicine cabinet. The files contain neatly divided sections, everything from bills to insurance, but nothing to do with Sunnycrest.

Come on, there has to be something.

I slump down at his desk. Most fathers have photographs of their family on display, but he only has one photograph of himself shaking hands with the mayor from when the asylum opened. In it, he's being presented with a giant check.

I wiggle his computer mouse and the screen blinks to life, prompting me to type a password. I try everything obvious, birthdays, names, anything I can think of, but nothing. This is useless! What am I expecting to find? In movies, people hide things behind paintings. In a last desperate attempt, I check behind each framed certificate, searching for a hidden safe buried in the wall, but there's only plasterboard.

I don't know whether I'm more disappointed or relieved to find nothing.

Suddenly, a floorboard creaks down the hall. I quickly fumble to put the frame back onto a nail, but it slips from my fingers and lands with a crash. The glass shatters, sending shards flying.

Heavy footsteps grow closer. I expect Aiden, Lex, or Eli to join me. Instead, my father looms in the doorway, looking angrier than I've ever seen him.

"Dad—"

He doesn't let me finish my sentence.

"What are you doing?" he explodes. Spit sprays from his mouth like a dragon shooting flames. "What are you looking for?"

"Nothing," I stammer, fear striking me to the core, "I was just—"

I've always been afraid of his angry outbursts, but after seeing what he's truly capable of, my bottom lip quivers in sheer terror. He shouldn't be back so early. Even if there was no accident, he usually stays at the asylum for hours post-event.

"Can you imagine my surprise when I got an alert to say that an intruder entered my office?" he blasts.

I didn't realize he'd set up surveillance equipment, although it shouldn't surprise me. He's paranoid and fiercely protective over his space, and now I understand why.

"I—"

"I've had it with you!" he shouts, striking me across the face so hard that I tumble to my knees.

I clutch my burning jaw. My skin is tender to the touch, but the bone isn't broken.

"Magnus!" Mom rushes in. Her cheeks drain of color, despite her blusher, as she sees me shaking on the floor. "What happened?"

He pulls me up onto my feet using my hair. "Another daughter being a disappointment, that's what!"

"Ouch!" I yelp. "Please—"

"First Sarah, and now you!" he continues. "After everything I've done for you girls, you continue to defy me. What are you looking for?"

"Nothing," I lie. "I was just... curious."

"Curious?" He releases his hold on my head and his hands move to my throat to grip my windpipe.

Being cornered by masked strangers is scary, but nothing compares to the fear of being held in my father's grasp. My life is in his hands.

"Magnus!" Mom yells hysterically. "Stop!"

He whirls around to face her, letting me fall. I clutch my throat and gasp for air.

"What did you say, Jocelyn?" he asks. "Are you questioning me?"

Mom opens her mouth to argue, then her features go blank. Her eyes glaze over, like she's been injected with a sedative.

"No," she says hazily. "I—"

He slaps her. Her head turns at an awkward angle and bangs into the wall with a thud, then she drops.

"Mom!" I scream, scrambling to get to her.

Blood trickles down the side of her face from a cut on her forehead.

Before I reach her, she sits up, putting a hand to her wound, and smiles serenely, like she's high as a kite.

"You should do as your father says, Erin," she says robotically, calmly rising.

"Are you okay?" I ask her. "Your forehead…"

"Oh, this." She looks at her bloody hand. "It's nothing." She laughs. "How silly of me. I better get myself cleaned up."

She pads away down the hall like a brainwashed zombie.

My anger rises. I've bitten my tongue for too long, but I won't anymore. With Sarah gone, it's time someone else stood up to him, considering Mom isn't able to.

"You hurt her," I scream. "You're a monster!"

I expect him to get angrier. Instead, he cackles, a deep rumble from the pit of his belly. It's the most I've heard him laugh for weeks until his expression turns completely deadpan in a flash, like a psychopath dropping his social mask.

"Be careful what you say next, Erin," he warns ominously.

I want to blurt out that I know what he's doing at the asylum and threaten to report him, but I resist, remembering my promise to stay quiet. Although I don't know what the guys are planning, any doubts I had about helping them are gone. Whatever it is, I want in. He must pay for what he's done.

Growing up, my father never showed us any affection. Yet, despite his flaws, I still loved him because he's all I've ever known. The familial obligation blinded me to his true evil nature. Now I have all the facts, and I'm sure he's involved in Sarah's disappearance somehow. I have to find out what happened.

Dad's glare scans me like an X-ray.

"What are you looking for?" he probes. "Tell me the truth."

"I…" I need to come up with an answer fast. "Pills."

"Of course," he says, unlocking the medicine cabinet. "You're just like your sister. First drinking, and now drugs—"

"It's not like that. I need to study for a test," I babble, trying to recover and stop him from sending me to rehab for the foreseeable future. "I thought you might have some Adderall to help me concentrate."

His eyes narrow in suspicion. I can't tell whether he really believes what I'm saying, but his temper seems to have dampened. "Do you think I'd leave medication lying around the house?"

"I… I didn't think," I stutter. "I was being stupid. I shouldn't have come in here."

"You're right. You shouldn't have." He hums while rifling around rattling pill bottles. "Aha!" He takes out a bottle and shakes it. "Here we are."

"I don't need to take anything," I say, edging toward the door. "Tonight was a mistake."

"The only mistake was me trusting you not to ruin this evening," he says, emptying pills onto his palm. "Take them."

"I—"

"Take the pills, Erin."

I can't get out of it. If I resist, he'll only force them down my throat like the last time.

He smiles as I swallow them down.

"Night, Dad," I say, turning to head out, oblivious to what drugs are now zipping through my system. I haven't eaten for hours, so it won't be long until they take effect.

Suddenly, he's right behind me.

"Remember, I'm doing this for your own good," he hisses.

A needle plunges into my neck like a beesting, then my entire body goes limp. I can't control my limbs, despite willing them to move, and slump against him. I try to object, but my mouth doesn't form words properly and I slur, drool dripping down my chin.

"Everything will be okay," he promises, dragging me through the house.

My bare calves burn from the friction of being pulled across the carpet.

He's taking me outside, and then… everything…

CHAPTER
TWENTY-THREE

ERIN

MY EYES TAKE a second to adjust to the darkness. Everything is slightly out of focus, and straight lines blur at the edges. Unfamiliar sheets scratch my skin, and I sit up in an uncomfortable bed. I put my hand to my forehead, groaning. My head weighs a ton, and it takes all my effort to look around at my unfamiliar surroundings: beige walls with flaking paint, a metal toilet, sink, and cracked tile floors.

Where am I?

I replay what happened leading up to this moment. The fundraiser, searching Dad's office, getting caught, and then...

Shit. I gulp as realization hits, facing the bolted door that's holding me prisoner. *I'm in Sunnycrest.*

This is my punishment for snooping. Perhaps it was inevitable that I'd end up here, the easiest place for my father to gain control of my life.

I take deep breaths, determined not to give in to my rising panic. Outside my room, screams and hysterical laughter echoes. I stay quiet. If I'm stuck here, the last thing I need is for the other patients to learn that I'm the daughter of the man mistreating them.

Suddenly, the door creaks open. I expect to see Dad, arms crossed and ready to deliver another lecture about how I need to be taught a lesson. However, to my surprise, an orderly in a white coat stands in silence.

"Hello?" I say to the unmoving silhouette. "Can I help you?"

He says nothing and doesn't make eye contact, then he nods to someone on his right and walks away, leaving my door open. Seconds later, Aiden and Eli march into the cell. Aiden's fists clench in fury, and Eli checks my body for signs of injury. They're wearing furious expressions, and the small space seems to shrink with them inside.

I shuffle until my back hits the freezing wall.

"What are you doing here?" I ask.

Aiden arches one eyebrow. The corner of his mouth tugs upward into a cheeky smile. "Would you rather stay?"

"N-no," I stammer. "But my dad—"

"Let us worry about him, Little Ghost," he replies, then taps his wrist. "Now move, unless you'd prefer us to drag you out by your hair?"

I scurry to my feet. Eli grabs my arm; his grip is firm, like he's afraid I'll slip through his fingers.

We follow Aiden down the hall. Heckles from surrounding cells goad and taunt us with each step.

"Who is that slut?"

"Eli! Come back!"

"Save yourselves!"

"I've been keeping my bed warm for you, Aiden," a girl coos. She presses her face against the glass of her room's window. "I've missed you."

Aiden stops sharply.

She licks her lips, pleased to have drawn his attention.

"Hi, baby," she purrs. "I knew you'd come back for me."

It's hard to make out fine details through the murky pane, but she looks beautiful. Thick black hair and big brown eyes, framed with long eyelashes.

"Come back for you?" Aiden laughs cruelly, then his expression turns somber. "You can rot in here, for all I care."

Her face crumples. "But we had something special. I—"

"Enough, Charlie," he hisses. His glacial stare makes her squeak. "You helped pass the time, but you're just another used pussy, and not even a good one at that."

"So you're hooking up with this princess whore, huh?" She narrows her eyes in my direction like I'm a piece of shit on her shoe. "What's so special about her?"

"Look at her like that again, and you'll regret it," Aiden warns. "Show some fucking respect and fall in line."

Charlie whimpers like a wounded puppy and shrinks away from the window. All the while, Eli stays silent, only tightening his grasp on me.

"Ouch," I yelp as he constricts my blood flow.

His grip eases, but he doesn't let go.

Aiden speeds off again. I take two steps for every one of theirs to keep up with their relentless pace.

"Won't someone see us?" I ask.

"No one who'll tell," Eli replies as Aiden swipes an access card to make a door open.

So much for the new security provisions that should make the building an impenetrable fortress.

"I thought you preferred to move around in the walls," I mumble.

It's not the time for jokes, but anything will help to make light of this crazy situation.

"Your father isn't the only one who runs Sunnycrest," Aiden says. "When he's away, everyone else knows who is in charge."

We pass a security station on our way to an exit. Much like high-security prisons, there are barriers and checkpoints to pass through to move from one area of the building. The guard on the desk snores as we pass; powdered sugar coats his top lip, and a box of donuts splays open in front of him.

We weave along different corridors that look the same and climb various staircases, sticking close to the walls and staying in the shadows.

"Shh." Eli yanks me into his chest and puts his gloved hand over my mouth. His cock stirs in his pants as I press into him. "Don't move."

Around the next corner, two doctors talk and compare patient notes. Apparently, not everyone is under Aiden's thumb. All it would take is a cough for them to find me, but I stay silent and hold my breath.

"Not far to go now," Eli promises.

As soon as the doctors are gone, we continue on. After proceeding through various doors using cards, keys, and codes, the chilly night breeze stings my cheeks.

"Where are you taking me?" I ask.

"Would you rather return to your cell?" Aiden sneers. "If I tell the other patients who you really are, they'll give you a warm Sunnycrest welcome."

I bite my lip. No questions, understood.

Eli squeezes my arm in reassurance. I look up into his eyes, and he smiles, as if to promise everything is going to be all right.

I want to believe him, but I don't.

"Get ready," Aiden says.

Before I can reply, Eli breaks into a run, tugging me along with him. I sprint, praying that my shoulder won't dislocate from Eli's force. Two motorcycles wait for us, hidden in a cluster of bushes on the concrete perimeter.

Aiden jumps onto one.

"Climb on," Aiden instructs, holding out a helmet.

I'm only wearing a flimsy white nightdress and socks. Without wearing proper riding gear, what will happen if I fall? Motorcycles are accidents waiting to happen.

My hesitation is clear.

"I won't ask again, Little Ghost," Aiden warns.

"Don't you trust us?" Eli asks, dropping my arm.

"I don't trust anyone," I answer. How can I, after all they've shown me?

"Just get on the fucking bike," Aiden commands, thrusting the helmet aggressively into my arms.

Reluctantly, I put it over my head and clamber on behind him.

There's no going back.

"Hold on tight," Aiden growls.

He takes off at speed. The rushing air makes it hard to snatch a breath. Wind tears at my hair, causing it to billow from underneath the helmet. On our left, Eli's engine roars as he passes us, racing through the open asylum gates. I don't question why no one stops us, assuming it's because of a bribe.

I wrap my arms around Aiden's waist, clinging on for dear life. My sweaty palms keep slipping on his leather jacket, so every twist of his hips makes my heart jolt, terrified I'll be thrown off. I clamp my thighs tightly around him. If this journey doesn't kill me, my dad will if he finds out where I am.

I open my mouth to scream but nothing comes out as Aiden skids around a tight corner, and the wheels wail in objection. Aiden cackles, enjoying making me squirm, and rides more recklessly.

"Soak in the night air, Little Ghost," Aiden yells. "This is true freedom!"

Up ahead, a lone pair of taillights illuminate a strip of road, completely out of place on the otherwise deserted mountain stretch. Eli swerves to a stop, and Aiden follows.

"Hang on," Aiden says.

His quick turn causes the bike to tilt at a ninety-degree angle. I squeeze my eyes shut, convinced this is the end.

Aiden's laughter lets me know I'm still alive when we finally come to a screeching halt beside the waiting car.

We dismount. I stagger and clutch my stomach, unsure whether I want to throw up or hoot with exhilaration because of the adrenaline surging through me.

A man gets out of the car to greet us. Even without his usual uniform, there's no mistaking him.

"What is she doing here?" Officer Blackwell asks, gaping at me like I'm an alien when I remove my helmet. "I swear to God, if she tells anyone, my career will be over. Brady will—"

"She won't say a word," Eli interrupts. He plucks a strand of my hair off my shoulder and rubs it between two fingers. "Will you, Little Ghost?"

I shake my head. Officer Blackwell glares at me, weighing up his options. He must realize that mutual silence is in both of our best interests. We all have our secrets.

"Do you have it?" Aiden snaps impatiently.

"Yes," Officer Blackwell replies. "But it wasn't easy."

He removes an evidence bag from his inner coat pocket. In the darkness, I can't see what's inside it. Aiden goes to grab it, but Officer Blackwell holds back.

"This is the last thing I'll do for you, understand?" Officer Blackwell says. "After this, we're even."

"It's a pleasure doing business with you," Aiden says, snatching the bag from him and stowing it in the under-seat storage before I get a proper look.

Blackwell gets back into his car without saying another word.

"Why did he owe you a favor?" I ask, unable to curb my curiosity.

"We know all about this town and its secrets," Aiden says mysteriously.

"What do you know about Blackwell?" I press.

"He helped conceal evidence," he says, patting the seat. "Evidence we now have in our possession."

"What kind of evidence?"

"You'll see," he says. "Now get back on the bike."

Eli must see the look of dread on my face and murmurs, "We don't have far to go."

I hope not. Grimacing, I climb on, and we hit the road again. Instead of continuing down the mountain into town, we take a right, hurtling down a short dirt path leading into the woods. It's a route only used by hunters, and even they are too superstitious to spend a long time in this section of the forest. This is the type of place where a serial killer would bury bodies and go undetected for years.

Mud kicks up the backs of my bare legs as we bounce off every stone, protruding root, and bump. The bike lights guide our way through the blackness, and the rustling trees cast strange shadows over the tightly clustered trunks.

We ride for what feels like forever. The guys expertly navigate the uneven terrain until, up ahead, a small wooden cabin comes into view.

A chill runs down my spine. Yep, this is definitely somewhere you'd chop up bodies and never find the pieces.

Light shines through the small cabin window, and Lex's face peers through it, watching. His face morphs into a psychotic grin when he sees me. Maybe a night in the asylum wouldn't be so bad after all.

"Home sweet home," Eli says, stopping.

When Aiden brakes, I practically leap off the bike. My feet land with a squelch in a muddy puddle, soaking my socks.

"So, this is where you've been hiding," I say, more to myself than to them.

"What's wrong, Little Ghost?" Aiden asks, tilting his head to study my reaction. "Not the luxury you're used to?"

"N-no, it's not that," I stammer. Obviously, they think I'm a spoiled brat because of my upbringing, but I've never cared about materialistic bullshit before. "You're just... closer than I thought."

"It's an old hunting cabin," Eli explains. "One of Acacia's friends owns it, but he doesn't use it anymore."

"Why did you bring me here?" I ask.

"We'll explain in good time," Aiden says, prodding me in the back to herd me inside.

The smell of fresh pine and a crackling fire hit me straight away. Dried dirty boot prints coat the wooden floor, which squeaks underfoot. Looking around, half-melted candles and dried wax droplets cover most surfaces, and mounted stuffed animal heads eerily follow my movements with their glassy eyes. To my left, a sofa and two armchairs with chunks missing sit around the fireplace. Moth-eaten blankets drape over the upholstery, signaling this is where they've been sleeping. To my right, a kitchen area with a small stove, a sink, and a table with four chairs. Knives are laid on the table, and next to them, three laptops are open, looking out of place among the dated decor.

"Did you get it?" Lex asks. He stands at the stove, monitoring the hissing copper kettle.

Aiden grins smugly and taps his inner pocket. "Right here."

Lex scowls and looks me up and down disapprovingly. He tips steaming water into a large bowl, puts it on the floor, and nudges it in my direction.

"Here," Lex says.

I look down in confusion.

"For your feet." He throws me a dirty rag. "You're covered in mud."

Eli pulls out a chair for me to sit down and forces me onto it. He kneels before me and removes my socks carefully, then steers my ankles into the waiting hot water. I bite my lip to stop myself from groaning. It feels heavenly.

"We're not animals," Eli says.

"You had me fooled," I grumble sarcastically.

I expect him to leave me to wash in peace, but he grabs a tiny bar of soap from next to the sink and kneels at my feet. He works the soap into a frothy lather between his strong palms, then takes my foot gently into his hands. He massages the suds into my skin, taking his time to clean my toes and knead the balls of my aching feet. I blush, stunned by the intimacy and care he's taking.

"So…" Lex talks to Aiden. "When can we open it?"

"Soon," Aiden promises. "First, we need to find out why our little ghost ended up in Sunnycrest again."

Their attention returns to me.

"I was looking in my dad's office for evidence," I say. "He caught me, and I made up an excuse about looking for pills."

"Not bad," Lex says. "For an amateur."

"He was furious," I say. "I don't think I'll get another chance to search his office again. He'll be watching me like a hawk if he ever lets me go home."

Eli rubs the arches of my feet, encouraging my rising anxiety to fade away. I've never had a foot rub before, but I could get used to this at the end of a hard day.

"You did well," Eli says.

"You were testing me?" I read between the lines, looking from Eli to Aiden. Their expressions confirm my suspicions. "Why?"

Eli removes my feet from the water, patting them dry with a rag, before going to empty the basin.

"We needed to know that you were serious," Aiden tells me. "Your father would never leave anything incriminating lying around for you to find."

"Great," I huff, crossing my arms. "So, you got me drugged and locked in Sunnycrest for no reason?"

"There's a reason behind everything we do," Aiden says, his eyes narrowing. "But that doesn't mean you're privy to it. The sooner you learn to stop asking questions and follow orders, the easier everything will be."

"I'll never stop asking questions," I say, daring to be defiant. "I don't want to be another pawn in your twisted games."

"Oh, really?" Aiden tips my chin up to face him. "And what do you want to be? One of us?"

"No," I answer. Too quickly.

Lex cackles while Aiden's lips curl, and he drops his hold. Eli slumps onto the chair opposite me, hurt flashes in his eyes as he hurls a clean pair of socks in my direction. They're three sizes too big and will come halfway up my shins, but they'll keep me warm at least. I open my mouth to speak, but Eli sharpening a knife tells me not to waste my breath. He's pissed. The scraping noise puts my teeth on edge, like sharp nails dragging down a chalkboard.

The truth is, I'm not sure what I want our relationship to be. Do I want to be someone they listen to? Someone who has their approval? More than just an object of their fascination, who gets picked up and down whenever they please? However, admitting I might want more means facing feelings I'm not ready to...

Aiden slaps the evidence bag he acquired from Blackwell on the grubby table with a flourish. My throat constricts. A worn red notebook with doodles adorning the front cover sits inside the plastic. I go to grab it, but Aiden slams his hand on top of mine to stop me, like a gavel crashing on a judge's podium.

He tsks. "Not so fast."

My heart thunders. "But it's Sarah's."

She didn't know I knew about her diary. A few weeks before she disappeared, I found it hidden in her closet when I was looking for a shirt. I only peeked inside the pages for a second before putting it away and feeling guilty, even though I didn't read it. Dad already invaded our privacy enough. When she went missing, I told the police about it, hoping it might give them some clues. But they didn't find it when they searched her room, or so I thought...

Lex rolls his eyes, always three steps ahead of me. "Obviously."

"I need to read it," I insist. "If there's something in her diary that will tell me what happened, I have to know."

"Poor Little Ghost," Aiden says. "Are you really still clinging to hope that your sister is alive?"

All the air zaps from my lungs. Although I can't see myself, I imagine I've turned a ghostly white as blood drains from my face.

"N-n-no," I gasp, as if I've been doused with a bucket of ice water. "She can't be. She ran away. She left home. I…"

"Your sister is never coming back," Aiden says bluntly, devoid of any sympathy. "She's dead."

I pull my hand out from under Aiden's and stand. My knees are too wobbly to hold my weight, so I collapse back onto the chair again. I'm not stupid. I've watched enough true crime to know the chances of Sarah being alive are slim, but I've still clung to hope. It's all I have.

"How do you know?" I ask, attempting to regain my composure. Aiden enjoys messing with people's minds. Another of his torturous tricks. "I need proof."

"As I said, we know all the town's secrets."

"Tell me what happened to her," I beg. "Whatever it is, I can handle it."

"Your biggest mistake, Little Ghost, is thinking we *have* to do anything," Aiden mocks.

"Fuck you," I snarl.

Instantly, a tension-filled silence sweeps through the cabin like an icy breeze. Eli exchanges a nervous look with Lex, shocked at my outburst. Contrary to what they think, I can stand up for myself when it's something I feel passionately about. Aiden's eyes narrow into murderous slits. Did my father hurt Sarah, or do they know Sarah is dead because they were involved? I wouldn't put it past them. They injured Nate and killed Gilsmear—how many other deaths are they responsible for?

"What did you say?" Aiden asks. His tone is calm, yet

hides a menacing undertone, warning me not to push my luck.

"I said, fuck you," I repeat, staring right into the inferno. I won't cower in the corner anymore when it comes to Sarah. I owe her that much, at least. "Sarah's my sister. You are going to tell me what happened. I have a right to know!"

"You'll learn everything you need to know when you return to Sunnycrest," Aiden says.

I lunge for the diary in desperation, but Aiden grabs it first. He holds it up high, waving it in the air to tease me.

"Give it to me," I demand.

He cackles, ignoring my request. I claw at his arms to lower them, but he doesn't react. I dig my nails into his muscles, tearing his skin until it bleeds. He doesn't budge an inch, remaining as still as a statue. He's holding Sarah's last words—doesn't he understand how much they mean to me? She was my everything! My twin! My other half! I scream in frustration and punch his unmoving chest.

Lex chuckles as my blows bounce off Aiden. My knuckles slamming into him are as useless as twigs beating against a brick wall, hurting me more than him. I won't stop, though. I keep going, pummeling continually until my chest heaves from the exertion of releasing every bit of my repressed rage.

"You bastard!" Hot, uncontrollable tears fall down my cheeks, and cruel insults shoot from my mouth with every pointless punch. "Sick." *Whack.* "Motherfucker." *Whack.* "Twisted fucking monster!"

I keep going, each hit getting weaker, until I have no strength left. Still, Aiden stands, unwavering, while Sarah's diary dangles tantalizingly above my head, promising answers.

"You've forgotten that we don't feel pain anymore," Aiden says. "Not after what your father did."

I double over, panting, with my heartbeat thundering in

my ears. I'd almost feel bad, if not for the secrets he was hoarding.

"It was a mistake bringing her here," Lex says, shaking his head in disappointment. "She needs more time."

"More time?" I direct my anger at him. "More time for what? To go without knowing what happened to my twin?"

"Lex is right," Eli says, like I'm not in the room. "She's forgetting who owns her."

"You don't own me!" Fury pours out of me. "No one does!"

Aiden stomps across the cabin, stashing Sarah's diary on top of a cabinet, then retrieves something from a box on the side. When he turns around, he's holding a strange object. It's hard to make out what it is. Something shiny and metallic appears to be attached to a hilt by duct tape.

"Get the ink, Eli," Aiden orders.

That's when I realize what he's twirling around his fingers.

"No," I stammer, "y-you wouldn't."

"We won't let you forget who owns you again," Aiden says, approaching me. "You'll leave with a permanent reminder."

I sprint for the door. No one makes any effort to stop me, but their laughter follows. I breathe a sigh of relief, finding the door unlocked, and fly into the night.

"Run, run, run, Little Ghost," Aiden calls. "But you won't get far…"

CHAPTER
TWENTY-FOUR

ERIN

I HURTLE INTO THE DARKNESS, leaving the cabin behind. My silky dress flaps in the wind, and its icy chill wraps around my limbs. I stumble in Eli's oversized socks, pausing for a second to pull them back up my calves. Each step is like wading through a vat of sticky caramel, but once I'm out of the mud, running on the grass flanking the dirt path makes it easier to cover more ground. It's slippery, but I grab tree trunks to support me, darting from one to the other like a pinball. I push aside my thoughts about other potential predators lurking in the shadows. They can't be any worse than the three men I'm running from.

All I have to do is find the road and follow it into town. But, despite my good sense of direction, it's impossible to see. Without getting down on my hands and knees to follow the indents left by motorcycle wheels, I'm led by pure instinct. It won't be long until morning, though. I can hide out until sunrise, right?

"Little Ghost!" Lex's voice echoes through the forest. "Come out, come out, wherever you are…"

I freeze and hide behind a tree, hugging its bark as if my life depends on it. A single beam from a flashlight slips through the leaves, and I back away from it.

Footsteps crunch through the undergrowth.

"You can't hide from us," Aiden says.

He's close.

I hold my breath.

The light swivels and turns away from me. I set off again, keeping each step light. Without shoes, I don't make much noise, but I'm still not quiet enough…

Another light appears, shining straight at my last hiding spot.

"Over here," Eli says.

I must get away. Adrenaline propels me forward. Branches tear at my skin, but I barely feel it. Aiden's news has numbed me, regardless of whether it's true.

The ground slopes, giving me some hope I'll be able to escape down the mountain. However, a bulky rock has other ideas. I trip, breaking the fall with my hands at the last second, and land on my knees.

I lose precious seconds, allowing the men to gain on me. Even though I'm ahead, I swear I hear them breathing down my neck. *Keep going, Sarah. Wait, did I just call myself Sarah?* My brain is rattled after their revelation and is doing anything to cling to her memory. I muster all my strength to pull myself up and sprint on. *You can do this, Erin.*

"You can run," Aiden yells. "But you can't hide."

Another tree branch tugs on my hair and makes my head jerk. Its thorny fingers hold strands captive, and I yank myself free, leaving a tuft behind.

They're too close.

In my panic, I make the mistake of looking back.

Three flashlights move fast.

Too fast.

I yelp and fall again. I tumble, rolling down the steep incline on my side. It reminds me of a snowy day from my childhood, filled with gleeful laughter when me and my sister threw ourselves down an untouched, white-topped hill. I couldn't be any further from that now.

I dig my nails into the earth, desperately trying to cling to something, but it's no use. Uprooted plants lie in my wake as I keep rolling and pick up pace. I might plummet to my death in a rocky ravine any minute. I whimper as my shoulders bounce off the rocks, and they skin my elbows. Twigs snap as I reach for them.

Thwack!

I hit the base of a tree and groan, coming to a harsh stop. Pain shoots up my spine. I wiggle my toes, thankful I only have bruises to worry about, but the worst is still to come…

A light beam hits my face.

They've found me.

I sit up and scramble back, wincing from the pain as another spotlight blinds me. I'm cornered with nowhere to go. Although I can't see, I hear them. Steady footsteps approach, mercilessly crushing anything in their path. Snapping sticks sound like snapping bones.

I tremble with trepidation as the lights suddenly go off, plunging us into darkness. My brain wills me to move, but terror grounds me.

The chase is up.

I shriek. Gloved hands grip my ankles and yank me forward. I resist, tossing and turning, grabbing fistfuls of leaves, but they force me to lie flat on my back. Someone steps over me, then strong thighs clamp around me, holding me in place as another pair of hands hold my wrists above my head.

"Don't resist," Eli says. He's on top of me. "You'll only make it more difficult."

"Let me go," I pant, struggling to get the words out due to his crushing weight.

Someone props a flashlight under the tree, illuminating

the canopy above. I can't see Lex or Aiden yet, but sense their presence.

"Can I punish her?" Lex asks enthusiastically from behind Eli.

"Fuck you," I snarl. "Fuck you all!"

My bitter anger boils to the surface. An anger that's been rearing its head more and more recently, and I'm no longer able to suppress it. Dad trained me to be a meek mouse, obedient and unquestioning. This fury is new. It's been lying dormant in a dark corner of my soul, and now it's finally unleashed.

A few months ago, I'd have been too scared to fight back, but I'm not the same person I was then.

"Don't fucking touch me," I yell. "I'll make you regret it."

"Oh, really?" I turn to the left and see Aiden's boots. He kneels and grabs my hair. He forces my head upward, tugging on my scalp, then slams me down again. "You're helpless, Little Ghost. You're at our mercy." He looks to his right. "Punish her, Lex."

Eli blocks my view of Lex, who forces my legs roughly open. I kick to bat him away, but he's already positioned between my knees. Any attempts to get him off will only give him better access. In the cold, the heat radiating from his flashlight warms my inner thighs as he subjects me to an examination.

"You think you're so brave," I taunt. "But you're all cowards! Is this the only way you get girls? By torturing them and taking them against their will?"

Aiden's hot breath tickles my ear menacingly. "Usually, girls beg us to pin them down." He catches my lobe between his teeth and bites hard, then withdraws. "You're fighting, but this is how you like it, Little Ghost."

"You don't know what I like," I hiss, spinning my head and gnashing my teeth.

"See? You like it rough." Aiden pushes my cheek into the dirt. "I bet your tight little pussy is dripping."

Lex pulls my slip up. He rips my panties off, tearing through the fabric like an animal.

"You're right," Lex says. I hear the grin in his voice. "She's soaking."

My face burns with shame as Lex parts my pussy and slides a finger between my wet folds. His scorching touch contrasts the otherwise freezing night. The hands of the devil fan my desire.

I kick out, but he pins down the lower half of my body with his knees, letting my legs fall open wide. Between the three of them, I'm completely immobilized.

"We'll show you how you like it, Little Ghost," Aiden promises. "Being fucked in the soil like a dirty whore."

Lex spits on my pussy like a cobra shooting venom. His searing spray sends tingles from my pussy to my toes as he massages my clit. He slathers me in his spit, then slips inside to fuck me with two fingers. I cry out as Aiden tightens his grip on my hair.

"Gag her, Eli," Aiden commands, using his hold to turn my face.

Eli's shadowy figure edges closer. He unzips his pants and releases his throbbing cock. When I open my mouth to hurl another insult in his direction, he squats over my face and forces his cock into me, silencing me instantly. Meanwhile, Lex's pumping grows more vigorous until he suddenly withdraws and replaces his fingers with a plastic cylindrical object.

I want to tell them to stop, but I can't. Tears stream down my cheeks as Eli forces his member farther down my throat. His shaft blocks my airways as he rocks into my face to muffle my screams.

Lex twirls the mysterious object around my entrance, stroking it against my wetness before pushing it inside me.

It's smaller than Eli's cock, but it's the first time I've taken something so large.

"You don't seem like a virgin to me," Lex purrs, fucking me aggressively with the object. "Look at our little ghost. Getting fucked by a flashlight in the dark."

Eli bucks his hips, and I gurgle on him. His balls slap into my chin, then they rise into his body, signaling he's about to blow. He grunts as he comes. Salty liquid spills down my throat. I gag, drowning in the wave of cum and swallow it down. Finally, he pulls out reluctantly, smearing any remaining semen over my lips with the tip of his dick like gloss.

At the same time, Lex forces my pussy to take the end of the flashlight. My body quivers, jolting with each motion. He holds me in place, leaving me with no choice but to accept it. With his spare hand, he rubs my clit, spitting every so often to keep me slick. The pressure on my clit is so intense that it's borderline painful, yet his warmth is akin to sitting next to a toasty fire. It's impossible not to succumb to the blissful sensation in the cold.

Eli stashes his cock away and moves aside. I gulp in the air, smelling the lingering dampness of fresh rainfall in the forest. Leaves scratch my ass, and I writhe around in them, my back arching with Lex's motions.

"You were too gentle, Eli," Aiden reprimands. "Hold her hands."

Eli grabs my wrists while Aiden shines his light down on my body, illuminating Lex crouching between my legs. My eyes widen, watching my pussy stretch while he defiles me with the flashlight.

Aiden takes Eli's place, his cock already in his fist. He slaps me across the face with it.

"You—"

He silences me with another whip of his dick. His hot

shaft rebounds off my cheek as he slaps me again and again. I turn to bite him but miss.

Aiden cackles, putting his hand to my throat and squeezing. "You'll regret that," he warns.

He pinches my nose, forcing my sealed lips to open, then shoves his cock into my mouth as I fight for breath. He pushes deep, having to release his hold on my throat to tip my chin back a little to give him the best angle. My gag reflex kicks in. I choke, battling the urge to be sick, but that doesn't stop him. He forces himself down my throat. My eyes bulge, ready to pop out of their sockets. That, and his weight bearing down on my chest, steal all my oxygen.

Suddenly, Lex's teeth sink into my sensitive inner thigh. The searing pain makes me shudder in a twisted mix of pain and pleasure. He does it again, biting and sucking hard, while continuing to fuck me with the flashlight.

My pussy tightens. How can I enjoy this? My body defies me at every turn as Lex's mouth brushes my clit and an intense orgasm blasts through me. It's all-consuming, transporting my body to another plane. I stay still, not wanting to give myself away. But I twitch involuntarily as my pussy spasms, gushing all over the flashlight.

"That's it," Lex praises, sensing my climax. "Come like the dirty whore we know you really are."

Aiden takes that as an invitation. He slams into me, fucking my face as hard as he fucked my ass earlier to teach me a lesson. As much as I try to fight back, they have a physical advantage, and they're not afraid to use it.

When I'm done, Lex removes the flashlight. He slurps loudly, licking my juices off it.

"So sweet," Lex says. His voice sounds faraway. "Delicious."

Aiden isn't finished, though. I'm dizzy, unable to catch my breath, as he continues to block my airways with his cock.

A light shines into my face. Behind it, Eli's darkened silhouette looms.

"She's going blue," Eli observes, frowning. "She's had enough, Aiden."

"I'll decide when she's had enough," Aiden snaps gruffly.

Eli says something else that I can't hear.

His comments only make Aiden fuck my throat more violently. My body convulses. Fuzzy dots swim before me. I'm a complete mess under his attack. He's obliterating me.

Darkness descends. A vision appears in my mind's eye. It's like a dream, yet it feels so real…

I'm in the woods again. This time, it's a warm summer night. Stars twinkle above, and moonlight slips through the lush green leaves. Aiden interlocks his fingers through mine, and I laugh at something he says. He smiles and tells me that this is somewhere we can call home. Lex is up ahead at the cabin, arranging logs into a neat pile to start a fire. I feel safe, like this is where I'm supposed to be, and then my vision fades…

"Stop, Aiden!" Eli's panicked cries pierce my eardrums, bringing me back to reality. "She's not breathing!"

Someone wrenches me into a seated position.

I cough up and retch, my shoulders shaking.

I can't think straight, let alone try to speak.

"See? She's fine," Aiden says coldly. "Carry her. We don't have long."

I look up to see Aiden storming away. Lex follows, lighter in hand, setting the tips of branches on fire as he walks. Lex's flames flicker for a few seconds, helping to guide their way, before they're extinguished by the wind.

Eli unzips his jacket and wraps it around me like a blanket, enveloping me in his scent, before scooping me up into his arms.

"You'll be fine, Little Ghost," Eli says. "You'll see."

Yet his words don't bring me comfort, only lingering dread as my eyelids flutter closed…

CHAPTER
TWENTY-FIVE

ERIN

WHEN I WAKE, I'm back at Sunnycrest in the same room Dad left me in. I startle and struggle to free myself from the tightly tucket sheets. I look around wildly, and my shoulders sag in relief.

They're gone.

Instead of my nightdress, I'm wearing a pair of gray slacks and a matching sweater. The same uniform all Sunnycrest patients are required to wear. Although it's not an orange jumpsuit, it symbolizes the same thing. We're prisoners.

While I don't remember how I ended up back here, I'm certain last night wasn't a dream. I recall the chase through the woods and flinch, putting a hand to my sore throat. Swallowing is hard, and I crave a warm drink to dull the pain. There are no mirrors, so I can't see what state I'm in, but my entire body aches. I gently massage the stinging base of my spine, which will be bruised. Underneath my clothes, scratches cover my arms, and I roll up a pant leg to see a Band-Aid placed carefully on my kneecap. They must have cleaned me up. Although I'm no longer dirty, I don't feel clean. The smell of soil lingers in my nostrils, reminding me of how Aiden pressed my face down.

A loud Klaxon-like siren blares through the building, and

a light bulb above my door flashes red. Moments later, the door opens and a doctor steps into my room. He's clean-cut, in his late thirties, and wears horn-rimmed glasses.

"Good morning, Erin," he says. "I'm Doctor Warner. Your father has asked me to look after you during your stay."

"Where is he?" I ask, peering over his shoulder and expecting to see Dad waiting in the wings. "How long will I be here? When can I go home?"

"Your father has explained to me the problems you've been experiencing," he says. "You will have a short, but intense, period of treatment while you're with us."

"But I'm not a criminal," I insist. "Or insane, like the other patients. Why can't I complete my therapy from home? That's what I've done before."

"Doctor Acacia feels a new environment will benefit your treatment," he explains. "I assure you, it's very safe here."

"I want to leave," I say. "You can't hold me against my will. I'm eighteen now. I have rights!"

"Involuntary admissions are acceptable if an individual is deemed at risk of harming themselves or others," Doctor Warner says, keeping his monotonous tone light. "As long as we deem you a risk, you will remain here."

I can't believe Dad did this to me. I understand him paying thousands of dollars for me to spend hours on a therapist's couch, but this? He's gone too far.

"What about school?" I ask, hoping to find a reason to make Dad change his mind. The Ivies don't look for applicants who've spent time in an asylum. "I can't fall behind. If you tell my father that, I'm sure he'll understand."

"You will continue your studies while you're here," Doctor Warner says. "Stonybridge Academy will send assignments to complete. We have incredible facilitators and resources on-site. However, it's more important that we focus on getting you well again. You've experienced a lot of trauma in recent years."

I nod in bleak acceptance. Resistance is futile.

"You're staying on a low-security ward," Doctor Warner continues. "This isn't a prison. You'll have plenty of freedom." He slides a sheet of paper into a mounted frame with rounded edges on the back of my door. "I'll leave your schedule here."

We're not prisoners, yet patients can't be trusted to hold a sheet of paper. Go figure. What do they expect us to do? Paper cut ourselves to death?

"Breakfast is served in the cafeteria, and communal showers are down the hall on your right," he continues. "Once you're ready, I'll see you for our first session."

On the surface, Doctor Warner appears to be kind, but his icy blue stare has a calculated edge, like he's rehearsing everything before he says it. I suspect he's only being nice because I'm his boss's daughter. My gut tells me I can't trust him.

"What if I don't want to do therapy?" I ask.

"Then you'll only extend your stay," he replies with a tight-lipped smile. "I'm sure you'll make the right decision."

I sigh as he leaves, then check my weekly schedule. It's a mixture of study time and therapy sessions. What will Mom say when she finds out where I am? Dad may have kept Sarah's time here a secret, but he won't be able to explain my sudden disappearance, especially after his angry outburst last night. Hopefully, she'll come to my rescue.

While I wait, as much as I'd like to stay in my room, I can't hide forever. Last night, we drew a lot of attention. How will the other patients respond to me? Aiden, Eli, and Lex have earned people's respect, so that could work in my favor. Although, after how we left things, I wouldn't be surprised if they asked other patients to make my life miserable.

I slip into the hallway. A few patients shuffle toward the smell of burning toast, so I opt to head for the showers first.

The asylum separates male and female sleeping quarters,

but the cafeteria and classrooms are shared, giving low-security patients the chance to mix during classes, group therapy, and mealtimes under supervision. However, I'm sure patients have their ways of getting around the rules and away from the watchful staff.

An orderly sits behind a desk at the entrance to the otherwise deserted bathroom, tapping her smoke-stained nails on the counter.

"Hi," I say. "I—"

Before I finish my sentence, she nudges her head at a stack of unfolded gray towels and a bucket with even grayer bars of soap.

"Is there any shampoo?" I ask.

"Shampoo?" She laughs, baring her yellow teeth. "You may be Acacia's daughter, but you won't get any special treatment here. You'll have soap, like everyone else."

Does Dad only recruit staff who have a mean streak? I cast a quick look around to make sure no one else heard her. Although, if the staff know who I am, it won't take long for word to get around. I feign a polite smile and pick up my supplies without complaining. Toilet stalls line one wall with sinks and mirrors opposite, and private showers span along the back.

I step into a cubicle. Mold fills the cracks between the ghastly green tiles, and clumps of hair protrude from the plug hole. I search for a shelf or hook, but there isn't one, so I sling my towel and clothes over the top of the door.

Lukewarm water dribbles out at irregular intervals. I have to punch a button every twenty seconds to keep it flowing, but it's better than nothing. If a patient wasn't insane before admission, contending with these showers daily would be enough to tip anyone over the edge.

I rub the back of my neck with the scrap of soap and frown. A patch of my skin stings and is raised to the touch.

"What the…"

A burst of laughter from the other side of the door makes me freeze. It takes a second to realize the reason for the noise. My clothes and towel are gone. Hysterical giggling accompanies the sound of slapping sandals across the wet floor.

A ringing bell signals the end of breakfast.

"Time to come out, Acacia," the unpleasant woman on the desk calls. "Breakfast is finished."

I peer around the door. "Can you bring me another towel, or anything else to wear? Someone took my clothes."

"What do I look like? A personal shopper?" The woman crosses her arms. "I can't abandon my station. If you've been careless enough to lose your uniform, you'll have to retrieve a fresh one from the laundry room. Next door on your left."

"You must have seen someone take my things," I say. "You were sitting right there the whole time."

"I saw nothing," she lies.

My cheeks burn. "But I don't want to walk down the hall naked."

She raises her eyebrows. "How is that my problem?"

"Look…" I take a deep breath, deciding to play the only card I have left in my arsenal. "I didn't want to say this, but if my father finds out—"

"That you're causing trouble?" she interrupts. "What will he do then? You may be a spoiled brat out in the real world, but here you're all just vermin to me."

I clench my fists. A rush of hateful fury surges through me. I give myself a mental shake and take a deep breath. *Where are these feelings coming from?*

"I'm only doing my job," the woman continues, checking her watch. "You're going to be late."

I grit my teeth as the image of me bashing her head into her stupid desk pops into my mind. This place must be getting to me. I'm not sure what shocks me most, the violent imagery or the underlying satisfaction I feel from wiping that shit-eating grin off her face.

I suppress my urges and step out of the cubicle, covering myself with my hands. Outside the bathroom, there's a flurry of activity. Instead of being empty, girls mill around chatting.

I hesitate for a moment.

"Hurry up," the woman jostles me along. "Move!"

I step into the busy hall under the stark, unforgiving white lights. Instantly, everyone stops what they're doing to stare. They point and cackle—obviously in no rush to get to their sessions.

"Look at the new girl," Charlie, the girl who begged Aiden to come to bed with her, exclaims. "She can't keep her clothes on!"

A camera flashes. Cell phones are banned in Sunnycrest, but contraband items seem insignificant compared to the twisted experiments my father's conducting.

"Fucking slut!"

"Where is her ass?"

"Flat-chested freak!"

The insults keep coming. I keep my gaze fixed on the floor, praying that it will swallow me up to save me from the humiliation. It doesn't take longer than thirty seconds to get to the laundry room, but it seems like hours.

After arguing with another grumbling staff member, I'm wearing a fresh uniform. It's scruffy with faded red stains around the cuffs and torn hems, but it beats baring all for the entire asylum.

When I reemerge, three girls hang around, waiting for me. The boldest, Charlie, stomps in my direction. In the daylight, I get a better look at her. She's stunning. Her dark shiny hair looks well-conditioned, and thick mascara frames her eyes.

"You." She points, looking me up and down. Her nose wrinkles. "Come here."

The rageful voice that's started speaking in my head responds. *I don't have to do what you say, bitch.* Yet, I keep my mouth shut and shuffle forward.

"I'm the one who makes the rules around here now," she says. "Aiden and the others can't protect you. Not anymore."

"I'm not here to cause any t-trouble," I stammer, regressing to the earlier version of myself who prefers to blend into the background.

"Yeah, right," one of Charlie's friends mutters sarcastically.

Charlie frowns in confusion. She mustn't be used to someone acting amicably. Most disagreements in Sunnycrest are likely settled with a fight.

"You're pathetic," she says finally. "I don't know what Aiden sees in you when he could have me."

Maybe he doesn't want a fucking psycho, the evil voice answers in my head, like a devil whispering in my ear. *Perhaps he wants someone with class?*

"We don't know, Charlie," her friend titters in agreement before turning to talk to the air. "Do we?" She shakes her head. "See? Hector doesn't know either."

"You can have Aiden," I say hastily. "I don't want him."

"Fucking liar," Charlie scoffs. "You have their mark tattooed on your neck."

I reach for the sore spot on my neck. "I…"

"Watch your back, Little Ghost," Charlie hisses.

How does she know the guys' nickname for me?

She storms past, bashing into my shoulder with her entourage in tow, leaving me staring after them and wondering what fresh hell I've got to look forward to next.

CHAPTER
TWENTY-SIX

ERIN

I STRUGGLE to get comfortable on Doctor Warner's lumpy couch. Faded landscape paintings hang on his beige office walls, and a metronome swings back and forth on his desk. The ticking is supposed to be relaxing, but it only makes me fidget more.

"Why do you think you're here, Erin?" Doctor Warner asks, reclining in his chair to study me.

People say talking about your problems helps, but it doesn't change the facts: Sarah's missing, Dad's a psychopath, and I'm... well, I guess I've always been whoever my father wants me to be. I've tried so hard to be the perfect daughter. Until now.

"Because my dad found me looking for Adderall," I lie. "I've been under a lot of stress recently with schoolwork."

"Hm..." He scratches his chin. "I understand it was recently the anniversary of Sarah's disappearance. Has that added to your stress?"

"Yes, it was—the anniversary, I mean—but that's not why I'm stressed," I say. "College is coming up, and I've had a lot on my mind. I was only looking for pills to help me study. I'm sorry to be wasting your time. You should be speaking to people who are actually sick."

Do I sound convincing enough?

Doctor Warner scrawls something in his notebook while the metronome ticks on. His unreadable expression gives nothing away.

"Why don't we talk about your sister?" Doctor Walker suggests. "It must be difficult having so many unanswered questions. It's natural for emotions to get repressed during times of immense trauma."

"I've already spent hours speaking to professionals about what happened," I say, putting an end to the subject. "There's nothing more to say."

I don't want to share my precious memories with another stranger. I want real answers, not hearsay speculations or cryptic clues from my psychopathic stalkers. Aiden claims I'll find out the truth about what happened to Sarah at Sunnycrest, but where do I start? He should have given me her diary. There must be something useful in there, if they went to the trouble of obtaining it from Officer Blackwell. Yet, as usual, Aiden seems intent on seeing me suffer.

"Humor me," Doctor Warner says. His impenetrable stare tells me he won't let this go. "What was Sarah like?"

"She was fun," I say. "She liked having a good time and always spoke her mind, even when other people didn't like it."

"Are you similar?"

"Me and Sarah?" I laugh. "No, we're opposites. I follow the rules, and Sarah liked to break them. She was the life and soul of the party, and I'd rather stay at home. She had lots of friends, and I've never been popular."

"I see." Doctor Warner takes more notes. "Your father claims you've been acting out of character recently. Has anything unexpected happened?"

"Nothing," I say. Well, unless you include three hot guys escaping from an asylum and invading every aspect of my life. "Dad's probably referencing a party I went to. I drank too much, and he was mad. Nothing out of the ordinary, though. Just normal teenage stuff."

"Hm." He nods. "I see."

"It was a mistake," I say. "It won't happen again. You can tell him that."

Doctor Warner puts down his pen, and his glasses slide down his nose. I squirm, uneasy under his scrutiny, and tune into the metronome. *Tick. Tick. Tick.* The noise slows my breathing, and I stifle a yawn.

"You've done talking therapies before, so perhaps a different approach will be useful," he ponders. "Have you ever undergone hypnosis, Erin?"

I shake my head.

"Let's try it," he says, taking out a tape recorder and clicking the record button.

Who even uses tapes anymore?

"You're recording our session?" I ask.

"There's a procedure to follow," he replies. "Lie down and get into a comfortable position. I'll dim the lights, and we can get started."

I shrug and do as he asks. Hypnosis can't be all bad, if it means not having to talk or answer more questions. He turns down the lights, and a mellow tune plays. It's comforting, almost lullaby-like, with gentle chimes.

"Close your eyes," he instructs. "You're in a safe place. All I want you to do is listen to the sound of my voice…"

He starts by taking me through a guided meditation. I visualize a golden orb hovering above the top of my head. His dull tone causes his sentences to drift into nothingness. I imagine an orb of light warming me, sweeping from my forehead to the tips of my toes. My tense limbs relax one at a time, releasing all my lingering tension, and I sink into the cushions below.

"Now, tell me what you see," Doctor Warner encourages. "Take me back to after your sister disappeared."

My mind wanders, rewinding back in time.

I'm in my bedroom, pressing my ear to the door to listen to my father and Sheriff Brady talking. Sarah didn't come home last night. She went to a party, and no one has seen or heard from her since. It's summer vacation. She's probably spending time with the guy she's dating, a jock from the hockey team. Dad doesn't know about them, and it's best it stays that way.

I can only make out snatches of their conversation, but they both sound worried, despite Dad's earlier assurances that Sarah will turn up.

"Very good," Doctor Warner says. His voice sounds far away. "Why don't you take me to an earlier time? A memory from childhood?"

I'm transported back again, watching my life like a movie.

Sarah and I are playing hide-and-seek in the park. We must be around six or seven. Mom waves at us to join her, beaming.

I haven't seen her smile like that in years. When was the sparkle in her eyes extinguished?

We race to be the first to reach her. Sarah wins, as usual, but I don't mind. We collapse in a giggling heap. Our chubby hands greedily reach for a slab of cake, stuffing it into our mouths and guzzling it down.

I can still taste it on my tongue.

Sweet vanilla sponge, a gooey strawberry jam, and sprinkled with extra sugar.

The picnic blanket is laden with an assortment of goodies that Dad doesn't let us eat. This is a special treat.

Sarah talks in a silly voice while she eats, spraying crumbs everywhere.

"*I wish I were like you, Sarah,*" *I say between laughs.* "*You're the funniest person in the whole wide world.*"

"*Come on, Sarah. Don't talk with your mouth full,*" *Mom chastises, but she's not angry. She wipes jam off Sarah's chin fondly.* "*Where are your manners?*"

"I don't have any," Sarah declares proudly. "Watch me do this, Erin!"

She jumps up to do a cartwheel, not caring that she's showing off her pink frilly panties. Unfortunately, she messes up her landing and skids, leaving a grass stain on her new pretty dress.

I clap my hands, then I turn to Mom.

Instead of smiling, Mom's expression changes. Her smile fades as she spots my father storming across the park. He must have come straight from work because he's wearing his smart suit.

Sarah, oblivious to Dad speeding up behind her, continues parading around. She twirls and dances like a clumsy ballerina, while I giggle behind my hands.

"What do you think you're doing?" Dad yanks Sarah's arms and spins her to face him. "You're making a fool of yourself!"

Sarah's face falls.

Our fun is over.

"What is this, Jocelyn?" He surveys our picnic in disgust. He picks up a bag of chips then launches it into the distance, making Mom flinch. "Junk! Pure filth!"

Mom's shoulders slump. "They've been good today. A little cake won't hurt them."

"We're going home at once," he snarls. "Throw this garbage away."

Sarah wails, and fat tears roll down her cheeks. "You're hurting my arm, Daddy!" she yells.

"Behave yourself," he hisses, dragging her away. "Why can't you be more like your sister?"

Mom smiles sadly, stroking my hair, then winks. She quickly wraps two slices of cake in a napkin and stashes them in her purse. "We'll save these two for tomorrow." She puts a finger to her lips. "It'll be our little secret."

I nod seriously. "Our secret."

The memory surprises me, and I feel a pang of sadness. I can't remember the last time my mother disobeyed my father's orders. Over the years, he must have stamped out her rebellious streak.

"Very good," Doctor Warner says as I recount the story. "Why don't we fast-forward to, say, high school? Tell me about that…"

Unlike recalling childhood, my memories are murkier the older I get, like they're shrouded in a dark smoke. I can recall vague events, but they're not vivid. The more I search for details, the blurrier they become.

"I don't want to do this," I blurt out. "Don't make me."

I can't explain my reaction. Aside from Sarah's disappearance, I've not been through anything especially traumatic, and my mind shuts off, stopping Doctor Warner from poking around in my head like a defense mechanism.

"Keep going, Erin," Doctor Warner insists. "Tell me what you remember."

"Piano," I say, settling on a safe memory. Yes, the sweet piano. The constant among the chaos. My salvation in sadness. Remembering music calms me instantly. "I remember playing piano."

"What else do you remember?" he presses.

"I spent a lot of time in the school library, reading books."

"What else?" he pushes.

"Swimming," I say. "I competed in a swim meet."

"What about outside of school?"

"I…" I struggle to remember, wading through the misty blur. I see snatches of family life, but can't pinpoint anything.

"Keep trying, Erin," he says. "Think."

Suddenly, I'm in the asylum again.

I'm in one of the rooms that the guys showed me during a previous visit, only it's not Lex tied down. It's me. Binds hold my legs and arms in place.

"Let me go!" I scream.

Dad doesn't listen.

He lowers a metal helmet-like object onto my head while someone else straps electrodes to the side of my face.

I thrash around to make their job as difficult as possible, but it's no use. I'm exhausted, and fighting is draining what's left of my strength.

"This is for your own good," Dad says.

"Don't do this," I whimper. "Please."

It's too late.

Zap!

Electricity courses through me. My body convulses. Someone shoves a rag into my mouth to stop me from biting off my tongue.

Zap!

"Tell me what you see," Doctor Warner commands. "Speak to me."

Say nothing, a voice in my head whispers. *He can't know what you're seeing, or you'll be trapped here forever.*

"I'm in math class," I lie. A bead of sweat drips down my brow. "I'm trying to get the hang of algebra, and I drop my pencil. The guy I have a crush on picks it up."

"That's enough for today." Doctor Warner sighs, sounding almost disappointed. "I want you to follow my voice as I count you out of the trance. Five, four, three, two… one. Open your eyes."

I sit up slowly, wiping my clammy palms on my pants.

"Are you okay?" Doctor Warner asks.

I nod. "I'm fine."

I mentally shake myself. I remember learning in psychology about unreliable memories. Eyewitness accounts are one of the least reliable forms of evidence in a court. People see what they want to. Whatever I thought I saw under hypnosis can't be real.

"Very good," Doctor Warner says, pushing a paper cup of pills toward me. "Here's your medication."

"What are they?" I ask, suspiciously eyeing the red and purple capsules.

"They help with stress and anxiety," he says with a nonchalant wave of his hand. "They're very similar to the medication you're already taking. Your father prescribed them himself."

I swallow them without question and open my mouth for him to check under my tongue.

"Very good," he says, satisfied. "You've had a busy morning. After lunch, I'll make sure your schoolwork from Stonybridge Academy gets delivered to your room."

I rise from the sofa. "Thanks."

"We've made progress today," he says. "You should be proud. I'll see you tomorrow."

I smile meekly, unsure what we've really achieved, aside from making me question my sanity.

As I exit, a boy, who is leaving an adjacent treatment room, crashes into me. We're around the same age. He's painfully thin with tufty yellow hair, sunken eyes, and weeping scabs from skin picking.

"Sorry," I say. "I didn't see you."

"Sure you didn't, Sarah," he mutters.

"Excuse me?" He has my full attention now. "What did you call me?"

His shoulders tense, and his eyes widen like a rabbit caught in the headlights.

"N-nothing," he stammers. "I didn't call you anything."

"You called me Sarah."

"Did not," he says, then scampers away.

"Wait!" I call after him. "Don't go!"

It's too late. He zips around the next corner, moving as fast as his scrawny legs can carry him, desperate to get away.

Doctor Warner appears behind me, placing a firm hand on my shoulder to stop me from following.

"Your room is that way," the doctor says. *Where did he come from?* I didn't hear him approach. "Hurry along."

Doctor Warner's stare burns into my back as I walk away.

Aiden said I'd find answers in Sunnycrest, and this is my first clue.

CHAPTER
TWENTY-SEVEN

ERIN

AFTER MY EARLIER ENCOUNTER WITH Charlie, I avoid the cafeteria at lunch, but I can't ignore my grumbling stomach when the siren yells again. I wait until the initial bustle subsides, hoping to slip in unnoticed while everyone's eating.

My hopes are quickly dashed. As soon as I walk in, everyone turns to stare. At Stonybridge, I blended into the background, until Nate paid me attention. Here, I stick out.

I join the back of the food line, keeping my head down. At first glance, it looks like any other school cafeteria. However, on closer inspection, I notice that the tables and chairs are stuck to the floor, and everyone eats with silicone cutlery. Patients can't be trusted to eat unsupervised, so security staff watch from every corner of the room, and a nurse doles out pills with food trays.

I spot Charlie. Her eyes narrow in my direction as she jabs a piece of pasta with her fork, probably pretending it's my face.

"Here." The nurse thrusts a small cup of pills into my hands and watches me wash them down before I continue. "Good."

"Next," an angry woman in a grubby apron snaps impatiently.

Unlike Stonybridge, which offers fresh food that caters to every dietary requirement and preference, the woman doesn't ask what I want to eat. There's no choice. She spoons a glob of rice onto my tray alongside a dollop of chili that smells like dog food.

A guy with red hair and a broken-looking nose swipes his fingers across his throat and mimes 'You're dead' to me across the room. I gulp and try not to take it personally. He must do that to everyone, right? I continue hunting for an empty table, or at least somewhere to sit where people don't look like they want to kill me, but my options are limited.

On one table, a group of patients talk to themselves and yell at imaginary figures. At another, an argument breaks out. A guy throws his tray and gets dragged off screaming by two white-coated men. Next to them, a group of greasy-haired patients stare blankly ahead. They chew with their mouths open and drool drips down their chins, too high on a cocktail of drugs to be aware of their surroundings or even know their own names. At the next table, I recognize Bea. She sits among a group of guys with buzz cuts, who are busy comparing cuts on their arms. Everyone else in the room avoids looking at me, hoping that I don't pick them to sit with. Dad portrays Sunnycrest as a positive place that offers rehabilitation and a fresh start, but it's a living hell.

My searching gaze stops on a guy at the back of the room. The same guy who mistook me for Sarah earlier. He tries to hide behind the broad shoulders of another patient, but it's too late. I weave through the tables toward him when, suddenly, a foot knocks my legs from underneath me. I have no time to react. I topple over, landing straight on my sore knees and spray chili all over my front.

Laughter rings in my ears.

I look up to see Charlie, one hand propped on her hip in a sassy pose.

"You should be more careful," she says, grinning smugly.

Even in asylums, you can't get away from cliquey, mean girls.

I drop my tray with a clang and stand, wiping sauce off my chin. My cheeks are ablaze, but to my surprise, not from embarrassment. There it is again. The simmering rage. My nostrils flare in fury. The violence and suddenness of the emotion surprises me, and I squeeze my nails into my palms to stop myself from wiping the smirk off her face. This place is getting to me.

Charlie backs away a little, her confidence waning as she senses a change in me. Something flickers behind her eyes. Fear, perhaps?

"Is there a problem?" A nurse appears. "We can get you another tray, Miss Acacia."

Anyone who didn't already know my identity does now, officially making me a social pariah and a potential target.

How many patients have been subjected to my father's cruel experiments and seek revenge?

"There's no problem," I say through gritted teeth. "Is there, Charlie?"

She glares back and shakes her head. I wonder why she's in Sunnycrest.

The woman beckons me away. "Come along."

I stay where I am.

"I want to speak to my father," I demand.

"Your father has given explicit instructions that you are to complete your treatment before you have visitors," she replies.

"He's not a visitor," I hiss. "He runs this fucking place!"

I'm acting entitled, but I don't care. This has gone on for long enough. I don't belong here with these people. I need to go home.

Her face pales and she stammers. "I'm only following orders."

"Relay my message," I say coldly. "And I'm going to eat in my room."

"We don't let—"

I shoot her a sharp 'don't mess with me' look. "I'm Doctor Acacia's daughter," I say. If everyone already knows who I am, there's no point in hiding it. "I'm sure you can make an exception this once. I expect a fresh tray waiting in my room after I shower."

The nurse's jaw drops, and I don't wait for her permission before stomping out.

"Bitch," Charlie mutters under her breath.

I rise above it… this time.

The same moody woman from this morning is monitoring the bathroom.

"Back again?" She looks down her nose at me. "You can only shower in the mornings."

I narrow my eyes. "I'm showering now, unless you want to look for another job."

She blinks hard, surprised by my transformation.

I hold out my hand. "Towel."

She mumbles something I can't make out, but hands me a towel, anyway.

"I want shampoo this time," I say. "And clean clothes."

She looks like she wants to tell me to stick the shampoo where the sun doesn't shine.

"I told you this morning—"

"I know you were lying," I snarl, not backing down again.

She scowls and reluctantly hands me a clean uniform and a bottle from under the desk. The shampoo isn't a luxury brand, but anything beats the smell of three-day stewed kidney beans. When I get home, I'll never take Mom's fancy toiletries from the spa for granted again.

As before, the water pressure is terrible, but I successfully wash the funk out of my hair and don't make the mistake of hanging anything over the side of the door.

Suddenly, a deafening siren blares through the facility. I put my hands to my ears, cringing as the sound vibrates my bones. A flurry of activity in the hall follows the noise. I peer around the door and watch two doctors race past, shouting over the alarm. I hear the words 'understaffed' and 'suicide'. A security guard stops by the bathroom, requesting help from the towel bitch, who points in my direction, torn about leaving her post.

"I'm about to head to my room," I say, rolling my eyes. "I'm sure I can make it a few steps without you watching me."

She can't hear me properly from her position, but seems to get the gist of what I'm saying. She hesitates for a second before following the guard.

A few minutes later, after drying and redressing, I hum as I step out of the cubicle, feeling victorious. As I do, the stall door on my left opens. Suddenly, freckled arms wrap around my neck and yank me inside it.

The redheaded asshole who threatened me earlier slams the door behind us, shutting us in the shower cubicle. A maniacal grin spreads over his sharp features as he brandishes a shiv. His blade is made from a jagged red plastic, likely from a broken lunch tray, and has been attached to a pencil with sticky tape.

"Your father has taken everything from me," he spits. "It's time I take something back. If you move, I'll make sure you'll bleed out."

I try to push him away, but he's deceptively strong. He swipes the plastic across the side of my throat. A warm trickle drips down my neck.

"Help!" I shout. "Someone help!"

No one will hear me over the noise, but it's better than doing nothing.

"Don't struggle," he hisses. His rancid breath fanning my face makes me want to hurl. "It'll only hurt more."

"Please," I beg. "You don't have to do this."

I raise my knee up to smash into his balls, but a slash of the blade against my neck makes me yelp.

"I said, don't fucking move," he warns. "I didn't plan on killing you, but I will, if you fight back."

He yanks my trackpants down, exposing my panties.

"Please, no," I whimper.

"No one will hear you scream," he says. "The doctors will be busy for a while. We've made sure of that."

I don't question who helped him. I'm sure Charlie will be behind this.

Tears spring to my eyes as his grimy, chewed fingernails paw my hips.

Separate your mind from your body, Erin.

Suddenly, the door flies open, and someone wrenches him out. The force causes me to lose my balance and land flat on my ass, leaving me face-to-face with a pair of biker boots.

A masked figure casts a shadow over my trembling attacker, whose face drains of color.

"Naughty, naughty," Lex growls menacingly from under a Ghostface mask, "you touched our property."

The hairs on the back of my neck stand on end, as Lex wiggles his finger back and forth.

The boy cowers, his entire frame consumed by violent shakes. He knows he's in deep shit.

"I...I ... I didn't know she was yours, Lex," he stammers. "I did what I was told. She's Acacia's daughter. After every-thing he's done, I thought—"

"You thought wrong," Lex replies. "If anyone touches a single hair on Miss Acacia's head, they answer to us. Do you understand?"

"Yes." He nods so vigorously that it looks like his head will snap straight off his neck. "I'll make sure everyone knows. I'll tell them."

"They'll find out for themselves," Lex says. "After you

pay for what you did." Lex pulls off his mask and throws it at me, flashing me a hot lopsided grin that makes my stomach flutter. "Go to your room, Little Ghost."

I grab his mask and stagger to my feet, pulling my pants back up.

"Please, no!" my attacker begs. "Don't!"

I should head back, but I don't. I linger and sniff the air. *Is that gasoline?* A bloodcurdling, guttural scream pierces my ears. A scream of pure agony.

Lex steps out of the stall, and the guy howls in pain behind him. His entire groin is ablaze as he desperately slams the shower button. Unfortunately for him, they are unreliable, and no water comes. He hurtles out, his dick still sizzling like a sausage on a barbecue. Much to my disappointment, a heat detector must sense the fire as sprinklers automatically power on from above, blasting us with stagnant water.

Lex grabs my arm and drags me down the hall to my room, leaving a wet trail of footprints in our wake.

Once inside, my chest heaves as I struggle to catch my breath, and I shiver through my soaked clothes.

"You..." My teeth chatter. "You... set him on fire... for me?"

"I'm the only one who can make you scream, Little Ghost," Lex says matter-of-factly with no trace of remorse. "He got what he deserved."

"You didn't need to do... that," I say.

Lex grabs my chin, wrenching my face to look into his crazy eyes. "Would you rather I stood by and watched while he raped you?"

Up close, I can see his scars properly for the first time. How one half of his face, smooth and marble-like, meets raised pink lines. He catches me staring. His hazel eyes appear to redden at their center, matching the fire he just started.

"What's wrong?" Lex sneers. "Scared of what you see, Little Ghost?"

Instead of shying away from him, I stroke his scarred cheek. He winces, but I don't move my hand. I swallow hard, fighting my fear, and trace my fingers along his bumpy skin.

"What happened?" I dare to ask. "Did my father do that to you?"

"No," Lex says, catching my wrist. "That's one of the few scars your father isn't responsible for." He breaks eye contact. "My family died in a fire. That's all you need to know."

"I'm sorry."

"Don't be," he replies bluntly, wiping his wet, dark hair out of his face. "I'm not."

I have so many questions, but I've already pushed my luck. Outside my room, there's a rush of wheels accompanied by a familiar scream that gradually grows fainter.

"You should go," I say. "If they find you here, they'll lock you up again."

"Do you really want to get rid of me so soon?" Lex asks, stepping closer. The tiny room shrinks more with him inside it. "The asylum is in lockdown. We're going nowhere."

"What about Aiden?" I ask. "He'll be wondering where one of his minions—"

Lex's jaw clenches. "I'm not a minion."

I've struck a nerve. I shouldn't annoy the man who has just set someone's cock on fire, but I can't help myself.

"That's not what it looks like," I say. "You and Eli follow Aiden's rules."

"Rules are made to be broken," he says. "You should know that by now. And besides, you owe me."

"Owe you?" I shake my head in disbelief. "After what you did last night, I owe you nothing."

"Don't pretend you didn't like it," he says, licking his lips. "I can still taste your sweet pussy on my tongue."

I back away from him until my calves hit the metal sides of the bed.

"Are you afraid?" His British accent makes everything sound better, even when it's a cloaked threat. "You should be."

"You won't hurt me," I say, hoping I'm right.

He's inches from me, and there's nowhere to run. His radiating body heat warms me through my wet clothes, and my nipples stand to attention, clearly visible through my sweater. He looks down, the corner of his mouth tilting into a twisted grin.

He arches an eyebrow. "Are you sure about that?"

Before I can respond, his lips are on mine. His fingers weave through my hair, and he pulls me closer. The lingering smell of gasoline goes straight to my head, sweeping me away in an inferno. His tongue plunders my mouth, and I wrap my arms around his neck, blaming my eagerness on the fumes.

He sinks his teeth into my bottom lip, forcing a groan from me. His scarred hands pull off my sweater, and I claw at his T-shirt, tearing the fabric around his shoulders. He pauses to remove it, giving me time to admire his body. The white light illuminates his pale skin, showcasing every scar and line of his delicious, defined muscles. I run my hands over his marks, and my heart sinks at the thought of what he's had to endure.

Lex pinches my nipple hard. His smoky scent engulfs me as he whispers, "Don't pity me."

I can't help it. His body maps his suffering. Knowing that my father is responsible is almost too much to bear.

"I'm sorry about what he did," I murmur, stroking the base of Lex's neck at the spot where his burns end and another scar begins. "I really am."

He crushes my windpipe in his grasp. With one hand around my throat, he propels my entire body around and slams my back into the wall, then slides his other hand into my panties. His fingers meet my wetness and spread me open.

"I said…" He slides two fingers inside me. My body jerks from the force as he fucks me with them. "Don't." His knuckles graze my pussy lips with each flick of his wrist. "Pity me."

I gargle, battling for air.

He smiles, satisfied I won't struggle as he releases his chokehold to unleash his cock.

"I'm a monster, Little Ghost," he murmurs. "A monster who breaks the rules."

"I—"

He withdraws his glistening fingers and rams them into my mouth to shush me, swirling them across my tongue and forcing me to taste myself.

I splutter as he pulls them out while he lines his cock up to my pussy, then grabs my ass, hoisting me into the air and pushing my back against the wall. Instinctively, I wrap my legs around his middle, clinging onto him, as my wetness slathers his throbbing shaft.

Fuck, why does he have to feel so good?

He's a monster, but my body still craves more.

"Aiden said you can't—"

Lex thrusts into me before I finish my sentence.

"Fuck the rules," he growls.

Aiden wanted them all to take my virginity together, but it's too late. Lex's cock pulses inside me, stealing my virginity with every buck of his hips. I gasp at the overwhelming fullness, but it doesn't hurt—not like how I expected it to. It feels… right.

"Fuck," Lex groans, pummeling into me with violent thrusts, like a wild beast losing control. My breasts bounce against him with each aggressive motion. "I've missed this."

How long has it been since he had sex with someone? My

question disappears as quickly as it comes when he grasps my ass to guide me. I'm powerless to stop him, even if I wanted to. Hearing the wet slap of our bodies turns me on even more and dulls the pain of my bruised back.

Everything around us, the sirens, screams, and running footsteps, fade into nothingness. Our ragged breathing synchronizes. Being one with him feels familiar, like coming home. His ferocious fucking unlocks my primal desires, and a heated friction builds as he grinds against my clit.

"Harder," I beg, clawing his broad shoulders. "Fuck, Lex…"

He spins me and pulls out carefully before throwing me down onto the hard mattress. His nine-inch cock twitches, and my gaze is drawn to a tattoo above his hip bone. A tiny, inked outline of a ghost. The same as Aiden's. The same design that I fear is permanently etched on my neck.

"You want more, Little Ghost?" he taunts, taking his cock into his fist and working it.

I watch him touch himself, mesmerized.

"Yes," I moan.

"Say please," he commands.

I spread my legs wide. "Please."

"I want you to beg for it," he orders. "Beg me to fill your tight, little cunt."

"Fuck me." My cheeks flush. "Please."

He tsks and shakes his head. "Not good enough."

Lex climbs onto the bed, positioning himself between my open legs. He teases me, rubbing himself against my entrance. He slaps the head of his cock on my clit, making sparks fly under my skin like an electric shock.

"I want you to…" Talking dirty is new to me, and Lex knows it. He's pushing me out of my comfort zone and enjoying every second. "Fuck me… hard."

"How badly do you want me, Little Ghost?" he taunts. "You need to make me believe it."

I wriggle, writhing my hips to try to maneuver him inside me. Lex laughs and pulls back to torment me further.

"Fill me, Lex," I plead. "I need you."

I moan as his cock glides over my clit again.

Our eyes meet, and everything shifts. It's as if an invisible thread has tied together in my mind, and I know exactly what he needs to hear.

"Make me scream," I demand. "Make me scream this fucking asylum down."

The look on his face tells me I've given him what he wants. He launches into action, seizing my ankles and resting them high on his shoulders. He enters me again. The angle intensifies the sensation as his cock rubs on a sensitive spot inside me. The pressure keeps building until I feel like I'm floating.

He props himself up using his elbows, thrusting deep enough to make the bed shake. I dig my nails into his back, leaving my marks on his skin as my climax arrives.

"Scream, Little Ghost," Lex purrs. "Scream for me."

An earth-shattering orgasm rages through me like an army finally bursting down their enemy's castle gates.

"Fuck!" I cry. "Fuck!"

I writhe around in bliss, not caring whether anyone hears us over the alarms. My pussy grips and squeezes him, wringing out every drop of pleasure. The orgasm seems endless; when one surge washes away, another crashing tsunami descends.

He drives me into the mattress. My thighs ache in the best possible way as he keeps going. I wail, feeling a small pop and a sudden release. A warm gush soaks my sheets. I blush, worried I've wet myself, but Lex's eyes light up.

"Look at you," he admires, fucking me more vigorously. "A filthy fucking whore squirting all over me."

There's no coming back from this. I'm ruined. His darkness has tainted me for good. No ordinary man will ever compare.

Lex groans, thrusting deep. He explodes and paints my insides with his cum. When he's done, he wipes his hair from his sweaty brow and smirks. After he withdraws, I expect him to redress. Instead, he grabs my hair and hauls me up to perch on the edge of the bed.

"Clean up," he orders. "If Aiden finds any trace of what we did, he'll punish you, too."

I look at him as I slide my tongue up his shaft, licking off the beads of salty cum pooling at his tip. He tastes of our sin and my undoing. I flick my tongue over every throbbing vein, until he yanks me back using my hair.

"All of me," he says, forcing me down roughly.

I stare at his balls, unsure what to do next.

"I said, clean up," he snarls.

I carefully take them into my mouth, one at a time, sucking gently to lick off my wetness. Finally, he pulls my head away, letting me know he's satisfied.

"No one can know about this," he says coldly, turning away to pull up his pants, leaving me shivering in our puddle of ruin.

I quickly put my soggy sweater back on, right on time for the light above my door to flash green.

"Lockdown's over," he says abruptly, reaching for the handle.

"Wait!" I say. "When will I see you again?"

He smiles. For once, it looks genuine and free from malice, then it vanishes just as fast.

"We're always watching," he replies.

"Aiden said I'd find answers here," I say, hoping to get some useful information before he leaves. "What did he mean?"

He sighs.

"You'll find out soon enough," he says, before disappearing into the shadows once more.

DOCTOR WARNER TIPS HIS METRONOME. "How are you feeling this morning?"

"Fine," I lie.

Internally, I'm still unpacking what happened last night. A conflicting mass of emotions swirls around my head, from horror and confusion to desire. And, most worryingly, being plagued by one question. If I don't regret what happened with Lex, what does that say about me?

"You seem distracted." He frowns. "You'll only prolong your stay if you're not being honest with me."

"I slept badly," I say, feigning a yawn. "That's all."

He scratches his chin. "I heard about an unfortunate incident last night. I assure you that accidents are rare here, and your father is dealing with it."

"That's good to hear," I say, having to bite my tongue to stop myself from sarcastically questioning how many other patients have had their penises turn into fireworks.

Despite the sickening display of violence, knowing Lex hurt my attacker to protect me makes me feel... wanted? I clench my aching thighs. On one hand, Lex's ruthless, but he hides a more vulnerable side that I caught a brief glimpse of. I'm intrigued to learn more about him. I didn't know it was possible to be terrified and turned on by someone at the same time.

"Why don't we try another regression?" Doctor Warner suggests, retrieving his tape recorder. "Looking back often helps us look forward."

"It's not like I have anything better to do," I grumble.

"This is for your own good," he says. "You'll see."

I recline on the sofa and shut my eyes. Relaxing music with twinkling chimes and gentle waves fills the room. It has a familiar, comforting tune, and I follow it, finding it easy to be lulled into a trance by Doctor Warner's dulcet drone.

My mind drifts away.

"Take me to a time when you were happiest," Doctor Warner says, cutting through the noise.

"The piano," I murmur, thinking of my safe place. "Before we moved to Pasturesville, we had a grand piano in the middle of the house. I used to play it for hours, looking out of the window across the garden."

"Very good," Doctor Warner says. "What was your life like then?"

"Every day was the same," I reply. "Home, study, piano, then swimming."

"What about school?" he presses.

"I spent most of my time in the library," I say. "That's where I ate my lunch."

"What was the library like?" he pushes. "Describe it to me."

"Nothing special. Lots of shelves… books…" I recall. "The air conditioning always broke, so it had a funny smell, kinda musty. No one else liked to hang out there."

I sought sanctuary between the shelves, hiding away from other people and nibbling on whatever salad Mom packed for lunch. Long gone were the days of her sneaking sweet treats into our brown bags without my father's knowledge.

"Did you have many friends?"

I shake my head, scrunching my eyes in concentration. Everything before we moved to Pasturesville seems foggy. My memories are within touching distance, yet they're fuzzy. My life is split into two parts: life before Sarah went missing and after. It must be my brain's way of protecting itself. Imagining her around is too painful to linger on.

Before Sarah disappeared and we moved to Pasturesville, Dad commuted to and from Sunnycrest. However, when the time he spent at the asylum kept getting longer, it made sense for us all to move closer. Sometimes I wonder whether we'd have all been better off if he left on his own and we stayed behind.

"What about Sarah?" Doctor Warner probes. "Did she have friends?"

"Yes," I say. "Loads of them. She went to every party."

A pounding bass suddenly pulses through my brain.

Strobe lights fill my vision, snapshots of people dancing, flitting from one scene to the next, too quickly to make out any details.

I laugh, throwing my head back.

Shots.

Liquid sloshes down my throat to the delight of a cheering crowd.

Clapping.

More laughing.

Dancing.

Twirling.

My hair swings around my shoulders.

I recognize a face in the darkness. A hockey player…

Max. That's his name.

His muscled arm wraps around my waist. He leans in.

I smell his aftershave, the liquor on his breath, and then I see it over his shoulder…

A white van.

"I have to go…"

"What is it?" Doctor Warner prompts sharply as the memory melts away. "What do you see?"

"I…"

Another image appears.

Dad.

He's shouting, red in the face.

For a change, he doesn't seem angry—more panicked. Hysterical, even. He's saying something. The same thing. Over and over.

"No. No. No. God no. Help me!"

He's not alone. There's another man. I can't see him properly, but I sense his presence. He's speaking, but his voice is garbled, like he's underwater.

My eyes crack open. The stark white room is so bright that my retinas burn.

Cold metal chills my spine as I turn my head.

It can't be…

To my right, Sarah lies on a metal-looking bench.

Her chest is still.

Her skin ghostly pale.

Her eyes frozen open in a haunting stare.

"What do you see?" Doctor Warner's voice rings through the haze. "Tell me."

I reach for her, extending my fingers, using all my strength, but Dad grabs my arm.

"It'll be okay, Erin," he says, stroking my cheek. "You'll see."

Back in reality, Doctor Warner's firm hands shake my shoulders.

I sit bolt upright, gasping for air.

"What happened?" he asks, his forehead wrinkling in concern.

"I…" I steady my breathing, knowing I can't tell him. How can I? "I saw Sarah and Dad arguing. She came home from a party, and he wasn't happy that she was late."

"Are you sure that's all you saw?" Doctor Warner probes. "You can trust me."

I put my hand to my head. "I think I've got a migraine coming on."

He opens his mouth to argue, then decides against it, and nods.

"Very well," he says. "I'll see you at the same time again tomorrow."

I hurry out of the room, unable to shake the vision. Has hypnosis unlocked a hidden memory? Can I really have known what happened to Sarah all this time? Or am I really going crazy? How do I know if what I saw was real?

I pace across the cafeteria, which I have to cut through to return to my room. I don't pay attention to where I'm going, flying out the door and colliding with a figure, who is rushing in the opposite direction.

"S-sorry," the guy stammers, then freezes as soon as he realizes who he's walked into.

It's him. The guy who called me Sarah and has been trying to avoid me since.

Before he has the chance to get away, I grab his arm.

"Wait!" I say. I'm taking a risk, but I can't let him slip away again. "Don't go."

His eyes dart around in fear. "I can't speak to you."

"It'll only take a second," I say. "Please."

"Do you know what they'll do to me?" he hisses, tugging himself free. "If they find out we've been talking?"

"Aiden and the others won't hurt you," I insist. "I'll explain that you were helping me. All I want is to find out what really happened to my sister."

"You already know," he whispers. "You don't need me to tell you."

"I can't remember—not properly, anyway," I confess. "You called me Sarah. That means you knew her, right? Was she here? Did you spend time with her?"

A slamming door ends my interrogation.

"Erin." My father's voice makes my blood run cold. "I

hope you're not upsetting my patients." His stare lands coldly on my, now cowering, companion. "Return to your room, Alfred."

Alfred bows his head, half trembling, taking any hope of getting more answers with him as he hurries away.

Two orderlies brandishing clipboards flank Dad, who marches toward me like a sergeant heading into battle. The temperature seems to drop a few degrees with each step he takes. It's the first time we've seen each other since I arrived, and his expression is filled with blatant disapproval.

"Doctor Warner informed me that you left your therapy session early," he says. So much for our sessions being confidential. "I was on my way to check on you. However, you must be feeling better, if you're fraternizing with male patients."

"I have a headache," I say. "I was going back to my room when I stopped Alfred to ask when lunch was served. He did nothing wrong."

"You should have checked your schedule," Dad says, unconvinced by my story.

"I forgot," I say lamely.

Dad glowers at me, his mouth settling into a frown that draws his eyebrows together.

"Can we talk?" I ask. "Alone?"

The orderlies gape, like I've requested something inconceivable. God forbid they be parted from their master for a single second.

Dad sighs, then reluctantly nods at the others to disperse. They remain close, hovering just out of earshot.

"Well?" he prompts, tapping his foot impatiently. "What is it?"

"When can I go home?" I plead. "I know you're mad because of what I did, but keeping me here seems... extreme."

"Extreme?" He scoffs. "Surely you can feel that you've not

been entirely yourself lately? You will stay for as long as it takes to complete your treatment. Sunnycrest turns people into the best versions of themselves."

As well as making them suffer and torturing them, I think.

"How is Mom?" I ask. "Does she even know I'm staying here? I'm not like the other patients. I'm not crazy!"

"Your mother is happy you've finally admitted you need help," he says. "In fact, she is coming to visit this afternoon. You'd know that if you checked your schedule."

"She's coming?" I blink in disbelief. "Here?"

"This isn't a prison, Erin." He narrows his eyes. "Although, if you're too ill to complete therapy, perhaps you're unfit to see her?"

He's caught me in my lies and he knows it.

"I'll be okay after I take some aspirin," I say hastily. "I want to see her."

He pauses, deliberating whether he wants to punish me more. Finally, after a strained silence, he checks his watch and addresses one of his minions. "Escort Erin to her room. Administer medication. Ensure she swallows all her pills."

"Is that all you have to say?" I ask. "Dad—"

He doesn't look at me.

"See to it that she gets a personal escort during visiting hours," he continues, pretending I'm not there. "Her mother will be here soon."

The orderly nods obediently.

Dad turns, his white coat swishing behind him as he glides away. A few patients jump back, pressing themselves into the walls like they're trying to hide as he passes them.

The orderly grabs my wrist.

"I don't need a babysitter," I say, wrenching it from him. "I can walk perfectly fine by myself."

At least I'll be seeing Mom soon. That gives me hope. Maybe she can get me out of here.

"How much longer will this take?" I seethe. "You've had two sessions already."

I grab him by the scruff of his shirt. He cowers, fear radiating from him, like a zebra caught in the jaws of a starving crocodile. He has a job to do, and my patience is waning. I want results, and I want them now.

"I'll tell you the same thing I told Lex y-yesterday," he stammers. "I'm trying everything. It's difficult with Acacia breathing down my neck. I need more time."

"You said you could do this, Doctor," I hiss, spraying spit over his glasses. I wouldn't leave his face intact if it wasn't for needing to avoid suspicion. "You claimed you could unlock her memories."

"And I can," he insists. "I just need more time. I thought we were getting somewhere today, but she's fighting it."

"She needs to remember!" I launch Doctor Warner across his office like a piece of trash. "She needs to know!"

He shakily brushes himself off. "You must be patient."

"We have been patient," I growl. "You said your methods would work."

"It's proving more difficult than I originally anticipated," he says. "Her memories are sealed away, hidden in her subconscious, just like he wanted. I've been gradually reducing her medication, which will help her see things more clearly. Taking it slow is the only safe—"

"We don't have time to do this slowly," I explode. "We can't wait!"

We have to leave Pasturesville. This town has stolen years of our lives already, but we can't leave without her. She's keeping us here, tying us to this perpetual hell. And until she knows everything, we'll never be together. Not how we should be.

"I'm doing the best I can. I want to help." Doctor Warner tries to use his therapist's voice, but I'm not falling for his bullshit. "What Acacia did was wrong—"

"Wrong?!" I smash my fist into the wall, leaving a dent in the plaster. "We had a deal!"

Doctor Warner is the only professional in the asylum to be appalled by Acacia's experiments, and he sympathized with us. We took advantage of that, exploiting his weakness to free ourselves, only the poor bastard never expected to see us again.

When we returned to Sunnycrest to demand his help with one final task, he looked like he'd seen a ghost. Perhaps he thought that Acacia disposed of us, like all of the other patients he's made disappear over the years. Despite agreeing to help, the stress is taking a toll on him. His rumpled clothes look slept-in, and he hasn't shaved. It serves him right. Although he doesn't agree with Acacia's experiments, his silence still makes him complicit. He's had every opportunity to raise the alarm, but he's too afraid. Too weak. Too fucking pathetic.

"This is a delicate matter," Doctor Warner says. "Her brain is fragile, and her grip on her reality is fragile. We have to be careful when dealing with repressed memories. One wrong move can—"

"She knows her sister's dead," I say bluntly. "I told her."

His brow furrows in concern. "I warned you about giving her too much information. The exposure could cause a psychotic break. To help her remember effectively, we must tread carefully. With another few months in therapy, she—"

Months? I expected results in days. We can't wait that long, and neither can she. As long as she's under her father's influence, she'll never be free. Who knows what else he'll do the longer she stays? She belongs with us.

"If you can't speed up the process, we'll do it our way."

"Aiden, I don't advise—"

"We won't be needing your help anymore, Doctor," I say coldly. "We'll take it from here."

We're getting her back, no matter the cost…

I HOLD my hands up in the air and rotate slowly, letting the security guard scan a metal detector over my body for the fourth time.

"How long will this take?" I complain.

"We can't be too careful, Miss Acacia," my orderly escort chirps. He hasn't left my side since my run-in with Dad earlier. Clearly, he wants brownie points from the boss.

"All clear," the security guard says.

"Finally," I grumble.

The orderly marches me into the visitors' room. My feet sink into the plush carpet. It's surprisingly nice here. Pretty landscape pictures cover the walls, and there is comfortable seating. If it wasn't for security guards loitering with batons and nurses poised with medication, it could be a café.

Only two other patients have visitors. Most patients live out of state, and it's difficult for their families to visit regularly. Others are deemed too dangerous to be permitted visitors at all. And, worse still, many don't have anyone who'd even want to visit.

I spot Mom instantly. She sits at a table in a quiet corner, as far away from everyone else as possible, wringing her hands in her lap. As usual, her hair and makeup are impeccable. However, her blush appears clown-like against the stark whiteness of her cheeks, and she's slathered concealer under her eyes to mask black circles.

She jumps up to greet me. "Erin!"

She pulls me into a tight hug, engulfing me in a cloud of expensive perfume. There's a lot of emotion wrapped into our hug, and words she doesn't dare say.

"You look..." She dabs her watery eyes. "Well."

Above us, the red blinking light of a security camera reminds us we're not alone.

Although Dad is intent on keeping me locked up, Mom has the power to intervene. If she found out that he was behind Sarah's disappearance, she'd finally be free from his spell. No matter how scared she is of him, I can't believe she'd do nothing, if she knew he was responsible.

"Why don't we sit down?" I suggest, keeping my expression neutral.

"How are you, darling?" she asks, then shakes her head. "Silly me, what a stupid question. Your father says that you're starting treatment?"

"I am." I lean in and drop my voice to a whisper, "You need to help me get out of here, Mom."

Her red lips stretch into a nervous smile, and she fidgets in her seat.

"Your father knows what's best," she says. "You'll be home as soon as you're better."

"You don't understand," I say. "I'm not ill."

"You've had a stressful time at school. Seeking help is nothing to be ashamed of. We're here for you, Erin." Her eyes glaze over, like she's repeating rehearsed words. "Everyone thinks you're spending the rest of the semester in Europe. You don't have to worry about anything."

"What about Mia?" I ask. "Don't you think she'll find it suspicious that I haven't called or texted?"

"I've spoken to Mia," she says. "She knows you'll be out

of touch for a while. All you have to worry about is getting better."

"But I'm not sick," I reaffirm. "Dad's only keeping me here to punish me because I snuck into his office without permission. You were there and saw what he did. If you tell them that I'm not a risk to myself, they'll have to let me go."

"I'm not a professional," she says. "Your father thinks you will really benefit from being in new surroundings."

"There's nothing wrong with me, Mom," I emphasize. "There's something else you should know, too. Dad had something to do with Sarah disappearing. I can't be certain, but—"

"You shouldn't make false accusations, Erin," she says. "Your father loved your sister very much."

Although, something stirs behind her eyes. Doubt, perhaps? Fear? Maybe I can get through to her. The mother I remember from my childhood is still in there somewhere. The same mom who gave us warm hugs, snuck us slices of cake, and took us to picnics. She would never let him hurt us.

"He did something to her," I say. "I don't know what happened exactly, but he's the reason she's missing. I think... I think he killed her."

"No," she mumbles. "You don't know what you're saying."

"Come on, Mom. Think about it," I say. "You know what he's like better than anyone. He hurts you, and he hurt her too."

Suddenly, her expression hardens. Any softness vanishes, like she's become a completely different person before my eyes.

"Your father loves us," she says, narrowing her eyes. "How dare you concoct such vicious lies!"

"Please, Mom," I say. "You're supposed to protect us. It's too late for Sarah, but you can help me now. You can get me out of here, and then we can report him. We can tell the sheriff what we think he—"

Her chair screeches as she stands.

"That's enough!" she yells, alerting the attention of the guards. "Your father is a good man."

"Saying it doesn't make it true," I say, reaching for her hand. "Wake up, Mom!"

"You're sicker than I thought," she hisses, jumping back like I'm infected with a contagious disease she doesn't want to catch. "Your father was right."

"No!" My voice cracks. "I'm not crazy!"

"Don't cause a scene," she warns. "People are watching."

I don't care. I cling to her as two guards approach. They grab my shoulders, but I don't let go. Mom wails as the front of her designer coat rips, leaving a scrap of fabric in my hands as they tear me off.

"No!" I yell, fighting against them. "No! Put me down! Mom!"

Mom shakes her head sadly. "Get well soon, honey."

"Help me!" I plead, thrashing against their firm grip. "He's a monster!"

"This is for your own good," Mom says.

I turn just in time to see a nurse on my left. She jams a needle into my neck, and my limbs go slack. I attempt to resist the sedative coursing through my veins, but it's too strong, and I'm sucked into a black vortex of nothingness...

CHAPTER
THIRTY-ONE

ERIN

"Little Ghost," Aiden's purr cuts through the hazy abyss. "Oh, Little Ghost…"

A drowsy heaviness drags me down, tempting me to succumb to a blissful sleep, but his voice beckons me back.

"It's time to get up."

"Go away," I groan. "I want to sleep."

"Wake up," he orders, pinching my cheeks. "Now."

I ignore him, sinking deeper into the murky waters of my subconsciousness, until he prises my eyelids open.

"Ouch!" I wail, squinting up at his masked face poised behind a flashlight.

"Follow me," he says.

I scramble to my knees from my fetal position on the floor and quickly assess my surroundings. I'm in a different cell. No bed or blankets, more locks on the door, and white padded walls.

My heart thunders. "Where am I?"

"Solitary confinement," Aiden replies, then heaves me up. "Move it. We don't have much time."

"Time for what?" I ask.

"You'll see," he says cryptically. "Put it on."

He hands me a soft, black balaclava. I stare at it blankly,

turning the ribbed fabric in my hands until he scowls and snatches it back. He shoves it over my head. It's tight, and the fabric sucks into my mouth with every breath.

My cell door creaks open.

"Hello, Little Ghost," Lex says from the doorway. A black-and-white checkered bandana covers the lower half of his face, and an unmoving orderly lays at his feet.

"Is he dead?" I ask.

"No," Lex says. "Unless you want him to be?"

"We have no time for games, Lex," Aiden snaps, shoving past him and dragging me out of the room.

I step over the orderly's body, and a noise from above draws my attention.

"Psst!"

A ceiling tile has been shifted to the left, revealing a gap where Eli crouches, waiting with outstretched arms.

"What—"

Before I finish my sentence, Aiden wraps his hands around my waist and hoists me into the air.

"Hold on," Eli says.

With Aiden supporting my weight from beneath, Eli hauls me into the ceiling. With one last heave, I collapse on top of him.

"Have you missed me?" Eli asks, grinning as I roll off him.

The cramped vent only leaves a few inches above Eli's head when sitting.

"Follow me," he instructs, flicking on the flashlight strapped to his head and crawling on all fours into the unknown.

I have no choice but to follow as Lex and Aiden join us, pulling the tile back into place behind them and condemning us to total darkness.

"Where are we going?" I ask.

My question echoes, but no one responds.

"Quiet," Aiden says. "Conserve your oxygen."

We settle into a rhythm and crawl for what seems like hours. We navigate tight bends and increasingly cramped vents that cover the length of the asylum. The faint noise of people talking below us grows louder the farther we go. Although I can't discern what they're saying, I recognize one voice.

Dad.

We make our way toward him. From his tone, he's annoyed about something. The vent widens, opening up to allow us enough space to sit upright.

Eli halts.

We've reached our destination.

"What did you say to her?" Dad rages beneath us.

Suddenly, the guys switch off their lights.

"Wha—"

Eli smothers my mouth with his hand, then pulls away to put a finger to my lips. Message received.

He shuffles to reveal a tiny shred of light coming from a gap where two pieces of steel don't quite meet. He wants me to look down. Gingerly, I lower myself, trying to stay quiet as I lie on my side. The metal chills my cheek as I peer through the hole at the scene unfurling below.

While I can't see the full room, I can tell we're in the secret part of Sunnycrest, where Dad conducts his vile experiments. I gaze into a white cell, watching Dad pace. Beside him, I see the heads of three other doctors who circle a chair in my direct line of sight where a patient is strapped down.

My stomach lurches as the patient struggles, bound by restraints on his hands and wrists. The victim's features are hard to make out. Strange lumps and pustules cover his face, like he's been attacked by a hive of angry bees. His only discernible feature is a mop of straggly, yellow hair.

I squeak in horror. It's Alfred. The boy I cornered for answers.

"Don't make me ask you a third time," Dad says. "What did you say to her?"

"I didn't tell her anything," Alfred whimpers, coughing up blood. "I swear, I didn't!"

Dad tsks. "It's a shame we've come to this, especially after making such good progress the last time you were in this chair."

He attaches electrodes to the sides of Alfred's head. Alfred wriggles around, making his restraints bite into his skin and draw blood, trapping him in place.

Dad walks out of my vision, presumably to a machine linked to the wires attached to Alfred.

"Stop!" Alfred croaks. His eyes wide with sheer terror. "Okay, I'll tell you! Just not that again. Please!"

Dad saunters back, wearing a twisted smile that shows the true psychopath he really is.

"Tell me," Dad probes. "What did you say?"

"All I said was that she already knows," Alfred says. "I swear, that's all."

Dad smiles and ruffles his hair affectionately. "Very good, Alfred."

"I promise I'll never speak to her again." Alfred sobs. "I won't say another word. She asked me the questions."

I bite my lip to stop myself from bawling. My father is evil. Seeing the tapes and hearing about his experiments was hard enough, but watching firsthand lets me see the pure pleasure he gets from causing others to suffer.

Dad strokes Alfred's bruised cheek tenderly.

His gentle gesture conjures a vision in my head.

The same fingers brush my cheek.

"It's going to be okay," Dad says.

I want to believe him. I really do. He dabs my forehead with a damp cloth. The coldness provides a brief reprieve from the burning sensation setting my skin on fire. However, despite his comforting words, I'm struck by more fear.

"You're going to be okay, Erin," Dad purrs. "Everything will be back to the way it was…"

"Everything will be okay, Alfred," Dad says.

Alfred's shoulders relax, buying his lies. Yet, I brace myself. Somehow, I know what's going to happen before it does.

Dad turns to another doctor and orders, "Maximum charge."

Alfred has no time to react as a thousand electric bolts shoot through his body. His eyes roll into the back of his head as his limbs convulse.

"Shall we stop?" a doctor asks as a machine bleeps like crazy. "His body won't sustain much more."

"No," Dad replies. "Keep going."

I want to look away, but I can't. I'm mesmerized by Alfred's twitching body and watch until a final drawn-out beep signals his heart has stopped. Even then, Dad keeps going, delighting in Alfred's dead body flailing around like a fish out of water. A puppet under his control.

Finally, when he's bored and Alfred's skin is steaming, Dad waves for the machine to be turned off.

"Take his body to the freezer," Dad says dismissively. He picks up Alfred's limp, burned arm to inspect it. "We can use his organs for our next experiment." Dad checks his watch and sighs. "I need to get home for dinner. My wife and I are hosting Sheriff Brady and his wife."

He hurries off and we remain in the vents, frozen, watching them wheel Alfred's corpse away.

He died because of me. If I hadn't hounded him for answers, none of this would have happened…

My mouth fills with the bitter taste of iron due to how hard I'm biting my lip. Silent tears soak through my balaclava. *He has to be stopped.* We need to put an end to my father's reign of terror for good. There must be a way to bring him down.

"Time to go," Aiden whispers.

He begins the journey back to my cell, but I don't move. I'm not only shaken by what I've seen, but by the fleeting memory that I've been here before, that I've been strapped to the same chair.

Eli gently nudges me.

"He's dead," Eli whispers. "Nothing will bring him back, and we'll all be dead if someone notices you're missing."

He's right.

My body enters autopilot, moving back through the tunnels. My ears are still ringing with Alfred's pleading. The crawl passes quickly. Aiden catches me as I drop from the ceiling, back into my padded cell, without saying a word.

I pull the mask off and slump to the floor, drawing my knees to my chest.

"We have to go," Lex says, peering around the cell door. "Or they'll find us."

"We can't leave her like this," Eli argues. "Look at her."

I rock back and forth.

That room…

The horrible smell of singed hair…

It transports me somewhere else…

"Wake up!" Dad's voice rings through the abyss. "Come back to me, angel."

Cold water douses my cheeks.

My entire body aches, and my eyelids feel like they're weighed down, but I open them. My irises burn from the stark light.

Machines whir.

White coats, clipboards, pens, squeaky shoes…

"There she is," Dad says. "Erin?"

"Yes?" I reply.

Dad's face lights up, smiling in triumph. "It's complete."

Others applaud. Doctor Warner stands among them, a strained smile on his face, feigning delight.

"I'm going to take you home," Dad says. "Everything will be fine."

"Where am I?" I ask.

"Don't worry about that now," Dad says. "You won't remember any of this. All you need to know is that I'm doing this for your own good."

"She's lost it," Eli says.

I cover my ears, sobbing as I rock.

I want these visions to stop, but they keep coming…

"Again!" Dad choruses.

They submerge my head in freezing water. Someone wrenches my head back. I gasp for air, just long enough to catch half a breath before I'm forced down. Water fills my mouth, and I scream silently, praying for the end, before I'm pulled out again, spluttering.

Piano music fills the room. It's almost deafening. I try to appreciate it, savoring the sound for a fraction of a second, before they shove my head below the surface once more.

"Again!"

I accept my fate. The water isn't clear. It's murky, with a yellow hue, and leaves a bitter taste in my mouth. I hope I'll drown. Anything to make it stop. The piano keeps playing, beckoning me closer.

Between my chattering teeth and the music, my thoughts are a jumbled mess. I can't tell what's real and what's not, or who I am. Everything is fragmented.

I'm wrenched up, dripping wet, and Dad drags me across the room toward the piano.

"Play," he commands.

Shaking, my fingers fumble with the keys.

"I said, play!" Dad instructs.

I keep trying, but I'm not good enough.

We always had lessons at the same time.

Sarah and Erin — the pianist twins.

I was never as good as she was, no matter how hard I tried. She was a natural, getting everything right the first time, but me? I had to work twice as hard. I never understood why we both had to play.

"I'm doing my best," I say through chattering teeth. "I really am. Please, Dad. I'll never be as good as her."

"You will!" He bangs his fist on top of the piano. "Practice makes perfect."

"I'll never be perfect," I say. "I'm not—"

He hauls me across the room again and plunges my head into the icy water.

"Enough, Erin!"

An earthquake rips through my brain, making it throb.

This isn't right...

This isn't me.

Eli shaking me pulls me back to the present. "Wake up!"

"Something's wrong," I mutter. "Something's wrong."

Mom was right. I really am sick.

"We have to leave," Lex says. "What if they find us here?"

"You two go," Aiden says. "I'll stay."

"You can't risk being seen," Lex hisses. "It's reckless."

"What's reckless is leaving her when we're so close," Aiden says. "I know the risks, and I make the fucking rules, remember?"

Eli hesitates. "But—"

"Go!" Aiden roars. "Now!"

The two of them scurry out, not daring to argue after seeing his thunderous expression.

I look up at Aiden. "Am I going crazy?"

He removes his mask and kneels by my side, smiling sadly. He holds my chin and tips my face up. I stare into his gray eyes, steeped in mystery and torment. Eyes that suddenly feel so comforting.

"We're all crazy," he replies.

"But the things I keep seeing in my head..." My sentence trails off. I squeeze my eyes shut to erase the visions, but they don't go. Not this time.

A few months ago, I was a star pupil at Stonybridge Academy. The most I had to worry about was a date to the Harvest Ball and college applications. Now, I'm unraveling. First, a simmering rage keeps rearing its ugly head. Now, visions that keep getting stronger the longer I'm in Sunnycrest. They feel real. Too real.

Aiden catches a tear as it slides down my cheek.

"What if I don't want to remember, Aiden?" I murmur.

"You have no choice," he says. "You need to come back to us. To finish what we started."

"Who am I?" My voice cracks. "Tell me the truth."

"You've always been ours." Aiden looks me in the eye. "*Sarah.*"

PART THREE
PLAYING WITH FIRE
THE PAST

I DANCE around the open firepit, enjoying the breeze on my skin. Music blares from a nearby truck. Everyone is drunk, high, or both. The monthly rave at the old campground is infamous in the area and has been for years. The cops turn a blind eye to the popular party site. They've all been young once, and hey! It beats parents getting their houses trashed by a bunch of adolescents who need to blow off steam.

Erin caught me sneaking out again, obviously. Every time I clamber down the trellis, her head pops out of the window to remind me what will happen if Dad finds out I'm gone. I've long given up on asking her to come with me. She's happiest with her stupid piano. I'd rather blow my brains out than sit through another of her classical renditions on a Friday night. Talk about dull. Thank fuck Dad doesn't pay for me to have music lessons anymore.

Everyone cheers as another truck pulls up with a fresh keg. A bunch of jocks gather, taking it in turns to stick their heads under the foam. Max Carter is one of them. He ducks out after swallowing a mouthful to a round of applause.

A girl I barely know swoons next to me.

"You're so lucky," she says, gushing over Max's display. "You're dating Max, right?"

"It's early days," I reply with a shrug.

It's nothing serious. Max isn't my usual type, but he has killer abs and isn't totally selfish in the bedroom, unlike a few other members of the hockey team I'd rather forget about. Better still, my darling sister has had a crush on him for years, not that she'll admit it, which makes screwing him even sweeter.

Some may argue it's petty to only date a guy because your sister likes him, and maybe I am. Being a twin means growing up in constant competition, and Erin usually wins every time. She's Daddy's little angel who does nothing wrong and gets whatever she wants at the click of her fingers, but me? I'm the fucking devil. The daughter he hates. The one he's determined to suck the life out of.

Much to my father's dismay, I'm a free spirit. Live, laugh, love, fuck, and drink until the sun comes up, or however the phrase goes.

Erin's my opposite. Studious, prim, timid. She gets straight *A*'s, and our entire house is a museum dedicated to showcasing her trophies boasting of impressive academic achievements. Despite that, she's basically a social pariah, which means I'm at least better than her at one thing. Although, hooking up with guys and partying doesn't look great on a résumé.

If Little Miss Perfect isn't already unbearable enough, she's recently started lecturing me about my behavior. If she kept her mouth shut, I wouldn't have felt obligated to hook up with Max. Ironically, if she actually admitted her feelings and got her nose out from under a book, they'd probably make a good match. Not that I'll tell her that.

"Sarah!" Max waves at me through the throng of partiers. "Wanna dance?"

I down my drink and shimmy over. We dance together; I grind on him in my tiny hot pants. God, I wish nights like this could last forever. Being at home drives me crazy.

Thankfully, Dad works away a lot, but he dropped a fresh bombshell at dinner. We're moving to Pasturesville at the end of the semester, so he'll be closer to the asylum.

I don't see why we have to go. We have everything we need here, but he's intent on making me suffer. Even worse, he wants to send us to a fancy private school called Stonybridge Academy. Naturally, Erin is delighted. It'll be the perfect place for her to thrive among a bunch of entitled assholes.

Dad has spent years rubbing shoulders with the most important people in Pasturesville, pretending he's one of them to build an image of respectability. I'm one of the few people who can see beyond his facade. He's a wife-beating faker. He desperately wants to fit in, but he doesn't. Just like Erin.

Sneaking out tonight is my big old 'fuck you' to his plans. I need to celebrate while I can.

"Come on," I whisper, grabbing Max's hand and pulling him away from the crowd. "Let's go somewhere quiet."

We stop at a private spot between the trees, out of sight from the others. He kisses me, and I slide my hands over the front of his pants.

Suddenly, Max breaks off.

I frown. "What's wrong?"

Usually, he's already under my shirt by now.

"I love hooking up with you," he says. "Don't get me wrong, the sex is fucking incredible. But maybe we can talk tonight?"

"Talk?" I laugh and kiss his neck. Anything to shut him up. "We can talk anytime."

My annoyance rises when he shrugs me off again.

"We've been dating for a few months, and I don't know anything about you," he says. "I mean, not really."

What a fucking bore. He's ruining the party vibe.

"What more do you want to know?" I sigh. "You know all

there is to know. I'm on the cheer squad, I'm failing math, and I love Mexican food."

"What about your family?" he prompts. "I've not met your parents yet. Every time I bring them up—"

"There's nothing to say," I say sharply.

"What about the marks on your thighs? The cuts?" he says. "I've not asked about them before, but I've seen them."

I shove his chest.

"Since when are you a fucking therapist?" I ask. "In case you've forgotten, we're at a party."

"I'm worried about you," he says. "I care about you."

This always happens. Guys are supposed to fuck without catching feelings, but that doesn't seem to be my experience. At the beginning, they're happy to have sex with no strings, and then they keep wanting more from me. More I'm unwilling to give. Neediness is such a drag.

"You're not my boyfriend, Max."

"I'd like to be," he says, his eyes shining with a false hope that I want to stamp out.

I don't want a boyfriend. Ever. If anyone got close enough to know what I'm really like, they wouldn't want to know me at all. They'd see how fucked up I am. How fucked up he's made me. Staying surface level is best. Pretending is easier.

"I've already told you, I don't do relationships," I say, kissing his neck. "Aren't you happy with things how they are?"

His face falls like a wounded puppy. It takes every ounce of self-control not to roll my eyes.

"But I thought—"

"You thought wrong," I say, stepping away with a disappointed sigh. "I need a drink."

Talk about clingy…

I return to the party and corner the local dealer. Typically, he's run out of pills. Why tonight? I'm craving something to take the edge off, and lukewarm beer isn't cutting it.

Laurie hurries to join me.

"Have you and Max had a fight?" she asks, masking her glee with fake concern after noticing us leave the forest separately.

Laurie is the cheer squad captain and the closest person I have to a best friend. Although she acts nice, she secretly hates me, along with anyone else she sees as a threat. Keep your friends close, but your enemies closer is my motto.

"No," I lie, not wanting to give her any ammunition. "We're fine, and we're not dating—remember? We're keeping it casual."

"Oh yeah," she says. "I forgot your dad doesn't let you date."

I don't add that it's also because I don't want to.

Up ahead, a blinding headlight cuts through the leaves. A few couples getting to third base scream as the car stops.

Fuck, I recognize the plate…

"Oh, shit!" Laurie chuckles. "Someone's in trouble."

Dad gets out of the car and marches over with a face like thunder.

"Sarah!" he yells. "Your sister told me I'd find you here. What part of 'you're grounded' don't you understand?"

Fucking Erin. Why can't she keep her mouth shut?

"The staying in the house part, it seems," I reply sarcastically.

"Get in the car," he orders through gritted teeth. A vein in his temple pulses. I wonder whether it's possible for someone's head to combust and what his brains would look like sprayed everywhere. "Right now."

I roll my eyes. "Fine."

I'm not in the party mood anymore, anyway.

I stomp away, leaving him trailing behind. It's not the first time he's shown up at a party uninvited. I slam the car door closed and cross my arms with a huff.

"You can save your breath," I say when he slides in next to me. "I get it. I'm a disappointment."

"You've been drinking," he states as we drive away.

"So?" I counter. "You're moving me away from all my friends soon. Aren't I allowed a little celebration?"

"You're not twenty-one."

"Who waits until twenty-one to drink?" I roll my eyes. "Don't you remember being a teenager? This is normal. You don't see other parents showing up."

"That's because their parents don't care what happens to them."

"Don't pretend you care about me," I snap. "All you care about is your precious fucking reputation."

Dad slams on the brakes, jolting us forward.

"I should sue you for whiplash," I mutter, rubbing my neck dramatically.

"That's it," he says, hitting the gas. "I've had enough."

Usually, Dad sticks religiously to the speed limit. Now, he hurtles around corners like a rally driver. I'd give him kudos if it wasn't dark and scary as shit.

"Where are we going?" I ask, clinging to my seat.

He ignores me as we set off toward Pasturesville.

Maybe I've pushed Daddy dearest too far this time.

A WOMAN'S high-pitched wail interrupts the whirring of machines that runs constantly in this empty part of the building, making us halt. We're on one of our usual midnight excursions to map the vents and plan our imminent escape. Below us, the rooms are reserved for storage. No one should be in them, especially at this hour.

"Is it a new subject?" Eli asks.

It's unusual for Acacia to admit someone new at night. Normally, it takes all day to check them in. They're forced to parade around in front of doctors and undergo many tests. Some don't even make it until sunset.

"I don't think so," I reply.

This feels different.

I creep a few feet forward and put my eye to a crack in the metal.

I see Acacia beneath me. He's soaked from head to toe, donning a long trench coat that leaves a wet trail on the concrete floor. He drags a girl by her hair. They've come straight from the parking lot, and they're followed by a gust of blustery wind from an open door.

The girl screams like a banshee. He tugs her hard, pulling her along like a dog on a leash. Black mascara runs down her cheeks, leaving dirty streaks behind. She's wearing tiny denim hot pants that show half her ass, and her fluorescent pink bra is visible through a white crop top.

"That's it," Acacia rages. "Enough, enough, enough! How many times do I have to repeat myself?"

"Get off me!" She claws his arms. "You're fucking insane!"

When she turns her head, I recognize her instantly. We've seen her before. In fact, we see her every year at Acacia's annual event.

"You bastard!" she shrieks. "Let go, or I'll tell Mom! Or are you so bored with hitting her now that you're gonna hurt me?"

"I'm doing this for your own good," Acacia says with a voice like ice, opening the door to a disused store room.

"Fuck you," she hisses.

He throws her inside. Her body careers into the wall, and she lands with a thud.

"I'll be back," he threatens. "We start your treatment tomorrow."

She scrambles up to escape, but she's too slow. He slams the door in her face and locks her inside. She bangs against the wood, pounding hard with her fists, but no one will hear her. She yells more vicious insults, but Acacia pays no attention and disappears into the night.

He should know better than to leave his daughter here alone.

My cock hardens as a shiver of excitement runs through me. Tonight's adventures are about to get a lot more interesting.

She's hot, I can't deny that. Her long blonde hair gives her a Barbie-like appearance, but she has the spirit of a wild tiger. She's exactly what we've been looking for.

"We should make her feel at home," I say.

Lex chuckles. "And welcome her to Sunnycrest the proper way."

"It'd be bad manners not to," Eli agrees.

We initiate all new patients in gen pop when they arrive. No matter what we force them to endure, it always ends in them swearing their undying loyalty to us. Nothing will bring me greater pleasure than having Acacia's daughter on her knees, begging us for mercy.

We can't rush, though.

We wait long enough to be sure Acacia isn't coming back, letting the anticipation build. It's hard to be patient when her screams turn into pleading. But he's not coming back. Not yet, anyway.

I carefully remove the screws from the vent.

"Dad!" she screams. "Let me out! You've made your point, okay? You just need to chill and have some fucking fun! I'm sorry I'm not your perfect daughter—"

I push the vent aside, and she freezes.

"Hello?" she calls. "Who's there?"

I wriggle myself through the gap and drop into the room.

She looks me up and down. A mischievous smile plays on her lips, drying her tears instantly.

"Oh, it's you," she says calmly in a tone edging on boredom.

When we show up in a patient's cell, their reactions usually range from screaming to tears to shitting their pants. Yet she barely blinks.

Lex and Eli drop to the floor next to me, and Acacia's daughter crosses her arms.

"You took my cigarettes," she says, pouting at me. "I want them back."

I laugh coldly. "You're in our territory now, Acacia. You don't get to make demands."

"Pity." She sighs. "I fancy a smoke."

Uneasiness settles in my stomach. This isn't how I expected our meeting to go. Where is her quivering bottom lip or begging for her daddy?

"Am I supposed to be scared?" she asks, reading my mind and stepping closer. She trails a red, manicured nail down my chest, sending a jolt of electricity coursing through me as her eyes meet mine in defiance. "Because I'm not."

For the first time in a long time, I'm speechless.

She looks over my shoulder. "Are these your enforcers?"

"Fuck you," Lex snarls in his most menacing voice. "You don't know anything."

She laughs, swishing her blonde hair.

"Does my dad know you skulk around the asylum at night?" she asks, raising her eyebrows. "This is the second time I've caught you. What're you locked up for, anyway?" She screws up her nose at my necklace. "Are those rat skulls?"

My fingers fly to my skulls. There are only three of them hanging on my chain. I have many more skulls stashed in our cell. I can't remember when I started collecting them. Until I had Eli and Lex, the rats were my only friends, and keeping a part of them with me brings me some comfort. I never take the necklace off and, no matter what happens, I'll never be alone again while they're with me.

"We don't have to answer your questions," I growl.

"No, you don't," she replies. "But it'll help pass the time."

She reaches into her bra to retrieve a cell phone.

"What?" She winks. "Do you really think I only have one phone with a father like mine?" She holds it above her head. "Shit. No signal."

"Aren't you worried about being locked up with three men who hate your father?" I ask. "Three men who'd do anything to see him suffer."

"If you wanted to hurt me, you'd have done it already," she says. "Besides, we're on the same side."

Eli splutters in disbelief. "The same side?"

"Doesn't sharing an enemy make us friends? We all hate

my father," she says. "I'm Sarah, by the way. If you don't remember."

"We'll never be friends," Lex hisses. "And we don't care what your name is."

She saunters over and whispers in his ear, "I think you do."

He flinches, but his eyes light up. He's intrigued. We all are, and I find myself jealous that he's gotten so close to her. Close enough to feel her breath on his skin. Close enough to smell her.

Fuck, I want her. No, I *need* her.

"The way I see it, you have two options," Sarah says, exuding the same arrogant self-confidence she did the first time we met. "You can keep up your little circus act by trying to get me to fear you, or we can spend the night really getting to know each other."

I clench my jaw. "What do you have in mind?"

She undresses slowly. First, she pulls off her wet T-shirt to expose her toned stomach and perky tits. Next, she unzips her boots, drawing attention to her toned calves, before wiggling out of her hot pants to reveal a pink thong. Fresh cuts cover the tops of her thighs, and a rush of protectiveness surges through me. She's damaged. Broken. Just like us. An unexpected burst of rage makes my hands curl into fists. Whoever made her want to hurt herself deserves to bleed out.

"You can put your tongues back in your heads. What did you expect? I'm soaking wet." She cocks her head. "I need to warm up before I catch a cold."

She's a fucking psycho. Perhaps even crazier than we are.

I wrap my fingers around her neck. "You don't know what you're asking."

She laughs as her hand glides down my body to stroke my erection through my pants.

"I think I do," she whispers.

We both lean in, and our lips brush. She tastes of cherry

lip gloss and rum. We don't kiss. Not yet. Our breaths melt together, and then she sinks her teeth into my bottom lip, biting hard enough to make me bleed.

I release her throat. "Fuck!"

She licks her lips. "Mmm."

"What's your game?" Lex snarls. "No sane girl would throw herself at three random guys from Sunnycrest."

"I never said I was sane." Sarah winks, unfastening her bra and letting it fall to her feet. "Don't you want to fuck Acacia's daughter raw?"

My cock throbs, dying to touch her, but still holding back.

"Maybe we don't want to touch a little slut who'll spread her legs for anyone," Lex answers.

She nods at the growing tent in his pants. "Liar." She turns to Eli. "Can you talk?"

Eli, thus far, has stayed silent. He isn't like me or Lex. Sex means something to him.

"Leave him alone," I say.

"Come on," she purrs. "Having fun isn't a crime."

"I could snap your neck in a second," I warn.

"Do it," she challenges. "I dare you."

I grab her throat. For a brief second, her eyes widen with fear. She isn't completely stupid. I push her against the wall and lift her up, and her toes skirt the floor as I squeeze the air from her lungs.

Crazy meets crazy when our pupils dilate.

We're the same.

Her nipples harden as she wraps her arms around my neck, and her thighs clench around my middle, drawing me closer.

Our mouths reunite with a new hunger. The metallic taste of my blood mixes with her sweet gloss. While she clings to me, I unleash my cock with my spare hand and slide her sodden thong aside. Fuck, it feels incredible to know how turned on she is, and I'm not gonna disappoint.

I don't wait for permission. Why should I? She's already soaking. It's easy to glide into her cunt with a single deep thrust. She claws my shoulders with every violent motion, and her pleasure-filled cries vibrate my throbbing dick. She's loving this as much, if not more, than I am.

She gasps as I choke her.

"Harder," she croaks. Her pussy tenses. "Harder!"

I've heard people say that they can pinpoint specific moments in their lives when everything changed. This is one of those moments. While I'm balls deep in this dirty slut, I know that life will never be the same because she's mine now. All fucking mine.

"Fuck, yes!" she moans as I claim her. "Yes, yes, yes!"

Maybe this is just a game to her. She's a bratty, entitled bitch wanting to fuck a few psychos to get back at her father, but it's not a game she'll win.

After tonight, I'll never let Sarah Acacia go.

HIS COCK FILLS ME COMPLETELY. He isn't like Max, or any of the guys from high school I've slept with. He's an animal. Fucking him taps into my raw, primal instincts. He isn't full of false bravado, like my ex-boyfriend, who wanted constant praise. This psychopath doesn't need any compliments. There's no pretense. He takes what he wants, and it's fucking exhilarating. Usually, I don't spread my legs until the third date but, for them, I'll make an exception.

I come hard, gushing all over him, while his friends watch. Knowing they're watching only makes me moan louder. The guys must be more than a little unstable to be in Sunnycrest, but they're not stupid. They sneak around under my father's nose undetected, which proves their intelligence, and hey, I'm a sucker for a rule breaker. After all, if I did what I was told, I wouldn't be here now.

He, their brooding leader, lowers me to the floor. His cum drips down my inner thighs. I slide my panties back into place casually, acting as if he hasn't just fucked my brains out.

I turn my attention to the silent brooder. He's hot with an intense look that hides a dangerous side. I reach for his face. He doesn't speak as I stroke his cheekbone and wipe a strand of his fair hair away. Suddenly, he catches my wrist, shocking me with the strength of his grip. If I twist at the wrong angle, he'll break it.

"Careful, sweetheart," he warns in his Southern drawl, conjuring an image of him in a cowboy hat in my head. His voice is deep and hearty, with a warmness that makes my skin tingle, but it has a sharp edge, adding an ominous air. "You don't know what you're getting yourself into."

"Yes, I do," I reply indignantly, then bat my eyelashes. "And don't call me sweetheart. I'm no fucking sweetheart."

He chuckles, dropping my wrist. "I see that."

"Just fuck her already," the smart-ass British guy says, rolling his eyes. "She's already Aiden's sloppy seconds."

"You shouldn't have said my name in front of her," the man who was inside me seconds before growls.

"Don't worry, *Aiden*," I say, flashing him a big smile and winking. "I won't tell, if you don't." I wag my finger at the obnoxious Brit. "What's your problem? Are you jealous because you didn't get to have me first?"

The guy flicks open a Zippo and waves it from side to side. The flame dances in the darkness. So far, he's lurked in the shadows, but he steps out of them now. The fire illuminates scars on the side of his face, and his eyebrows lower in fury because of my teasing. He clearly has a massive ego, which will make annoying him more fun.

"Watch that pretty mouth of yours," the scarred, dark-haired monster purrs. "Or we'll cut your body into little pieces and send it to your mother in gift-wrapped boxes."

I snort, holding back a laugh. Maybe I'm being reckless. He could be an actual murderer—he wouldn't be the first killer to stay in this asylum—and this might be a real threat. However, it's refreshing to be around a person who says what's on their mind with zero bullshit.

"Unless you put my limbs in Cartier boxes, my mom won't be interested," I say.

The cowboy snickers and extends his hand. "I'm Eli." He nods his head at my British nemesis. "That's Lex."

"It's a pleasure." I shake Eli's hand. His giant palm dwarves mine. Rough calluses cover his fingers, but his grasp is surprisingly soft. He raises my hand to his lips and kisses it, making Aiden bristle at my side.

"The pleasure is all mine," Eli says.

"Please," Lex scoffs. "You only want to get your dick wet."

I whirl around to face Lex. He leans against the wall leisurely, exuding an alluring arrogance. He's gorgeous with angular features, and his scars only make him more interesting. I'm tired of normal boys. Lex has obviously been through serious shit, and that draws me in.

Lex arches one eyebrow. "Like what you see, *sweetheart*?"

"And here I thought British guys were supposed to have manners," I say. "Obviously, I was wrong."

"And here I thought the daughter of a famous psychiatrist would have class," he mocks. He'd be more infuriating if he didn't have a face that begs to be sat on. "Do you fuck anyone as soon as you meet them, or is it just us who have that honor?"

"I never said I'd fuck you," I say, despite my pussy tingling with anticipation.

Fucking guys isn't something I have a problem with, but wanting to fuck them a second time? Well, that rarely happens, but these men? They're different. I feel like I'm standing on the edge of a cliff and they're daring me to jump, and I want to. Oh God, how I want to…

"Let's not pretend," Lex says, continuing to wave his lighter around. I approach and whip my hand quickly through the flame, fast enough not to burn myself but slow enough to register the heat. Lex's eyes light up. "You like games, huh?"

I lean in close, and whisper, "You have no idea."

He stares straight into my soul when I pull away.

"Why are you here, Sarah Acacia?" he asks.

"Because my father can't control me," I reply. "No matter how hard he tries."

Eli nods. "She's like us."

"No," Aiden says with a scowl. "She's not. She'll never understand."

"Can you swim, Sarah?" Lex asks, stroking my collarbone. "Because I think you're trying to stay afloat. You're kicking your legs, bobbing above the surface, but every so often, you're dragged down. You keep kicking, hoping no one notices that you're secretly drowning. You're drowning because you're afraid you'll never know what true happiness is. Drowning because you're worried you don't know how to feel at all. Drowning because no one sees you until you're splashing, causing a scene, gasping for air. By then, it's too late. Until then, they don't see what's happening underneath... but I do."

I gulp, swallowing hard.

Maybe this is a mistake.

Sex is one thing. It's easy to separate my body from my mind, but Lex has managed to pinpoint how I feel, even though I struggle to articulate it myself. If a crazy psychopath from Sunnycrest understands, what does that say about me?

"Am I right?" Lex prompts.

I don't answer.

"We understand you," Lex says, brushing my lips with his thumb to make them part. He slides a finger into my mouth, and I lock my lips around it. "Mmm. I see right through you like you're a ghost. You want revenge, don't you?"

I suck his finger, pretending it's his cock, without breaking eye contact. Lex's erection twitches in his pants.

"I'll take that as a yes," Lex says.

Eli creeps up behind me and sweeps my hair around to

the front. He licks along the curve of my shoulder from behind, making me moan while sandwiching me between him and Lex.

"We're going to make you ours," Eli murmurs.

"Yes," I whisper, basking in the longing for them. "Fuck… yes…"

I don't hesitate, despite having never been with more than one man at once before. Being pressed between them makes me crave more. A desperate need blooms inside me, growing stronger the longer I'm wedged between their bodies.

Lex pulls the edge of my thong away from my skin, then holds his lighter to it, setting the thin string alight. I don't wince, my desire overshadowing any fear of being licked by flames.

"Careful," Lex says. "Or you'll get burned."

The smell of singed fabric fills the air as the side of my panties falls away. He moves the flame to the other side, watching my reaction like this is some kind of test. Again, I don't move.

My burned underwear drops to the floor.

"There's no going back now," Eli whispers, leaving me completely naked.

Aiden watches from the side of the room, crossing his muscular arms. I meet his gaze, and he grins.

"We see right through you," Aiden says. "You don't know what you're getting yourself into."

I run my hands through Lex's black hair, then kiss him passionately. I open one eye to look at Aiden as if to say, *Does this look like the face of a person who doesn't know what she's doing?*

I groan as Eli's fingers slip between my legs. I gasp into Lex's mouth as Eli circles my wet entrance, then he slides two fingers inside me, covering himself in my wetness and Aiden's cum.

"Who's going first, Eli?" Lex asks like I'm invisible.

"I'm not a sex toy," I hiss. "And for that comment, you're going last."

I spin to face Eli and trail a finger down his chest. He's ripped; his abs feel like they're carved from stone. He's hotter than any player on the hockey team and makes Max look weedy in comparison.

"Careful," Eli drawls in his delicious accent. Him riding on horseback will be my fantasy the next time I'm touching myself alone. "Lex doesn't like being told what to do."

I pout, and say, "Neither do—" *Fuck!* I yelp. Lex grabs my hips and yanks me back to his impatiently waiting cock. "You bastard!"

"A bastard you're wet for," Lex mocks, rubbing his hardness between my ass cheeks.

"You can save the best for last," Eli says, stroking my hair. "But while I wait…"

Eli wraps my blonde hair around his fist like a boxer taping his hands before a fight. He tugs hard to force my head lower while unsheathing his cock with his other hand. He's big and girthy, twitching from arousal. Above it, his defined V-line muscles are surrounded by scars that I get a brief flash of as he pushes me down until I'm head-to-head with the tip of his dick.

Lex takes advantage of the opportunity, entering me from behind in a slick movement with a grunt. I gasp in surprise, and Eli seizes the chance to force my mouth onto his velvety shaft.

My tits jolt with Lex's violent thrusts, and I groan onto Eli. I gag as he rams his cock farther down my throat, making my jaw widen to where it feels like it'll break. Their combined movements make tears stream from my eyes as I struggle to catch my breath.

"Fuck yeah," Lex groans in victory. "She's so fucking tight. How is the little slut's mouth?"

"So." Eli holds my head with both hands to face fuck me

with maximum control. "Fucking." I choke, slathering him in my spit. "Good."

Eli slows, giving me a second to glance at Aiden. *Where is he?* I can't see him, yet my skin prickles, knowing he's still watching.

My legs quake as Lex pounds into me aggressively, making a slapping noise. He and Eli move in perfect synchronicity, timing every thrust to coincide with my mouth working on Eli's cock.

"Come for me," Lex commands.

Usually, I never follow orders, but this time, I do as instructed.

"Good girl," Eli purrs.

My orgasm unravels, like a twisted coil finally snapping, and my pussy clamps onto Lex's cock. Eli's thighs clench, letting me know he's close as my muffled screams vibrate his body. He doesn't come yet, though. He's saving himself.

I tense and quiver, suspended in a state of pure bliss as Lex reaches around to stroke my clit as I come. His probing touch adds pressure to prolong my pleasure. I guess he isn't that selfish after all…

When my peaks of pleasure fade from a blinding explosion to a simmering warmth, Lex spanks my ass and jolts me back to reality. That'll leave a red handprint behind. He pulls out, almost all the way, leaving an inch skirting around my entrance.

"Hold it there for a sec," Aiden says. I can't see what he's doing, but I don't care. It feels too good. "Perfect."

Lex plunges into me slowly, again and again.

"Hurry up, Lex," Eli growls. "It's my turn." He yanks my head off his cock and forces me to look up. He smiles. "Jesus, you're so fucking beautiful."

Beautiful? Although I can't see myself, I'm sure I look a mess. Makeup runs down my face, and my eyes will be bloodshot from choking. Yet, he still looks at me like I'm the most precious object in the world. My heart flips. Fucking them was only supposed to be a way to pass the time, but Eli's expression fills me with such an intense high that it makes it almost impossible to look away. A high like that is addictive. Something I'll do anything to chase. I'm in deep shit…

Lex shatters our moment, grasping my hips with a guttural roar. He thrusts deep, spilling his devil seed, then withdraws with a satisfied sigh.

"She's all yours, Eli," Lex declares proudly.

I stand up straight, and Lex's cum dribbles down the insides of my legs. Eli doesn't care. He laces his fingers through mine while Lex makes a retching noise.

"Do you want me to make you feel good?" Eli whispers.

"I didn't think you guys asked," I say. "Don't you take what you want?"

"Oh, we do," Eli says, drawing me closer until my tits press against his chest. "But I'm still a gentleman."

I forget the others are watching as Eli sweeps me away. His tongue coaxes my lips open, and our kiss hits like a tidal wave as his fingers weave through my hair, clinging on tightly like he never wants to let go. Then, just as fast, he pulls away, leaving me breathless, and spins me to press my back into the wall.

He hoists my thigh to wrap it around his body and strokes my leg, teasing me with his gentle swirling motions as he makes his way to my pussy. I tingle with anticipation as he circles my clit. The aftershocks of my earlier orgasms make every touch ten times more sensitive.

I no longer care about why these men are patients. No one knows how to pleasure a woman like they do.

"Just fuck her already," Lex says.

Aiden clicks his tongue impatiently. "We're running out of time."

I peer around Eli in irritation, prepared to tell Aiden to stop getting his balls in a twist and find him holding a phone.

My jaw drops in horror. "Are you filming?"

What are they going to do with it?

Worse still, what happens if it gets into my father's hands?

Aiden approaches, and I breathe a sigh of relief to see it's my cell phone.

"Call it a memento to remember us by." Aiden grins, then addresses Eli, "Hurry the fuck up."

Eli lifts me into the air, and I squeeze my legs around his torso. His cock slides effortlessly inside me. He uses me, moving me up and down his shaft like I'm weightless. His pace quickens, fucking the life out of me, while Aiden captures my expression on camera. I smile and wink at the lens, enjoying being the star of my own porno.

"How does it feel?" Aiden prompts.

"So fucking good," I moan. "He's so big."

"Fuck her good, Eli," Aiden orders. "Pound her pussy hard enough that she won't be able to sit down tomorrow."

Eli doesn't need any encouragement. His earlier tenderness vanishes in an instant, and a new wildness sweeps through him, like an untamed beast who has just escaped from its cage. His blue eyes darken, like a demon has crawled underneath his skin to possess him. The sudden shift makes my mind whir, questioning what else he's capable of...

Eli's panting makes the hairs on the back of my neck stand on end. My fear and desire mingle together, creating an intoxicating mix. If I love this, what's wrong with me? I'll have to question my morality later because, right now, my body has other ideas. My pussy clamps down, chasing the dangerous high again.

"You're all ours," Eli whispers.

His husky words tip me over the edge. He comes at the same time.

Black dots cloud my vision, leaving me a trembling mess.

When he's finished and my tremors have eased, he gently lifts me off.

"Time to go," Aiden says, tapping his wrist.

"You're gonna leave?" I ask incredulously. "Just like that?"

"What's the matter?" Lex teases. "Three cocks weren't enough and you're wanting more already?"

I scowl. "Fuck you."

"Enjoy your gift," Aiden says, returning my cell phone with a grin. A grin that makes my insides quake. "But, make no mistake, this isn't the end."

"What do you mean?" I ask.

"You're ours now," Aiden says. "All fucking ours."

He scans my body and licks his lips like I'm a meal he wants to devour. His brooding intensity should make me feel uneasy. Instead, it captivates me. Before now, I've never wanted a relationship. No one has been worth my time, but tonight has changed that. Although I won't admit it to them, I want to be owned by these monsters more than I've ever wanted anything.

"I belong to no one," I say, despite my instincts.

"You do now," Aiden says possessively. "You're all fucking ours. We will see you again soon."

"Not if I see you first," I promise.

"Unbelievable." Lex shakes his head. "We spend all of our time trying to get out of this place, and she already wants to come back."

He's right. It's crazy to want to return here, but if I get a welcome like I had today, then sign me the fuck up. Besides, my home isn't so different from Sunnycrest. I'm not locked up, but I basically live in a prison under my father's control. We're more similar than they realize.

"We won't be here for long," Aiden says. "She will help us get out. She hates her father as much as we do."

"If I came back to Sunnycrest, how would you know?" I

ask, anticipation already building at the prospect of seeing them again.

Aiden snickers. "We know everything that happens here. Your father isn't the only one who runs Sunnycrest. We do."

Eli scoops up my singed panties from the floor and stashes them in his pocket. He smiles. The lingering crazy in his eyes that came to the surface when we fucked has already faded.

"See you soon, Sarah Acacia."

HE BRINGS her here as a punishment. It's been four months since our first encounter, and we've seen her almost every other weekend. He locks her in the same room, hoping that it will somehow lead to a miraculous breakthrough. One time, when he was particularly angry, he integrated her with the general population for a weekend. She ate with the rest of the patients in the cafeteria which, he hoped, would frighten her into submission. Instead, Sarah picked a fight with Charlie and asserted herself as the rightful queen of Sunnycrest within a matter of minutes. Acacia is at a loss. He underestimates her. He seriously believes that she's not clever enough to conceal her tracks when breaking his rules. However, he doesn't know she has an ulterior reason for wanting to be caught.

"What did you do this time?" I ask.

I've been in Sunnycrest so long that I've become institutionalized. Hearing stories about the outside world provides a welcome break, and Sarah's rebellious acts are my new favorite source of entertainment.

"Another party." She shrugs. "Erin told him where I'd be. It turns out her being under Daddy's thumb isn't so bad, after all. How are the others?"

"That reminds me," I say, reaching into my pocket and taking out a rat skull. "A gift from Aiden."

Her eyes light up and she stashes it in her purse. "I'll have to show him how thankful I am next time I see him."

"I guess I'll just have to do until then," I mutter sarcastically.

"Hey!" She grabs my face, and her voice softens. "You're enough on your own, you know. You don't need Aiden. Let's forget about him and Lex. Right now, it's just me and you against the world."

She always knows what to say to make me feel better. I pull her into a tight embrace and breathe in her sweet jasmine shampoo, craving how her warm body feels. Being with her always leaves me wanting more. More kissing. More fucking. More talking. More everything. If I had my way, I'd never leave her side.

I love her. I feel it deep in my bones, even though Aiden and Lex tell me I can't be sure what love is. Love is whatever *this* is. It's wanting to crawl under her skin and wear her because I'll never be able to get close enough. She's mine now. Ours. Aiden and Lex refuse to admit it, but they feel the same way. Why else do they keep rejecting the queue of girls begging to fuck them? They haven't been with anyone else since our first night with Sarah.

The others can't see her tonight. A change in guards has made our nighttime explorations more challenging, and they're working on a new angle. They're going to visit a new doctor. Unlike the others, Doctor Warner appears to sympathize with our cause, and we have to exploit any sign of weakness in Acacia's regime.

"Does it hurt?" Sarah asks, frowning at the fresh scar around my throat that looks like a red choker. A gift from her father's latest experiment. "It looks painful."

"This is nothing, sweetheart," I say dismissively. "I'm fine."

It's good that Aiden and Lex aren't here. They're in worse shape than me. Lex's shoulder is a wreck from being dislocated and put back into place repeatedly, and Aiden's left eye is swollen shut.

Acacia recently offered complimentary sessions for potential investors, and we're the subjects he gives them to, to torture for fun. It's nothing too bad, though. He keeps the worst punishments for paying customers. This afternoon, he paraded around his new subjects in a grim death march. They are the ones who will be subjected to his worst experiments, and we are his poster boys. Hurting us is less fun now that we're desensitized to pain, but we're still favorites to some regulars, who have watched us for years, hoping to see us finally break.

"Did my father hurt you?" she probes. "Did he do this?"

We haven't gone into detail about her father's real work here or the experiments he conducts. I'd tell her in an instant, but Aiden doesn't trust her. Not yet. He's cautious, and it's something we've argued about. She has a right to know who she's living with. She's told us how he beats her mother, but she'll still be shocked at the true depths of his depravity. Aiden's not sure she can handle the truth. However much she hates him, he's still her father.

"I can't talk about it," I say. "We don't have long, sweetheart. Why waste our time talking?"

I like having her all to myself. Sharing is fun, but it's more special when it's only the two of us.

"None of you ever answer my questions," she says, turning her head as I lean in for a kiss. "Something bad is happening here. I'm not stupid. Every time I see you, you all have fresh scars. Whatever it is, I can handle it. You can't hide it forever!"

"Not forever," I say. "But not yet."

Although I don't agree with Aiden, I will never defy him.

"You mean, Aiden says you can't tell me," she mutters

sarcastically. "I keep coming back, don't I? Doesn't that show I can be trusted?"

"Partying and flirting with hockey players isn't hard work," I say bitterly, unable to keep the jealousy from my voice. "There's more to trust than fucking someone."

"That's all I am to you? An easy lay?" She crosses her arms. "I think you should leave."

"Sarah—"

"No, Eli," she snaps. "You've made it perfectly clear what you think of me. Maybe I'll stop breaking the rules for a while and be a good girl. You can all find some other slut to fuck. I'm sure there are plenty in here."

My face falls. She notices. A smug smirk plays on her lips. Bitch. She's playing me, and I've shown my hand. She knows I need her just as much as she needs me, if not more.

I grab her throat. "You will never stop breaking the rules, Sarah Acacia."

"What aren't you telling me, Eli?"

I let go of her with an exasperated sigh. Questions. Questions. More fucking questions!

"We'll tell you when the time is right," I say. "Isn't that good enough?"

"I'm not very patient." She taps her foot. "I did everything you asked. I searched my father's office. I listened to his conversations. I recorded his calls. And, for what? What exactly do you expect me to find?"

"Someone has to stop him!" I explode. "We need to find evidence that'll put him behind bars!"

"So he does hurt you," she says. "The scars. The injuries." Her face pales. "I know what he does to Mom, but if he's hurting his patients too…"

"This goes beyond beating," I say. "What he does is… twisted."

"Tell me," she says. "I'll speak to the sheriff and report him anonymously. I—"

"No!" I yell, making her jump. "You can't. Not yet. I've already said too much."

"You can't expect me to sit back and do nothing."

"This is bigger than you," I say. "It's complicated. We have to get this right. There are dangerous people here who can hurt—"

"I don't need your protection," she interrupts. "I want to help!"

As strong as she thinks she is, Sarah's lived a sheltered life. Despite growing up in the house of a monster, she's had the best of everything. Her fragile mind won't be able to comprehend such brutality.

"You are helping," I insist. "Just do what Aiden says."

"Fine," she relents, realizing it's an argument she won't win—not tonight, anyway. "But I want to know the whole truth."

"And you will," I say, stroking her soft cheek. "Soon."

Her eyes light up and flood with desire. That look will never get old. I'll never get enough of her and her body.

Suddenly, a bang from behind makes us freeze as our lips meet.

"Sarah!" Doctor Acacia yells, bursting in and causing us to spring apart.

"Dad," she stammers, "i-it's not what it looks like…"

It's the first time he's returned within an hour of leaving her. We've gotten cocky. Reckless, even. The only solace is my coming to see her alone, hoping it'll spare Aiden and Lex any punishment.

"Twenty-Five," he addresses me. His glacial stare makes me shiver. "How did you get in here?"

I have to think fast. Thankfully, I covered the vent opening behind me. If he finds out we've been crawling around in the ceiling, it'd ruin everything.

"An orderly left my cell unlocked by mistake," I lie. "I was exploring and heard a girl in here. I thought…"

His eyebrows lower menacingly. "You thought you'd take advantage of my daughter?"

"He didn't do anything," Sarah intervenes. "I'm the one who tried to seduce him."

Acacia unclips the pager from his waistband and requests assistance. For a second, I debate smashing his face. However, that'd be too easy. Public humiliation and revealing the truth will be our true revenge.

"I thought bringing you to Sunnycrest would help you see the errors of your ways, Sarah." He shakes his head. "But you're much sicker than I first thought."

Running footsteps echo down the corridor, then three orderlies barge inside.

"Take Twenty-Five to my lab," Acacia commands.

They grab my arms.

I don't fight. I need to conserve my strength. After touching his daughter, whatever punishment I face will be his worst yet. Maybe he'll finally kill me…

"Where are you taking him?" Sarah asks in frantic panic. "Don't hurt him! It was my fault!"

"He's ill," Acacia replies. "He needs treatment."

I can't risk saying anything to Sarah as they haul me away, but our gazes meet for a moment. I shake my head as she opens her mouth to argue. Tears well in her eyes. Getting involved with Sarah Acacia was asking for trouble, but it was worth it. If her face is the last I ever see, I'll die happy. If that isn't love, then I don't know what is.

WEEKS LATER...

LEX HOLDS up one of the tubes feeding a mystery cocktail of drugs into Eli's arm.

"What shit is this?" Lex asks. "I've never seen Acacia spend so long on one experiment."

It's been three weeks since Acacia took Eli hostage. Despite Acacia's usual diligence, there are no cameras installed in this room, which makes me more worried. He always documents the worst of his gruesome torture. What is he doing to Eli that's so bad he doesn't want to keep any record of it?

Eli's suspended in a coma-like state and doesn't respond to anything. Still, we try to visit him every day. We've bribed a few orderlies to get more information about what Acacia's doing, but no one knows anything. The other complicit doctors are all Acacia's loyal disciples. They won't be black-mailed into giving out details, which leaves us oblivious to what Eli's going through.

I cautiously pull back the threadbare blanket covering Eli's lower half. There are no casts or bandages. We know Acacia gets his kicks from causing pain. In the absence of physical injuries, he must be messing with Eli's mind, which is far more dangerous.

"We have to get out of Sunnycrest soon," Lex says. "We can't wait much longer. He'll be looking to turn us into vegetables next."

"We're not going anywhere without Eli," I say. "We stick together. Whatever happens."

"What if he doesn't wake up?" Lex questions. "He could be stuck like this forever."

I can't allow myself to think that losing Eli is a real possibility. He's my brother. He and Lex are the only family I have. I remember when Eli first came to the asylum. He was the only subject, after me, who made it through Acacia's first test and remembered his own name. That's when I knew I'd finally found an ally, right when I was losing hope. I'll never give up on him.

"He'll wake up," I say. He has to. "It won't be long now."

Our escape plan is almost ready. We know the route, how to time everything perfectly with staff shifts, what ruse we'll create, and even have transportation lined up. All we're waiting for is the right opportunity and a safe place to go to.

"I thought I heard the phone," I say, changing the subject. "What did she say?"

Although they're banned, there are ways to get cell phones into any institution. Until now, we haven't needed one, but keeping in touch with Sarah has been useful. Acacia hasn't brought Sarah to Sunnycrest since he caught her and Eli together, and not seeing her is driving me crazy. He's keeping her locked away like a princess in a tower, and I fucking crave her.

"Apparently, Acacia's recent dinner party was a bust. The fucker's too good at covering his tracks," Lex says, impatience creeping into his tone. His scowl turns into a smile as he reads on. "She's found some useful documents. Financial records.

This could be it! The proof we need to show the world what he's done and who he's working with! There's more too…" He talks more animatedly, daring to get excited. "There's a hunting cabin in the woods not far from here. Acacia's associate uses it in the summer, but he's working abroad for the next year."

"Get her to send coordinates for the cabin," I instruct. "Arrange to meet there on Friday."

"You mean, actually leave the asylum?" Lex stutters. "What about Eli? You just said—"

"You should be happy. You're the one who keeps saying that we need to get out of here," I snap. "We need those documents."

"Don't you want her to smuggle them in or hold on to them?"

I shake my head. We can't use a third party and risk them getting into the wrong hands, and every posted letter gets checked before it's delivered. Acacia monitors Sarah closely. What if he finds out she has them? No, we have to meet. It's the only way.

"We can't risk any screwups," I say. "We need to do this ourselves."

"Do you really think our plan will work?"

"Of course it will," I say, extinguishing any doubts he has. "We've spent years perfecting it. All we need now is a plan for us to get back in."

"You mean, we'll come back?" Lex's shoulders slump. "But I thought—"

"How many fucking times? We're not leaving without him," I snarl. "He goes where we go. End of discussion."

Lex nods. Despite his resistance, he cares for Eli as much as I do. We're a team. We're all we have. Meeting Sarah is a risk, but one I'm willing to take.

"What if we get caught?" Lex asks. "This could be our only chance at freedom."

"We better make sure we're not caught then," I reply with a smirk.

Seconds later, the cell phone buzzes.

"She'll see us there," Lex confirms.

Everything is finally coming together. Our plan has to work. It's got to. If we can make it in and out, it's only a matter of time before we can leave Sunnycrest forever with the evidence needed to take down Acacia's entire regime.

I GROAN and touch myself while watching the video of Lex and Eli fucking me for the first time. I listen to my moans as Aiden zooms in on Lex spreading my ass cheeks and captures the moment he enters me.

Fuck.

I bite my lip and come hard over my fingers.

As soon as the wave of pleasure tapers, a deep emptiness replaces my momentary bliss. I miss the guys. Until I see them again, the video is all I have to satisfy my desires.

I reread Lex's text for what feels like the hundredth time. I have two phones—one that Dad monitors and my real one. I've had two since I realized that he installed hidden software to read my messages, which has come in handy.

Since Dad caught me and Eli together, I've been under house arrest. He escorts me and Erin to and from school. He's locked my windows to stop me from climbing out at night and positioned motion-triggered alarms on every door to the outside, so he knows if anyone leaves the house. When I'm not at home or school, I'm in different therapists' offices. He's trying everything to stamp out my 'rebellious' nature, but he doesn't understand that I'm just being me.

I text Lex.

Can't wait to see you.

I only have to wait two more days. The secluded hunting cabin will be a perfect meeting spot. In the meantime, all I have to do is figure out a way around Dad's security measures.

"Sarah!" Mom calls up the stairs. "Breakfast!"

I groan. "I'm not hungry."

Boxes are piled up in my room. We're officially moving to Pasturesville next week. Our move has been delayed a few times because of building renovations. Secretly, I think Dad's been delaying things purposefully until he 'fixes' me. He doesn't want his daughter showing him up at the posh academy we're starting.

I quickly check under my pillow to make sure my diary is there before going to hide it in my secret spot in the wardrobe. I'm not the type of girl who keeps a diary—that's more Erin's thing. However, since helping the guys search for evidence of what's happening at Sunnycrest, I decided to start keeping evidence of my own. If anything ever happens to me, I want a record of what Dad's done; the nights he's locked me in the asylum, his fights with Mom… all of it.

A knock on my door makes me throw a pillow across the room.

"I told you, Mom," I yell. "I'm not hungry."

The door inches open, and Erin pokes her head around it.

"What do you want?"

She shuffles inside and shuts the door quietly behind her.

"What are you wearing?" I frown. "You look like you're going to a funeral."

Her black shapeless below-the-knee dress and buttoned-up cardigan do nothing for her figure. Mom's taken Erin shopping countless times, but they always return with the same type of clothes. I've seen less conservative outfits at a Sunday church service. When Mom and I go shopping, we burn through Dad's platinum credit card with glee, but Erin treats it as a chore. Considering how miserable he makes us, we may as well take advantage of the opportunity.

"It's the last day of school." Erin blushes and plays with the hem of her dowdy dress. "I thought I'd dress up."

"Seriously, Erin, you look like a nun," I say. "Why don't you borrow something? We're the same size."

I jump out of bed, wearing only a crop top and panties. Her eyes bulge at my tiny lace thong. She probably wears huge white bloomers.

"I don't think that's a good idea," Erin murmurs. "We don't exactly have the same style."

"We're almost eighteen, not eighty." I roll my eyes. "It won't kill you to look or act your age. We're moving soon. Why don't you leave with a bang?"

She chews her bottom lip thoughtfully, the way she always does when she's conflicted about something.

We used to be close when we were kids. Her quiet personality complemented mine. I was the performer, and she was the perfect audience. She always encouraged me, clapping when I danced and did silly things, but she was too shy and self-conscious to take part herself, even though I could tell she secretly wanted to. For identical twins, I seemed to have got all the confidence genes.

"What is it?" I ask. She's obviously holding something back. "I know we're not as close as we used to be." I soften my tone. "But you can still talk to me."

She stays quiet.

"Come on," I encourage. "Spit it out then."

"Is it true that you and Max have split up?" she asks, her eyes sparkling with hope. "I heard some girls talking about it yesterday in gym class."

"We were never really together," I reply. "We went on a few dates. That's all. He's not my type."

Her lips twitch into a tiny smile. "Oh, okay…"

"You like him, don't you?"

She quickly glances over her shoulder, even though the door's closed.

"Don't worry. Dad's already left. He's away for the weekend, remember? Some business trip." That's why this weekend will be the perfect time to meet the guys. "I won't tell him that his little angel has a crush."

"Well, I wouldn't call it a crush…"

"You can't lie to me," I say. "It's written all over your face. You like Max. Admit it."

I still don't get Max's appeal, but I can understand how a clean-cut hockey player seems enticing to Erin. She's watched too many movies about sports stars falling for the nerdy girls.

Erin would get a lot of male attention if she put herself out there. Her ugly clothes and lack of effort don't help. Appearance is everything in a school like ours.

"I guess Max is cute," she says reluctantly.

"So borrow a dress," I say. "He'll notice you then."

"I'm not like you, Sarah." She sighs wistfully. "Your clothes won't look good on me."

"Have you looked in the mirror lately? We're identical twins!" I say. "What looks good on me looks good on you."

"I don't know…"

"Did you hear about the party on Friday night?" I ask, getting an idea that could be advantageous for us both. "A final blowout to celebrate the end of the semester."

Her eyes narrow in suspicion. "What about it?"

"You should go," I say. "Everyone's invited."

She shakes her head vigorously. "No, I can't." Her eyes almost pop out of their sockets. "And neither can you! What if Dad finds out? The cameras will see you. He'll be watching."

"Relax," I say. "First, he's out of town. And second, I'm not going to the party."

"I can't go alone," she says. "I never go to parties. I don't know what to say to people."

I flick through the many outfits hanging in my closet and pick out a dress I know Max likes. It's a navy slinky bodycon. I wore it on our first date, as it's the hockey team's color. That'll draw his attention. I hold it up against Erin. It'll be perfect.

"Do you remember the game we used to play when we were little?" I ask. "Twin switch?"

Back then, it was almost impossible to tell us apart. Since I started dying my hair blonde and wearing makeup, it's made it easier.

"Yeah." Erin giggles. "That was fun."

Sometimes, we'd switch places. Mom and Dad never noticed. For a wallflower, Erin did a great job of coming out of her shell when she pretended to be me.

"Why don't we play it again on Friday?" I wiggle my eyebrows. "You pretend to be me at the party and see Max?"

"That'd never work." She gasps. "Plus, we have different hair. People will know."

I rummage around in the back of the closet and find a box of bleach.

"We have time to give you a makeover before then," I say. "We can pull it off."

"But I'd be lying," she says.

"So what?" I roll my eyes. "We're moving to Pasturesville. This will be the last time we ever see these people. What's wrong with having a little fun for one night?"

"What do you get out of it?"

Erin's not stupid.

I bat my eyelashes innocently. "What do you mean?"

"I know you, Sarah," she says. "If I'm at the party pretending to be you, I know you're not gonna stay home and do homework. What are you planning?"

"What I'm doing doesn't matter," I say. "Let's just say it'll be mutually beneficial."

"If I agree, and that's a big if," she says. "How will we get out? The front door's alarmed and your window's locked."

"Your bedroom," I say, excitement bubbling in my stomach. If Erin agrees to break the rules, this will work. "He hasn't locked your window. We can climb out onto the garage, then shimmy down. Mom will be busy drowning her sorrows with a bottle of wine and won't notice we're gone, and we'll be back by morning. Easy-peasy!"

"I don't know…"

"Live a little!" I shake the blue dress enticingly. "You could be making out with Max in a few days." I thrust the dress into her hands. "At least try it on."

She beams, and her entire face lights up. "Fine. I guess trying it on won't hurt…"

It's been a long time since she's smiled like that. Maybe we should spend more time together. Dad's constant comparison game has created a divide between us. This is the first step to rebuilding our relationship.

When she's dressed, I wolf-whistle. "You look hot."

She rotates to see herself from all angles in the mirror.

"Don't you think it's a little…" She looks at her cleavage. "Revealing?"

"You're pretending to be me, remember? It's perfect," I say. "We just need to dye your hair, and I'll do your makeup. No one will know. If Dad finds out about the party, I'll be the one getting in trouble—not you. You've got nothing to lose."

"Twin switch," she says, nodding. "One last time. And you have to promise to re-dye my hair before Dad gets home."

"Consider it done," I say, holding out my hand.

We shake on it.

Both of us will get what we want on Friday night.

CHAPTER
THIRTY-EIGHT

SARAH

"Are you sure about this?" Erin asks. "Do you really think it'll work?"

"Of course," I say. "If I can hardly tell us apart, no one else will."

After giving Erin a makeover and style re-haul, looking at her is like staring into a mirror. Our eerie likeness is unnerving.

"What if Max can tell?" she says.

"Boys don't pay real attention when they're trying to get into your pants," I say. "Just smile and laugh at whatever he says. You'll have him eating out of the palm of your hand in no time."

She giggles nervously, and her cheeks flush. When was the last time I saw her this happy? I'm struck by a sense of pride. Maybe I'll turn my obedient sister into a rebel after all.

Erin shakes her head. "I still can't believe I'm doing this."

"You'll do great," I say, adjusting the hairline on my itchy wig.

With Erin pretending to be me, I needed a disguise. I cut a black wig I once wore for Halloween into a sharp-cut bob, like Uma Thurman in *Pulp Fiction*.

"Are you still not telling me where you're going?" she asks.

We wait under the streetlights on a street corner a few blocks away from home, waiting for two separate cabs to take us to our next locations. Climbing out of Erin's window and sneaking through the backyard was easy. Mom has friends over—they're too busy drinking and complaining about another woman in their book club to notice our absence.

I shake my head. "I told you, where I'm going doesn't matter."

"Well, I hope he's worth it," she replies knowingly.

I can't help but grin. They are.

The first cab comes to a stop in front of us, and I give Erin an encouraging push.

"Have fun," I say.

"I'll see you tomorrow," she says, pausing before getting in. "And, Sarah?"

"Yes?"

"Thanks for… you know."

I wink. "Don't do anything I wouldn't."

I watch her drive away as my cab arrives seconds later.

"Where to?" the driver asks. He frowns when I give him directions. "The highway to hell isn't safe for a young girl at night. You know what they say about that stretch of road."

"I can take care of myself," I snap, although I sense his lingering hesitation. Before he objects further, I wave a wad of bills in his face. "I'll pay double."

His reservations vanish instantly. Cash is king, after all.

Thankfully, he doesn't talk for the rest of the drive, giving me plenty of time to think. Being close to the guys is the only good thing about our upcoming move to Pasturesville.

My stomach flutters with excited butterflies as we get closer, and I reapply my lipstick for the third time. I'm not the only one taking a risk tonight. The guys are risking everything to see me. They've planned their escape for years, and this will be their first time out of the asylum's walls.

The cab slowly climbs the mountainside. We pass many warning signs, urging drivers to be careful around sharp bends and steep drops. A sign directing to Sunnycrest has been graffitied over with the warning 'Abandon all hope, ye who enter here'. The same text that sits over the Gates of Hell. Spooky.

"You can stop here," I say, checking the map on my phone.

We're close to the trail where we're meeting. From there, we'll hike through the woods to the cabin.

"Here? Are you sure?" the driver asks. "The crazy house is a few miles up ahead. They say you can hear them screaming at night. Lock 'em up and throw away the key, I say. I can still turn around…"

"Here's fine," I insist firmly.

After passing him the cash, he shakes his head. "Look after yourself."

"I plan to," I say, stepping into the night.

I zip up my black leather jacket. The cold nips my knees, making me regret my choice not to wear tights with my high-waisted tartan skirt. At least my Doc Martens should withstand the walk through the undergrowth.

The cab's rear lights vanish down the hill. Aside from the rustling trees, it's ghostly quiet. I check my phone. Still no word from Lex. They should be here soon. I don't know how they're planning to travel from the asylum, but I assume they've arranged some kind of transport.

I slink into the tree line to wait, hoping they won't be much longer. Twigs snapping behind me makes my head whip around. Is it a bear? I clutch onto my tiny purse, cursing myself for packing mascara instead of bear spray.

Silence descends once more, and goosebumps pop up on my arms. I squint into the dense woodland but see nothing. I step forward, edging closer to the road, back to safety. Maybe the cab driver had a point…

Without warning, a shadowy figure lunges and wrenches me backward. Hands smother my mouth to muffle my scream, and I stare up at a masked face. My heart thunders, thinking that I'm about to die, until I breathe in the familiar smell of burning wood.

"Shh," Lex purrs. "I prefer you blonde."

Explosive giggles erupt from my mouth as he releases me, and I punch his shoulder playfully.

"You scared the shit out of me!"

"You need to be careful in the woods, Miss Acacia," he says. "Bad men could be lurking around."

"I was kinda banking on it," I reply, attempting to regain my cool composure but not fooling him.

Lex snickers as another masked figure emerges from the trees. He's wearing a Ghostface mask with a large white mouth and eyes that seem to glow. Judging by his height and broad stature, I can tell it's Aiden.

"Where's Eli?" I look for him, hoping he'll appear too.

"We're still working on getting him out," Aiden replies.

He reaches to pull up his mask, but I grab his wrist.

"Leave it on," I say, running my hand over his body, from his chest down to his hard cock bulging against his pants. "I like it."

"As much as we'd love to fuck you right here, right now, guards use this road at night. We need to be out of sight," Lex butts in to kill the mood. "Let's move."

"Follow me," I say, holding up my cell phone to light the way.

I lead them to an opening in the undergrowth. The track is seriously overgrown, but we should be able to make our way through it.

"I'll go first," Aiden says.

"I'll lead." I stand my ground. "This is the twenty-first century."

To my surprise, he doesn't push it, and we fall into a line. I stroll quickly. The sooner we get there, the sooner I'll be able to rip their clothes off.

"How much farther?" Lex complains after we've been walking for five minutes.

"Quit whining," I say.

I start to wonder whether I'd misheard the directions or took a wrong turn when my light finally settles on a cabin roof peering over the top of the twisted branches ahead.

"There." I point. "See?"

Aiden storms forward, shoving past me to get to the cabin first. He charges down the door with his shoulder, making a massive bang that causes sleeping birds to caw.

I arch one eyebrow. "There's a spare key under the mat."

Although, I can't deny his manly display of strength was kinda hot.

"Fuck that," Aiden says, although I can tell he's grinning underneath his mask.

As I approach, he scoops me into his arms. I squeal as he carries me over the threshold like we're newlyweds.

Lex follows and flicks on the light switch to no avail. "Generator's out."

This place hasn't been used for a long time. I stifle a cough from the dust, but at least no animals have taken over.

"It's a good thing you know how to start a fire then," I say, propping my cell phone on a dusty table for light and gesturing at the hearth. "Look, there're candles here."

Lex acts swiftly, like a soldier called to arms, and begins setting alight anything he can find with his trusty lighter.

I gaze up at Aiden, seeking his approval. "It'll do, right?"

"It's perfect," he replies.

I roll up the bottom of his mask. Immediately, our mouths

crash together in a desperate frenzy. I don't know which of us needs this more.

"Fuck," he groans. "I've been dying to taste you."

I lean to kiss him again, but he turns his head and pushes me onto the sofa with full force.

"Spread your legs," he orders, removing his mask fully and hurling it aside.

I do as he asks and spread my legs slowly. To my right, Lex is busy fanning embers in the fireplace that give off a soft, orange glow.

Aiden lets out a low whistle and drops to his knees to admire my pussy.

"No panties," he says, crawling to me.

Just as he reaches me, I snap my legs closed. "Aren't we gonna talk first?"

"Talk?" he scoffs. "We can talk after you've come all over my tongue."

Who can argue with that logic? He wrenches my knees apart, and his head disappears under my skirt to nibble my inner thighs.

Lex chuckles. "You're starting without me, huh?"

Aiden growls possessively, grabbing my hips and pulling my pussy onto his face. He licks down my slit, lapping up the pool of wetness at my entrance. He pushes his tongue deeper, fucking me with it, and tasting me from the inside. I tug his hair, holding him against me, then gyrate onto his face. The friction against my clit makes me tremble as we move in tandem, and I chase the pleasure that only he can give.

"I need more, Aiden," I beg. "Please."

"No," Lex says. "You're getting exactly what you need."

A pleasure-filled night with psychopaths. What more can I possibly want? I clamp my thighs around Aiden's head as he explores me, while Lex sits next to me and removes my jacket. He kisses my neck, sending shivers down my spine. Slowly, Lex undoes the buttons on my crop top until it falls open. I'm not wearing a bra, and my nipples harden as he brushes his fingers over their peaks.

Lex picks up the brass candleholder that's balanced on the coffee table. Wax is already collecting in the little dish, and he tips it from the holder, dripping a drop onto my chest.

I flinch. "What—"

"Shhh," Lex purrs, silencing me with a kiss. "Close your eyes."

The combination of the wax and Aiden eating me out is in stark contrast to the chilly night breeze.

"If you put that candle anywhere near my ass, I'll slap you, Lex," I joke.

My hips buck as another drop of wax hits me as Aiden flicks my clit with his tongue.

"An idea for another night then…" Lex teases. "Do you like the wax?"

His icy fingers tweak my nipple before dropping another blob onto my skin.

"Yes," I moan. "Fuck, yes."

My thighs quiver. An orgasm nears, but I try to hang on to it, biting my lip and letting the sensation build. My toes curl as I cling to Aiden's hair as if my life depends on it. I want to hang on to this moment forever. Hang on to them.

"Don't hold back," Lex says, reading my body language. "Come for us. Then we'll make you come, again and again."

I cry out, unable to keep my orgasm captive for any longer. Aiden holds my clit in his mouth, sucking in short, rhythmic bursts to coax more pleasure from me, before the point of his tongue finds salvation inside me. Every probing motion causes a wave to break through, soaking him.

Lex drips the wax between my breasts. It scorches for a few seconds, intensifying my pleasure, then dulls as it cools. I open my eyes as he puts the candleholder down to pay attention to my nipples. He pops one into his mouth, sucking gently, while kneading my other breast. It sends a burst of bliss through my body from him to Aiden, like an invisible thread is linking them.

I turn my head to kiss Lex, while Aiden withdraws.

"It's time to mark her," Aiden declares.

Lex pulls away, his eyes sparkling with excitement. "Fuck yeah."

"Mark me?" I frown, still panting from my orgasm.

"We always mark our property," Aiden says, rummaging around in his deep pants pockets and retrieving a needle, ink, thread, tape, and a pen. He lays them down on the coffee table.

"A tattoo?" I question, sitting upright. "You can't be serious. I'll get an infection."

Lex flicks on his Zippo and waves the needle tip through the flames. "Happy now?"

"What if my dad sees it?" I ask, realizing I sound pathetic.

"He won't," Aiden says. He runs his finger between my shoulder blades, making circular motions, then pauses. "This is the spot."

"But—"

"You want to be ours," Aiden cuts in. "So prove it."

I take a deep breath while Lex wraps the thread around the needle, creating a bulb toward the end, then he tapes it to the pen.

"Fine," I say with a determined nod. "Do it."

I wince as Lex jabs the needle into my skin. It's hard to describe how it feels. There's an almost popping-like sensation as he pokes the needle in and out in short bursts. He uses his T-shirt to wipe away loose ink every few seconds. It's less painful than I thought, but it still stings.

"What is it?" I ask, fearing that they're inking a penis onto me forever.

"A triangle," Lex replies. "One line to represent each of us."

"Tattoos are Lex's specialty," Aiden says, watching on and

licking his lips. His cock hardens, getting turned on by my virgin skin being tainted.

I squeeze my eyes shut. "Is it nearly done yet?"

"Almost," Lex says, finalizing the line work.

It can't be big. I'd guess it's around the size of the tip of my little finger.

"There," Lex says, giving my skin one final wipe. "Finished."

"Nice work," Aiden says. "Now you're all ours, Sarah."

There's no going back. I'm theirs.

"And you're mine," I say. "All of you."

Aiden grins, making the white scar on his cheek dance, as he undresses, distracting me from any lingering pain. He's built like a professional athlete with a dangerous, rugged edge, and… he's all fucking mine.

Overcome by a primal urge, Aiden grabs my legs and moves me to recline across the length of the sofa with my head balanced on its edge. Lex rises to watch. The sofa isn't wide enough for Aiden to lie on top of me, but he kneels between my legs and hoists my ankles over his shoulders.

He thrusts inside me with no hesitation. Although I'm soaking wet, I still have to stretch for him to fit. Lex stands near my head, whipping out his cock to wipe his salty pre-cum over my lips. I open wide, showing him exactly where I want him to be. I need to be filled by them both.

I tip my head back a little to make it easier for Lex to slide into my mouth while Aiden thrusts. The two of them use me in tandem.

Out of nowhere, Aiden stops abruptly and pulls out.

Lex follows his lead.

"Hey!" I object with a moody pout. Are they crazy? I can already feel another orgasm nearing. "Why'd you stop?"

They exchange glances, communicating in their own silent language, before reaching a conclusion and nodding in mutual agreement.

"Wha—"

Before I finish my sentence, Aiden picks me up and throws me onto the rug in front of the fire.

"Don't move," Lex threatens as he and Aiden fully undress.

They lay on either side of me, facing me like I'm the center of their universe. Aiden rolls me onto my side to kiss me. This time, our kiss is slower, more intimate, packed with unsaid words. He and the others don't talk about their feelings often. Their language consists of rough sex and revenge, but there's more behind this kiss. A hidden tenderness and care layered in his lips.

Lex sweeps my hair from my shoulder and licks along it, his teeth grazing my skin and setting my nerve endings on fire. It almost tickles. I wriggle around and wetness drenches my upper thighs as Aiden's cock pulsates against my stomach, while Lex's nestles between my ass cheeks.

"I need you," I whimper. "I need you both."

Aiden takes my leg, positions his arm behind my knee, and grasps my thigh to lock me in place and give himself leverage. His wet cock glides into my pussy effortlessly, while I turn to Lex, who nuzzles into my neck.

"There's room for you in here, Lex," Aiden groans.

My pussy clenches in a heady mix of desire and trepidation. Is there enough space for the two of them? Is that even possible? Aiden senses my reluctance and obliterates it with a violent thrust.

"You can take us," he growls.

Lex slips two fingers into my mouth and twirls them around, coating them in spit, then finds a home for them between my legs. He edges one finger inside me alongside Aiden's cock. I gasp as another one follows, slowly sliding against Aiden's shaft to stretch me and make space. The sensation is all-consuming, but once the initial shock subsides, I relax and succumb to my desires. I don't know what's hotter, knowing they're both in my pussy at once or that Lex is inadvertently stroking Aiden's cock, too.

Lex pulls his fingers out.

"You're going to take two big cocks like a filthy slut, aren't you?" Lex's breath in my ear sends tingles down my spine. "That tight pussy is going to be filled with our cum."

"Yes," I groan as Lex positions himself behind me and grabs my ass for support.

Aiden stops moving, leaving only the tip of his cock inside me. He and Lex are on their sides, each with one leg bent to give them greater control of every movement.

"Say please," Aiden commands. "Beg. Tell us what you want."

"I want you both to fill me," I say. "Fill me with those massive cocks. Fill me with your cum."

Lex lines himself up beside Aiden's cock and enters me. I squeeze my eyes shut, sinking my nails into Aiden's shoulder and moaning.

"Our dirty little whore," Lex compliments. "What would Daddy say?"

I can't speak. Being fucked by them overpowers all my senses as they move together and thrust with the impeccable timing of synchronized swimmers. They delve deeper, one inch at a time. Aiden holds my leg higher, spreading me wide open, while Lex's grip on my ass grounds me.

The three of us merge into one. They plunder me, taking everything I have, and get showered in my wetness. The rest of the world fades away. After this, I'm not sure whether one guy will ever be enough.

Now that I'm fully comfortable, they quicken their pace. My tits jolt as their hands slither all over my body. We're a cluster of panting limbs; I don't know where I end and where they begin.

A deep ache builds inside me, making me feel like I'm about to implode.

"Come," Aiden grunts. "Soak us."

I let go of everything I'm holding on to. Uncontrollable tears run down my face as an orgasm catapults me into a state of pure bliss. My pleasure amplifies, reaching an unparalleled high, and I squeeze their cocks simultaneously. The sheer fullness makes it a thousand times more intense, and I gush all over them. The wet slap of our bodies and my moans drown out the whistling wind outside. We're in a different world. Our world. A world where no one can touch us.

Another orgasm descends, crashing through me like a freight train. My pussy releases and tightens, trying to push them out and hold on at the same time.

"Fill her, Lex," Aiden orders.

Lex bucks violently and comes with a long guttural sigh, then Aiden does the same. A hot burst of warmth shoots inside me. When they're finished, they don't pull out straight away. They stay, unmoving.

"Fuck," I say eventually. "That was..."

For once, I'm lost for words.

"Do you think we're done already?" Aiden says. "We're only getting started."

From across the room, my ringing cell phone interrupts our moment.

"Ignore it," Lex urges.

Aiden kisses me in agreement.

However, as soon as the ringing stops, it starts again. I break away from our kiss, but he turns my head back to him.

"They'll stop soon," he whispers.

I assume the caller will get the message after ignoring their call for a second time, but it keeps going. Lex huffs in agitation.

"Answer it," Aiden says. "But know you're going to pay for that interruption later."

"I'll turn it off," I say. "To make sure we're not interrupted again."

"We better not be," Aiden warns.

Still shaking from being ravaged, I crawl to my jacket and rummage around in the pockets. The ringing keeps going. Whoever it is must really want to talk. I frown when I see that it's Erin. It's not even midnight. The party won't be over yet.

"I have to take it," I say begrudgingly. "It's Erin. It might be important."

Usually, I'd choose multiple orgasms over speaking to my boring sister, but my instincts urge me to answer.

Aiden smirks. "You'll pay for that decision."

I wink at him. "I'm counting on it." I turn my attention back to the phone and answer. "What is it, Erin?" I snap in annoyance. "I'm kinda busy right now."

She mumbles something, but I can't make out what she's saying due to the patchy signal. Although, I can tell from her high-pitched tone that she's panicking.

"Problem… party… Dad…"

My ears prick up. Call it twin senses, but I instantly sense that something is wrong.

"Slow down," I say. "I can't hear you. Say it again."

I put her on speaker, so the guys can listen in.

"It's Dad," she says breathlessly as the connection improves. "I think he showed up at the party, but now I'm not sure…"

My heart sinks. He's supposed to be away for the weekend. How did he know?

"Tell me exactly what happened," I say.

"I was at the party, hanging out with Max on the front lawn, when I saw Dad watching from a van. At least, I think it was him. He wasn't alone either. There was a young guy with him. We're gonna be in so much trouble if he catches us!"

Aiden and Lex exchange concerned looks, communicating in their secret language again. Only this time, I seem to know what they're saying as I've already reached the same conclusion.

"What did he look like?" I ask. "The guy that was with him?"

"It was hard to tell in the dark. I didn't get a good look. He was around our age with shoulder-length wavy hair," Erin says. "There was something… not right about him. I can't describe it, but he gave me an off feeling. I know it sounds crazy, but I think he might be a patient. Why would Dad take a patient out of the asylum? He wouldn't, right?"

"Where are you now?"

"I got so spooked that I got Max to drop me a few blocks away," she says. "I'm home now. I just need to climb back inside."

"You need to stay calm, okay?" I say. "Just sneak back in and wait for me. Where's Dad? Can you see him?"

"I don't know. There's no sign of him," she whispers. "Maybe I imagined the whole thing?"

"It'll be okay, Erin," I reassure her. "Even if you weren't imagining it, he won't know it's you. I'll be the one to get in trouble."

"Going to the party was a stupid idea," she groans. "I should never have agreed. He'll kill me if he finds out I went along with it."

"Don't panic," I say. "And be careful, okay? You don't know what he's capable of."

A bang from the other end of the line makes me jump as Erin drops her phone. She's not alone. I hear the distant rumble of a male voice. Erin whimpers "No," then it sounds like there's some kind of struggle, as if someone is bundling her in a wad of fabric.

"Erin?" I yell. "Erin?"

The line goes dead.

"I have to go," I say, scrambling to gather my clothes. "I'm sorry, I—"

They're already redressing, donning serious expressions. They know the consequences for breaking my father's rules better than anyone.

"We're coming with you," Aiden says. "If Eli's with him, we have to help. We don't know what Acacia's done to him. If they're together—"

"No," I cut him off. "If you're caught, he'll make sure you never leave Sunnycrest again. You have to go back and wait. Trust me."

They look torn but know I'm right. They have no choice, if they want to return and escape with Eli.

"Fine," Aiden reluctantly agrees. "But call us when you can."

I nod.

A shiver slithers down my spine, like someone is dancing on my grave, and a crushing dread presses on my chest like a pile of bricks.

Something bad is about to happen.

EARLIER THAT NIGHT...

I WAKE up choking and gasping for air. A burst of adrenaline shocks me into an upright position. Acacia looms, bearing an empty injection from the shot.

"We're going on a field trip, Twenty-Five," he says menacingly. "Rise and shine."

He's never taken a patient out of Sunnycrest before, unless they're in a body bag. Why start now? My heart sinks. What twisted experiment will I face next? I start counting back from one hundred in my head to regain control. Losing control is akin to signing a death warrant here, and it only worsens any pain. I learned that the hard way.

"Where are we going?" I ask.

"That is not your concern, Twenty-Five," he says. "Don't ask questions."

He clutches a small gadget that looks like a remote control. I gulp, knowing its function. Whenever he presses the red button in its center, a dose of a mystery drug is administered straight into my bloodstream by the new implant in my arm.

Experimental drug use should be reserved for the rats, but

I've become his new subject since being held hostage. When I'm not sedated, he's been using me to test a strange chemical concoction. I'm not entirely sure of the drug's purpose, only that I am compelled to obey Acacia's orders whenever he pushes the button. The side effects range from general confusion to recalling strange memories of events that I have no recollection of, making me lose grip on reality. At least being tortured is simple. Handling pain and healing physical wounds is easy compared to questioning who you are and being warped into a compliant soldier.

"Put these on," he commands, handing me a white orderly outfit.

I stare at the clothes in confusion. "What—"

"I said, no questions." He presses the red button. A calmness whooshes through me. My limbs move of their own accord, quickly dressing, eager to follow his orders. He gives me a once-over and places a baseball cap on my head before nodding in satisfaction. "Good. Follow me."

We're the only two people in this part of the asylum. He's been carrying out the bulk of his experiments on me alone. As I've drifted in and out of lucidity, I've watched him tinkering with chemicals and formulations, making rushed notes between mixing them together like a mad scientist.

"This will show her," Acacia mutters, more to himself than to me.

My brain wants to question who he's talking about, then halts. Whenever I have an original thought, a mental roadblock shuts it down in a flash. I'm Acacia's puppet, and sheer willpower isn't enough to fight it.

"You will do exactly as I say," Acacia says. "Understood?"

"Yes."

He leads me out of the asylum. I inhale the crisp fresh air, and the wind caresses my cheeks for the first time in years. Imagine how good running would feel. Numbness sweeps through me, making my limbs tingle, and extinguishes any thoughts of escape.

"This way." Acacia heads to a white van that's usually used for making deliveries or moving patients between facilities. He opens the door. "Get in."

Once buckled in, he locks us inside and turns the key in the ignition. The last time I was in a vehicle, someone was bringing me to this hellhole under false pretenses.

I stare blankly out of the window. For a brief second, I think I see my younger self looking back. An innocent boy, full of hope, with his entire life stretching ahead of him. I put a hand to the cold glass, wishing I could turn back time. When I blink, the little boy is gone.

I return my gaze to the road. We're jostled back and forth, trundling across the uneven road surface. Acacia swears under his breath in exasperation, one eye ahead and the other on his cell phone. His knuckles turn white, gripping the steering wheel with steely determination.

We reach the bottom of the mountain and join a stream of other cars. They are a colorful blur, streaking across my vision like shooting stars in dazzling rays of red, blue, and gray. It's surreal, watching ordinary people go about their lives, stopping at the gas station, visiting grocery stores, going to the local diner. I knew there was a world outside Sunnycrest, but it may as well be another planet. It's been so long since I've been a part of civilization that even the mundane is mesmerizing. Acacia clicks the red button again. Any wonder evaporates and is replaced by another fresh wave of nothingness.

Eventually, we come to a stop on a normal-looking street.

Acacia points at a group of teenagers partying on the lawn. "Do you see her?"

The group dances to loud music and they pass around red cups, laughing between themselves. A beautiful blonde girl in a blue dress stands in the middle of them, beaming.

"Sarah…"

I lunge for the door handle. My desire to protect her overpowers whatever medication pumps through my veins. I have to warn her! Another click of the dreaded button makes me slump backward. I'm not going anywhere.

A handsome guy with a perfect smile wraps his arm around Sarah's shoulders and whispers something in her ear that makes her giggle. My fists clench in anger. My first instinct is to smash out every single one of his white teeth, but I don't know why…

"Keep your eyes on her," Acacia orders, clicking the button to eradicate my anger. "Don't look away."

Sarah turns in our direction. Our eyes meet. Her jaw drops in horror, like she's seen a ghost.

"Dammit," he curses, hitting the gas and speeding away. "Change of plans."

I check the mirror to see Sarah grabbing the guy's arm, worry written all over her face, and tugging him to a waiting car.

We drive around for a while, weaving through the streets with no clear destination in mind. Acacia doesn't speak, but he grinds his teeth in fury and occasionally slams his hands on the wheel, while checking his cell phone like an obsessive stalker.

"That should do it," he mumbles, coming to a stop outside an ordinary house surrounded by a high gate.

My stomach drops as I squint to see a familiar figure in the darkness, creeping around the side of the building toward the garage and out of our view.

"Time to go, Twenty-Five."

Acacia gets out, and I follow. We slink around the back of the house to catch up with Sarah, who's talking on the phone.

"Grab her," Acacia instructs, jamming the button three times. "Now!"

I lose all sense of who I am. His words are all I can

comprehend. I dive at Sarah in the darkness. She squeals as I get her in a headlock then spin her to face Acacia.

"You've already had your last warning, Sarah. Enough is enough," Acacia spits, striking her hard across the face. "Follow me, Twenty-Five."

Sarah resists as I drag her through the garden. She digs her heels into the grass, but it's no use. I haul her through the back door, smothering her mouth so no one hears her screams. She claws my arms, thrashing to free herself, but it's a losing battle. She stands no chance against me. I'm stronger and will always have the upper hand.

"Drop her," Acacia hisses.

Sarah falls to the cold tiled floor, her hair flops forward and covers her face. We're in a pristine kitchen. There's no light aside from various appliances on standby, making it difficult to see.

"Dad, please!" Sarah sobs. "You don't understand…"

Her shoulders shake inconsolably from her hysterical sniveling.

"Enough!" Acacia roars. "'I've tried everything, Sarah. I really have. I've given you chance after chance, time and time again. Therapy didn't make a difference. A stint in Sunnycrest didn't help. What choice do I have when you still insist on defying me? You're beyond saving."

She grabs my ankle and yanks on my pant leg, as if she's pleading for my help.

I don't look down.

"Twenty-Five?"

I stand to attention, ready to do whatever he asks. Acacia's word is all that matters. "Yes, sir?"

"Snap her neck," he orders.

He watches me closely, checking for any sign of resistance, but there is none.

I step closer. Sarah's cries echo around the empty room as

she crawls away, backing herself into a corner against the kitchen cabinets. There's no escape.

Suddenly, a voice buried deep in my subconscious screams at me to freeze.

"No." I halt. "I can't."

"Twenty-Five." Acacia lowers his voice in warning. "That was an order." He jabs the red button on the remote multiple times. So many times that I lose count. "Kill her!"

I blink.

Acacia's orders fill every crevice of my mind, echoing like a mantra.

Snap her neck.

Snap her neck.

Snap her neck.

I corner the crying girl. She begs for her life, but her words are nothing more than background noise. All that matters is doing what Acacia wants.

Kill her.

A quick twist, snap, and jerk is all it takes.

"Very good, Twenty-Five," Acacia says. "Very good."

His praise fills me with pride while Sarah's lifeless body lies at my feet.

He hands me the keys. "Wait in the back of the van. I'll be with you soon."

Wait. I step over her corpse, putting one foot in front of the other. *Wait in the back of the van.*

All my emotions are muted. I'm aware of what I've done, but I can't do anything about it, nor do I feel any guilt—or anything at all, for that matter.

I wait in the back of the van in the pitch black, as instructed, until Acacia returns. I'm not sure how long he takes. It could be ten minutes or an hour. When he cracks open the doors, he's red in the face, struggling to haul a long object wrapped in black plastic by himself.

"Take this end," Acacia instructs.

I wince as the package hits the van floor with a thunk. Together, we heave it into the back.

"Don't make a sound," Acacia warns. He shows no remorse or sadness for his daughter's death, only impatience. "I'll be back."

A strand of hair pokes out of the edge of the black plastic, and my stomach churns.

Her body is still warm.

Sarah. The girl I love. *Dead.*

Acacia returns a few minutes later with a shovel. He throws it at me, then slams the van door closed and leaves me with her.

I'm catapulted to an early memory, recalling my mother's lifeless body lying at the bottom of the stairs after my father pushed her. I pull Sarah's head onto my lap and stroke her hair as we drive. It's the last time I'll ever touch her. I want to be able to cry and apologize. I want to tell her how much she means to me and make these last precious seconds together count, yet numbness swallows me once more. I say and feel nothing.

I cradle her as the van speeds over bumps, trying to protect her, even though I know it's too late and I couldn't save her when it really mattered. The silence is punctuated by Acacia raving outbursts from the front. Usually, he's so controlled and meticulously plans every action. Now, he could be one of his patients.

The journey seems to last forever and take no time at all while I'm suspended in a surreal cerebral state, unsure whether this is even happening. Eventually, we stop, and Acacia wrenches the doors open. Moonlight streams in. Sunnycrest looms behind him like a sinister background in a gothic horror. We're parked in an unloading bay, although it's usually canned goods people are carrying instead of corpses.

"Carry the package." His words come in a breathy rush, and craziness lurks behind his wild eyes. "Fucking move!"

I sling her body—the package—over my shoulder, and follow him. He stalks through the building, and I struggle to keep up with his relentless pace. We weave through the empty corridors. Our footsteps, my breathing, and Acacia's swiping key card admitting us into a restricted area are the only sounds I hear.

"In here!" Acacia beckons me into the morgue. "Quickly!"

This is where he keeps the bodies of subjects who died in his experiments before throwing them into the furnace, if their organs can't be farmed. I shiver, suddenly grateful that drugs are suppressing my emotions.

There are nine compartments in the mortuary cabinet, and I wonder how many are empty…

Acacia wrenches a lever to open one and pulls out a steel rack.

He points at it, and says, "Dump the package here."

I place her down with a thud, and Acacia quickly stows her away. As soon as she's hidden behind the silver panel, he inhales deeply. His chest puffs out dramatically while he regains his composure. When he exhales again, any signs of frantic panic are replaced by his usual impassive, stony expression.

"Twenty-Five." He narrows his eyes. "If you speak a word of what happened tonight to anyone outside of these walls, I'll make sure the world knows what you really are. A killer."

I'm a killer.

I'm a killer.

I'm a killer.

He puts his hands on either side of my head. "Say it."

"I'm a killer," I say, burning the message into my brain like a brand.

"Again!"

"I'm a killer," I repeat.

"Again!"

"I'm. A. Killer."

CHAPTER
FORTY

SARAH

APART FROM MOM'S CAR, the driveway's empty. That's a good sign. This is the first time Erin's broken Dad's rules, so paranoia is to be expected. Still, I gingerly push the door open, psyching myself up for what I might face on the other side. Was she right about Dad returning from his business trip early? If he confronted her, does he know that we switched places? Will he be waiting to interrogate me? Instead of facing the firing squad, the house is quiet. Too quiet. Somehow, that makes me more nervous.

I kick off my boots. My feet ache after hiking halfway down the mountain to meet a cab because the driver was too superstitious to venture up the highway to hell. On the drive, I called Erin multiple times, but it went straight to voicemail.

"Erin?" I shout. "Erin? Are you home?"

Someone flicks the hallway light on.

"What is it, honey?" Mom calls. She hovers at the top of the stairs in a robe with her hair wrapped around giant rollers. "Do you know what time it is? It's too late to be shouting."

"Where's Dad?" I ask.

She yawns. "He's at a conference, remember? Go to bed, Sarah. It's late."

I bound up the stairs, taking two at a time. I push past her and race to Erin's room. Her bed hasn't been slept in. The curtains are open. An unfinished essay lies on an impeccably tidy desk alongside neatly folded laundry waiting to be put away.

I call Erin again.

Nothing.

Where is she?

The pit of dread in my stomach intensifies, unable to shake the feeling that something is wrong. Very wrong.

"Mom, he has her!" I announce, running into her bedroom, where Mom's busy applying a fresh layer of anti-wrinkle cream. "He has Erin!"

"What are you talking about?"

"Dad's got Erin," I say, tripping on my words because I'm speaking so fast. "She was pretending to be me. Something bad has happened. We need to call the police. We have to look for her!"

"Your father's in Washington, and Erin's probably reading somewhere." Mom shakes her head and stifles a yawn. "You've been drinking again, haven't you? Your father won't be happy if he finds out. Go to bed and sleep it off."

"Erin's not here. Her bed's empty," I say. "Check for yourself, if you don't believe me."

"Enough with your ridiculous stories!" She holds up a finger to silence me, then reaches for her sleeping pills. "Now, shoo! Not everything is about you, you know. Have you seen my crow's feet lately? I need my beauty sleep."

I sigh in exasperation and stomp out. It looks like I'm in this alone.

I return to Erin's room and sit on her bed, surrounded by her childhood plushies. I watch the clock on her wall. The hands tick on; seconds stretch into minutes, then into an hour. I hit redial again and again. Still no answer.

Where could they go at four a.m.? Has he locked Erin in

Sunnycrest? Guilt gnaws at my insides. Erin's fragile. She's not like me. Taking her to that godforsaken cell will traumatize her for life, and it'll be my fault for manipulating her into switching places.

Suddenly, a noise downstairs draws my attention. I sneak out, pressing my back against the wall, and tiptoe down the stairs. I stay in the shadows, watching Dad slink in. Alone.

I fumble around for my phone and call Erin.

Ringing echoes through the hall, and I gasp as Dad fishes her cell phone out of his pocket. If he has it, where is she? Panic takes over, and I'm about to dial 911 when the phone slips from my sweaty fingers. It hits the wooden step with a bang, and the screen cracks, blowing my cover.

Dad whirls around. "Erin?"

I only have one chance to escape.

I make a break for the front door, but I'm too slow.

Dad's surprisingly fast. He grabs my arm and yanks me back, almost dislocating my shoulder.

I wrestle to free myself, sinking my fingernails into his skin. "What did you do to her?"

"Sarah?" Dad's jaw drops in horror. All the color drains from his face like he's seen a ghost. "But you're…" His mouth opens and closes like a bewildered fish. "Where's Erin?"

"You tell me," I snarl.

"I don't understand," he mutters. "You were at a party…"

"Erin went to the party instead of me," I say. "Remember that game we used to play when we were little? We swapped places. All Erin wanted was to have fun for a change, instead of staying here like a fucking prisoner. Where is she?"

"No, no!" Dad wobbles on his feet. His eyes mist over, and his face crumples in devastation, like his entire world has collapsed. "Not my Erin…"

"What did you do?" I demand. "Where's Erin, Dad? Did you hurt her?"

His pained, guilty expression says it all.

"It can't be," he murmurs. "No… it's not possible… my Erin can't be…"

I stagger back, fighting the urge to throw up.

"She's dead, isn't she?" I whisper, daring to voice my worst fears. "You killed her."

Dad's entire demeanor changes in a flash, from a broken man into a monster. A new menacing determination crosses his features. He lunges at me again, grabbing my jacket, and searing me with a stare full of pure hatred.

"This is your fault." His lips curl into a vicious sneer. "I did nothing, it is you who killed her!"

Even though the guys dropped hints that Dad did awful things to patients, I never thought he was capable of something like this…

"Let me go!" I scream. "Mom, help!"

"You're not getting away with it this time," he hisses. "I won't let you."

I push him and manage to knock him off-balance for a second. I seize the opportunity to grab a nearby vase and swing, aiming for his head, but I miss. It crashes to the floor, shattering into hundreds of pieces.

"No!" I yell as he throws me to the ground.

"My angel's dead," he hisses. "It should have been you."

"Sorry to disappoint you," I say bitterly.

He wraps his hands around my throat and squeezes.

"I won't lose her," he says, crushing my neck. "I won't!"

"Magnus?" Mom calls down, causing us both to freeze. "Is that you?"

Mom turns on the light and stands at the top of the staircase, watching the scene unfold. Our eyes meet, and she freezes.

"Mom!" I croak. "Help me."

She squeals in horror. "Magnus, what—"

Dad abandons strangling me and grapples around for what looks to be a remote control in his jacket. He jams a red button, and Mom's hysteria dissipates instantly. Her eyes glaze over, giving her a spaced-out appearance, like she's taken a long drag on a joint.

"Go to bed, Jocelyn," Dad orders.

"I'll buy a new vase tomorrow. A blue one, maybe? Fresh flowers too." Mom smiles serenely. "Yes, that'll be perfect." She blows me a kiss. "Sweet dreams, Sarah."

What. The. Fuck?

"Mom, please…"

But she's already gone.

This is it.

He's going to kill me too.

AT DAYBREAK, an orderly throws Eli into our shared cell by the scruff of his neck. He staggers in, swaying on his feet, in a haze. His skin is sallow with a yellow hue, and he's fighting to keep his eyes open. He's lucid. Just about.

I spring up just in time to catch him as he slumps forward. Lex grabs his other arm, and we drag him to the bottom bunk before he sags to his knees.

Eli's entire body shakes uncontrollably like he's crying, but no tears fall from his bloodshot eyes.

What the fuck did Acacia do this time?

"Eli?" I kneel before him and give him a hard shake. "Can you hear me?"

No response.

"Move," Lex says. "Let me."

He rolls up his sleeves, then slaps Eli hard.

Eli's face lolls to the side, staring vacantly ahead, looking right through us.

"Again," I demand.

Lex keeps hitting him until Eli's cheek is blazing red. Eli still doesn't respond. He's here in body, but his mind is elsewhere.

"Come on, Eli," Lex growls, hitting him again, hard enough to bust his lip. "Snap out of it!"

Blood drips down Eli's chin, coating his light stubble. His head snaps up, finally seeing us, and I sigh in relief. Thank fuck. He's back. I've seen too many people reduced to brainless zombies at Acacia's hands. We can't lose Eli. Not now that we're so close. After last night, I can almost taste freedom.

"Eli?" I say. "What happened?"

"Sarah," Eli rasps. "She's…"

"We were with her last night," I say. "She's okay."

Her perfume still lingers on my skin, and I haven't washed her sweet juices from my cock. If I try hard enough, I can even imagine exactly how she felt, how her toned thighs clamped around my head as she gushed over my tongue.

"Acacia found out she snuck out," Eli mumbles. "He took me with him. He… made… me…"

He lies back and curls into a ball, drawing his trembling knees up to his chest.

"It was Erin!" Lex, hotheaded as usual, jumps straight to conclusions. "It had to be! Sarah always says Erin tells her father everything. She set her up. She must have called her to lure her home."

"We don't know that," I say calmly. "What did he make you do, Eli?"

"Acacia fucked with my head," he confesses, tears rolling down his face. "He's been testing a new drug on me."

"What does it do?" I ask.

His expression darkens. "It's some kind of super drug that makes you do whatever he says. First, he gave me an implant." Eli brushes his wavy hair from his neck and pulls his skin taut to reveal a strange rectangular object lodged underneath the surface. "After that, all he has to do is press a button to dose me."

"Shit, man," Lex groans. "That's some seriously screwed-up shit."

"I d-didn't mean to..." Eli stammers. "I had no choice... I..."

"Just get to the fucking point," Lex snaps, his patience waning. "Spit it out. What did you do?"

I glare at Lex and soften my voice. "It's okay, Eli. You're safe now. You can tell us what happened."

"She's dead. Sarah's dead," Eli whispers. "I didn't want to... he made me..." He sobs into the pillow. "I killed her."

"Call her," I order Lex. "Right now."

He's already dialing.

"Well?" I demand.

Lex shakes his head. "She's not answering."

It's perfectly plausible Eli's mistaken. He's not in his right mind. Right now, he's acting more insane than Bea, and she eats razor blades for fun.

"Her body's in the morgue," Eli whimpers. "I'm a killer... I'm a killer..." He keeps repeating it. "I'm a killer." He hits his forehead. "A killer. A killer." He keeps going like a broken record while hurting himself. "A killer!"

I grab his wrist to stop him. "It'll be okay," I promise. "We'll remove the implant."

Lex climbs on top of our toilet to loosen the screws on the vent cover. "I'll go to the morgue. I know the way."

It's not a good idea. The last time one of us snuck out solo, Acacia found Eli and took him hostage. But I won't stop him. Even if I order him to stay, he won't listen. Lex doesn't show his emotions outwardly, but fear emanates from every pore in his body. I can smell it. Visiting the morgue is the only way to corroborate Eli's story. He has to go.

"Be careful," I say.

Lex nods solemnly before scampering up the wall into the vent and disappearing.

"It's my fault, Aiden," Eli whimpers. "I loved her. I really fucking loved her."

"I know," I say, stroking his hair while sliding my other hand underneath the mattress.

I fumble around to find a shard of plastic that I've fashioned into a blade from a broken lunch tray. I always keep one stashed for special occasions and emergencies. This is one of those times.

"A killer," Eli mumbles. "I'm a killer."

I pull out the pillow from underneath his head.

"Bite down on this," I instruct. "I'm getting that chip out of your neck."

"Okay," he says, looking up at me wide-eyed, with no hesitation.

Cutting his implant out without hitting an artery is going to be a challenge, but it's better than leaving it in there. I won't let him be used again. He's better off dead than becoming Acacia's puppet.

Eli winces when I make the initial cut.

"Don't move," I urge. "Stay really fucking still, okay?"

He freezes as I carefully pull back a flap of his skin. Blood spews down his neck, covering my hands. Judging by the volume, I've not hit anything important. I scrunch up my nose in concentration and take a deep breath before poking my finger into the hole and grappling for the alien object.

"There," I declare, finally getting a grip on the metal tube. I yank it out in a flourish, like I'm ripping off a Band-Aid, and hurl it across the cell. "It's gone."

Eli cups his neck, nodding dazedly. He holds a blanket against his wound to stem the bleeding. He's suffered worse injuries than this.

"Lie down," I say, climbing into bed with him, the same way I did when we were kids.

I wrap my arms around him. He sobs into me, more

hysterically this time, and I stroke his back. His tears soak through my shirt, mixing with his blood.

"What're we gonna do next?" Eli says between sniffles.

As much as I want to tear out Acacia's throat for what he's done, I hold in my fury, locking it away in the little box in the back of my brain where I hold all my repressed feelings. They exist as demons, lurking in the shadows of my subconscious, but I can't face them. Not yet. The others are depending on me to get them out of here.

"We'll get revenge," I say. "Acacia will pay for this and everything else he's done. We'll expose him as a monster, and we'll get his beloved daughter to help us. We'll turn Erin against him. She will be his undoing, and we won't stop until we get what we want."

PART FOUR
NEVER ALONE
PRESENT DAY

My SKULL RATTLES, imploding from the weight of a lifetime of memories crashing into me like a tsunami. I remember everything. Childhood. High school. Partying. Erin and I swapping places that night, Dad finding me, and then my last recollection before I lost myself bowls me over...

I'm not dead. Not yet, anyway. Although, I may as well be in hell.

Sunnycrest Asylum is as close as it gets.

I'm not in the same room Dad usually locks me in. I'm somewhere new. It's an operating room with sterile, white walls and an antiseptic smell. I'm strapped to a table, my ankles and wrists locked in position.

Dad peers down at me. At his side, a doctor with horn-rimmed glasses frowns.

"Are you sure about this, Magnus?" the strange doctor asks.

"Am I paying you to question me, Warner?" Dad spits. "We're running out of time. Memories have a short lifespan."

I rattle my restraints.

"Should we sedate her again?" Doctor Warner asks, playing with the lanyard around his neck nervously. "She's coming around."

"No," Dad snaps. "We need her awake to improve the transfer outcomes."

"But—" Doctor Warner objects,

"I didn't bring you here to question me," Dad snarls. "You're here to work."

I catch Doctor Warner's gaze. He looks away, refusing to meet my pleading stare as he inspects the wires feeding into my body. There are so many of them, red, yellow, green...

I attempt to look around, but a metal brace locks my neck in position. I open my mouth to yell, but I can't. My entire face is paralyzed, except for my eyes that flit side to side.

"Switch one," Doctor Warner says. "On."

An electric shock ripples through my head, accompanied by a grating, high-pitched noise that vibrates my bones and causes my limbs to seize.

What the fuck? It stops for a second, giving me a brief reprieve to inspect my surroundings again. I follow the wires. They lead to a machine that's being monitored by Doctor Warner. Strange symbols flash on its small black screen. He taps away on a keyboard, a frown on his face, clearly unhappy at whatever he's seeing.

More wires come out of the machine on the other side. They stretch across the room like long shiny tentacles. I follow them. What the...

It takes a second to realize that I'm not having an out-of-body experience when I see where they lead to.

I choke down vomit.

Erin.

She's lying on an identical operating table. However, unlike me, she's completely motionless. Her lips and fingers are a ghostly bluish shade. Her chest is still, and her head is twisted at an impossible angle, tilted in my direction. Her gaze is dead and glassy, fixed in a permanent state of unblinking terror.

If seeing my sister's dead body isn't horrifying enough, it gets worse. Someone has drilled holes into her temples and poked wires into the sides of her head. Wires that connect the two of us through the alien machine.

What the fuck have they done to her?

"Switch two!" Dad cries before I have properly processed what I'm seeing. "On!"

A buzz fills the room, like an angry swarm of bees battling their way through a cloud of static. The binds around my ankles and wrists heat up and make my skin prickle uncomfortably. Suddenly, a second surge of electricity whips through me, causing my legs to twitch and spasm uncontrollably.

"Seizures shouldn't happen," Doctor Warner says. "I think we should stop. It's not working."

"Do I need to remind you that it was your paper that provided the theoretical basis for this procedure?" Dad snarls. "You will bring her back to me."

"The thesis was purely theoretical. Memory implantation is unreliable at best. This technology is still in its infancy. We don't know the long-term effects. It's not safe," he says. "You could kill her."

"My daughter's already dead," Dad says. "What have I got to lose?"

Me! *I want to scream.* I'm your daughter, too.

"We could try conditioning. It's a gentler approach," Doctor Warner says. "We have Erin's memories stored in the machine. If we use them in tandem with your new influencing formulation, we could hope to achieve similar results. The drugs worked well on your first two subjects. We can force Sarah to accept a new version of herself, as long as she keeps taking the medication. Trying to erase a lifetime's worth of memories and replace them is far more complex. We're stretching the realms of what's possible. We're years off being fully ready."

"We don't have years. We have one night!" Dad blasts. "There's no going back now. This will work. It has to."

Doctor Warner opens his mouth to argue, then fear crosses his face, and he nods in reluctant resignation. He might disagree, but *my father scares him too much to stand his ground. Fucking coward!*

"If we increase the voltage, we will have a better chance, but the results could be unpredictable," Doctor Warner says. "We can't guarantee they'll be permanent. From my research, the procedure will bury her real memories deep inside her subconscious. However, for all we know, one small event could trigger their return—"

"Yes, yes," Dad says dismissively in his pompous 'I know best' voice. "And she'll need to continue taking the medication. We know that works."

"Are you certain you want to proceed, Doctor Acacia?" Doctor Warner asks. "Do you really want to risk losing them both?"

Dad strokes my cheek with a tenderness he's never shown me before. Thank fuck. He's finally coming to his senses.

"It's okay, Erin," he coos, making me recoil. "I'll bring you back." His eyes darken, and his lips twist into a maniacal smile as he turns to Doctor Warner. "Do it."

The machine powers on.

A blinding light fills my vision, and I fade away...

Back in the present, I cry out and squeeze my eyes shut. My hands fly to my temples. It's too much...

"Sarah?" Aiden squeezes my shoulders. "Do you remember?"

"Y-yes," I stammer. "I mean, I think so. But I'm not the same, Aiden. I'm not me anymore, and I'm not Erin either. Who am I?"

The pain comes again. I crumple, falling into Aiden's embrace and succumbing to the memories...

"Erin?"

I wake in my bed, surrounded by cuddly plushies.

"Dad?" I rub my eyes as he draws back the curtains. "What time is it? I thought you were away for the weekend at a conference."

He tilts his head, looking at me with a strange expression. Do I have something stuck to my face? I sniff my hair. It smells weird, ammonia-like almost. Nothing a shower won't fix, though.

"I got back early," he says. "Have you heard from your sister?"

I check my phone. No messages. That's not unusual, though. Sarah never tells me where she's going. For once, I can't remember her sneaking out, either.

"No," I reply. "Why?"

"Sarah didn't come home last night," he says. "Did you see her?"

I shake my head. "No."

His stare bores into me. "Where were you last night?"

"Here," I say. "I watched a movie, then studied, like every other night."

"Very good." He smiles. "I'm sure Sarah will turn up soon enough."

I nod in dazed agreement. It wouldn't be the first time she stopped at a friend's house without telling us. Although, something feels different this time. Call it twin instinct, but I can't shake a lingering dread settling in my stomach.

A vague recollection comes to me from out of nowhere.

A phone call.

Did I speak to Sarah last night?

I should call Dad back into the room and tell him, but my gut tells me to stay quiet.

I check my call log and frown. There's no trace of any call taking place. What the hell? Maybe I'm imagining it.

A shiver runs down my spine as I vividly recall her saying, "You don't know what he's capable of…"

"He used me," I whimper as Aiden cradles me. "He…"

"We've been trying to help you remember," Aiden says. "You know the truth."

My bottom lip trembles. "Erin's dead."

"I know," Aiden says. His heart thuds against my cheek, confirming that he's not a figment of my imagination. "But now you've come back to us."

"It was my fault," I say. "I made her switch places. I saw her body…"

Although Erin and I were never best friends, she was still my sister. My twin. I always hoped we'd get closer again if she plucked up the courage to go against Dad. Now, he robbed us of the chance.

"He thought he was killing you," Aiden says. "Never forget that."

I pull away from him violently and wipe my eyes. The thudding in my head dulls, making way for a torrent of fury. "Why didn't you tell me before?"

"We didn't know what consequences breaking the delusion would have, and neither did Doctor Warner," he says. "We wanted you to reconnect with your true self. It was the best way to help you remember."

"Maybe not knowing would have been better," I say bitterly. "At least then I had a chance of living a normal life as Erin." I shake my head. "I don't know what's real and what's not anymore."

My thoughts are a scrambled jumble, whirring and blurring together, making it hard to wade through. Although my old memories are coming back, I see snatches of Erin's memories, and her thoughts mix with my own. Whatever Dad did changed me forever. He tore down the very foundations of who I am, and Erin? She's dead, but I can still hear her…

"We'll help you. We'll—"

"How long have you known?" I snap.

Time didn't stop when 'Sarah' died. Aiden, Lex, and Eli creeped into Erin's—my—life and terrorized us.

"Lex saw your tattoo first. He thought he was imagining things until I saw it for myself the night we showed you the videos in the asylum. You had no idea who you were, so we had to put the pieces together," he explains. "It didn't take much persuasion for Doctor Warner to fill in the gaps. Before then, we all thought you were dead. Lex saw your body in the morgue. If we knew, we'd—"

Putting together timelines in my head is difficult. They learned the truth after Dad locked 'Erin' in the asylum. After they escaped. After they…

"Before you found out I was alive, you were still fucking my sister!" I explode. "You stalked her around town, crashed her ball, and left her creepy gifts. What's wrong with you?!"

I spring to my feet and turn on him. Aiden steps forward, but I shove him hard in the chest.

"I admit, we handled it badly. At the beginning, we only ever wanted to use her to take your father down. Seducing her was part of the plan to win her trust," Aiden tries to justify himself. "Then, she started to act more like you, and maybe it felt like you were still with us in some strange, fucked-up way…" He sighs. "We fucked up, okay? But we really thought you were dead. How could we not after Eli…"

"After Eli, what?" I ask sharply as his voice trails off.

"He didn't mean to hurt her," Aiden says. "Look, your dad drugged him, he—"

"Eli did it?" I want to vomit. "*He* killed Erin?"

"Acacia killed her!" Aiden growls. "Eli was under his control. He couldn't fight it."

"Now it makes sense," I say. "All his ranting and raving over the last few months. He's fucking crazy! You all are!"

Aiden reaches out, but I slap his hand away. "Sarah…"

"Don't fucking touch me," I snarl, crossing my arms. "Did my dad drug you? Is that why you seduced her, or is that all on you?"

"Acacia brought her—you—to the asylum. He gave us an opportunity, and we wanted to get close to her," he says. "As soon as we found out the truth, we started working with Doctor Warner to bring you back, so we can finally be together again. You don't understand—"

"You're twisted!" I spit. "Shit, Lex even made me—Erin—

believe he was taking my virginity. How was that helping get my memories back, huh?"

"Lex did what?" Aiden asks. His eyes glaze, and his jaw hardens. "When?"

"A few days ago," I say, waving my hand dismissively. "Why do the details matter? He creeped into this cell, pinned me against the wall, and fucked me right here. Did you all have a good laugh about it after?"

"We made a deal that none of us would do that," he whispers. "Not until you knew the truth."

"Well, Lex broke your little pact." I narrow my eyes. "But that's not a surprise, because that's all you seem to do."

"You have to believe me," Aiden pleads. "We thought you were dead. Erin was… she wasn't you… but she was the closest we were going to get. She could help us get you justice!"

"By stalking her and taking over her life? Fuck you, Aiden!" I scream. My inner rage fully takes over now. "You're as bad as my father. Your lies, your twisted games. You're sick —all three of you! I always thought Dad was wrong about you, but he wasn't. You belong here. In Sunnycrest."

His head jerks as if I slapped him. "Little Ghost…"

"Don't!" I snarl, jabbing my finger into his chest. "That's your nickname for her, not me! Did you like her more? Perfect Erin, the better twin, the one who can do no wrong. See? You're just like him!"

"No… Sarah… I…"

"Stop, Aiden." I turn away, unable to listen to any more lame excuses. "Leave. Now."

"But—"

"Go!" I yell.

He sighs deeply, realizing there's no point in arguing. He pauses at the door. "Before I go…" He throws my diary onto the floor. "This belongs to you."

"Just fucking go," I whisper, using all my willpower to

hold back tears. I won't give him the satisfaction of seeing me break. "And don't come back."

He doesn't argue. He clicks the door closed quietly behind him. As soon as he's gone, I sink to my knees.

What now? Erin's dead, my brain's fucked, and the three people I thought I could trust have shown me their true colors. I thought I loved them, and this is how they treat me? Like I meant nothing to them? Like I'm replaceable! They told Erin they were monsters, and they were right.

If I had the energy to move, I'd smash my fist through the wall. Instead, I scream as loud as I can. It's freeing. My blood-curdling screech bounces off the bricks as I release all my pent-up emotions, fury, bitterness, sadness, guilt…

I scream until my throat burns and goes hoarse, until I'm unable to make another sound.

How could *he* do this?

How could *they* do this?

How is anyone supposed to come to terms with the fact they've returned from the dead alongside the revelation that their twin sister is gone forever? It's fucked up. Beyond fucked up. This kind of thing wouldn't be out of place in a B-rated sci-fi movie, but it's real life. My life. And I don't know how I'm going to move forward.

"It's okay, Sarah." Erin's voice comes out of my mouth. Her words. Her intonations. It's her. "You're not alone."

This is more than a figment of my imagination. It's like she's really here.

"Erin?" I ask, my voice shaking. "Is it really you?"

I can hear her in my head while my mouth moves.

"I'm still here," she says. "And I'm not going anywhere. I'm part of you now. A part of you that'll always be here."

I feel myself slipping away as she comes to the surface. If she bursts out, I feel like I'll disappear again, so I cling to my sense of self, stopping her from overpowering me. It's a delicate balance and a battle for control. She needs to speak and be heard—and I want to hear her—but I can't lose myself again…

"What did he do to us?" I ask.

"He merged our minds," she says. "He wanted to bring me back to life by transferring my consciousness to your body."

"This can't be happening," I say. "I must really be going crazy after everything that's happened…" I go to hit myself in the head, then my arm suddenly stops, as if someone else has taken over.

"No!" Erin says. "Stop!"

"It's my fault you're dead," I say. "If we hadn't swapped places—"

"You didn't know what was going to happen," she says. Even when suspended in a liminal state, she's rational. "We had no idea how far Dad was going to go, and what he's done. The guys have shown us that."

"They did terrible things to you, Erin," I say. "It's my fault they came into your life."

"I'm glad they did," she says. "They showed me the truth. They taught me to be fearless, more like you, or maybe that was you coming out… I don't know. Either way, I know who Dad really is now. We know the truth."

"What now?" I ask. Erin's always been the smart one. I'm spontaneous and reckless, always thinking with my heart over my head. "I don't know what to do next."

"We show the world who he really is," she says.

I'm a broken shell, cracked into a thousand tiny pieces. Pieces that will be impossible to put together. Yet, despite the blurry haze of not knowing who I am, a new calmness comes over me as my next steps firm up.

I may not know a lot, but the one thing I know for sure is that I can't let my father know my memories have been restored. He's been able to erase them once before, and I've somehow retained my sanity. I don't know if I'll be able to survive another round of his twisted experiments.

"You're right," I say. Of course she is. "We have to make him pay."

"And you can't do it alone," Erin says.

"I'm not alone," I say. "I have you."

"That's not what I meant, and you know it," she replies.

"But they…" My eyes fill with angry tears. "They hurt you. They hurt us."

"But they love us too," she says gently. "You need them, Sarah."

AIDEN BURSTS into the cabin like a hurricane. The wooden walls shake as the door slams closed, almost torn from its hinges.

"What happened?" I ask. "Does she know?"

"You!" Aiden ignores me and sets his sights on Lex. "How could you?"

Lex, still oblivious, leans over the sink. He sets strips of paper alight and watches the ashes flutter down the drain.

"What's wrong?" Lex looks up. He arches an eyebrow and smirks. "Didn't get your dick wet?"

Without warning, Aiden barrels forward and tackles Lex to the floor. "You bastard!"

"What—"

Lex doesn't finish his sentence before Aiden punches him square in the jaw. What's wrong with him? He usually saves that level of ferocity for others. We never turn on each other. We're united. A team.

"Aiden!" I grab Aiden and try to haul him off. They're a blur of thrashing limbs. "Stop!"

Aiden doesn't listen. Instead, he keeps pummeling merci-lessly like he's trying to put Lex's face through the floorboards. In the frenzy, Lex manages to wrap his leg around Aiden to get some respite.

"What're you talking about?" Lex rasps, tilting his head to avoid another whack. "I don't—"

"You fucked Erin!" Aiden yells. "We had a deal!"

"What?" My eyes narrow. "Seriously?"

We had an agreement. We made it when we began tormenting Erin, and then reaffirmed it when we learned she was Sarah. We planned to wait until Sarah learned her identity. Of course, Lex couldn't control himself. Selfish fucker.

"It just happened," Lex wheezes. "Okay?"

While Aiden's distracted, I grab his shoulders and heave him off, even though I wouldn't mind seeing Lex with a broken nose.

"We can't turn on each other," I say, ignoring my simmering resentment. "Not now. We're so close."

Aiden's nostrils flare, but I seem to have struck a chord and brought him to his senses enough to reconsider letting Lex go. He stands and readjusts his crumpled shirt, then takes out his remaining frustration on the chair. He boots the wooden leg, causing it to splinter away from the seat. I guess that's progress.

"She knows her real identity," Aiden pants. "And she's angry."

"Of course she is," I say. "She's just learned her father reprogramed her."

"It's not just that," Aiden says. "She's mad at us."

I frown. "But we've helped her realize who she is…"

"She remembers everything that happened when she was Erin," he mutters. "Everything."

"You mean, she's jealous," Lex adds, wiping his mouth and spitting blood.

"We have to make it up to her," I say.

"You didn't see her." Aiden's shoulders slump. "She never

wants to see us again." His eyes meet mine. "And she knows how Erin died."

Fuck. My heart skips a beat. It was inevitable she'd find out. Still, it doesn't hurt any less. I wanted to tell her what happened myself. She has to know it haunts me every day. The gnawing guilt is chewing me up from the inside, as well as the burning shame of knowing I wasn't strong enough to beat Acacia when it mattered.

"Killer," I mutter. "I'm a killer. Killer. I'm a—"

"I told her it wasn't your fault," Aiden interrupts. "I explained you had no choice. It was all Acacia, but—"

I shake my head to stop myself from spiraling, then mutter, "You did what you had to."

I'm not sure whether I'm talking to him or to myself. Probably both.

"It's over," Aiden says in bleak resignation. "She doesn't want us."

He's willing to let her go?

Lex's brow furrows, having the same thought. This is the first time Aiden's given up. Even after hours of torture, Aiden kept his spirits up, clinging on to hope when there was none to be found. He's an unbeatable force. An unbreakable man, or so I thought.

"It's not over until we say it's over," Lex says firmly.

I take a deep breath and nod in agreement. For once, Lex is right. I'm not ready to give up on her, even if Aiden is. We'll win her back. We have to.

"She's angry, but we can't lose her now. We won't," I say. "She belongs to us."

"Don't you get it? She's not Erin anymore!" Aiden says. "Sarah doesn't do what we say. She won't listen."

Erin was easy to manipulate. For months, we found fun in that. Plaguing her and making her suffer gave us a sick sense of satisfaction, knowing we were messing with her and Acacia. Yet, it's different with Sarah. We didn't love her because she obeyed. We loved Sarah because she never shied away from us. She walked into our hell and never wanted to leave. She risked it all to help us escape. Now we have to risk it all to save her. She's alone and confused, not sure what's coming next. We need to give her a reason to live. Just like she did for us.

"Maybe her sending you away is a good thing," I say. "It shows she's really back."

"She's not the same person, Eli," Aiden says with a pained expression. "She doesn't know who she is. She thinks she's broken. After everything Acacia did to her, maybe she is…"

Lex laughs. A crazy maniacal laugh.

"Listen to yourselves," Lex mocks. "We're all fucking crazy, or haven't you realized that by now? We'll never be sane!" He rolls his eyes. "We're not like normal people. We won't get to live happily ever after. We're cursed. We always will be. Acacia made sure of that, but we still have a chance at freedom. That's what we want, isn't it? That's what *she* wanted."

Aiden cracks a tiny smile. My shoulders sag in relief. He's back again.

"We're breaking her out," Aiden says with a newfound determination. "She's our fucking property, and we're bringing her home."

I grin. "Yes!"

"And then we finish what we started?" Lex asks.

Aiden nods. "Acacia's going down, then we're getting the hell out of Pasturesville and away from Sunnycrest for good. All four of us."

CHAPTER
FORTY-FOUR

SARAH

I PORE OVER THE DIARY, reading about my punishments and the times Dad locked me in Sunnycrest to stamp the spirit out of me. It's easy to see why Dad paid Officer Blackwell to dispose of my diary, and even easier to see why Officer Blackwell kept it. This is pretty damning evidence. It lays out what a monster he is. If anyone read it, they'd be sure to question my father. Maybe Blackwell is sharper than Erin thought.

When writing, I omitted any details about the guys and our hookups to avoid getting them into trouble. I regret that now. I can't trust my own memory, and I'd like to remember exactly how I felt back then.

Although returning, my memories are still a little fuzzy, but the more I recall, the sharper they become.

Our relationship revolved around sex at the beginning. I liked knowing we were doing something forbidden, as well as getting the best orgasms of my life. It soon turned into more than that...

I continue flicking through the pages, laughing at how he thought letting me stay there for one weekend would change who I am. I chortle as I read a passage.

Dad took me to Sunnycrest this weekend. He wanted to show me what would happen if I broke his rules again. I was terrified! I was sleeping in a cell next to murderers and psychopaths! One of them threatened me with a knife. I thought I was going to die!

Okay, so I had a flair for the dramatics. In fact, the truth was very different. Another memory comes back from that weekend…

"Seriously?" I face off against Dad as he hauls me into a cell. "You're going to leave me here?"

"It's only for the weekend," Dad says. "I want you to see what could happen if you don't change your ways."

I huff and flop down onto the firm bed, where a mound of disgusting gray clothes lies in wait.

"I'm not wearing that," I say, picking up the sweatshirt and dropping it in disgust. "It's not my color."

"This is a hospital." Color creeps up Dad's neck as he tsks in exasperation. "Not a catwalk!"

"Clearly," I mutter sarcastically. "Look, it's bad enough that you're making me stay here. It doesn't mean I'm going to look terrible doing it. I don't care whether this is a hospital. I'm not sick, remember? I'm just a disappointment."

Dad looks like he wants to tear the clothes off my body and force me into the horrible shapeless items. Thankfully, a knock on the door spares me another tirade of abuse.

"Enter!" Dad barks impatiently. He checks his watch and frowns.

"We need you, Doctor Acacia!" An orderly barges in, then casts a nervous look in my direction. "We have a… new arrival… who needs orientation before this evening."

"I'll be right there," Dad snaps, then narrows his eyes at me. "You will see the therapist this afternoon. Lord knows, they may help you." He points at me menacingly. "If I find out you've caused

any trouble in the meantime, you will pay dearly. Do you understand?"

"What're you going to do? Send me to Sunnycrest?" I arch one eyebrow. "I'm already here."

His lips purse like he's sucking a very sour lemon, then he scowls and stomps away. I hear him picking faults with the orderly as they get farther away.

I run a hand through my blonde hair and shake my head to give it added volume. Annoyingly, Dad confiscated my purse, so I can't reapply my makeup.

The cell door isn't locked, and I saunter into the hall. I'm greeted by a swarm of identically dressed girls. Silence descends. Obviously, they all know who I am. Their stares are full of curious intrigue, anger, and a sprinkling of bitter resentment. Maybe they just like my outfit. My denim shorts and crop top are better suited to a frat party than an asylum.

"What're you staring at?" I ask, putting my hands on my hips.

Being Acacia's daughter won't win me any favors, but I'm not gonna kiss their asses.

"You think you're so special, don't you?" a pretty girl with dark hair dares to answer. She's flanked by two minions wearing smug smirks. "Your dad owning this place doesn't mean shit. Here, you're not untouchable."

I pout, looking her up and down in bemusement.

"Is that supposed to be a threat?" I laugh. "You'll have to do better than that to scare me."

Her eyes widen, taken aback. Did she expect me to quake and fall to my knees, begging for surrender? Puh-lease. Her groupie's draw a sharp breath, horrified someone sassed their queen.

"You…" the girl stammers. "You should be scared."

She's regained her composure, but it's too late. I've already seen through her mask. I know girls like her. Girls who are so insecure that they tear down everyone else to make themselves feel better. Unluckily for her, I've heard better teardowns from fellow cheerleaders. Petty jealousy is rife on the squad, and there's always some kind of drama.

"Seriously?" I roll my eyes. "Is that the best you can do?"

She steps forward and slides a shiny object out of her sleeve. I don't get the chance to see it properly, as we're suddenly cast under a massive shadow. The minions dart back against the wall, and one of them squeaks like a terrified mouse.

A hand grabs her wrist and wrenches the gleaming object from her grasp.

"I'll pretend I didn't see that, Charlie," Aiden growls.

Lex and Eli lurk behind him. Some girls watching on bite their lips nervously, while others smooth down their hair. I can smell their fear and lust a mile off. Unfortunately for them, the guys are already mine...

Upon Aiden's arrival, the girl—Charlie—has a miraculous change of heart. Her entire expression changes, first freezing, then batting her eyelashes and smiling.

"I wasn't gonna use it." She simpers like an idiot. "This is the new girl. Acacia's daughter. I wanted to make sure she knew the rules—"

"The rules?" I interrupt. "I make the fucking rules."

I wrap my arms around Aiden's neck and pull him in for a kiss. He responds hungrily, wrapping his giant hands around my waist possessively. His tongue darts into my mouth, sweeping me off my feet, not caring that we have an audience.

Lex's wolf whistle breaks the moment. Reluctantly, I pull away and see Charlie hasn't moved. Her shoulders are tense, and her arms have gone weirdly rigid, like she's internally combusting.

"Why are you here? Run along." I shoo her. "You're dismissed."

Charlie's jaw drops, completely stunned. Her cheeks flush in anger, and she casts a longing look at Aiden. "But—"

"You heard her," Aiden says, threading his fingers through mine. "Get out of our girl's way."

The way he says 'our girl' makes me tingle in all the right places. Charlie's eyes fill with tears, and she scurries off to whatever *wretched hole she wormed out of. Good fucking riddance. Usually, I think public humiliation is unnecessary, but there's nothing sweeter than making a mean girl pay.*

Aiden chuckles fondly. "You've been here less than an hour, and you're already running this place."

Lex smirks. "She won't be popular."

"So?" Eli says. "She doesn't need to be. She has us."

They lead me into the cafeteria.

"Welcome to Sunnycrest!" Lex says, extending his arms and twirling around.

Every head turns to face us, including the staff. I notice a few raised eyebrows, and people whispering behind their hands. One glare from Aiden shuts everyone up instantly.

I slip my fingers out of his grasp.

Aiden turns in anger. "What—"

"If Dad sees, I don't want you getting in trouble," I say.

"It's nothing I can't handle," Aiden says, but he doesn't hold my hand again.

Maybe part of him knows I'm right, or he knows better than to argue with me.

"We'll just have to sneak into your room later when he won't have eyes on us," Lex says, winking.

"Is that a promise?" I tease.

Eli's eyes trail down my body, fucking me with his eyes. "You bet it is."

He leads me to a table and pulls out a chair like a true gentleman.

"Thanks," I say, sitting with a smirk.

Dad thought a weekend at Sunnycrest would scare me. Somehow, I don't think he banked on three monsters treating me like a princess.

"What did you do?" I ask, half teasing, but also curious. "It's like you rule this place."

The three of them exchange a look. The same look I've become accustomed to. A look that means there's more they could say but won't.

"They know what we're capable of," Aiden replies cryptically.

Before I can probe him further, he beckons a boy over. The boy reminds me of a scarecrow with straw-like, yellow hair and a clumsy walk. He lollops toward us like a dog being whistled by his master.

"Yes?" the boy asks, half panting. "What can I do?"

"Go to the kitchen and bring Sarah a proper meal, Alfred," Aiden orders. "Cook will know what to do."

"Yes, Aiden," he says, bowing his head as a mark of respect. "Coming right up, Sarah."

"You don't have—"

Lex holds up his finger to silence me. "Go!"

Alfred squeaks and scuttles away, almost tripping over his own feet in his haste.

"You can't rule the masses without a little fear, sweetheart." Eli smiles lazily, and his hand creeps under the table to stroke my thigh. "You'll learn that soon enough."

I throw the diary away and cup my ears. Erin stirs under the surface. I sense her wanting to speak, probably to say something comforting, but I push her down. I want to be left alone with my thoughts. I don't need her to make me feel better or attempt to condone what they've done. And, most of all, I don't want her seeing the darkest thoughts in my head.

I love Erin, but there's an innate competitiveness between twins. It's natural when you're brought up together and compared. Erin always won out with our father. The guys were mine first. Is it so wrong that I didn't want to share them with her? While I know it's not her fault—she didn't ask to be stalked—I can't help being mad that she took something that was mine.

I remember when I first met the guys. They were fiercely protective, and I loved the feeling that they would do anything for me. It was addictive. Still, despite getting to know them, I always struggled to get them to open up fully.

They always held something back. They never divulged all the details about what happened to them during their time in the asylum, yet they told Erin. Why couldn't they talk to me?

"They'd have told you eventually," Erin whispers.

"Are you sure about that?" I ask, giving way to her consciousness.

I thought I knew them well...

Aiden's an alpha. He'll do anything, including killing, for the people he loves. He's strong, makes the rules, and likes to get his own way, but not because he likes to control people—not all the time, anyway—but because he tries to help them. I once asked him about the rat skulls he wears around his neck. He told me how they used to be his only friends and serve as a physical reminder of how far he's come. Perhaps that's why he clings to those he loves so tightly...

Lex is a total heathen, and I always loved that about him. Like me, he's not afraid of causing trouble. He's a rebel who uses dark humor to hide his emotions. In fact, he likes to pretend he doesn't have any feelings at all, but there's more to him. In his gaze, I sometimes caught sight of a hidden vulnerability. I don't know exactly how he got his scars from the fire that killed his family, but he plays up to the idea of being a monster. How much of that is real?

Eli is easier to read. He's the most sensitive of the group and wears his heart on his sleeve. If it wasn't for everything Dad put him through, he'd be the definition of a perfect gentleman. He has old-fashioned values, yet his obsessive tendencies give way to darker desires that lurk under the surface. That's why he likes trophies, hair, underwear... anything to keep his latest obsession close. Conflicting thoughts pop into my head when I think of him. I know now that he killed Erin, but he wasn't operating under his own free will. Can I ever forgive him?

"I forgive him," Erin says.

"Of course you do," I mutter sarcastically. "You're too nice for your own good. He killed you, remember?"

"Dad killed me," she corrects. "Not Eli."

"You've had my body for a year," I snap, hitting the side of my head, as if the action will somehow get her to fall out of my head. "Can I get a little fucking peace for a minute?"

She must have listened as a deadly silence follows, making me instantly regret my outburst. Being truly alone is even worse.

Suddenly, my cell door bursts open. Bright lights from the hall flood in, making me squint to see an ominous outline in the doorway. A masked figure steps inside, and I jump to my feet. Two more masked men follow him, and the door closes behind them with a bang.

I clench my fists and hold them up like I'm preparing for a fight.

Lex chuckles from behind his black balaclava. He's the one on the left.

"Come on, sweetheart," Eli says to the right of Aiden, who stands in the middle. He raises his hands. "Don't make this harder than it needs to be."

"I'll scream," I warn. "The orderlies will come. My father will find you. He'll lock you up and throw away the key!"

"No one is coming," Lex says. "We've made sure of that."

"I'm not Erin," I hiss. "You can't intimidate me."

Aiden steps forward. "We know you're angry, but—"

"Fuck you!" I cut him off. I'm not playing by his rules. Not anymore. "I'm not going anywhere with you. Wasn't I clear enough the first time? Leave me alone."

"We can't do that," Eli says. "We're the only ones who can help you."

"I don't want your help," I hiss indignantly.

"You don't have a choice," Aiden says. "Your father will find out you're back soon."

"I'm a good actress," I say, but my voice quivers.

How long can I really pretend to be my sister? I can't lose control again or let her take over.

"Not that good," Lex says. He takes out his cell phone and holds it up. "You need to watch this."

"What is it?" My lip curls. "Another video of you fucking Erin?"

"You can't hold that over us forever," Aiden says impatiently. "We thought you were dead."

"That doesn't justify it," I snap. "You aren't crazy enough to think we'll pick up where we left off, right? Too much has happened!'

Lex thrusts the phone into my hand. "Just fucking watch it!"

I snatch it from him and hit play.

It's a video of Doctor Warner's office.

"We installed hidden cameras, so we could watch your sessions," Eli explains.

"So much for patient confidentiality," I mutter sarcastically.

In the video, Doctor Warner sits behind his desk, shuffling through papers. He looks terrible. He struggles to keep his eyes open and drinks a coffee before putting his head in his hands. If he wasn't partially responsible for trying to erase me from existence, I might actually feel sorry for him.

"Another depressed doctor? Big deal!" I say. "If you haven't noticed, this place is full of them."

"Keep watching," Lex urges.

Doctor Warner's office door swings open, and my father steps inside. He opens the door with enough force for it to hit the opposing wall. Doctor Warner jumps up, and his blood-shot eyes widen in fear.

"This video was taken an hour ago." Aiden points. "Look at the time stamps."

I turn up the volume and keep watching.

"Something's off," Dad says. "She's not acting how she should be."

Doctor Warner adjusts his tie nervously, and a bead of sweat drips down his forehead. For a psychiatrist, you'd think he'd be better at feigning confidence. I'm not a body language expert, but even I can tell he's acting shady.

"W-what do you mean?" Doctor Warner stammers.

If Dad finds out about Doctor Warner working with the guys and reducing my medication, he'd find himself the subject in my father's next twisted experiment. Luckily for him, Dad seems too distracted and annoyed to notice Doctor Warner's nerves.

"She's not my Erin!" Dad blasts. "The rule breaking… the back talk… what she said to Jocelyn during visiting hours… it's her. Sarah's breaking through. I can feel it."

"Erin's going through a rebellious phase," Doctor Warner suggests. "It's common at her age. She seems fine to—"

"You don't know her like I do!" Dad picks up Doctor Warner's metronome and hurls it against the wall, smashing a framed painting. "This isn't how Erin behaves. Make preparations for repeating the procedure."

"But, Magnus, that's madness," Doctor Warner says. "The upload of Erin's consciousness will have disintegrated since the first procedure. The consequences could be disastrous. Think of the age gap alone. She'll have no memory of anything from the point you moved to Pasturesville."

Dad grabs Doctor Warner by the collar and sprays spit over his face as he yells, "I said, make the preparations!"

"But…" Doctor Warner whimpers, and his face reddens as he struggles to breathe. "It would almost certainly kill her."

My heart thunders.

Dad drops his hold, and Doctor Warner splutters, massaging his neck.

Dad takes a deep breath. I think he's about to come to his senses, then he says in a chilling tone that makes my blood run cold, "I've told you once before, my daughter is already dead. I will do anything to get her back."

"Magnus… we have to stop… we…"

"No!" Dad blasts. "I make the rules! If you don't comply, I will destroy you, Warner. I'll make sure you never see the light of fucking day again. Your career, your life's work, and your reputation will be gone in an instant. Do I make myself clear?"

I hope Doctor Warner will finally grow a pair of balls, but he only snivels and nods warily. Spineless coward.

"Okay," he says. "But it'll take time. I need to tweak the machine."

"You have twenty-four hours," Dad says. "We'll do it tomorrow."

Lex gently extracts the phone from my sweaty palm.

"Do you see what we're up against now?" Aiden asks.

"What I'm up against," I correct him. "I don't need your help."

Aiden strokes my cheek. "So fucking stubborn." I hear the smile in his voice as the black fabric covering his mouth stretches. "You really are back."

My body responds involuntarily to his touch, and a tremble of longing shoots between my legs. What's wrong with me? I turn my head and bite his finger hard. That's better.

"Ouch," he hisses, yanking his hand away and scowling.

"Wise choice," I say.

"We spoke to Doctor Warner on our way here," Eli says as Aiden glowers at me. "We have a plan. A plan that, if it works, will give all of us what we've been waiting for."

"See? You're always thinking of yourselves," I mutter scathingly.

"We're on the same side," Lex says. "You may hate us, but you hate your father more. We're not just doing this for us. Don't you want justice for Erin?"

My rage boils over in another furious outburst as I jab my finger into his hard pec. "Don't you dare say her fucking name!"

"Let us help you," Eli says softly. "I know it won't change what happened, but we can make this right."

"Says the guy who murdered my sister," I snap.

Eli steps back like he's been sucker punched. His haunted eyes sparkle with guilt. I sense Erin's disapproval prickle under my skin. I've always had a quick temper. Act first, ask questions later is my motto.

"It wasn't his fault, Sarah," Aiden growls protectively. "And you know it."

"She's right, though," Eli says. "I'm a killer. A killer. Killer. Killer." He falls into a robot-like trance. "A killer. Killer. Killer. I'm a killer."

He never used to be like this. My stomach knots with guilt over triggering him. He's hurting just as much as I am. Erin must agree, as she bursts to the surface like a volcano erupting.

"I forgive you, Eli."

Erin's words leap from my mouth, and everyone freezes.

Eli's jaw drops. "E-Erin?" he stammers, putting his hand on my shoulder. "Is that you?"

"Yes," she says. "And I mean it, Eli."

Eli's face crumples. "Erin, I'm so sorry..."

"That's enough." I blink hard and take a deep breath to suppress her, then hiss, "This isn't about you, Erin."

I'm the one who died, she responds in my mind in her annoying know-it-all way. *It's very much about me. Thank you very much.*

"Shut it," I command. "Can you give me time to think for a second without butting in?"

Thankfully, she fades, although her lingering disapproval eats away at my conscience. The sensation of having her stuck in my head is hard to describe. She's getting a front-row seat to my life while being stuck in a room in the back of my brain. She will appear when called, and I can push her back if I try hard enough. However, if she feels strongly enough about something, she's able to burst through of her own accord.

"She's still in there?" Aiden asks, obviously stunned. "I thought when you came back, she—"

"She'd disappear forever? No." I ignore his probing gaze that has an unnatural skill for knowing what I'm thinking. "It doesn't seem to work like that."

"All the more reason for us to work together," Lex insists. "If we don't stop him, who knows what he'll do next?"

"Let us help you," Eli says. "Both of you." He wipes his watery eyes pleadingly. "Please."

They know my father's twisted ways and this asylum better than anyone. They may be the only chance I have to not lose myself again, even if it means swallowing my pride.

"Fine," I say. My jaw hardens, resolute in what I must do. "We'll work together. Just this once. After that, we're done. What's the plan?"

"So…" Aiden begins.

WE BRIEFED SARAH. Obviously, she wasn't happy about it, and neither am I. Having to leave her in the asylum unprotected is like torture. I don't want her trapped there any longer than necessary, but Aiden keeps reminding us that picking our moment is important.

"She's not alone," Aiden says, like he can read my thoughts. "She has Erin."

"Yeah, because her sister's voice in her head is going to help her," I mutter sarcastically.

It was a petty thing to say, but it still makes me feel better.

How is it even possible for Erin to still be living in Sarah's head? I can't stop replaying her words. Erin forgives me. I never thought I'd get to apologize to her. Although it was comforting to hear from Erin, it hasn't got rid of my guilt. Forgiveness or not, it'll follow me around like a black cloud forever. I'm a killer—yet another thing I have Acacia to thank for.

"Hello?" Lex waves his hand in front of my face. "Anyone home?"

We're standing in a cleaning closet. Between the mops and vacuum cleaners, there's little space, and we're squashed shoulder to shoulder, counting down the minutes.

Aiden checks his watch and nods. "It's time."

They are leaving the asylum, while I stay a little longer. There's one last job to do, and I'm the best person to handle it.

"Are you sure you don't want me to stay, Eli?" Aiden prompts, jerking me from my daydreams.

"What?" I say, then shake my head to avoid dwelling on Erin's words. None of it matters if we don't get her out. "Yes, of course."

Aiden chews his lip. I know what that means. He's having second thoughts about trusting me with something so important.

"I can do this, Aiden," I insist, more lucid and eager to prove myself. He's done so much for us. I won't let him down. "I know I can."

"Don't take any risks," he says. "Get what we need and leave, understood?"

I nod firmly. "Understood."

"We'll see you on the other side, brother," Aiden says, clapping me on the back.

"We're so close." Lex rubs his hands together gleefully. "I can almost fucking taste it!"

"It's not over yet," Aiden reminds him grimly.

We know what happens when you get complacent or cocky; mistakes happen and people die. A higher power has never looked out for us before and won't start now. We're all we've got. Sticking together is our only way to survive.

"I've got this," I say. "I'll see you soon."

"Remember, no risks, Eli," Aiden says again, right before he and Lex scramble up into a vent.

"No risks," I chirp back dutifully, screwing the vent cover closed behind them.

Next, I'm going to pay Doctor Warner a visit.

We have an agreement, and I have to ensure that he makes good on his word. There's no room for errors. Not this close to the end.

I stick to the shadows as I weave through the asylum. This reminds me of stalking Erin at Stonybridge Academy. It was only child's play, but I smile fondly at the memory. It was fun to break in and make her squirm. We were almost spotted by other students a few times, but it's surprising how little people pay attention. No one likes to stare into the shadows for too long. They're scared of what they'll see looking back, and for good reason.

Around the next corner, I hear two doctors talking. A pair of Acacia's most loyal followers.

Shit…

We had made arrangements with the relevant orderlies and bribed a security guard to give me a clear route to Doctor Warner's office after hours, but Aiden's warning makes me think twice about continuing. Instead, I head in the opposite direction. The ceiling it is, then. I find another vent to climb into and crawl on my stomach through the familiar tunnels. Even the cramped space doesn't seem as claustrophobic as usual when I know this will be one of the last times I'm here.

Almost there…

I see lights at the end of the tunnel.

Doctor Warner is waiting.

I peer through the slats in the metal and prod the grate with my little finger. It falls with a bang onto the floor below. Doctor Warner flinches at the sound but doesn't look up from his book as I drop into his office. Unfortunately for him, impromptu visits from maniacs have become the norm lately.

He looks even worse than the last time I saw him. He has a vacant, glazed look from lack of sleep, he's not shaved in days, and his suit is riddled with creases. Maybe we've broken him.

"No smile?" I mock. "I thought you'd be happy to see me."

"I already told Aiden." He sighs deeply, pushing his slipping glasses wearily back into position. "We're on track."

I don't like his abrupt tone and slam my fists on his desk, making him jump. He shrinks back in his seat, remembering his place. We're in charge, and he better remember that.

"I don't need to remind you how important this is," I snarl. "After tomorrow, we're gone. All four of us. That's what you want too, isn't it?"

"I did everything you asked."

"And the car?"

"All sorted," he says, passing me a set of keys. "All the preparations are made. Does Sarah know?"

"Yes," I say. "Aiden wanted me to remind you of what will happen if you screw us over. Your wife's pregnant, isn't she?"

His face pales. "How do you—"

"We know everything," I interrupt. "A bouncing baby boy is on the way. A mini Doctor Warner! We all want to make sure that he grows up with parents, don't we?"

"Everything is sorted." His bottom lip trembles. "I promise."

Threatening his family is a low blow, even for us, but nothing is off limits when our freedom is at stake.

"Good," I say. "And the supply of drugs?"

He opens the top draw of his desk, fumbling around with shaking fingers to retrieve a box. "Everything you need is here."

"Now I need you to explain exactly how it works," I say. "The dosage, the effects, how long it will last. Everything."

For our plan to work, I need to be prepared. I already have some understanding following my time as Acacia's test subject. When Acacia held me hostage in the lead-up to Erin's death, I spent days drifting in and out of consciousness. During my stretches of time awake, I took in my surroundings. I paid careful attention to the chemical names, watching how he mixed them together, and what he muttered as he made notes. Naively, I had hoped that by understanding how

Acacia's drug worked, I'd be able to reverse its effects. However, it was too strong, and Erin died before I had the opportunity.

"Do you have any questions?" Doctor Warner asks after spending almost an hour explaining in painstaking detail how the drug worked. It was easy enough to follow. If Sunnycrest hadn't stolen my potential, I'd have made an excellent scientist. My mind works logically, and I have a natural understanding of the subject.

"Only one," I say. "Do you have any spare implants?"

"Spares?" He frowns. "Well, I guess so, but I don't see why you'd need them."

"We'll need some of those," I say. "Just in case."

There's no room for error. I've let down the guys once before—it's my fault Erin died, and we lost a year with Sarah. I won't let that happen again. I'm not losing her, and I'll do whatever it takes to keep her.

CHAPTER
FORTY-SIX

SARAH

I STARE at a crack on the wall, waiting for them to come.

Underneath my skin, Erin stirs, unable to express her anxiety. I wish she'd give it a rest as keeping calm is already difficult enough without dealing with her jittery energy.

"I thought you said we could trust them," I say in accusation.

"You can!" Erin replies.

"Then will you calm the fuck down?" I snap. "You're making me antsy."

I've always been short-tempered and quick to act, while Erin was more patient and calculated.

"I can't help it," she replies.

"Well, cool it, or I'll think you out of existence," I threaten.

Her smile stretches over my mouth. "I don't think that's possible."

"You know you only exist because of me, right?"

"You can trust them, Sarah," she says, seeing past my confident bravado. Hiding anything from her is fucking impossible when she has a front-row seat to every single one of my emotions. "We want the same things. They'll stop Dad, so he can't hurt anyone else."

"But they're bad people," I say. "Don't you remember what they did to you?"

"Who wouldn't be damaged after being stuck in Sunnycrest for most of their lives?"

"Save it for someone who cares, Mother Teresa," I say.

"But the videos…"

Although I didn't see them myself, I caught a glimpse of Erin's memories. I clench my jaw to shut the images out. I'm already nauseous at the thought of what's coming next, and I need a clear head.

Erin senses my discomfort and a comforting feeling sweeps through me, like I'm getting a hug from the inside.

"We're starting afresh when we get out of here," I say, putting my focus firmly on the future again. "We'll start over, away from them. That's our deal."

"You can't lie to me, Sarah," she says. "They hurt you, but I know your feelings for them are strong."

"Hurt?" I snort. "The only thing hurting me is a headache because of your constant chatting!"

She sighs and falls into a huffy silence. She doesn't know my own feelings better than I do.

Before I get into another argument with my twin, my cell door flies open suddenly.

This is it.

An orderly with a screwed-up face and slapped-ass expressions steps inside.

"Come with me, Miss Acacia," he barks.

He's flanked by two other orderlies, who look like small gorillas and have sullen scowls.

"Where are we going?" I ask, playing ignorant. They need to think I don't know what's happening. "Am I going home?"

"Get her arms," one commands.

The other two grab me and roughly tug me to my feet.

"Hey!" I yell. "Keep your hands to yourself!"

Careful, Erin warns in my head, *you're supposed to be me, remember? I'd follow without a fuss.*

The orderlies don't pay any attention to my comments, though. They have about three brain cells between them, so I doubt they'd notice any changes to my temperament.

"Get the mask," one gorilla says.

While my arms are held, they put a thick, black band of material over my eyes, pinning them closed.

"What're you doing?" I ask as darkness descends. "I need to see! What if I fall?"

The other gorilla loosens his grip.

"Acacia's orders were clear," another says. "Mask and straitjacket!"

I gulp, tempted to knee them in the balls and run, but I wouldn't get far before I'm caught and plied with sedatives. I can't miss the moment my father finally gets what's coming to him.

They force the straitjacket over my head and fold my arms across my front in an uncomfortable position.

Stay calm, Erin soothes me. *It won't be long now.*

"Ready to go," the orderly says.

Between them, I'm dragged through the deserted hallways like a rag doll. It's hard to have good footing when you can't see where you're going, and I pray I don't trip and smash my face. With my movement restricted and sight robbed, my other senses heighten. My heart thuds in my ears. They're treating me like a criminal being led to the gallows. I swallow hard. If our plan doesn't work, then that's exactly what I'll be facing…

"*I'm right here with you*," Erin says in my head. "*I'm not going anywhere.*"

Despite our earlier disagreement, I'm grateful she's here now. We're facing this together.

"Erin," I reply through my thoughts. "*If this goes wrong and I die, I want you to know that I'm sorry.*"

"You have nothing to apologize for."

"I wasn't the best sister," I say. *"I kept trying to push you out of your comfort zone. It's my fault you died. I guess…"* It's time for total honesty. This could be the last chance we get. *"I guess part of me has always been jealous because you were the twin who always did everything right. You were the perfect one, and I was… a disappointment."*

"Jealous?" The gravity of her shock floors me. *"I was always jealous of you! You've always been so confident and brave, never being afraid to say what you think. You stood up for Mom when I didn't. I'm sorry I didn't see the truth sooner. I wish I had. Maybe then, things would have been different."*

"We can't change the past, but we're trying to fix it now," I say. *"That's all we can do."*

Whatever happens, at least we've made amends, and we're facing my father in solidarity.

Our bonding moment is rudely cut short by an orderly dragging me around a corner. I stumble, but a flabby arm catches me before I fall.

"What's happening?" I say.

There's a series of beeps, the sound of cards being swiped, and then my father's voice makes my blood run cold.

"Thank you for escorting her," he says. We've reached our final destination. "Return to work."

"Yes, Doctor Acacia," the orderlies respond in tandem.

Suddenly, my mask is ripped away. My first instinct is to shut my eyes because of the blinding white light. After being locked in solitary confinement, it's like staring straight into the sun, and my retinas burn.

"Dad?" I squint up at him. "What's happening?"

We're in the operating theatre. A surge of adrenaline rushes through me, willing my legs to run, but I stay frozen. This is where it started, and this is where it has to end.

"Hello, Erin," Doctor Warner greets me. I hadn't noticed him lurking around, looking like he'd rather be anywhere but here. "You're here to complete the final phase of your treatment."

I search his gaze, looking for a flash of reassurance. However, it doesn't come. He can't even look at me.

Panic sets in.

What if Doctor Warner can't be trusted?

My bottom lip trembles. "I want to leave."

My fear is no longer an act. It gnaws deep into my bones and grips my core, while the various machines around the room hum ominously. These same machines somehow transferred my dead sister's consciousness into my head. Machines that could kill my soul forever.

"Sit on the edge of this table, and we'll remove the jacket," Dad orders.

Begrudgingly, I do as he asks while he studies me closely. I'm not sure what he's looking for, but his scrutiny makes me uneasy, and my skin prickles.

Doctor Warner removes the jacket, and I flex my fingers, grateful to have regained control. While I'm enjoying the temporary relief, a sharp sting on the side of my neck makes me yelp.

"What the fuck?" I gasp, turning to stare at Doctor Warner, who is brandishing an empty syringe.

"See?" Dad jabs his finger in my direction. "More proof that she's not acting like herself. My Erin doesn't curse."

"The medication will relax you," Doctor Warner says. "Lie back."

Do as they say, Erin's thoughts come to me. *They'll be here…*

My arms and legs don't feel quite right. They're heavier, and it takes great effort to move. My stomach rolls. Doctor Warner was only supposed to inject me with saline, but there was definitely something else in that shot.

My eyes dart to the doors, willing them to open. "But I don't need a procedure."

"Please lie down," Doctor Warner says.

"Do as the doctor says, Erin," Dad snarls.

"I don't want to," I say.

Where are they? They should be here by now! Aiden promised I'd never have to lie on the operating table.

"Just relax," Doctor Warner pleads. "This won't take long."

"No!" I say, trying to stand. Shooting pins and needles makes me sit back down again. "I don't want to!"

Dad sighs, then pulls a filled syringe from his shirt pocket. "I had hoped we wouldn't need to fully sedate you."

My eyes widen with panic. "No!"

A crash cuts my scream short as the theatre doors burst open. Aiden, Eli, and Lex enter. All of them look thunderous and ready to tear someone's head off.

"Sorry we're late," Aiden says, glaring at Doctor Warner. "It appears there was a problem with our key cards."

Doctor Warner whimpers like a wounded puppy. "I…"

"Enough," Lex snaps, grabbing Doctor Warner's wrist like a limp piece of lettuce and twisting. His bones make a horrible snap. "Now, we're even."

Doctor Warner slumps to the ground at Lex's feet, sniveling and cradling his wrist like a baby.

Eli grins at me apologetically. "Sorry for the delay, sweetheart."

"See?" Erin declares in triumph. *"I told you so."* I'm too relieved to chastise her for gloating.

Dad freezes as his mind turns a thousand miles an hour to figure out what's happening. While he's distracted, Aiden swipes the syringe from his grasp in a slick motion.

"We'll be taking this," Aiden says.

He tosses it to Lex. Doctor Warner senses what's coming and tries to scramble away. In the process, he snags a wire and wrenches it out of the machine, causing a deflated, fizzing noise.

"No!" Dad yells as the machine's screens power off. "Put it back!"

It's too late. Lex has already injected Doctor Warner, who is now sprawled across the floor, unconscious.

"Erin?" Dad looks quizzically from me to Aiden. "Do you know these patients?"

"We've become well acquainted in recent months, Doctor Acacia," Aiden hisses.

"You've had your fun, Zero," Dad says. "You should have stayed gone. Why return?"

"Maybe because they have a conscience?" I suggest. "Unlike you."

Dad isn't stupid. He's outnumbered, and fighting isn't an option.

"I don't know what these men have told you, but they're lying," Dad says, opting to manipulate his way out of the situation. "You can't trust them, Erin."

"No," I say, rising to my feet. My legs are still a little shaky, but I refuse to have this conversation with him looking down at me. "The only person I can't trust is you."

"You don't know what you're saying," Dad says. "I know you're mad, but, Erin—"

"Don't you dare say her name," I hiss. My voice is as cold as ice, but my boiling fury erupts to the surface. "Erin's dead."

Dad's cheeks turn ashen gray as realization dawns on him. His act is up.

"I know everything," I say.

"Whatever you think you know is wrong," Dad says. His pathetic excuses won't work. He can't worm his way out of the corner he's backed into. Perhaps he realizes that. "You don't understand."

Lex and Aiden grab his shoulders and haul him to the operating table. Dad thrashes to free himself, but it's no use.

The guys are strong and effortlessly bind his wrists and ankles to the table.

In the corner, Doctor Warner stirs and crawls into a seated position. He's thoroughly disheveled with his glasses askew on his face.

"Warner, raise the alarm!" Dad orders. "They're back!"

"I can do this without you, Warner," Eli says, extending his hand. "But it'll be quicker with your help."

"I'm sorry, Magnus," Doctor Warner mumbles, letting Eli pull him up.

"What are you doing?" Dad asks, watching in horror as Doctor Warner moves to the workbench. "Warner! I'll fucking destroy you for this!"

Doctor Warner ignores him. His hands shake as he crushes various pills into powders, measures liquids in various glass containers, and starts mixing them together.

"Don't even think about using a low dosage because I'll know," Eli warns as Doctor Warner carefully adds a few droplets to turn the clear liquid a lurid green. "If it doesn't work, we'll strap you to the table next."

"Call for help, Erin!" Dad begs, still feeding his disillusion. "I'll take you home. You'll never come here again. You can play piano—even study music at college! That's what you want, isn't it, Erin?"

Pathetic.

"Too little, too late," I mutter.

He controlled every aspect of our family's life for years, but he never truly cared about us. We were just like his patients. He's a psychopath with a superiority complex. It's only fitting he meets his demise like this.

"This is your final warning," Dad says. "If you don't do as I say, Erin…"

Of course he's resorting to threats because bribery didn't work.

"Stop calling me Erin!" I scream. "I'm Sarah!"

Dad's lips twist into a cruel sneer.

"You!" he spits, searing me with a look of pure hatred. "What have you done to her? My Erin would never do this."

The inferno building inside me finally explodes.

"You killed Erin!" I scream. "She's dead because of you!"

"I got her back," he says coldly, with zero remorse. "You're the one who killed her for good."

Please, let me speak to him.

"It's too risky," I say. "He won't listen. He never does."

I need to do this.

"Who are you muttering to?" Dad asks. "See? I was right to bring you to Sunnycrest. You're just like your mother. You never do as you're told."

"No one will ever have to follow your orders again," Aiden growls. "She'll be free. We'll make sure of that."

"And you three misfits think you can look after her?" Dad scoffs. "You, the kid whose whore mother didn't love him, or what about him? The boy who burned his house down and killed his family! And don't get me started on Twenty-Five. If you think you'll skip off into the sunset, you're wrong."

I don't have time to dwell on what Dad said as Erin claws her way to the surface. My skull feels like it's about to crack in two.

"Ouch!" I yelp, clutching my head.

The pain.

It's too much…

"Sarah!" Aiden catches my arm to steady me as I wobble on my feet. "Are you okay?"

Suddenly, I'm not in control anymore.

It's Erin.

I'm simply a spectator watching the scene play out, powerless to do anything.

Erin, I think. *Stop it!*

"I need to do this," she says aloud.

"Erin…?" Lex asks, sensing the shift.

She smiles. My furious shakes stop, and my shoulders slacken as her calmness washes over me.

"Erin?" Dad's face softens instantly, noticing the change of my demeanor. "Oh, darling. Is it really you?"

"Yes," she replies. "It's me."

"Your sister has got me into this horrible mess, and these men? They're criminals," he says. "I need your help."

Erin doesn't move.

"Why was nothing ever good enough for you?" she asks.

"What?" He frowns in confusion. "We can talk about that later, now—"

"I always looked up to you," she interrupts. "I believed you loved us, that you did bad things because you wanted to protect us. That was before I learned the truth. You tried to kill Sarah, and you torture your patients."

"That's a lie," he says. "I don't know what these men have—"

Even in this moment, when he's tied to an operating table and has no hope of escape, he still chooses not to take accountability for his actions.

"I saw videos of your experiments," Erin says. "I watched you kill Alfred." She wipes a tear from my cheek. "Did you ever really care about us? About me?"

"Of course," Dad says. "You're more important to me than anything. I'd do anything for you."

"And Sarah?" she says.

"Your sister is sick," he sneers. "She always has been."

"Why are we wasting time talking?" Lex snaps impatiently.

I agree with him. This is a waste of time. Anyone can see he's irredeemable.

"Give her more time," Aiden says. "She needs this."

"You don't know what she needs," Dad hisses. "I tried to save you, Erin." His voice breaks. "I wanted to bring you back. Can't you see I did it all for you?"

"If you love me, you'll do the right thing," Erin says. "Turn yourself in and close Sunnycrest for good. It won't erase the pain you've caused, but it's the first step. Will you do that for me?"

"Pain?" Dad snorts. "No one cares about the patients here or what happens to them." He looks coldly around the room. "They're disturbed!"

I can't watch anymore.

"Goodbye forever, Dad," Erin says sadly.

I feel her pain and resignation as she retreats. She wanted to persuade him to do the right thing, but he's beyond saving. She always sees the best in people, but there's not an ounce of good left in our father. You can't reason with evil. This isn't a story where the villain has a sudden change of heart. He's rotten to the core.

"Erin!" Dad struggles, arching his back to sit up, but his binds are too tight. "Please—"

"Erin's gone," I snarl, reclaiming my place and channeling my inner strength. "And the only reason they are 'disturbed' is because you made them that way."

"It's ready," Doctor Warner says, holding up a vial. "Do you remember what to do, Eli?"

Eli nods. "Of course."

"I'll destroy you, Warner," Dad threatens. "If you want to take my memories—"

"Take your memories?" Aiden laughs. "Is that why you think we're here?"

Dad hesitates, and his forehead wrinkles in confusion.

"As much as we'd like to put you through every twisted experiment you inflicted on us, we have bigger plans," Lex says.

"We're not going stop your reign of terror," Eli says, taking a remote control with a red button out of his jacket pocket. "You are."

Fear flickers across Dad's face. "No!"

Aiden and Lex hold him down while he struggles like a flailing fish, and Doctor Warner approaches.

"Hold his arm still," Doctor Warner says. "Pull his sleeve up."

Their backs are turned, so I can't see exactly what they're doing, but when Doctor Warner withdraws, a small patch of blood stains my father's white shirt.

"Let's see if this works," Eli says with a twisted grin. He clicks the button on the remote. "Tell us how Alfred died."

Dad's face reddens. He bites the insides of his cheeks to stop himself from talking. Eli clicks the button again. The urge to speak is too strong to overcome.

I watch in fascination as words burst from Dad's mouth in a breathy gasp. "He was electrocuted!"

"How do you like having to do what I say?" Eli smirks. "Not fun, is it?"

"Can I g-go?" Doctor Warner stammers.

Aiden looks like he's having second thoughts, but I step in.

"Let him leave," I say. "We got what we wanted."

Aiden clenches his fists, but nods reluctantly. "Go, before I change my mind."

Doctor Warner doesn't need telling twice. He bolts away, skidding and almost tripping over his own feet in his hurry.

"What're you going to do now?" Dad hisses.

Despite his menacing glare, there's a glimmer of something else behind his eyes—fear. He's finally learning exactly how he made his victims feel.

"You're going to tell us where to find Erin's remains and your records," Aiden says. "The real records. The ones that document every experiment you've ever done. You're going to take them down to the station and confess."

"I won't," Dad sneers.

"You have no choice," Eli says, passing the remote to Aiden.

Aiden clicks the red button. "You won't attempt to escape or run."

Dad grits his jaw as Lex undoes his binds. His face contorts, like he's in pure agony, but his free will is gone. His own weapon has been turned against him.

"Kill me," Dad says. "You want to see me suffer, so kill me."

"Trust me, I'd like to," Lex purrs. "But killing you would be too easy."

Dad turns to me. "Sarah, think of what this is going to do to your mother."

"She already knows she married a monster," I say. "She'll be safe when you're locked up. You're finally going to get what you deserve and, while you're rotting in jail, your career, reputation, and everything you've built will be destroyed."

His cruel stare zeroes in on me. "You have always been my biggest failure."

Even though he knows his life is over, he still uses the last of his energy to make me feel small.

Lex lunges, but Eli grabs him before he lands a punch. Shame. I would have been happy to see him with a broken nose.

"No!" Eli says. "We can't have the cops asking questions."

"But—"

"Eli's right," Aiden says, returning his attention to my father and clicking the red button. "You will never speak or look at her again. You'll only speak again when I tell you to."

Lex scowls. However, he takes out some of his aggression by roughly hoisting my father up and tying his hands behind his back. Although restraints shouldn't be necessary, it doesn't hurt to have a backup measure in place.

"Before we leave, you have a decision to make, Sarah," Aiden says. He hands me the remote. "You can return to your old life, or you can make yourself disappear."

I stroke the smooth plastic object in my hands. It's virtually weightless, but it holds so much power…

"Disappear?" I look down at it. "What do you mean?"

"Your father killed Erin," Eli says. "He could have killed you both."

"You choose what happens next," Aiden says. "We said we'd give you freedom. It's up to you how you want to spend it."

If Sarah and Erin Acacia both die, I'm free to start over. Or, I could return to Mom and pick up the pieces of the life I left behind as the daughter of a criminal. The decision is easy.

"You killed both of your daughters," I say, clicking the red button. "You will confess to your crimes." I toss the control to Aiden, not wanting to see my father again. "Can we go now?"

"Take Sarah to the cabin and wait for us there," Aiden says.

"I'm not coming with you?" I ask.

"You're dead, remember?" Lex says. "You can't be running around Pasturesville."

"Come on." Eli wraps his arm around my shoulders. His embrace is warm and comforting. "It's time to go home."

CHAPTER
FORTY-SEVEN

SARAH

I CLING TO ELI, hanging on for dear life as the motorcycle takes dangerously quick swerves. Usually, I'd be screaming into the air and enjoying the ride, but even the adrenaline rush doesn't seem to improve my mood. After everything that's happened today, my energy is completely drained.

Aiden and Lex will gather everything they need and force my father to memorize the meticulously planned script they've put together. After that, they'll turn him over to the cops, and we'll never see him again. I should be elated, but I'm left with an empty numbness and tightness in my chest. His life is over, but so is mine.

Soon, everyone will think I'm dead. I can't stay in Pasturesville. I need to get away from here before I'm seen. Going with the guys seems to be my only viable option, at least until we cross state lines, but spending time with them will be tough. I still haven't forgiven them for what they did to Erin. I thought I'd feel differently after we apprehended my father, but I'm still festering in a cloud of bitter resentment that's impossible to shake. Maybe I never will.

After bounding over the rough terrain and avoiding getting hit in the head by branches, Eli comes to a sharp stop at the cabin. His feet barely touch the floor before I jump off.

"Hey!" Eli catches my arm to stop me from stumbling. I guess the meds are still in my system. "Let me help you."

"No!" I shake him off. "I don't need your help. I need to get used to being on my own."

"Sarah…" Eli's face falls. "Don't say that."

"Haven't you been listening? As soon as we're out of here, we're done," I snap, turning on my heel and stomping to the cabin.

Thankfully, the door's already open. I scrunch my nose at the mess inside. Half-eaten food containers litter the surfaces, threadbare blankets are draped over chairs, and random computer parts are strewn over the table. I can't believe they've been living like this.

"It's not exactly an upgrade from Sunnycrest," I snipe, knowing I'm acting like a brat but not giving a shit.

"It's the best we could do while we were waiting for you," Eli murmurs. He dashes to gather up some of the garbage, but it doesn't make a difference. It's a total dump. "Our next place will be better. You'll see."

"I won't," I say, picking my way over empty beer cans to the sofa and sitting down, hoping I won't catch a disease from it. "We're going our separate ways."

"Do you really mean that?" he asks. The hurt look in his eyes almost makes me feel bad until I remember everything he's done. "You really want to leave us and move on? After everything we've been through? After everything we've done to be together?"

"Moving on shouldn't be difficult for you," I say. "You seemed to manage fine before, remember?"

I'm mad, not just at Eli, but at the whole situation. Erin took over my body for an entire year, and my father used his final moments of freedom to remind me that I'm a fucking disappointment. Even the men I thought loved me shacked up with my sister the moment they thought I was dead. On my own, I'm never enough.

Eli's whole body stiffens. His usual kindness vanishes, and something inside him snaps.

"You can't leave us," he says. His voice is harsh and unrelenting, as if he won't take no for an answer. "You can't. You're everything. You're ours. You're mine."

His possessive psycho act won't fly with me. Not anymore. I used to find it endearing, but I'm done with someone else telling me how to live my life. I'm not losing control again.

"I'm not yours," I say. "I'm only here because I have to be. I'm not your fucking property, and if you don't see that, then you're as bad as my father."

"Don't say that," he yells, launching himself across the room and wrapping his hands around my throat. "Never compare me to him."

"Or, what?"

His pupils dilate, then his mouth descends on mine hungrily. There's so much emotion wrapped in our kiss, anger, hurt, lust, and, most powerful of all, his desire to claim me. I should push him away, that'd be best for everyone, but my body has other ideas. I lean in closer, wanting to be devoured. If I try hard enough, maybe I'll even forget how we ended up here.

His tongue pillages my mouth. Taking from me. I taste his desperate longing and toxic obsession. It's fucking addictive. I shouldn't want him, but I do, and I hate myself—and him— for that.

I rake my hands through his dirty blond hair. His rough hands slide down my back, grabbing a handful of my ass before hoisting me up. I wrap my legs around his middle, tightening my thighs around his muscles and ignoring my instincts screaming that this is a terrible idea. I bite his lip hard, but he doesn't back away, and the metallic taste of his blood fills our mouths.

"I hate you," I murmur.

His cock hardens.

"I love you," he says.

A fuzzy warmth blooms between my legs. I rationalize that succumbing to my urges is a healthy way to release my pent-up frustrations. It sure beats the anger management classes Dad used to make me attend. I claw Eli's broad shoulders. He doesn't mind. While I scratch and leave my marks over his skin, he nips my neck, biting and sucking, then pushes me back into the wall.

"You're mine," he growls. His hot breath sends a chill down my spine. "All mine."

He lowers me to the ground and slips his hands underneath my clothes to seek out my wet heat. He groans as his fingers meet my dripping entrance, then he slides two inside me.

"Fuck," I curse.

I hate how good it feels. I reach for the button on his pants, craving more. Why does the damn thing have to be so fiddly? I huff in frustration until I finally free him. His cock springs loose, and I wrap my fingers around it. I forgot how big he was.

"Off," he commands, tugging down my pants. "Now."

I wriggle out of them and pout, noticing how his eyes blacken at the sight of my lace panties. Why does he have to be so hot? It's infuriating!

"All off," he growls.

Fucking to forget has always been one of my mantras. It doesn't have to mean anything. I've had sex without strings before. This is on my fucking terms.

"I'm not sure Eli thinks like that," Erin chimes in.

Not now. I will her into submission, and it seems to work. For now, I can't even feel her lingering presence, and it's liberating. This is my time with Eli. I don't need to listen to her comments or performance reviews.

Eli takes off his clothes and tears off the rest of mine until we're both naked.

"Fuck…" He looks at my body in appreciation. "You're perfect."

I push him onto the sofa, asserting my control. There's no way in hell I'm lying on that flea-ridden mound, so I mount him. My plan to ride him until I can't think straight is going off without a hitch.

"Sarah," he groans as I sink onto his shaft. "You feel…"

I lick the smeared blood around the edges of his mouth, then catch his bottom lip between my teeth and suck on it while gyrating my hips. I take him inch by inch, enjoying how he stretches me. So fucking full.

"God, I've missed you," he says, tipping his head back.

I seize the opportunity. I clap my hand around his throat and squeeze. His eyes widen in surprise, but he's not angry. His cock twitches, letting me know he likes it. His giant hands cup my ass, squeezing hard to encourage me to quicken my pace, but it has the opposite effect. I slow, sliding up and down his cock at a tortuous speed, relishing every second of his torment.

"You're killing me," he whines.

I smirk and tighten my grasp on his throat. This is exactly what he deserves. I chase my pleasure, using him like an object. My pussy flutters, getting closer to climax, when Eli suddenly decides he's done with being submissive.

He pulls my hair and yanks my head closer, causing me to release my grip on him. We kiss again, a dizzying blur of panting breaths and regret tinged with false hope. Our ragged breathing synchronizes, and neither of us can hold back. I come hard, releasing a loud, primal moan as my pussy holds him hostage. As I unravel, we're blasted by a cool breeze from the opening cabin door.

Lex's jaw drops at what he sees when he walks in.

"Well, shit," Lex says. He's already pulling off his T-shirt. "You've started celebrating without us."

I'm too busy panting from my seemingly endless orgasm that I can't think of a witty quip to rebut with. The sight of Lex's scarred, sexy body sends a fresh surge of lust through me. I've entered an animalistic state where physical sensation trumps everything and all my intrusive thoughts have been temporarily banished.

Aiden shuts the cabin door behind him. Despite his grave expression, I sense a change in him, like he's finally rid himself of a massive weight that's been dragging him down. He watches me and Eli with an unreadable expression.

"Fuck," Eli gasps as I climb off him. His cum trails down the inside of my leg as I stand. "That was… incredible."

Lex saunters over with his massive boner swinging. His presumptuous arrogance makes me consider telling him to befriend his hand, but we've got limited time left together. I may as well benefit from him while I can.

"Take a good long look," I say. "Because this will be the last time you'll ever have me."

Lex grabs my face and holds my chin between his thumb and forefinger. "We better make it count, then."

He bends me over the sofa, giving him a perfect view of my pussy, still dripping with Eli's cum. Lex's fingers feel like flames licking down my spine, stopping to rest on my tattoo. A tattoo that he gave me. A tattoo that was supposed to signify our commitment to each other.

I shudder and push aside old memories as his cock enters me roughly. A sex-crazed demon takes over him as his violent thrusts make my body jerk from his relentless force. I close my eyes, entering a dazed state, until he spanks my ass to bring me back, demanding my full attention.

His next slap sends a judder of pleasure jolting through me like a lightning bolt.

"Our little whore," Lex says. "You're not sweet like your sister. Oh, how I've missed you."

How dare he mention Erin right now! I buck against him in anger, but that only makes Lex cackle and hold me in place firmly. This is the reaction he hoped for.

"Fuck you," I sneer.

"Hate me all you like," Lex purrs. "But I'll still make you scream."

His cock rubs against my G-spot, creating a dizzying spin of friction. I clench my fists, willing myself not to come, but the harder I resist, the more the intense sensation builds.

I gasp as Lex spanks me again.

"Sarah…" I turn my head to Aiden's voice. He's watching us, still fully clothed. His erection strains in his jeans, but his eyebrows scrunch in concern.

I look away and focus on the feeling of Lex's cock instead.

"Come help our girl out," Lex calls to Aiden. "I'm sure she wouldn't mind you eating her pussy."

Aiden doesn't move.

"I'm not your girl."

"How about you, Eli?" Lex drafts him in. "Do you want to taste her sweet juices?"

Eli eagerly accepts the challenge. While Lex plunders me from behind, Eli crawls between my legs and licks my clit from the front. The two of them catapult me into another realm.

"Sarah," Aiden says again.

I tear my head around to face him. He looks almost… sad.

I force myself to look away and close my eyes, finally succumbing to my pleasure. An orgasm crashes through me. Even though the tidal wave of pure bliss is incredible, it's tainted with the knowledge that this is the end. This is it. We'll soon go our separate ways. It's what I want, right?

"I'm going to fill you with cum," Lex grunts. "My dirty little whore."

He grunts and empties his load with a giant thrust, while Eli's tongue flicks over my clit and makes my thighs shake. When they're done, Lex withdraws, leaving me a quaking mess. As soon as I stand up, indifference takes over. All my fire has been extinguished, leaving only ashes.

Lex collapses onto the sofa. "That was something else."

"It really was," Eli agrees, licking his lips.

"Remember what I said," I say. "That was the last time." I turn to Aiden. "Do you want your turn?"

Instead of accepting my offer, Aiden scoops up my discarded clothes. He thrusts them at me, and whispers, "Get dressed."

His rejection stings, and I blink away tears, hoping he doesn't notice.

"Come on, Aid. It's time to party," Lex teases. "Acacia's in jail, and it won't be long until the story breaks. We've got everything we ever wanted."

"Not everything," Aiden murmurs.

"It's your loss," I say, feigning that I'm okay and redressing.

Fuck him. Does he think he's too good for me all of a sudden?

"You've made it clear what you want, Sarah," Aiden says, only speaking to me again once I'm fully clothed. "We'll take you somewhere safe and give you enough cash to start over."

Eli blanches. "You can't be serious."

"We had a deal," Aiden says. "A deal I intend to keep. We've been prisoners all our lives. I'm not forcing Sarah to stay with us against her will."

"But she's ours." Eli's bottom lip quivers. "All ours."

"I told you already, I'm not yours," I correct him, then turn to Aiden. "Thank you."

He nods curtly, like we've completed a business deal. "We'll leave as soon as we've taken all the necessary precautions." He points at my neck and frowns. "You're bleeding."

I shrug. "It's nothing."

"Eli." Aiden goes into leader mode and dishes out orders. "You still have supplies from the asylum, right? Patch her up." Next, he addresses Lex. "Load up the bikes. We'll get everything ready for the road."

"But I can hardly feel it," I say. "I'll be fine."

"You can't just walk into a hospital anymore," Aiden says. "The last thing you need is an infection. Let Eli help."

I guess he has a point. A dead person can't exactly rock up in the emergency room.

"Have you got the hair dye?" Aiden asks Eli. "Do that too."

"Hair dye?" I question. "What're you talking about?"

"You need a disguise," Aiden says, talking to me like I'm stupid. "We thought dying your hair would be best to avoid you being recognized."

"What color?"

"I picked it," Lex says. His eyes glint cheekily. "Red."

Of course the fire king would pick red. It's not my usual bottle blonde, but it'll have to do.

"Make it quick," Aiden says. "They'll interview Acacia for hours, but it won't be long until the news breaks in a town like this. We need to get ahead of this."

I wonder how three men with no identification and money have been able to get by, but I'm sure I'll have time to ask questions on the journey. I need to learn as much as possible from them, if I'm going to make it on my own.

"This way," Eli beckons.

I follow him into the grimy bathroom, where a box of dye is waiting. I guess the color will be okay. It's the first time I've gone red, and it feels fitting, like a phoenix being reborn from the ashes.

"Let's sort your neck first," Eli says.

I perch on the edge of the ancient bath.

"It really doesn't hurt," I say. "Warner must have nicked me with the needle."

"Let me take a closer look," Eli says, gently sweeping my hair out of the way. "I'll get this cleaned up." He rests a box on the nearby sink. "I'll fix this."

"Make it quick," I grumble.

"It might sting a little," Eli warns. "You should probably shut your eyes."

"Just get it over with it already," I complain. "Quit dragging it out."

"Shut your eyes."

I do as he asks, too tired to argue.

I wince as he wipes my wound with a cool wipe that smells of strong disinfectant.

"I'm sorry, Sarah," he murmurs. "But it's the only way to make sure I can keep you safe. It'll only sting for a moment."

Suddenly, there's a sharp, searing pain that spans all the way down my neck.

"Ouch!" I yelp.

"There, there," Eli purrs, dabbing the area. "All done. How do you feel?"

Despite the initial sting, the pain has dimmed immediately. I didn't think I had such a low pain tolerance. Maybe today has made me extra jumpy.

"I'm fine," I say, wishing he'd stop fussing like an old woman. "Are you going to dye my hair or not?"

Eli seems to have cheered up considerably and beams at the prospect. He's always had a strange fascination for hair.

Less than an hour later, we emerge from the bathroom. They don't own a blow-dryer, but from my initial inspection, Eli seems to have done a decent job and applied the color evenly.

"We're ready," Aiden says as soon as he sees us.

In our absence, they've cleaned out the cabin. All of their

laptops, screens, and junk are gone, along with any trace of them ever living here.

"We'll leave you in the first town over the border," Aiden says. "Does that sound good?"

Before I answer, Eli steps in.

"Actually, Sarah's changed her mind," Eli says. "She wants to stay with us. It's safer if we stick together."

"I..." I don't remember having a change of heart. A sudden wave of calmness sweeps through me and crushes my doubts until I find myself agreeing with him. "Yes, it is."

"Are you sure about this?" Aiden asks.

"Yes," I say, suddenly surer than I've ever been about anything. "Positive."

How did I ever think I could start over by myself? It makes no sense. Why would I leave them? They're all I have.

Aiden's moody scowl turns into a rare smile, transforming him into a completely new person.

"See?" Eli says. "I told you."

Lex arches an eyebrow. "What fumes were in that hair dye?"

"Fuck you, Lex," I hiss. "I can make my own decisions."

He chuckles. "I guess the fumes weren't that strong then."

"You won't regret it," Aiden says earnestly. "We'll stick together. Until the end."

Erin's approval buzzes under my skin. I guess this is what she wanted too...

CHAPTER
FORTY-EIGHT
AIDEN

I LOOK BACK at Sarah in the rearview mirror and grin, drinking in the sight. She's fast asleep, her head leans against Eli's shoulder as he strokes her freshly dyed red hair. The color suits her. He inhales a strand of her hair, getting high on her scent, while Lex lights matches and throws them out the truck window, letting them catch the wind and leave a trail behind us. She looks at home with us. At home with the monsters. I guess that's what she's been used to.

We cruise past the sheriff's station. It's not on our way, but I can't resist. When I was a kid, I drove old cars around the trailer park as soon as my feet could reach the pedals. Although I'm rusty, I'm good enough to get by. The truck was a parting gift from Doctor Warner—a small price to pay to get rid of us for good.

We watch the mayhem from across the street. Journalists and local news crews have already flocked to the scene to hear the sheriff make an announcement. Someone must have tipped them off. I notice Officer Blackwell standing outside the station. The tip-off we gave him will cement his career. All he had to do was provide me with a list of addresses in exchange.

Cameras flash as Sheriff Brady comes outside to stand on the station steps. I crack open the window to hear him speak into a microphone.

"Earlier today, we charged Magnus Acacia, the lead psychiatrist of Sunnycrest Asylum, with the murder of his two daughters: Sarah and Erin," Sheriff Brady starts. "We recovered the remains of, who we believe to be, Sarah Acacia on the asylum grounds. Acacia has confessed to his crimes."

I glance at Sarah—serene, but very much alive.

A few cop cars speed past us with blaring sirens. They'll be heading to search the Acacia house, where we've moved his records and some of the tapes—the full collection was too large to relocate. His office safe will be the first place they look.

It won't be long until the true horrors of Acacia's crimes come to light. We, and all the others, will finally get justice. How will *he* like being locked in a cage?

When they find out about everything he did at the asylum, no one will question whether he could kill his daughters, even without finding a second body. The case will be airtight, coupled with his confession. We've compelled him to tell the truth. Ironically, this is the first time I've been grateful for his experiments.

"What're you waiting for?" Lex says impatiently. "We've got everything we need."

He's right. There's nothing left in Pasturesville but bad memories and lost years. What we've been through will never leave us, but at least now we might have a chance.

"I'll never let you go," Eli murmurs, stroking Sarah's cheek tenderly. "All ours."

Eli's often underestimated, but he's the most dangerous of the three of us. I see the possessive look in his eyes when he watches her. A look that says he'll do anything to keep her.

No, he wouldn't…

I push the nagging doubt from my mind. Nothing will ruin this. I won't let it. This is what we deserve and what we wanted from the moment we met Sarah.

The four of us. Together. Forever…

Finally free?

EPILOGUE

SARAH

FOUR MONTHS LATER…

I WAIT for the gas station attendant to finish ringing up the pile of candy and potato chips. He's annoyed that I've interrupted him and keeps casting glances at his games console. A deflated bleep chimes.

"Shit," he curses. I guess he's lost. "No fucking fair!"

I rifle around in my purse for cash. Outside, the guys are waiting on their new motorcycles—swapping the truck for them was our best decision yet.

We've not stayed in the same place for more than a few days since leaving Pasturesville. After being locked up for years, it's understandable the guys want to keep moving. It suits me just fine too. I enjoy seeing the country and visiting different places. Running feels safer.

But we've not left every part of our past behind. While hopping from town to town, we've been on a new mission. The guys remember the names and faces of my father's clients—the sick fucks who tortured them for fun. With the help of Officer Blackwell, we've been paying them visits.

Showing up at their mansions unannounced has been fun.

Their reactions have been priceless when they realize who we are. Lex would prefer to kill them, but Aiden insists that blackmail is more beneficial. With them bankrolling our travels in exchange for our silence, we can go anywhere. Although, after what we've endured, money is the least of our worries.

I slide the money across the counter. Behind the attendant, a small television mounted in the corner of the shop plays. I freeze when a familiar face flashes on the screen.

My face.

The guy notices me staring and turns to see what caught my attention.

"That's some fucked-up shit," he comments, shaking his head at the old photograph of me and Erin filling the screen. "How didn't they know he was a crackpot before he killed his daughters, huh?"

"Beats me," I murmur, glad that I'm still wearing my helmet.

Even with my red hair, I've noticed a few people look at me strangely, like they're trying to place where they know me from.

He turns up the volume.

"The entire nation has been gripped by the case of the monster psychiatrist," the reporter says. She's standing outside the gates of Sunnycrest Asylum. "Magnus Acacia confessed to murdering his twin daughters, and new disturbing tapes have also been discovered that involve the abuse of patients in Sunnycrest Asylum."

The camera pans to show the cops hauling giant boxes into their vans.

"Our sources say that these tapes show brutal acts of torture and even murder," the reporter continues. "It's rumored that Acacia forced minors to participate in twisted experiments going back years. His reign of terror on his patients seems to know no bounds. Acacia's arrest and shocking crimes have drawn international attention, leaving everyone asking the same question, how did no one know?"

"Sick fuck," the gas attendant spits. "He won't get away with it. He has one of those faces you can't trust, you know? Maybe they'll make a movie about it."

"Maybe," I reply vaguely, looking back at the screen.

A montage begins, showing clips of various people from our old life talking.

Nate Holt's chiseled face flashes over the screen. "Erin was my date at our Harvest Ball," he says. "You know, I think she might have been my first love..."

Fucking asshole.

Next, it pans to Ms. Chi, Erin's favorite teacher at Sunnycrest.

"Erin was a talented student," Ms. Chi says, dabbing her eyes. "I thought she was quiet in class because she was struggling to cope after Sarah disappeared, but I know now there was so much more to it. I keep wondering what signs I missed and whether there was more I could have done..."

Finally, it zooms in on a sobbing Mia. "I knew there was something wrong!" Mia says. "Erin's dad was always controlling and overprotective. He gave me the creeps!"

It cuts back to the reporter. "Yesterday, Jocelyn Acacia was cleared of all charges..."

My mouth goes dry as a shot of my mother being escorted by police officers from the station appears. Her usually pristine hair has been pulled into a scruffy bun, and she's wearing giant sunglasses to hide her face.

"New medical evidence has found that Jocelyn is also a victim in this case," the reporter says. "Our sources claim that Doctor Acacia tested experimental drugs on his wife for over a decade..."

I tune out the news, my mind reeling after this latest revelation. I always believed that Mom's spirit was stamped out after years of abuse, but the drugs explain why the fun mom I remember from childhood disappeared. Did he start drugging her because she wanted to leave him? Maybe I'll see her again one day and ask...

"How didn't we see it?" Erin speaks in the back of my mind. *"I should have done more..."*

"Not now," I whisper.

My sister's guilt is harder to swallow than my own. I don't hear her as often now, but she still comes through occasionally, and I sense her presence, especially when she has strong emotions or reactions. I don't know if that'll ever change. It's both maddening and comforting to know I'll never be truly alone again.

The attendant gives me a strange look. "Did you say something?"

"No," I lie, then spot a pack of Swedish Fish. I grab it and add the pack to the pile of snacks. "These too. Keep the change."

I get out of there as quickly as possible. Aiden, Lex, and Eli smile as I approach them.

"Got everything?" Aiden asks.

He's different from the man I first met in Sunnycrest. They all are. Darkness still lurks underneath their smiles—maybe it'll always be there—but there's now a small crack of hope peeking through stormy clouds.

"All set," I reply.

"Swedish Fish?" Lex raises one eyebrow. "What did you do now?"

I hate them, but they're Erin's favorite candy. Sometimes, I like to treat her or use them as a peace offering when I've been too harsh or dismissive. But, after finding out about Mom, she needs cheering up.

"Do I need a reason to be nice to her?" I ask. "Maybe I'm just in a good mood."

Aiden frowns. His uncanny knack of being able to see through me is fucking annoying, and I shake my head a little, just enough for him to know that I don't want to talk. Not now.

"Come on, sweetheart," Eli says, patting his seat. "Let's go."

I climb on behind him, breathing him in. The smell of home. Safety.

"Race you!" Lex says, kicking off.

Aiden tears after him, then Eli and I follow. I whoop into the air. Maybe we'll never stop running. Maybe we'll never put the pieces of ourselves back together that my father broke, but we're together, and we're going to be okay... I think.

I'm truly a ghost.

Their little ghost.

AUTHORS NOTE

This book was as much of a journey to write as it is to read.

It took one year of blood, sweat, and tears, navigating pregnancy, birth, and the newborn trenches. I started writing as one person and came out another—a mother. Oddly befitting, don't you think?

Thank you to Ben, as always. You've shaped this book more than any other. You've listened to me, been my sounding board, and my rock. You've pushed the pram while walking for hours, helping me figure out some of the finer plot points with endless patience. You have made this book what it is.

Thank you to Ria. My incredible, talented, and kind friend. You kept me going with your words of encouragement and advice during my lows.

A special mention to Sauieh - for naming Robert. I hope you enjoyed his grizzly death as much as I liked writing it. He needed to die.

Finally, thanks to you. For choosing to suspend your reality and get lost in my twisted story. You're the best.

ABOUT THE AUTHOR

Holly Bloom has a degree in English Literature, but don't let that fool you... she would pick a steamy romance over a Shakespeare play any day!

Holly writes contemporary romance - the dark, gritty and twisty kind. She loves creating badass babe characters, who aren't afraid to speak their minds, and writing about the men who can handle them - often, there is more than one! Why choose, right?

When she isn't working on her next project, Holly spends an unhealthy amount of time watching true crime and roaming around the woods near her home in the UK.

As well as gooey chocolate brownies, Holly's favourite thing in the world is hearing from her readers - her characters may bite, but she doesn't! Promise!

Find out more and sign up to Holly Bloom's newsletter to receive a free book at:
www.hollybloomauthor.com

www.ingramcontent.com/pod-product-compliance
Lightning Source LLC
Chambersburg PA
CBHW031738180726
48283CB00005B/1558